The Unbinding of
Edward Tremenhere

The Unbinding of Edward Tremenhere

A Cornish Complication

Kim Sancreed

Cover Design www.kaspar.co.uk

For all my friends in politics.

Chapter One

"Two identical manilla envelopes"

For the third time in as many days, Edward Tremenhere awoke to the sound of accordion music drifting up from the street below. The playing was light and sweet. The melody was unfamiliar, but might have been French. He lay for a while in a state of growing perplexity, for his bedroom gave out not onto a Parisian street corner but an undistinguished main road in Roskear, a former mining town in the far west of Cornwall. Roskear had known better days, and accordion music was not its usual dawn song. Edward stretched his long frame, threw off the covers and reached for his dressing gown. Something told him that if he took time to dress properly, he would be too late.

He pushed his bare feet into a pair of ancient Chelsea boots, and hurried down the broad wooden staircase of the Count House. The front door was only a short distance from the street, but by the time he opened it, the music had stopped. The camelias and rhododendrons that surrounded the property obscured any view of the street or the musician. Edward took the path in four impatient strides, yanked the gate open and stepped onto the pavement.

It was a fine March morning, but still early, and being a Saturday there was little traffic. A paperboy on a skateboard rolled nonchalantly past, mouthing to whatever was coming through the brightly coloured headphones clamped to his ears, and drawing Edward's eye momentarily in the wrong direction. He turned and looked back towards town. There! That must be her. (If it was a her - his glasses were still on his bedside table). Sixty or seventy yards away a slim figure with a bulky backpack was walking quickly away from him. He had an impression of jeans, Doc Martens or something similar, a tight-fitting leather jacket and cropped hair, startlingly blonde, under some kind of cap. A vertical streak of vivid pink there too. Edward grimaced slightly. He considered hair colouring of any sort a lapse of good taste, even in a busker.

He could have caught up with the musician in a minute if he had wanted to, and he took a couple of steps with that intention before remembering that he wasn't really dressed for town, even by Cornish standards. He raised his hand, and considered calling, but what would he call? "I say!" would sound pompous. "Hoy!"? Too aggressive. "Yo!" was not part of his vocabulary. He watched the figure for a moment or two as it continued its progress along Roskear's wide main road, past the large, slightly down-at-heel villas that were a remnant of the town's glory days of mining wealth. Then he turned and walked back up the path, retrieving the Saturday Guardian from the letterbox as he went.

The grandfather clock in the wide wood-panelled hall struck eight as he went in. He noted with disapproval the mud on the Minton tiles, a trail of which led to where Murdo's bike was propped against the banister. Another matter to raise with the occupant of the basement flat. He sniffed speculatively, for there were rules too around which substances his lodger might and might not imbibe, but the air seemed clear enough. He paused to adjust the angle of a framed print on the wall – the commissioning letter he had received from the Queen in return for a spell of naval service in his early twenties. It was the sole memento the house contained of a brief but intensely happy period of his life.

He considered dressing, but the crispness of the morning had given him an appetite for coffee. Even at this hour the conservatory on the rear of the Count House would be passably warm in the sunshine. In the large kitchen he set about the construction of an espresso, grinding the beans – locally roasted – and adjusting the settings a touch to suit the mood that the accordion music had awoken. It was an unconscionable amount of fiddling for a very small beverage, but he found the ritual soothing. He recognised that with the passing of the years a natural conservatism was in danger of hardening into inflexibility.

As he had anticipated, the sun was glancing through the mildewed glass of the sun porch, creating a pool of warmth at one end. Perhaps in the Easter break Murdo could be tasked with cleaning the conservatory up a bit. It might be pleasant to sit beneath the magnolia in a Panama hat and watch the lad toiling shirtless up a ladder, doing something useful for a change. He settled himself on the battered settee and glanced at the front page of the newspaper before laying it to one side. He wasn't yet ready to put the matter of the accordionist completely from his mind.

Three mornings now. On the first occasion he had barely noticed the oddity - there had been a greater volume of traffic, and without giving the matter much thought he had dismissed it as something escaping from a car window. The repetition on the Friday had struck him more forcefully at the time, but he had the morning's routines to negotiate, and a day's teaching to think about. By the time he returned from his shower the music had stopped.

But this third occasion put things into a quite different light. The musician, whom he now thought of as female, had, on the face of it, no conceivable reason or business to be playing outside his house at that or any hour. It was a residential street, too far from the town centre to be any good for busking, and in any case who busked at that time of the morning? A conviction grew in him that, for whatever reason, the music was intended for his ears.

He tried to piece together the remembered fragments of melody – that gallic lilt. Was that a clue? Edward had spent time in France some decades previously, when certain events in the school where he had been a young Head of English – innocent, misinterpreted, but nonetheless *awkward* events - had necessitated a prolonged leave of absence. He retained a deep fondness for the country, its language (which he spoke fluently) and its culture. It all seemed a very long way from Roskear and his fifty-fifth year.

The girl might, of course, be one of Murdo's consorts. It would be just like the boy to put her up to some kind of prank. But he had heard his lodger come in the night before, and was

9

fairly sure he had returned alone. There was only one way to settle the matter. On Sunday morning he would be up and dressed in good time to ensure the young troubadour could not slip away without explanation. Edward drained his coffee and picked up the newspaper.

Twelve miles south of Roskear, on the opposite coast, Kate Porteous, who taught in the same English department as Edward, reached the far end of the beach and turned for home. It was not much of a run, for unless the tide was well out there was only half a mile or so of sand, but this was not intended as serious exercise so much as a statement of joyful intent to kick off what promised to be another sunny weekend, much of which would be spent in the open air. Kate was three months into a new relationship with Dave Singleman, who lived above her in the converted engine house on the cliff top.

She ran barefoot, padding easily back along the line of her own footprints in the sand. She would shower when she got in, then she would make fresh pancakes with the batter she had already mixed, and they would eat them on Dave's balcony with sheep's yoghurt and blueberry jam if the wind up on the top wasn't too chilly. This was Kate's first Cornish spring, and if somebody had told her when she moved down the previous autumn that she would be sharing an ancient stone tower above a beach with a lean, brown surf dude like Dave Singleman, she'd have laughed in their face. A no-nonsense Yorkshire lass, she had come to Cornwall to work, to advance her career. In a sense she had also come to get away from men, and as a result Dave had not found the wooing easy. The fact that they taught at the same school, and then found themselves living cheek by jowl with only the gulls and the crashing of the winter seas for company, had sometimes seemed to him as much of a hindrance as a help.

Kate climbed the steep footpath that led from the beach up to Wheal Prosper. The Engine House enjoyed spectacular views across the wide bay, but she also loved this moment, as she reached the top of the path with her back to the sea, when her home rose into view before her. Built square and uncompromising of Cornish granite, there were nonetheless pleasing subtleties of design: a slight tapering as the structure rose to its second story; the arched windows; the stub of a chimney at one corner. A hundred and fifty years ago it had housed the enormous steam engine that drove the pumps, and those in turn kept water out of the mine workings that still stretched their subterranean fingers far out beneath the seabed. Although there were dozens upon dozens of disused engine houses in west Cornwall, relatively few had been successfully converted, and Kate knew how lucky they were to have the tenancy of Wheal Prosper.

There was no sign of Dave on the balcony. She stood for a moment to draw breath, noted in herself a slight sense of pique that he wasn't watching for her return, and immediately dismissed it. He liked his bed. She liked his bed too, but she also liked her independence, and it suited her that the configuration of the two apartments meant that they retained a degree of separation. At her insistence bed sharing was a weekend activity, although the definition of the weekend might, when occasion merited it, be stretched to include Thursday evening. This was a stipulation that Dave occasionally moaned about, but which he recognised was not going to change until Kate was ready.

She climbed the outside stair and poked her head into the flat. She could hear Dave in the shower, so she flopped on the sun-lounger and closed her eyes briefly against the morning sun as the light breeze dried the film of sweat on her forehead. Then she leaned forward and peered down critically at the surf, or lack of it. The broad bay was largely flat, with slow curling waves little more than a foot high licking gently in from the southwest at six-second intervals. Sunday was forecast to be better.

She remembered the day she moved in, at the start of the previous autumn. Back then, she had only had the crudest idea of how the sea actually *worked*. She had been a county swimmer in her youth, but in landlocked Harrogate that had meant ploughing up and down lanes in the competition pool in Leeds, where the temperature seldom varied and the only swell came from the exertions of other swimmers. Now, she understood neeps and springs, and the rule of twelfths; how tides related to the phases of the moon; how surf was affected by wind direction, and the contours of the sea bed, and storm activity thousands of miles away. All this she had learned from Dave Singleman.

She heard the door open behind her and turned as he came out on to the balcony, a towel round his narrow waist.

"Blimey," he said. "It's a bit parky out here. Good run?"

"Mmmm," she smiled, closing her eyes and puckering her lips for a kiss. He duly obliged and she tugged gently at the corner of his towel.

"Oy!" he said. "I'll catch pneumonia. And I've just had a shower."

"Singleman," she said, "you're all mouth and no trousers."

"I'm just about to do something about that," he said, stepping out of her reach. "Are you ready for breakfast?"

"I'll have a shower first," she said. She hauled herself off the lounger and walked past him into the flat. "Don't attempt to do anything with that pancake mixture."

"Okay boss."

Dave cast his eye over the bay and reached the same conclusion about the surf as Kate had a few minutes earlier. He rose and followed her indoors, thinking, as he did on a daily basis, that he was very lucky indeed to have her in his life. For years the flat below had been occupied only by a succession of holiday makers, and his breakfasts had been solitary, spartan affairs that never involved pancakes.

He didn't see or hear the postman's van grind on to the gravelled parking area at the back of Wheal Prosper, and was unaware of the two identical manilla envelopes, one addressed to each occupant, that were deposited in the wooden letter box at the foot of the stair.

Chapter Two

"Stanley Baxter outta Janey Godley"

On the days when he was not pursuing his degree in politics, the emergence of Murdo McAndrew from his den in the bowels of the Count House seldom occurred before midday. When he did venture up to the kitchen the young Glaswegian was invariably taciturn, unwashed and ill-tempered. Should he encounter his landlord at such times, the exchanges were reminiscent of Prospero's berating of Caliban in Act One of the Tempest; Edward waspishly critical and Murdo monosyllabic and foul-mouthed.

On this particular Saturday, the Saturday of the third accordion rendition, Murdo had the kitchen to himself, Edward having walked into town to pick up some shopping. He helped himself to a large bowl of cornflakes and wandered into the conservatory, now pleasantly warm from three or four hours of sunshine. He belched loudly and with satisfaction, lowered himself onto the settee, and picked up Edward's Guardian, turning immediately to the editorial pages.

A committed socialist and a fully paid-up member of Momentum, Murdo regarded the Guardian as hopelessly liberal, and was particularly incensed by what he viewed as its hostility to the Corbynite wing of the Labour party. Like most millennials - a term that he himself despised – his main source of news was his mobile phone, and he regarded Edward's reliance on a physical newspaper that was never less than twenty-four hours out of date as mildly hilarious. Nonetheless, he took a perverse pleasure from scanning its pages, and often played a kind of mental game, where he imagined which stories would catch his landlord's eye, and how they might be received.

The sound of the front door opening caused only the briefest break in his concentration, and he carried on reading while Edward brought the bags of shopping into the kitchen and placed them on the table. For Edward's part the sight of his young tenant's coppery curls through the kitchen window aroused the usual ambivalence. He placed the fresh items in the fridge, noting the careless spillage of milk on the worktop, and debated whether, and in what tone, to open the day's conversational jousting.

He decided that it would better serve him to think warmly, rather than critically, of the boy, and he wiped up the milk himself before setting about dealing with the rest of the groceries. He had had the benefit of the fresh air from his walk into town, and was in a forgiving mood. Murdo for his part had enjoyed his cornflakes and solitary moments in the sun, and when he came in from the conservatory with his empty cereal bowl he greeted Edward more or less politely.

"Aw right big man?" Six months in the far southwest had done little to refine Murdo's accent or his style.

"Yes thank you," replied Edward. "Are you rested?"

"Aye, pretty much. What time is it?"

"It's a quarter past midday. I'm putting some soup on if you'd like some."

"Naw yer all right. Got any bread?"

"There's a granary loaf in the bag."

"Is there none of that white left?"

"I don't know," said Edward. "As you are, to my knowledge, the only consumer of refined flour in the house, you are probably best placed to answer that yourself."

"Aye well you say that. Ah wouldn't put it past you tae feed it tae the fuckin' ducks."

Edward winced. He had no philosophical objection to four-letter words, but he held that they should only be used when the time and the place were appropriate. The Count House at mealtimes was neither of these. It was often difficult to tell whether Murdo's frequent breaches of the linguistic house rules were an involuntary consequence of his upbringing or a calculated attempt to provoke.

Murdo held up his hand. "Sorry. Wash ma mouth out." He wandered over to the bread bin and fished out a crust.

Edward set about getting the soup on, while Murdo applied butter and jam to his bread. As a minor act of contrition he carefully replaced the lids on both jam jar and butter dish.

"There was something I wanted to ask you," said Edward, when he had joined Murdo at the large deal table.

"Uh-huh?" Murdo looked vaguely defensive.

"Have you seen anyone hanging around the front of the house recently? A busker, or anything like that?"

"You mean the bird wi' the squeezebox?"

"A young woman with an accordion, yes."

"Short blond hair? Skinny arse?"

Edward nodded wearily. He could see what was coming. Murdo put his finger to his chin as if in contemplation, then,

"Naw. Nobody like that. I did see a midget wi' a banjo if that's any use."

Edward smiled patiently.

"Remind me which Glaswegian comedian you are descended from."

"Stanley Baxter outta Janey Godley."

"She's nothing to do with you then, this accordionist?"

"Not yet. I'm working on it though."

"So you've spoken to her?"

"We've exchanged pleasantries. She was outside Friday morning when I went for ma bus. Ah was in a bit of a rush so there wasn't time to fully implement stage one of the infallible McAndrew seduction strategy. Why the curiosity? She's a bit young for you, I'd have thought?"

Murdo might have added that there were other reasons why she wouldn't be Edward's cup of tea, but the matter of his Landlord's long-standing bachelor status was, as yet, an area beyond the scope of their otherwise wide-ranging conversations.

"I'm a little curious, that's all. The last three mornings she's been playing her accordion beneath my bedroom window. Why would anyone do that?"

Murdo leaned back in his chair and yawned. His tee shirt rode up to reveal a washboard stomach, and he beat a brief tattoo upon it with his fingers.

"How do you know she's not playing it outside *my* bedroom window?"

Edward opened his mouth, and closed it again. There was really no answer to that question, except that it hadn't occurred to him. Murdo's basement flat was indeed lit from a barred window at the front of the property, albeit one sunk in a concrete trough a few feet wide. And it was perfectly possible, or even probable when you considered it, that the music was intended for Murdo's ears. Not for the first time, Edward felt wrong-footed by his tenant.

"You know sometimes Edward, for a man who's been to Oxford, yer no' all that smart."

Edward decided to ignore the inaccurate allocation of his *alma mater*.

"It's a fair point, I suppose. The music is being played beneath my bedroom window, and, if we're being strictly accurate, above yours. It is a little odd, though, don't you think?"

"Ah wid say it is refreshingly liminal, yes," said Murdo. "Those of us who live in that contingent and serendipitous space where happenstance is a joy, rather than a threat, delight in such ephemera. And given that said accordionist, from my initial assessment, comfortably meets the McAndrew threshold of minimal attractiveness, I am happy to undertake to investigate further."

"I'm only curious to know what draws her to the Count House," said Edward. He found Murdo's rapid switches from semi-aggressive monosyllables to flights of rhetorical fancy difficult to keep up with, and more than a little irritating.

"Nae bother," said Murdo. "Leave it with me. Now I've got to be off. There's a protest up at the hospital this afternoon. You can come and join us if you like. Or are you all sorted with private health care?"

"I rely on the NHS and will defend it to the hilt," said Edward, "as I think we have established through previous discussion. I am, however, on duty at the Food Bank."

"Aye well mebbe the day will come when there will be no need of foodbanks," said Murdo. "But until then, by all means ease yer liberal conscience with a bit of charity work, if it keeps you out of mischief. Ah'm not in for tea tonight by the way."

"Nor am I," said Edward, who was not in the mood for political sparring. He was the scion of an old Cornish Liberal family, with a great-uncle who had represented a neighbouring constituency at Westminster, and he retained an interest in County politics. It all seemed rather remote from the aggressive energy of Murdo's convictions, but it made, at times, for interesting conversation.

He finished his soup and rose from the table. "In that case, I shall see you when I see you."

He placed his dishes in the sink, then came back for Murdo's cereal bowl.

"So you will," said Murdo, and pushed back his chair. Edward watched his short, broad frame as he left the kitchen, the long russet curls bobbing slightly with his gait. He heard him tripping down the stairs to the basement, and the closing of the door at the foot of the steps. He turned on the tap and reached for the washing-up liquid. Somehow the matter of the mud on the Minton tiles had been overlooked.

The Pascoe family's ancient white-and-rust Nissan pickup slowed to a halt outside the car-park of the small hospital that served the Newlyn and Penzance area of west Cornwall. The three occupants of the front seat leaned forward simultaneously to make sense of the scrum of bodies and placards that blocked the entrance.

"Woss goin' on here then?" said Viv.

"Some kind of demo," said Maisie. She was a matronly woman whose broad, cheerful countenance balanced out her husband's sharp features. The third occupant of the front seat, who sat between the two adults, was a skinny lad of fourteen with lank, mousey hair. Sammy Pascoe's face had the same narrow lines as his father, but he had inherited the large friendly eyes of his mother, and this gave him a certain urchin charm. He said nothing, but craned to read the placards.

Viv wound down the window as a youth with corkscrew red hair approached the pick-up.

"Can I give youse a leaflet?" he said.

"You can let us into the bleddy car park," said Viv. "We got an appointment in ten minutes." His tone was sharper than

17

it might have been, partly in response to the protestor's unfamiliar accent.

"Aye, sure," replied the youth. "You'll get in no bother. But we want to make sure this hospital is here for all your future appointments, too."

He handed Viv a leaflet, who passed it, without looking at it, to his son. Sammy studied it with interest. Then the youth moved back into the crowd, calling something incomprehensible to the front rank of demonstrators, who parted like the red sea to allow the pick-up through.

"Flamin' cheek," said Viv. "They're not about to close the hospital, are they?"

"It's the minor injuries unit," said Maisie, who was a parish councillor, and more in touch than her husband with the reality of how and by whom such decisions were made. "They're looking at some kind of rationalisation of emergency provision, and we all know what that can mean."

"Who's "they"?" asked Sammy.

"Good bleddy question," said his father. He parked the pickup in a disabled space and he and Sammy disembarked, and began the process of unloading Maisie's wheelchair from the back, where it lay, secured by a length of bungee cord, between a wheelbarrow and a cement mixer. Sammy helped his mother down from the pickup – a considerably easier operation than the one required to get her in in the first place – and into the wheelchair. Viv lit a skinny roll-up.

"Right," he said, his mood improved slightly by the tobacco and the fact that they were now safely at the hospital in good time. "How are we going to do this?"

"I'm meant to be meeting Issy at two," said Sammy. "I did mention that."

Viv looked as if he might be about to object, but Maisie caught his eye.

"Well, we don't want to get in the way of that," he said with a wink at his wife. "But I've got some bits and pieces to do as well, so you'll need to be back here by three in case your Mum's not through."

"OK, thanks," said Sammy. "That's no problem." He gave his mother a hug, jammed his hands in the pockets of his windcheater, and set off through the crowd of protesters in the direction of town.

Viv watched him go, then pinched out his rollup and lodged the remnant behind his ear. He took the handles of the wheelchair and tipped it back to negotiate the kerb.

"So how's the love affair of the century going?" he asked, as they made their way along under the covered walkway to the rheumatology department, where Maisie was due to receive some routine injections.

"I'm not altogether sure," said Maisie. "It's all gone a bit quiet."

The love affair referred to was, in truth, barely worthy of the name. At the St Petroc's junior disco the previous November, Sammy had, to his great surprise, ended up snogging in a dark corner with his long-time childhood companion and current debating partner Isadora Brunel, and that appeared to have started something, the nature of which wasn't entirely clear to him. Looking back on it, he wasn't sure how it had happened in the first place; where the impetus had come from, not to mention the mastery of technique. OK, mastery probably wasn't quite the right word. You knew what snogging was supposed to look like, of course, both in its gentle and more vigorous forms, but there had been something very strange about engaging in the practice with Issy Brunel. It seemed completely unconnected with their relationship up to that point, as if, out of the blue, they had randomly started playing croquet together.

Whatever it was that had begun on that day in November (approximately the same time, as it happened, that two of their favourite teachers, Mr Singleman and Ms Porteous, had finally got it together), it was still, just about, going. The relationship, if that was what it was, had been lent substance initially by a couple of Christmas parties, at which it was understood by their peers that they were "an item". It had limped along through January and February largely in the form of such meetings as had been arranged today, plus occasional cycle runs, with additional snogging (and some experimental fumbling) when the weather permitted. The fact of the matter, mused Sammy as he approached the coffee shop, was that the best and least complicated bit was probably the chatting, and they had always been pretty good at that anyway.

Through the glass door of the café he could see Issy at a table in the corner, her long fair hair falling forward over the book that she was reading. He pushed open the door and went in.

Chapter Three

"I've definitely just been dumped"

St Petroc's Academy (A Marcato Trust School, Head Office 1760 John Newton Tower, Bristol), where both Sammy and Issy were Year 9 students, and where Edward, Dave and Kate were all members of the English staff, was largely empty and silent on a Saturday afternoon. Once the town's grammar school, it occupied a commanding position on top of a rise, and enjoyed views of the harbour to the southwest, and St Michael's Mount to the east. It had its share of modern teaching blocks, but at its heart was the old grammar school building, an unpretentious but dignified granite structure with a wide frontage and a modest clock tower. For a decade or so St Petroc's had also enjoyed the use of a well-equipped theatre. This facility was shared with the community, and had been funded partly by parental subscription, and partly by the Chairman of the Marcato Trust, whose wealth had been acquired through the trading of quality used cars. Edward Tremenhere's father, who had been a keen amateur thespian and was himself educated at the grammar school, had made a considerable contribution towards the project shortly before his death.

All this was ancient history, and of little interest to the sole member of the Senior Management Team in the building on that Saturday afternoon. This individual occupied a square, white, and oddly unadorned office in the old school block. At first glance he might have been thought to be the Head of PE, for apart from the obligatory desk, chairs, and low table, the only item of furniture was a large cylindrical punch bag in one corner. This vaguely obscene sausage of red vinyl was suspended from a strong point in the ceiling, and had been fitted, at the occupant's request, along with the stainless steel bar set high into the lintel of the doorway.

It was from this bar that Anton Killick, Senior Deputy Head and Director of Studies, was currently suspended, his chin at bar height and his arms held at right angles so that his handsome biceps bulged and shivered slightly. He exhaled slowly and lowered himself gently and with perfect control before hauling himself up for the fiftieth and final time to chin the bar. He then dropped to his toes on the floor, tilted slowly to one side, took a kind of controlled shuffling hop into the room on his rearmost foot and lashed a karate-style kick at the red punch bag, which shook with the smack of the impact.

Killick straightened himself, bowed solemnly at the vinyl sausage, still vibrating upon its moorings, and returned to his desk and his MacBook. He was conducting a detailed analysis of the Year 11 mock results, an analysis which would result in several spreadsheets, tabbed for reference and colour-coded for clarity. These in turn would be cross-referenced with the same cohort's Year 9 test results. In this way the notional value-added to each student could be calculated (as if an adolescent were a financial product, rather than a complex cocktail of hormones and potential). This current cohort did not, sadly, have the benefit of the further battery of tests he had recently introduced in Year 7, for Anton Killick had only been at the school for eighteen months, and the full effect of his reforming zeal would not be enjoyed by St Petroc's students for some years to come.

He was not entirely alone in his office. In a small cage on the window ledge two white rats scratched about in their straw. These were Leon Trotsky and Josef Stalin, who normally were left at home. They had been brought into the office today because Anton was a little concerned that Leon Trotsky was not entirely himself. Killick was sometimes perceived by colleagues to be a cold man, but those colleagues were ignorant of the care and compassion that he lavished upon his rats.

He turned his attention to the results for the English department, in which he took a particular interest. This was not because it was his subject – he was a physicist - but because he harboured a suspicion that his efforts were unappreciated in that quarter. In fact he was fairly sure that in some regards they were actively resisted. This alone might have been dealt with easily enough – Anton was not a man to be crossed, nor to be lightly put off – but there were other factors involved. The previous term he had made tentative overtures towards one of the female members of that department, and had been rather summarily rebuffed. To add insult to injury, Kate Porteous, the colleague in question, to whom Anton had also offered valuable and generous professional encouragement of various sorts, had taken up with the slacker Singleman. Then, to cap it all, Singleman had been awarded a promotion – against Anton's clearly expressed wishes - to a pastoral position for which he was manifestly unsuited. This had all brought the autumn term to a highly unsatisfactory conclusion for the Senior Deputy.

Now Killick stared in irritation at the data on the screen before him. There was a blank column where a set of figures should have been - somebody had failed to enter their results. He scrolled to the top of the sheet, where the initials DS told him what he might easily have guessed. Dave Singleman's results for component three of the language paper were missing. This was despite a full week in which to mark the papers and enter the data, and several reminders via email and staff meetings.

Anton held up his hands in frustration, as if in mute appeal to the education gods, and let them fall to the desk. Without Singleman's figures, the fine detail analysis of the mock results would be incomplete. He considered ringing the man there and then – his contact details would all be on the management system to which Anton had access - but even he knew that calling a member of staff over a weekend for anything other than a pastoral emergency was simply not done. Instead he punched out an email.

I have come into school this afternoon with the express purpose of completing the analysis of the mock exam results, in order to present them to the Heads of Department meeting on Monday. It appears I am missing your paper 3 language figures. Can you please remedy soonest.

He considered leaving it at that – the email programme would automatically apply his signature block – but it was a point of principle with him to always leave the door open to resolution, and so he finished with his customary salutation:

Kind Regards
Anton.

He stabbed the send key with a force that belied the sentiment, and flicked back to PowerPoint. He would not allow this irritation to prevent him from using his Saturday afternoon school time efficiently. He could usefully spend forty minutes or so tidying up the presentation he planned to make to the Head on "St Petroc's – Stripped for Action".

It was a bold, imaginative scheme about which Anton was quietly excited.

Perhaps as a result of the pleasant weather, Costa was relatively quiet, which made the delicate conversation in which Sammy and his girlfriend were now engaged a little awkward. He sat across from Issy, a half-drunk glass of cola in front of him. She had returned her copy of *Pride and Prejudice* to her bag, and was sipping a cappuccino. Although their birthdays were only a month apart, Issy might have been two years older. She was tall and athletic, and a seriousness of expression leant maturity to her features.

"So, does this mean we're like," Sammy glanced round and lowered his voice, "*breaking up?*"

"I don't know. I just want to get straight in my head what it's all for, I suppose."

"Don't you like me being your boyfriend?"

"It's not about *you* Sammy. You've always been my best buddy. I'm just not sure I see the point of it being a big *thing*. You know, that everybody knows about, and talks about. People keep asking me how it's all going. Do they ask you that?"

"Yeah and it is bloody irritating." The boys in the class asked him other things as well, but he wouldn't tell Issy that.

"Well, I just wonder, can we maybe ease off a bit? Just go back to being friends?"

"You're *dumping* me."

"No Sammy, really I'm not. I wouldn't do that to you. I'm…I'm opening a dialogue."

For a moment there flashed in him a defensive anger. Should he just walk out of the café now? Was that what you did? He could slam a couple of pound coins down on the table, in a magnificent, sarcastic gesture, but of course they had already paid for their drinks, or at least Issy had paid for them. *That* now seemed significant, and reminded him of all sorts of other complications about the difference in their situations. He looked at her. She was looking back at him kindly, beseechingly, even, from those clear hazel eyes. He, Sammy Pascoe, at the age of fourteen, had a gorgeous girlfriend that he was just about to lose.

"I'm really not dumping you."

He sighed.

"OK. You're not dumping me. So…suppose we do go back to being friends. I mean *just* friends. That means no more…you know…"

"Well, whatever. It's not the most important thing, is it? I mean it's not as if we're going to stop giving each other hugs…"

"I suppose." In all honesty it might be a relief not to be worrying about what exactly they were supposed to be doing with each other, which got all tangled up with what they weren't supposed to be doing.

"Can I think about it over the weekend? I mean…I don't want to carry on with it if you're not comfortable. And of course, being friends with you is more important than… the other stuff. I just don't want to be *dumped*, is all. I don't want to have to tell people that."

"Well I'm not going to tell people that."

"Can I ring you Sunday night?"

"Yes, of course. Look – I've got to go. I'm meeting Phoebe out of ballet, then Mum's taking us clothes shopping."

She stood up, five foot eight in her trainers. That was another awkwardness. Suddenly Sammy couldn't face walking out of the café next to her, the disparity of height on display for the counter staff to smirk at.

"Actually I'm just going to hang on here. I'm meeting my parents in a bit, too."

Issy looked momentarily distressed.

"You OK?"

"It's fine, Issy, honestly. I'll call you tomorrow night."

"OK, then." She leaned down and hugged him. Then she was walking out of the café, her leather shoulder bag swinging on her hip as she pulled at the door.

I've *definitely* just been dumped, he thought, as it closed behind her.

Half a dozen miles to the west, the romance of Sammy and Issy's respective form tutors was enjoying a more harmonious spring outing. They had parked Dave's MG halfway down the steep wooded valley that led to the rocky cove at Lamorna, and had walked, hand in hand, first through the woods, where the pale dappled sunshine picked out star-like clumps of celandines and anemones, then along the cliff path above the stony beach to where the choughs were. Now they were sitting on the balcony of the café, where Kate picked contentedly at the remains of a slice of carrot cake. Dave had already demolished more than his fair share.

"I suppose we'd better think about heading back," he said. "What time is Frances expecting us?"

They were due to have supper that evening with their Head of Department.

"Not till seven thirty," said Kate. "It won't take me long to get ready. Let's not rush it."

"You're right," agreed Dave. "The day's too good to waste. It's so much easier to relax on a Saturday than a Sunday."

"I don't know. We should get most of the day on the beach tomorrow."

"Yeah, but it's the knowledge of what lies at the end of it. It starts to settle in the pit of my stomach around three o'clock."

"Have you got much to do this weekend?"

"A couple of hours' worth. I've still got to put my paper 3 mock marks on."

"Ooh Singleman. The deadline was Friday, wasn't it?"

"Close of play Friday. Which means in effect first thing Monday morning. I suppose yours are all done?"

"Of course."

"Inky swot."

"You know you love me for it."

"I do. I love you and I need to learn from you, but…maybe not just yet."

They bantered on in this easy manner for another half an hour, then began the climb back to the car. Dave had left the roof down, and they kept it that way for the short run back to the Engine House. It was a little chilly but he kept a supply of scarves and beanies jammed behind the passenger seat, and they wrapped up for the brief trip. Kate's own car was nearly new – stylish in its own way and considerably more reliable than the forty-year old MG, which she had regarded initially as symptomatic of Dave's laid-back and vaguely chaotic approach to life. In time however she had grown fond of the little blue sports car. She liked the way he drove it, too – not recklessly, but with a kind of zest, his long legs stretched out before him, the one nearest to her dipping and lifting in time with his punchy, decisive gear changes. She would have enjoyed driving it herself, but he hadn't yet offered, and she was a little afraid to ask. Along with his surfboard it was one of the few material possessions to which he showed any real attachment.

They swung onto the gravelled parking area of the Engine House and pulled up beside Kate's Fiat 500, which they used for evening trips. Dave fiddled with the roof of the MG while Kate went on ahead to open up – they had keys for each other's flats, and tended to use Dave's at weekends because of the balcony and the mezzanine sleeping deck with its stunning views. When Dave had finished securing the car, however, Kate was still at the foot of the stair, standing by the wooden letter box.

"Anything interesting?"

"These look a bit ominous." She held up the identical manilla envelopes. "One for me and one for thee."

Chapter Four

"A dabbler and a drifter"

Dave took the envelope and glanced at it.

"Looks like it could be from the agents," he said. "Shall we open them inside?"

They climbed the stairs to Dave's flat in silence. They rented their apartments at the Engine House from Issy Brunel's parents, who owned several properties in the area. Dave had lived in the upstairs flat for a number of years, but Kate, who had only moved in downstairs a few months previously, knew that her apartment had previously been used as a holiday let, and might be again. They had recently renewed their six-monthly leases, so that their tenancies were secure until the autumn. Beyond that the future was uncertain.

In the upstairs flat Dave put the kettle on; an instinctive response to the slightly charged situation. He watched as Kate opened her envelope and scanned the letter.

"Looks like I'm getting the heave-ho," she said glumly. "You might be too, I'm afraid. They want to do up the Engine House over the winter."

Dave opened his letter and read the contents aloud.

Dear Mr Singleman,

I am writing to inform you that under the terms of your short-term tenancy agreement, and pursuant to Section 21 (4) (a) of the Housing Act 1988, the Landlord requires possession of the property after the day upon which a complete period of your tenancy expires, this being 30th

September next. This is to facilitate refurbishment and improvement of the property over the winter period.

Yours sincerely etc."

He made a face.

"Same as mine," said Kate. "We're being evicted."

"Well it could be worse," said Dave. "We've got six months to find somewhere."

"Yes. At least we'll have the summer here."

But even as she said it, the implication that it might be the only summer they would enjoy in their idyllic cliff-top hideaway seemed unbearably sad.

"Do you fancy some tea?" asked Dave.

"Yes please," said Kate. "I think I'd like a biscuit too, if you've got one."

Dave brought the mugs of tea and a half-opened packet of hobnobs over to the sofa, where Kate was re-reading her letter with pursed lips.

"It must be worse for you," she said. "I always knew this was only a short-term let. But it's been your home for years."

"Yes, it has," said Dave. "But it was always on the cards that they might decide to do it up one day. It's really scruffy by holiday-let standards. They could make a mint out of it, given the location, if they spent some decent money."

For a moment or two they sat in silence, torn between the comfort of sharing memories of the autumn and winter that they had spent as neighbours and lovers, and the necessity of looking ahead into an uncertain future.

"You don't seem that upset," said Kate.

"Well…I don't suppose I am. In some ways I had been kind of preparing myself to move on anyway. Before we got together, I mean."

"But now that we *are* together…"

"Well it's not exactly an ideal set-up for a long-term relationship, is it? I mean it's very lovely that this is where it all happened, and I'm sure it will always be a special place for us, but I never imagined we would carry on living above and below one another in separate flats for ever and ever."

"I dunno," said Kate. "It works for me."

This was a tease, but one rooted in truth. For Kate, the relationship as it stood was already a massive step in a direction she had never envisaged taking. Pragmatic and focused in all her affairs, she was surprised at the extent to which she found herself caught up in the romance of their present situation, and how much she was enjoying it. She found herself reluctant to look beyond it to any more settled future, and this was something of a fault line between them.

"Well," she said, draining her mug of tea. "Lots to think about. I've got a few chores to do downstairs before we go out."

"OK," said Dave, who was by now used to his partner's need for solitude, and who recognised that the news they had received had unsettled her and would need to be absorbed. They embraced briefly and then she was gone, through the door onto the balcony and down the wooden stair. He sat for a moment listening to the sound of her front door opening and closing, and her faint footsteps beneath him as she moved around in her own flat.

At thirty years old, Dave Singleman was experiencing something of a transition in his attitude to life. Rewind to the previous summer, and he would have been easily characterised as a laid-back surf dude, a dabbler and a drifter, moving lightly over the earth and beholden to no-one. He enjoyed teaching English to teenagers and was good at it, but he had little time for the current obsession with data and the striving for continuous improvement that dogged maintained schools in England. His resistance to some of the initiatives at St Petroc's, particularly those attributable to Anton Killick, was well known.

Then Kate arrived on the scene. Kate with her neatly tailored, professional suits, her serious demeanour and smart little car, all belied by a spectacular tattoo that few got to see. They had not exactly hit it off at first, but whether he realised it or not, Dave was ripe for a change of direction. By degrees, and not always straightforward ones, he had fallen in love with his downstairs neighbour and departmental colleague. By the end of the term, and partly in an effort to convince her that he was a serious prospect, he had applied for and secured a promotion to Head of Year. This wouldn't take effect until the following September, but it was now Dave who had a plan for the future, and Kate who was not entirely clear as to what she wanted. To Dave, an enforced departure from the Engine

House at Wheal Prosper represented an opportunity as much as a threat.

There were six of them at supper that evening at Frances Fivey's town house in Penzance. Their Head of Department had a long-term partner who was also an Ofsted inspector, but Inga was visiting family in Scandinavia, so Edward Tremenhere was there, along with the d'Allesandros. Raphael d'Allesandro was the head of drama at St Petroc's and his wife Rona was the Head's secretary. Both had dark, Italianate features and they might have passed for brother and sister, but while Raphael's accent was neutral home counties, Rona spoke in the broad and unapologetic tones of her native Glasgow. They were in their early forties and they made a striking couple.

Frances's house was filled with a tasteful but eclectic mixture of prints, fabrics and *things* that all somehow worked together without any obvious scheme or style. Sometimes Kate felt as if she were inside a pre-Raphaelite painting. Then her eye would light upon some Nordic artefact that seemed perfectly in place, or a piece of driftwood picked off a north coast beach. Everything was either beautiful or interesting. They sat now round the dark oak table, grazing at a generous cheese board as firelight and candlelight set competing shadows on the walls.

"So how's my nephew doing?" asked Rona. The question was directed at Edward.

Kate had heard something of the arrangement that had been agreed between Rona and Edward to accommodate her young relative when his flat share had fallen through. She understood Murdo to be something of a character, and had been a little surprised at Edward's willingness to enter into the arrangement. The lofty, patrician demeanour of her bachelor colleague, which at first she had found a little off-putting, made him seem an unlikely inn-keeper to waifs and strays. She was curious to hear how things were working out at the Count House.

"Young Murdo," said Edward carefully, "is a most interesting and intelligent young man."

"He's also a cheeky wee bampot," said Rona. "I hope you're not taking any nonsense from him."

"He's quick-witted, and quick-tongued, I grant you. His political views I find a little extreme. But he has yet to beat me at chess."

"Well it's a great relief to me that you're keeping an eye on him," said Rona. "I can't say I was thrilled when I heard he was coming down. I'm afraid I made it quite clear he couldn't stay with us. I mean we don't have the room."

"The transport links are poor too," said Raphael. "I just didn't feel he'd have much of a student life."

A glance passed between the two.

"It suits me well enough," said Edward. "I like to keep the basement flat let if I can. And I do have some sympathy for this generation of students. My lot had it easy by comparison."

There were nods of agreement round the table. Frances and the d'Allesandros were just old enough to have escaped the imposition of student loans, but both Dave and Kate were carrying tens of thousands of pounds of notional debt.

"And what about life out at the Engine House?" asked Frances. "Are the pinks out on the cliffs yet?"

"It's beginning to feel like spring, isn't it?" said Dave, glancing at Kate. "The gorse is certainly glorious. But we had a bit of news this afternoon. It sounds as if we might have to look for somewhere else next term." He explained the gist of the letters, to general murmurs of sympathy.

"You'll find it difficult to match the Engine House for location," said Raphael.

"Yes, I don't think you get that lucky twice," said Dave.

Frances was watching Kate, who merely nodded.

"Do you think you'll rent again, or might you buy?"

Dave looked at Kate again.

"Well I don't know. We really haven't had time to take in all the implications."

"We literally got the news a few hours ago," said Kate.

"But you'll look for something together," said Rona, then immediately realised that the assumption might be premature. "I mean…sorry…maybe I'm speaking out of turn."

Dave said nothing. Kate looked about to speak, and hesitated. Frances rescued the conversation.

"Well I guess the positive thing is, you've got plenty of time. And it's a lovely time of year to be looking at property."

"Roskear is worth considering, if you're thinking of buying," said Edward. "It may be the butt of jokes but a lot of young professionals are moving in, and there's a bit of an arts scene."

"I don't think I've ever been there," said Kate. "It's on the railway line, isn't it?"

"It is," said Edward. "Twenty minutes from Penzance, twenty minutes from Truro. And property's relatively cheap."

The conversation moved on to the advantages or otherwise of various locations within commuting distance of St Petroc's, and the question of Dave and Kate's future domestic arrangements wasn't revisited until they were on their way home.

It was Kate who brought it up as they drove onto the parking area at Wheal Prosper.

"I know what you're thinking." She turned off the engine.

"What am I thinking?"

"You're thinking, wouldn't it be nice to buy a little house together."

"Yes, but I'm also thinking, Kate's never going to be up for that. Not yet, anyway."

There was a silence, in which they could hear the Fiat making its soft ticks and sighs as the engine cooled.

"*Not yet* would be more accurate than *never*."

He smiled. "I remember Not Yet."

"And look where your patience and persistence got you."

"That's why I'm curbing my enthusiasm."

Kate leaned across and kissed him gently and slowly.

"Let's see whether we can't rekindle it. We can talk all this through tomorrow."

On the train back to Roskear, Edward Tremenhere reflected upon the evening. He had enjoyed the company. Raphael crewed regularly on Edward's boat, and was a good friend, and Frances both respected and understood him, as he did her. Dave and Kate he had less in common with, although he liked the quiet seriousness of the newest member of the department. What must it be like, in this day and age, to be setting out together upon the uncertain waters of a serious relationship, with decisions about marriage, property and children all in the future, a future so much more freighted with

33

uncertainty than his own had been. When he had graduated in the eighties it was fairly cut and dried for most folk – you got a job, then a mortgage, then you settled down to raise a family, unless there were clear reasons not to. Probably his own decision to join the Navy on a short commission had been a way of escaping those tramlines, and if so, it had worked – they now marked out routes that other people followed, while Edward remained an interested observer.

The train – one that Edward often caught after an evening in Penzance - was the sleeper that ran on up to London. He stepped down onto the long, deserted platform at Roskear, and waited as he always did by the level crossing for the train to set off once more on its overnight journey. He had a fondness for trains. The giant snub-nosed locomotives that pulled the sleepers – this one was the *Pendennis Castle* – always seemed to him like monsters that must have been subdued and harnessed by some primitive act of heroism. The driver was leaning now from his high window looking back down the platform at the guard, who was checking the doors. Edward suppressed an urge to wish him good evening. Then the whistle blew, the driver withdrew his head, and the engine note rose as the huge train inched forward. Edward watched the darkened sleeper carriages slide past as it accelerated, then he followed the red pinpricks of light on the back of the train until they disappeared round the slight bend at Pengegon, three quarters of a mile down the line. Only when darkness and silence returned did he set off on the ten-minute walk home to the Count House.

Chapter Five

"A half-remembered line from his parents' record collection"

On Sunday Edward was awakened by his alarm at seven o' clock. It was just becoming light. He listened carefully but there was no sound from the street, so he showered quickly and dressed, pulling on jeans and a warm sweater. He padded downstairs and quietly opened the front door. Nothing. He walked carefully down the path and peered over the gate, but the street outside was deserted.

He was unsurprised – the accordionist had never begun her performance quite this early before. He returned to the kitchen and made himself a cafetiere of coffee and some toast, which he took into one of the two large front rooms of the Count House – the one that in theory served as a living room, although much of the actual living was done in the kitchen. He opened one of the broad sash windows an inch, and listened again, but could hear nothing but birdsong. It was still not yet half past seven. He selected a volume of Tacitus from the vast pine bookcase that took up most of the back wall, and settled himself comfortably in an armchair. He could be out of the house and down the path in ten seconds if required.

The minutes passed. The house was silent except for the deep, slow tick of the grandfather clock in the hall. From outside he could hear the passing of an occasional car. The birds were settling down now, their dawn chorus subdued to a general warbling. Edward finished his breakfast and, when eight o'clock struck, put down his book. He went outside once more and surveyed the empty street.

He knew quite suddenly that the girl would not appear. Of course she wouldn't. He began to think that he had never really believed she would, that he was caught up in some strange enchantment, the pace of which he could not and should not force. The best response was patient compliance, until whatever was to be revealed to him should be revealed. Although a rationalist, the solitary life that Edward had led inclined him occasionally to magical thinking where his own destiny was concerned.

He considered his options. He could comfortably make the nine o' clock service at St Jude's, for which there was no need to change. Before that there was time to mop the floors. Both activities held a certain soothing attraction. He listened at the top of the basement stair before extracting the mop and bucket from the hall cupboard, but there was no sound from Murdo's quarters. Probably the boy had stayed out overnight.

St Jude's was the large Anglican church that lay a quarter of a mile further along the main road into town, and Edward was an irregular attender. At times he felt inclined to abandon it altogether, for he had no personal faith to speak of. He found it painful to watch the philosophical and behavioural wriggling that the Church of England and its more thoughtful adherents were put to as they attempted to reconcile first century theology with twenty-first century sensibilities. And yet, and yet…

It seemed to him that to break with the church at this point in his life would be a wilfully destructive act, and besides, there were things about it that he greatly valued. The building was architecturally impressive but was decorated internally in the low Anglican tradition of whitewashed walls and minimal ecclesiastical clutter. St Jude's was blessed with an exceptional organist and choir-master, and Edward had a deep appreciation of choral music. The rector was a cheerful, intelligent man in early middle age who seemed to be energised by the very dilemmas that daunted Edward, and who combined an active programme of social action with a fearless intellectual scrutiny of moral and theological questions.

It seemed to Edward that on balance the existence of this building, and the odd challenges that it both faced and offered, were an asset to his neighbourhood. And so he supported St Jude's financially, assisted with some of its social programmes, including the food bank, and perhaps once a month attended the early service, a small enough sacrifice of his time that he never regretted.

He sat now on the thinly carpeted wooden pew as the vicar began to wind up his sermon, which today had reflected on the challenges and opportunities presented to Christians by social media. Edward did not engage with social media in any shape or form: as far as he could see it merely added to the sum of envy, anxiety and fear that dogged modern life. He knew however that it was the principle means of communication employed by his students, and he was happy enough to learn a little more about its workings.

Attendance at St Jude's also offered the opportunity to spend some time in contemplation of Anna Parminter. Anna was Edward's solicitor, and was, as usual, seated two rows in front of him and a little to his right, her long back straight and her head tilted attentively to one side. She was in her late forties, and her dark hair, which she wore in a longish bob, was greying a little. Anna had a husband, whom Edward found a little boorish, and who didn't attend St Jude's, and two children at different stages of university education. She was also the Chair of the local Liberal Democrats, and in this latter capacity Edward had from time to time worked with her on political campaigns of various sorts, although it was some years since he had been an active member of the party.

He often thought that Anna was the sort of woman he could have married, and that they might have been happy. He knew that after the service they would talk over coffee, and that there would pass between them an unspoken charge of recognition that would both comfort and unsettle him. He had no idea what effect it had on Anna Parminter, but he did not doubt for a moment that she felt it.

The vicar concluded his remarks, and the congregation rose for the closing hymn.

That same Sunday, Dave Singleman and Kate Porteous, in company with another dozen or so committed surfers, were taking advantage of the improvement in the conditions that had occurred overnight. They had not been late back from Frances's house, and in any case it was worth getting up early, even on a Sunday, to get in a decent spell on the water. They bobbed on their boards now, sixty metres out on the slow, green swell, waiting to catch a wave. The sea was at its coldest at this time of year, and Kate was glad of her wetsuit, although it still felt strange and cumbersome. She was at home in the water, but wasn't used to hanging around getting chilled.

"Here we go!" said Dave.

She glanced behind, and could see the wave he was hoping to catch building suddenly and with surprising speed thirty metres beyond him. She adjusted her position on her board and began pulling herself toward the shore with long, powerful strokes. This was the bit she was good at.

Out of the corner of her eye she could see Dave already starting to pull himself up to a crouch. He had been surfing for years, and while she was improving rapidly she still couldn't match the ease with which he popped up at the critical moment, nor his judgment. There he went! He caught the wave beautifully, while Kate, in spite of her paddling, was left bobbing behind it as it slid beneath her. She sighed and watched with mingled admiration and frustration as Dave weaved his way elegantly towards the shore. One day she would get him in a competition pool and they would have a race. Just so he didn't get too cocky.

She belly-boarded in to join him on the next half-decent wave.

"Fancy a coffee? I seem to have temporarily lost the knack."

"Sure."

They undid the velcro cuffs and wrapped the leashes round the boards, carrying them the two hundred yards along the beach to the café, newly opened after the winter. It was here that they had first shared a drink together, as colleagues and neighbours, on a glorious September evening when Kate, at least, had no thought in her head that anything romantic might develop between them.

Dave got the coffees and they found a table on the terrace that offered the benefit of the weak sunshine and shelter from the breeze. There were a few dog walkers around, but no holiday makers as yet, and the café was quiet.

"So," said Dave. "Tell me your thoughts. About our eviction situation."

They had had no further discussion of the issues raised by the agent's letters, but Kate knew some kind of assessment of the options ought to be made before the working week began.

"My thoughts," she said, briskly, as if it were a simple matter of choosing which restaurant to eat at. "Well I guess it's fairly straightforward. We either look for somewhere to rent together, or we look for somewhere separately."

"And...what about buying? There are some good first-time buyer deals around."

"You mean together? I...I just don't think I'm ready for that. I mean even renting together would be a bit of a step for me."

"We're practically renting together as it is."

"In some respects, yes. But at the end of the day, if I have work to do, or I'm feeling a bit...hemmed in, or whatever, I've got my own space. Having you upstairs is a lovely bonus, but the downstairs is still mine. When you're there, you're there by invitation."

Dave jutted his lower lip, but said nothing. He loved Kate for her independence of spirit, but you could have too much of a good thing. She reached across the table and put her hand on his.

"I'm sorry. It's not about us – really it isn't."

"That's good."

"Maybe I just need to get my head round the idea."

"What if we could rent somewhere big enough that we each still had our own space? I mean we should be able to get a lot more by pooling our resources, and we'd be saving on bills."

"That's true." The Northerner in her was not immune to arguments based on financial advantage. "What about you? What would you do for choice?"

"Well if it was just me, I'd certainly consider buying. I'll have more money coming in from September, and for me, this would be the obvious time to make that step. I'd never be able to afford anything right on the coast, but there are some good solid little houses in Penzance or Newlyn that are probably within my range. My old man has always said he'd help with a deposit."

Kate felt she had said all that needed to be said on the matter of buying. Dave continued,

"But it's just me. You know I'm in this for the long haul. So I guess I'll settle for renting together, if we can find somewhere that gives you the space you need. We need to see what's out there."

"And do our sums," said Kate gloomily. "I don't have much in the way of savings, and I'm still paying off the car." She looked up to the top of the cliff, where the upper storey of the Engine House was just visible. "It's kind of heart-breaking to think we've only got another six months of this."

"But we're so lucky to have had it," said Dave. "And we'll always have the memories."

He was about to add something sententious about nothing good lasting for ever, but realised in time that a half-remembered line from his parents' record collection was probably not what the situation required.

Sammy Pascoe spent much of his Sunday thinking miserably about the imminent demise of his relationship with Issy. He helped around the house with some chores in the morning, then after lunch he took himself off on his bike. The Pascoes lived in a small terraced cottage in the village of Eglos, a few miles outside Newlyn, and there was open countryside more or less on the doorstep. No shortage of hills, but he was as fit as any Cornish teenager who had spent much of his childhood out of doors. He set himself to the long steady climb that would take him up to the quoit known as the Gurnard – an improbable stack of flat slabs of granite, each the size of a small car – that sat on the crown of a gorse-covered knoll high above the coastal settlements.

An hour later, having left his bike in a pile of bracken and climbed via a path that no tourist would ever find, he was perched on the topmost slab, whose scalene mass gave the quoit its name. From here the whole coast from Lizard Point to Porthcurno was laid out before him. The castle on St Michael's Mount sat like a delicately carved ornament in the bay, and tiny vessels of various types plied their separate courses over the wrinkled blue canvas of the sea. Sammy barely noticed any of it as he tried to order his thoughts.

Was he desperately upset? No. He could be philosophical about it. And he recognised that theirs had always been an unlikely alliance. He had known Issy since infant school, so their friendship was deep and well-founded, and this latest romantic complication was something of an oddity. He had been aware for some time that they were all growing up physically, that this happened at different rates, and that he, Sammy was not in the vanguard of their year group's relentless onward push to adulthood. Issy on the other hand, was apparently striding effortlessly into her future self on her long, sun-tanned limbs. They had not been an obvious couple.

Let it go then. Be grateful for what it had been, whatever that was. Issy had said that the friendship would continue, and surely that was the most important thing. He lay back on the slope of the granite slab, letting the sun warm him. Holding his phone up against the light, he squinted at the screen, and expertly punched out a text with his thumb.

Happy to call it a day. All cool. Do we still sit together on the bus?

Chapter Six

"Sir, there's something on the whiteboard"

Monday morning was cloudy and cold, with a restless breeze coming in off the sea. Edward shivered as he climbed the hill from the railway station, regretting that he had not brought a coat. He was a religious checker of weather forecasts, and his time in the Navy, in addition to many years of sailing in small boats with less than reliable engines, had given him an understanding of weather patterns that meant he was seldom caught out. He wondered if he was going down with something.

There had been no sign of the accordionist that morning, and this also unsettled him. There had now been three days with early morning music, and two without. Perhaps the whole matter would simply slide into the past – an oddity that would soon be forgotten, and not, after all, a message from the universe.

As he approached the school gates the odd knots of St Petroc's students, little more than disinterested fellow-travellers on the long road up from the town, converged with others from the large housing estate next to the school, and those the buses had disgorged at the disembarkation area further down the hill. As always at this point in his daily commute, Edward began to feel himself no longer an individual, but part of some greater living entity that was in some sense, even in its subdued Monday morning state, not entirely at ease with itself. He wondered, as he increasingly did these days, how much longer he could or should continue to teach.

On the face of it, there was nothing to keep him at the school. He was still some time off retirement age, but the rules were such that a teacher could go a year or two early in exchange for a reduction in pension. In fact the pension was not the main consideration – there was Tremenhere money still, albeit much reduced these days, in odd bits of property and land. Edward was in any case something of an ascetic, and required little in the way of creature comforts. He had his books, and his music, both of which were inexpensive pleasures. He kept a small, practical car in his garage at the Count House, and a small, rather less practical boat on a swinging mooring near Falmouth. The Count House could do with some maintenance, but there were funds set aside for that. Even if he retired early there should be enough money to travel on the Continent, which was as far afield as he wished to go.

What then kept him at his post, teaching English to adolescents in the challenging environment of a comprehensive school? He supposed it was a reluctance to accept that he was ready to be moved up the line towards what Larkin had skewered as "age, and then the only end of age", to being identified no longer as a working professional, but as a retiree, filling out those empty decades at the end of life with some bespoke combination of idleness, self-indulgence and personal development. There were, and would be, no grandchildren.

Edward knew too that he would miss the social network that school provided. Although to junior students and younger staff he appeared aloof and solitary, he was an established figure in the school, and had friendships – often surprising ones – whose roots lay back beyond the memories of most. These were based on odd connections or shared interests that were not immediately obvious – the Head of Art was married to a Tremenhere cousin; a caretaker sang tenor in the same choir; the great-uncle of a junior member of the history department had once had a share in a fishing boat with Edward's father. Some of these relationships of course might be continued beyond St Petroc's, but there was comfort and security in seeing these people day by day, even if no words were exchanged.

Registration and the first lesson of the day went smoothly enough. On Monday breaktimes the entire teaching body crammed into the staffroom for the weekly briefing, but Edward had some time ago secured that slot as his staff duty, which meant that he could grab a quick coffee and excuse himself, spending the time instead supervising the middle school playground and the adjacent teaching block. This meant he was often under-informed as to what was going on in the wider life of the school, but that was not something he found to be a problem.

Still feeling a little chilled, he wandered in desultory fashion from classroom to classroom, conversing occasionally with students who knew him, and snuffing out, usually with little more than a cold stare and a raised eyebrow, any incipient mischief. Incipient mischief on a Monday morning was relatively rare, which was another reason why this particular duty slot suited him.

The bell rang for the end of break, and he made his way back to the staffroom to return his coffee cup. This involved swimming against the tide of teachers who were leaving the briefing, and inevitably delayed him a little, so that by the time he embarked upon the journey back to his classroom, the school was for the most part at lessons. As he walked along the long corridor of the main teaching block he could hear the rising hubbub of his year nine group, who would be lined up on the stair outside the classroom, and he felt his irritation mounting. In all other classrooms along his route students were settling to work, so that the noise of his class was even more conspicuous. He weighed up whether to administer a bollicking, or acknowledge the inevitability of the behaviour and assume the situation would resolve itself upon his arrival. He caught a glimpse of a face – Toby Trott's, he thought – that appeared briefly round the corner and disappeared swiftly, no doubt to sound the warning of his arrival.

The furore died down rapidly as he approached, so that the class were largely silent by the time he reached the door. He paused before opening it, and made eye contact with a few notable individuals. Toby Trott returned his gaze with innocent insolence, and Edward had a momentary fantasy of boxing the boy's ears.

"This," he said, "is the level of noise that is expected whether the teacher is within sight, or not. Now enter the classroom quietly, and have your books and equipment out and your bags under your desks without my having to say anything further."

He paused to ensure that the message had sunk in, then opened the door and strode to the front of the classroom. The students filed in behind him in more or less respectful silence. A little too respectful, thought Edward as he stood behind his desk and watched them settle, removing books and pencil cases from backpacks. He had a sense that something was afoot.

Trott's hand went up.

"Sir there's something on the whiteboard."

Edward turned to the board. Scrawled in green marker pen was the single word PEEDO.

He turned back to the class. There was an attentive, interested silence. Nobody was giggling. Edward suddenly felt very weary. He pulled his seat out from behind his desk and placed it in the centre of the teaching space in front of the board. He sat down and eyeballed Toby Trott.

"Stand up please, Toby."

Trott looked a little surprised, but rose to his feet without argument.

"You have been in my class since September. Is it my practice to clean the board at the end of each lesson?"

Trott looked less sure of himself. "I dunno Sir."

"Let me put it another way. Is it unusual for there to be writing on the board at the start of a lesson?"

Trott shrugged. He understood where this was going.

"Anybody?" Edward's gaze swept the class. There were shakings of heads; some muttered negatives.

"No. There is frequently writing on the board at the start of my lessons, so I am bound to ask why you saw fit to comment upon it this morning."

"Well it's just," said Trott, collecting himself, "that it isn't the sort of thing I would expect a teacher to write."

"Quite so," said Edward. "It is, of course, the sort of thing you might expect a student to write, as a rather unpleasant kind

45

of practical joke. And you, Mister Trott, are currently my number one suspect. By drawing my attention to it you would be, in effect, returning to the scene of the crime."

"Sir it wasn't me that wrote it."

"I am afraid the jury is out on that one for the moment. And whether or not it was you that wrote it, it is you who will rub it off. NOW!"

The interrogation up to this point had been conducted in measured, if slightly menacing, tones. The class recognised that their teacher's mood was finely balanced, and the atmosphere was tense. But Edward's temper was fraying, and his actions now were conditioned not only by the events of the morning. His unmarried status and the lingering whiff of a decades-old scandal all fed in to the muddled adolescent mythology that exists in every school. For the most part Edward lived with it, and these days it only rarely surfaced in incidents such as this one. It was the accumulation of the frustration of years, combined with the extraordinary and widely acknowledged capacity of Toby Trott to irritate, that caused him to bellow the final syllable. The class jumped perceptibly, and Trott blanched. For a few seconds it looked as though he might attempt further argument, but under Edward's baleful gaze he rose from his seat and did as he was asked.

"And now, said Edward, reverting to his dangerously calm voice, "Turn to chapter three of *Animal Farm.*"

The rest of the morning passed without incident. An unusually good lunchtime pasty helped to restore Edward's equanimity, and to dispel the lingering chill in his bones. In the afternoon he had a free lesson, and was in his classroom marking books when Frances's head appeared round the door.

"Hello Edward, do you have a minute?"

"Of course. Grab a chair." He put down his pen and sat back.

"That's all right, I'll perch." Frances was tall, and striking to look at, and used both to advantage when controlling a class. She sat elegantly on one of the desks in the front row.

"I've had Toby Trott's mother on the phone."

"Really? What does she want this time?" Mrs Trott was an inveterate telephoner and emailer. A certain mismatch between her own perceptions of her son's brilliance and nobility of character and the boy's actual achievements and behaviour meant there was no shortage of material for her communications.

"She claims you verbally assaulted Toby in his English lesson today. She says that he rang her at lunchtime in considerable distress, because he had tried to be helpful and you accused him of something he hadn't done, and shouted at him in an intimidatory manner."

Frances was one of a small number of teachers at the school who held Edward in high regard. They both knew that parental complaints happened from time to time, that they were sometimes rooted in fact, and that they had to be followed up. Her tone was only lightly ironic, but it was enough for Edward to know she was on his side.

"I shouted a single word in what I suppose you might call an intimidatory manner," said Edward. "For the rest, my tone was sweetly reasonable, particularly given the circumstances. And I didn't accuse him of anything. I merely pointed out that he was acting suspiciously."

"And the circumstances were?"

Edward told her.

"Ah. That's unpleasant. Are you all right?"

"Yes, I'm OK. I think. I just wasn't feeling a hundred percent, and it took me by surprise. It's been a while since anything like that happened. Actually the class were pretty good. There was no sense of it being a group effort."

"Do you think it was Toby that wrote it?"

Edward shrugged.

"It was mis-spelled, though that hardly narrows the field. I'm happy to let it go, so long as it doesn't turn out to be the start of a trend."

"You should formally report it."

Edward looked at her sceptically.

"Well it's up to you. At any rate, you can leave Mrs Trott to me. I just needed to hear the whole story."

"Thank you. And I'm sorry to add to your workload. Do you ever get this sort of nonsense?"

"From time to time. Last year somebody wrote "Fivey is a dyke" on a desk in my room. I turned it into quite a good lesson. Simple sentence, assonance, power of the stressed monosyllable. Then I set them an essay on the potential of language to wound and diminish."

"How did that go down?"

"Well I thought it went down very well. Then at the end I asked if there were any questions. Jasmine Tregunna put up her hand and said, "So Miss, *are* you a dyke?""

Edward smiled. "As only Jasmine Tregunna could. I don't think it would have been wise to offer 9K the chance to ask questions."

The problem, thought Edward as he waited for the train back to Roskear, was that unlike Frances, who was gloriously and unarguably "out" in an age when such things were, at least officially, beyond reproach, his own quite strong instinct was to keep his ambiguous sexuality to himself. In his early days at the school it had been a different matter. He was then in his early thirties, a dashingly handsome and recently promoted Head of English, with a First from Cambridge and a short service commission in the navy behind him. He had felt invincible, carefree, and careless of the opinions of others. That had resulted in him leaving his job.

"All right Mr Tremenhere?"

A diminutive year seven student from his form had joined him on his bench, and sat now with his legs swinging as he licked his ice cream.

Edward smiled. "Yes I'm fine thank you. How are you?"

"Not too bad. That's Monday done, eh?"

"It is indeed. And that's always a good thing."

"Can you do that thing with the coin again?"

Edward occasionally entertained his form group with a simple piece of sleight of hand that he had learnt from the Master-at-Arms on a Type 21 frigate.

"Ask me another time. The train will be here any minute."

"Right on. Here it comes now!" And the child jumped up and wandered off down the platform to re-join his friends.

Chapter Seven

"A St Laurent scarf round the neck of a traffic warden"

Sammy and Issy sat side by side in silence as the school bus rattled back along the road to Eglos. They had said little to one another on the morning journey, although they had hugged briefly at the bus-stop as they always did. They were in different forms this year, which meant that they were in different classes for most of their subjects. English was an exception as they were both in a top set. At breaktime Sammy had wandered vaguely around their usual haunts, but Issy was nowhere to be seen, and he had begun to suspect that he was looking lost and needy, and that maybe hanging out together at break was something that would inevitably disappear down the cracks between a friendship and a relationship.

He was discomfited by not knowing what people knew, or what they might guess, and when he would have to acknowledge that he was no longer going out with Issy. There would be the inevitable questions about who dumped who - fourteen-year olds are not delicate in such matters. Perhaps everybody would just assume that he was the dumpee. He wasn't sure whether that was a comforting thought or not. At lunchtime he decided to cut his losses and join the tech team in the theatre. They would be making plans for the junior play soon, and he was keen to signal his interest. Mr d'Allesandro had been pleased to see him, and Sammy felt a little guilty that he had let his commitment slide in recent months.

Now he sat staring out of the window of the bus, watching for the occasional flashes of primroses on the verges as they barrelled along the main road. Then, as the bus turned off towards Eglos, Issy said,

"Mum and Dad are going to do up the Engine House."

"Oh. OK. Does that mean Singleman and Porteous will have to move out?"

"Yup."

"Will they let them back in again?"

"Dunno. Dad was a bit cagey. If they do they'll probably put the rent up."

"Right. Bit harsh, isn't it?"

"Not really. Not if Mum and Dad have invested money in it to make it nicer to live in."

Sammy thought about this. He was in Ms Porteous's form, and he and Issy had watched the uneven courtship of their teachers unfold the previous term. Or rather Issy had watched, and offered Sammy a running commentary, mostly on the bus to and from school. He hadn't really been that interested, though he liked both teachers, and in a generalised way he wanted a happy outcome. He was sensitive to the arbitrary and apparently undeserved power that the Brunels wielded as a result of their wealth, but this had to be balanced against their friendliness towards him. The Brunel family home was opulent, but Issy's parents had always gone out of their way to make him feel welcome.

"Do they know?"

"Yeah, they've had letters. They don't have to be out till the autumn. Keep it quiet, though, will you?"

"Yeah, sure."

Issy's father believed in explaining to his elder daughter how their property business operated. She was under strict instructions to maintain confidentiality, and Sammy, in whose discretion she had absolute trust, was the only person to whom such information was ever imparted. He took the sharing of this latest nugget as a kind of peace offering, a gesture from Issy to reassure him that the friendship was still on course.

The bus pulled into the Eglos layby, and they alighted with half a dozen other St Petroc's kids. The Brunel Range Rover was parked across the road. There was another brief hug before they went their separate ways.

Well, that's day one of the new normal out the way, Sammy thought, as he walked up the lane to the cottage.

Edward's walk home from Roskear station to the Count House took him through the town centre, which was convenient for picking up odd bits of shopping. Today he had some letters to post, one of which would need to be sent recorded delivery. There was a queue at the Post Office, which was now situated at the back of WH Smiths, and he stood in line patiently, trying to remember how the premises had been set out before the alteration. How long ago was it now? How quickly one forgot. How quickly years slid by.

The queue moved slowly forward. Two spaces in front of him was a large man with a shaved and tattooed head, and even with the advantage of his own height Edward's view of those at the counter was impeded. In any case he was in pensive mood. He pondered upon the odd conjunction of the graffiti on his whiteboard and the unabashed friendliness of the Year Seven boy at the station. How long before some helpful adolescent or older sibling initiated him into a bastardised version of the scandalous past of Mr Tremenhere?

He was nearing the front of the queue, and his reverie was disturbed by a growing awareness of a French accent. Somebody was enquiring about postage rates – a young woman's voice, light and quick – the English perfectly good. She thanked the assistant, and the queue advanced again.

The man with the tattooed head, his own business complete, passed him on his way out of the shop, closely followed by the young woman with the French accent. It was the accordionist, ash blonde hair under the same hippy cap, her bulky back-pack carried with apparent ease on strong young shoulders. It was the first time he had seen her face, and he was struck by the contrasting presence of youth and wisdom in her expression. She must barely be out of her teens, but there was an assurance there, a confidence in her own unanswerable vigour and beauty that was somehow very French. In the workaday surroundings of Roskear Post Office, at the back of WH Smith's, she stood out like a St Laurent scarf round the neck of a traffic warden.

For a moment Edward stood, unsure what to do. He was now at the front of the queue; and the woman ahead of him at the counter was fastening her purse and opening her handbag. He needed to catch the post that day, and yet – he craned round. The young woman was at the door, stepping back nimbly to allow someone to enter before she herself left the shop. A robotic voice was calling him forward. He stepped out of the queue and turned back towards the door.

As if on a well-organised film set, the aisles of magazines and stationery now filled with an assortment of awkwardly shaped and slow-moving browsers. Ahead of him Edward could see that the girl was now on the pavement, the glass door swinging to behind her. He muttered apologies as he threaded his way through the tangle of customers. As he reached the door the man with the tattooed head reappeared, returning for some forgotten item. There was a moment of absurd sashaying between the two large men before Edward was past him and out into the chill of the early evening.

He glanced quickly up and down the street, which was busy with early evening shoppers, but he could see no sign of the girl. Fifty yards down the road, on the other side, the St Ives bus was taking on passengers, and he had a sudden conviction that she would be on board. There were cars coming both ways so he ran down his own side of the road until he was almost level with the bus. Yes! There she was, slipping into a seat on the top deck. He went to cross the road but a blast from a car horn forced him back onto the pavement. The bus began to move.

Edward stood helplessly and watched as the double decker pulled out into the flow of traffic. As it drew past him, the girl on the top deck turned and held his gaze. She gave no indication that she recognised him, seeming instead to stare right through him. Then the bus was past him, fifty, a hundred yards down the road. There were traffic lights a quarter of a mile away, and for a moment he considered pursuit. Then the folly of the situation struck him, and he turned and walked back to WH Smith's where he joined the end of a now considerably longer queue.

Edward avoided Murdo on his return, retreating instead to his upstairs study until the clattering in the kitchen suggested that the boy was starting on supper. The catering arrangements at the Count House were flexible. Murdo paid rent that covered his rooms and a share of the bills, and the original assumption was that he would cater for himself as and when. It had become apparent however that despite his frequently appalling diet, he was a perfectly capable cook, and occasionally he would offer to produce a meal. Edward had responded cautiously at first, but to his surprise the food had been perfectly tasty, and Murdo had settled into a routine of cooking for them on a Monday evening. Tonight it was what his lodger insisted on calling "mince and tatties", a visually unappealing but nonetheless appetising dish which Edward was happy enough to eat provided it was accompanied by some kind of green vegetable. Murdo invariably grumbled about this, dismissing it as middle-class affectation, and insisted that Edward attend to his own broccoli.

These logistical complexities were now behind them and they were seated at the deal table in the kitchen, the main course dispatched and Edward in the process of peeling a banana, while Murdo scraped the remains of a Tesco chocolate pudding from its plastic tub.

"Pretty shockin' about old man Narabo, eh?"

Edward looked up. "What about him?"

"Did you no hear? He only dropped down dead in the Council chamber this afternoon."

"Goodness. He can't have been more than sixty."

"Sixty-two. So that'll be a nice juicy by-election on our doorstep."

Edward was genuinely taken aback. Vincent Narabo had been the Conservative councillor for a largely rural ward that began just outside Roskear and extended south to include both St Petroc's school and the neighbouring Penhale estate. He was also a governor at the school. A colourful figure with colourful opinions, he had aroused devotion and loathing in equal measure. Edward had known him vaguely. As is often the case in politics, however, sentiment at any sudden demise was almost immediately displaced by calculation.

"What's his majority?"

"A couple of hundred ahead of you lot. But it's an odd one. The opposition was split four ways last time, and they all got a decent vote. I reckon Labour could take it if they put the work in."

Edward chewed reflectively on the remainder of his banana, then folded the skin neatly on the side of his plate.

"I hate to disappoint you, Murdo, but Labour don't do terribly well down here. Not in local elections. It's Lib Dem, Tory or Independent, plus a few Cornish Nationalists."

"That's because people have forgotten what Labour stand for. They just need tae be reminded. And there's an army of activists up at the Uni ready and willing to do just that. You wait."

If Murdo was expecting a good gnarly argument with his landlord, he was disappointed. Edward rose from the table and began the clearing up. When Murdo proposed a game of chess after the dishes were done, he declined, saying that he had marking to do. He needed to think.

Ten miles away in the tiny terraced miner's cottage in Eglos, Sammy and his parents were also eating supper, not at a table, for that was covered with Maisie's parish council papers, but seated around the small cheerful fire that was kept up for most of the year.

"You know this house?" said Sammy.

"I should do – I've lived here long enough" said his father.

"We don't own it, do we?"

"No, we rent it."

"Who do we rent it from?"

Viv Pascoe glanced at his wife. In fact the property was owned by the Tremenhere family. Sammy had never raised the matter before, and they weren't sure how he might feel about having one of his teachers as a landlord.

"Well we deal with an agency in Roskear," said Maisie. We never see the actual owner."

"Why d'you ask, Sam?"

"Well could the landlord, or the agents, or whoever, just decide they don't want to rent to us any more? I just heard of that happening to somebody. Like, they were given a few months' notice, and they had to leave." He was mindful of the confidence he had promised to Issy.

"Well in theory they could," acknowledged Maisie. "But we rent from an old Cornish family who own two or three houses in the village, and they don't treat their tenants like that. The only family I've ever known be evicted were a real problem, and they gave them ever so many second chances before they kicked them out."

"So when you say an old Cornish family," said Sammy, who sensed that his parents, for whatever reason, were unwilling to make full disclosure, "it's not the Brunels, is it?"

"No son, it's not the Brunels. Though I'm sure old man Brunel is a decent enough landlord. He's a very fair employer."

Sammy nodded but said nothing. He had never been very comfortable with the fact that his father worked for the Brunels, albeit on an occasional basis. He was glad they were not also their landlords, able on a whim to kick them out, do up the cottage, and only re-admit them on a higher rent. Although he could not have articulated it so precisely, the moment marked the awakening of a political sensibility in his young mind.

"Terrible news about Councillor Narabo," said Maisie, changing, as she thought, the subject.

Chapter Eight

"As if the world were open before him"

Sammy did not find that week particularly easy. Rumours that the romance of the previous term had run out of steam had begun circulating on Wednesday. At first, nobody said anything to him, but there were some sympathetic glances, which was bad enough. Then at breaktime on Friday, Donkey Doggett, unlikely poster-boy of the Year 9 Aspiration and Achievement programme, slouched up to him. The two had never been friends but Donkey had of late been enjoying his new status, and was making something of an effort to moderate his more loutish tendencies.

"All over then with you and the maid?"

Sammy tried to look unconcerned.

"Well – there was never that much to it, to be honest."

"How far you get with her?"

"That's a kind of personal question."

Donkey grinned. "Not very far then."

Sammy said nothing.

"I heard she dumped you?"

"Did you? Well there you go."

"Well, did she or didn't she?"

"It was kind of mutual."

"Thassa yes, then. Was it 'cos she fancies somebody else?"

"Donkey, do us a favour will you?"

"Whassat?"

"Just fuck off. Go and write an essay or something."

Donkey grinned again, less pleasantly this time.

"You wanna mind your manners Pascoe. You and I both know that I could punch your twatty little head for you, and nobody would be any the wiser. But I've got a position to maintain, so I'll let it go this time. You've told me what I need to know."

And with that he wandered off, hands in pockets.

Dave and Kate had agreed that on Friday after school they would hit the letting agents in town. They had already been on the websites, but it was clear that not all the available property found its way online. They split up for efficiency, working into the centre from opposite ends of the High Street and meeting for a drink to compare notes on completion.

The understanding at this stage was that they were looking for something to rent together, and Dave conscientiously collected details for properties that fitted this description, ones with enough spare room to accommodate Kate's need for space. He had also cast his eye over one or two that he thought might be within his budget to buy outright, although from what he could see from a cursory glance he knew that Kate would regard them as far too cramped. These he left on the shelf.

Kate took a different approach. She was not being dishonest when she had assured Dave that her commitment to the relationship was solid, but that did not, in her mind, mean that they had to cohabit seven days a week. In fact she was pretty sure such an arrangement at this early stage of their romance would be a threat to their long term future, rather than cementing it. She was therefore not averse to some discreet investigation of other options. Now she was standing outside the window of Fox and Penwerris, eyeing up the details of the Net Loft, a bijoux apartment to let on the waterfront at Newlyn with a small rear sun terrace. She entered the shop, and when she re-emerged a few minutes later, the details of the Net Loft were tucked in an inside zip pocket of her bag.

They met as agreed at the Clipper on Chapel Street just before six, and Kate found a table in the corner while Dave ordered the drinks – a pint of Betty Stoggs for himself and a ginger beer and lime for Kate. He set the glasses down carefully, for the tables in the Clipper were notoriously wobbly, then he pulled out one of the small barrels that, with the welcome addition of an ancient velvet cushion, served as a seat.

"So," he said. "What have you got?"

"Well…" Kate didn't bother trying to sound too upbeat. "Not a lot that thrills me if I'm honest. I've got half a dozen or so that are within our price range, and reasonably well-located, but they're just a bit…I dunno…uninspiring I guess."

"We need to not keep comparing them to the Engine House," said Dave. "That's a one-off, believe me."

"No, I get that," said Kate, trying to push the Net Loft from her mind. "But I really don't think I can face a modern flat, or anything on a housing estate. My soul would just shrivel. And the fisherman's cottages are sweet, but a bit small for the two of us." She flicked through her sheaf of papers dismissively. "I mean, have a look if you like. It's all a bit depressing."

Dave studied the leaflets that Kate had collected. The unworthy thought crossed his mind that perhaps she hadn't been trying very hard.

"This one's quite a decent size. It's got a bit of garden too."

"Dave, it's a bungalow. I'm only twenty seven. I'm not quite ready to start cultivating azaleas in my spare time. I only put it in to make up the numbers."

"Fair enough. Well, I see what you mean. But I think I've found a couple that are better than these."

He passed across two of his finds that had rather more character than Kate's uninspiring collection. She examined them critically, quizzing him on the locations. He knew the area much better than she did.

"This one's only got two bedrooms." They had agreed that a third bedroom was essential.

"Yes but they're a decent size. And it's got this studio thing in the back. I thought maybe that could be a retreat for you if the proximity was all getting a bit much." There was indeed a substantial summerhouse in stained wood, which had been kitted out attractively with cushions and hammocks.

"And it's got a garage for the surf gear," he added, a little hesitantly. He was wary of over-selling.

Kate looked at him.

"Oh Dave." He was unsure whether she was expressing frustration or affection, then he saw that her eyes were soft behind her glasses.

"You OK?"

"Yes, yes I'm fine. And you're very lovely."

"Maybe we could make an appointment? Just for that one? I mean you can't really tell from the details."

"Maybe. Look, shall we go home? I need to get out of my school clothes. I've picked up something nice for supper."

They finished their drinks and left the pub.

Edward Tremenhere was also in a pub that Friday evening, a quiet inn a mile outside Roskear. He was sitting opposite Anna Parminter, whose dark eyes seemed particularly soulful in the soft evening light. They had met at Edward's request to discuss the Liberal Democrats response to the by-election that would inevitably follow from Vincent Narabo's sudden and unfortunate passing. Edward had been rather semi-detached from the party in recent years, but he continued to support it and had remained a member. Anna had seemed happy enough to spare him an hour. Perhaps the boorish husband, whose name Edward could never recall, was up country on one of his regular business trips.

"So. The end of Vincent Narabo. Must have been a bit of a shock for the councillors."

"I think most of them were nodding off. Vincent was apparently halfway through a long and rather dull speech on the need to free up planning restrictions. Those who noticed thought at first he had just paused for effect. We've sent our condolences to Mrs Narabo, of course."

"Any idea when the by-election will be called?"

"Well they'll want to avoid Easter, so there's no rush. I imagine they'll go for early May. Don't tell me you're thinking of standing?"

"Is that such an outlandish idea?"

"Not at all. But you know…we have approached you once or twice in the past, and you've never been interested."

"Yes, well. For everything there is a season, and all that. I could never have done the job properly while I was teaching full time, but I'm now at the stage…" He nearly said "age", but some streak of vanity prevented him, "…where I'm looking at other options."

"Well…that's welcome news. Of course we would need to run a formal selection. And you would have to go through approval first – not that that would be a problem."

"Is there anybody else who might be interested in standing?"

"Well nobody has come forward yet, but it's early days. Trevor Williams stood last time, but we had to twist his arm."

"He did all right though."

"Oh yes. There's a solid Liberal vote in the ward, but we need to get another couple of hundred of them to turn out. And the Tories will chuck everything at it."

"My spies tell me Labour think that it's winnable too."

"Well that's wishful thinking. But they'll take votes from us if they put up a sensible candidate."

"So…where do we go from here?"

"The first thing is for me to email members looking for expressions of interest. You need to formally respond to that. In the meantime you could start reading up on the ward. You don't actually live in it, do you?"

"No, I'm about half a mile outside. But the school's in the ward."

"Ah! Now that could be a problem. Is St Petroc's a local authority school or an academy?"

"It's an academy," said Edward, in a tone that suggested a lack of enthusiasm for the concept.

"That's all right then. You're technically not an employee of the council. Good! Well obviously, I'll be delighted if you're the candidate, but there are the usual hoops to jump through first."

"Of course. I'm assuming nothing. Would you like another drink?"

Their eyes met briefly. The meeting up to now had been perfectly business-like, but for a second there was that familiar feeling of connection.

"I'd better get back. I've no idea what I'm cooking tonight."

"I'm going to eat here, I think. I might have another glass of wine and take the bus home."

"Oh. That sounds rather a nice idea."

"Why don't you join me?"

"Well…would you mind?"

"Of course not."

Presumably, then, there was nobody at the Parminter residence waiting to be fed. That was interesting.

They stayed in the pub until just before nine, when the bus was due. They shared a bottle of wine with the meal, and Edward noticed that Anna kept pace with him as they drank. They talked a little more about politics, and a lot about Cambridge, and the differences between their experiences there, which were almost a decade apart. They split the bill without argument.

The bus stop was across the road from the pub. Anna took his arm as they crossed, and in the glow of the alcohol it seemed no more than a companionable gesture, or a response to the trailing edge of winter that could be felt on the March wind. They stepped instinctively into the darkness of the bus shelter, and here the conversation dried a little, as if, with the crossing of the road, the situation had moved into new and unfamiliar territory. Then Anna said,

"Julian's having an affair."

Julian! That was the boor's name. At first Edward could think of nothing appropriate to say in response. Then he started to say he was sorry, but Anna cut across him.

"I don't know why I said that. I mean, it's true, but…sorry. You're the only person I've told."

"Well…I'm glad you did. That's horrible. How did you… I mean…"

"He told me. He wants a divorce. The children don't know yet. I suppose we'll tell them when they come back for Easter."

"Well I'm very sorry to hear that. I mean I've never been a particular fan of Julian's, but you've been married a long time."

"Twenty five years this summer."

"Were you…happy?"

"Oh God, I don't know. What does happy feel like? It was fine. We lived well. I suppose I never stopped to look too closely." She gave a short laugh. "Well, clearly I didn't."

At that point the bus came into sight, its swaying double storey of lights illuminating the trees and the hedgerows as it ground towards them. Edward put his arms round Anna and held her close. It felt a little strange, but it seemed the right thing to do. He could feel the quality of her woollen coat against his chin and he could smell what he knew was expensive perfume. She leaned her head briefly against his shoulder.

"Thank you," she said, and they broke apart as the bus pulled up next to them.

They paid with their cards and climbed up to the top deck. The front seats were both empty and there was an odd moment when it was unclear whether they would share, or take a seat each. Anna slid into the one on the left, and moved close to the window, and Edward took this as permission to join her. He felt suddenly young again, as if the world were open before him and everything was possible once more. They were silent as the bus sped along the main road towards Roskear. Anna lived on the nearer side of town, Edward on the farther. They would soon be at her stop.

Anna said quietly,

"Will you come in with me Edward? Please?"

Chapter Nine

"The jewels in the crown of number fourteen"

On Friday evening, Dave and Kate had taken a more considered look at the six or seven properties that could not be immediately ruled out. 14 Penmere Terrace, the one with the studio and the garage, was the only one that Kate was willing to consider. It was agreed however that they would try to find another two on the internet, so that by Monday they would have looked at three properties, and at least have moved matters forward to that extent. Dave had a game of golf arranged for Saturday afternoon, which he was willing to cancel, but as it turned out they were able to arrange a viewing of the Penmere Avenue property for eleven o'clock on Saturday morning. Two further viewings were scheduled for the following day.

Now it was Saturday, and they were driving slowly along Penmere Terrace, a narrow lane high above Newlyn harbour, with cars parked bumper to bumper along one side of the road.

"Parking isn't going to be easy," said Kate. Then, catching Dave's eye, "Sorry."

They had agreed there would be no negative comments until after the viewing was complete. Eventually they found a space a hundred yards or so from number fourteen.

"Nice view," said Dave by way of evening the score as they walked back along the narrow pavement.

There was indeed a fine view of Newlyn's busy fishing harbour, from which faint boaty sounds and faint fishy smells floated up on the breeze. The effect was rather pleasant. Kate noted the short front gardens, many with recycling bins tucked under the living-room windows. Clearly, space was at a premium. There was however a kind of cheerful, community feel to the road. She imagined there might be a mix of young professional couples, some with small families, and older more established residents. Grudgingly, she acknowledged to herself that the location at least was acceptable. It was a few minutes' drive from the school.

Number fourteen was clearly identifiable by the letting agent's board in the front garden, and by the letting agent standing beside it. This was a tall, genial young man by the name of Tim, who swayed like a sunflower as he greeted them. He looked a little out of place with his suit and clipboard amid the Saturday morning clutter. Kate felt very conscious of how coupley they themselves must look, and was sure she could sense Tim sizing up their letting potential. So long as he didn't say anything about there being room for a growing family (which in any case there clearly wasn't). She found herself deliberately making space between Dave and herself as Tim fiddled with his keys. She glanced around the small front garden. It was tidy enough, spruced up no doubt for the re-letting. The house was one in a long, terraced row, but a little wider than the fisherman's cottages nearer the harbour. The front doors of those opened straight into their living rooms, but when Tim finally did get the door of number fourteen open, it gave onto a narrow hall.

It took only ten minutes for Tim to sway and duck his way around the property, pointing out an original feature here, an open fireplace there, and for Kate and Dave to establish that the rooms were square, clean and empty, and approximately the size that had been indicated in the details. Tim cautiously offered the opinion that the back bedroom, while not having the advantage of the view, would be fine as a guest bedroom, office *or nursery*. This, Kate pretended not to hear. The bathroom had been recently and rather tastefully redone, and would certainly be an improvement on her current

64

arrangements at the Engine House, although she reminded herself that she would be sharing it with Dave. While he was not what you would call a slob, he had one or two habits that might need to be discussed. The kitchen was perfectly serviceable, with a functional breakfast bar.

"So where are the garage and studio?" asked Dave, a little anxiously. He knew that on the evidence so far presented, Kate would be unconvinced.

"Ah, yes," Tim swayed a little, and Kate began to feel mildly seasick. "The jewels in the crown of number fourteen. They're across the lane at the back."

They followed Tim out of the kitchen door and across the small back courtyard. Sure enough there was an unmade lane, reasonably wide, and on the other side of this a further area of land with the garage – not large but sufficient for either one of their two vehicles, and the wooden studio, set back on a small area of patio with some tired looking winter pansies in terracotta tubs. The studio had its own small veranda, which caught the late morning sun. Inside however it was not like the photograph. The hammock and cushions, presumably the property of the previous tenants, or borrowed for the photograph, were absent, and there was a smell of damp. There was power and light, however, and with a little imagination you could see that it might be pleasant in the summer.

As they wandered back through the ground floor to the front of the house, Tim ventured a shift in tone from vaguely deferential chumminess to something more business-like.

"Are you looking to move soon?"

"We're not in a rush," said Kate before Dave could respond.

Tim swayed a little, but was undeterred.

"And what are your initial feelings about number fourteen? Might it fit your needs? It's a great position."

Dave and Kate exchanged a glance.

"Well we wouldn't rule it out, said Dave, "but we've got a couple of others to see, and as Kate says, we're flexible in terms of timing."

"Just be aware our rental properties aren't hanging on the market," said Tim, his voice lowering a little as if imparting privileged information. "This will be gone by next week."

"Sure," said Kate, "Understood."

"Excellent," said Tim, brightening again, and turning his sunflower face to the sky, as if checking for omens, or an incoming flight of the Red Arrows. "Well, I'll give you my card. Give me a ring if you want to take things further. I'll just go back and make sure everything's locked up."

They said their farewells and walked back to the car in silence. The difficulty of negotiating Newlyn's narrow streets gave them sufficient excuse to defer discussion until they were out on the coast road.

"What did you think?" asked Dave, in neither hope nor expectation.

"Well. I mean the location was quite good - it'd be handy being able to walk into town. And it's nice that it overlooks the harbour. But I can't say my heart leapt at the accommodation."

"No, I know what you mean," agreed Dave. "If we were desperate, then probably we'd consider it, but we don't actually have to move till the autumn, so…"

"It would be quite cramped," said Kate. "That studio might be nice in the summer, but not really all the year round. And the back bedroom was a bit small."

"I guess," said Dave carefully, as they pulled onto the gravel parking area at Wheal Prosper, "that if we were to share the front bedroom, we could use the back as a kind of overflow space. Which could be mainly yours if you like. I mean – you could make it quite cosy, like a den, or something."

"Hmm," said Kate. "That's a bit of a leap from our current arrangement." She had not yet committed to the idea of full-time bedroom sharing, as Dave well knew.

"Yeah, I get that," said Dave. "Ah well. We've made some progress. Let's see what we think of tomorrow's offerings."

Murdo McAndrew climbed the long hill from the railway station in Penzance, chewing on a pasty and talking animatedly to his immediate companion. This was an older man in a black beanie, who nodded along, but said little in response. They were part of a larger group, and many of them wore the colour red somewhere about their persons. It was in fact the same route that Edward took every working day, but this did not strike Murdo until they reached the school, and he noticed the name, and put two and two together. This brought a brief hiatus in the conversation, and the older man spoke.

"What you have to remember," he said, "is that it's been an uphill struggle for Labour down here over the years, even for Westminster elections. We find Jeremy doesn't go down all that well on the doorstep."

"Aye, but this estate's, what…eight hundred houses?" countered Murdo. "If we can get even half of them to turn out for us, we'll take the seat. It's just a matter of raising consciousness."

"Well let's see how we get on today," said his companion, who was a man named Mallinson. He was a member of the executive of the local branch of the Labour party, and one of a number of possible candidates for the forthcoming by-election. He was also Murdo's politics tutor. "One thing's for sure, Narabo's done nothing for them for the past few years. You'll probably find nobody's heard of him."

They were past the school now, and nearing the entrance to the Penhale estate, and they paused to let the stragglers catch up. They were a disparate bunch. Around half of them were unmistakably students, but there were several older activists, including a couple of deceptively mild-looking grey haired ladies, one of whom carried a bulging Guardian tote bag. There were a good many badges on display , some worn on lapels and some on hats. A few of the group were long-standing members, but most of the students were relatively new to politics, inspired by the cult of Corbynism to give up their Saturdays in pursuit of a better world.

"Right," said Mallinson, as the group gathered round and the chatter died down. "Just a few pointers for those who haven't done this before. We're after two things here. Voting intention, and topics of concern. Offer the householder some literature, and leave a leaflet if there's nobody in. I'll be running the board so report back to me after each contact, and don't go to a door until I send you. If you get any aggro just politely wish the householder good day and move on. Don't get into an argument. Close any gates on entering or leaving the property. Anyone who wants a spatula can get one from Jenny."

"What do we do with the spatula?" asked one of the students.

"You fold your leaflet round the spatula so," said Jenny, demonstrating, "then you push it through the letter box. In case of dogs."

"Spatulas?" said Murdo derisively, as Jenny handed them out. "Where I come from yer no an activist if ye've still got all your fingertips."

One or two of the students giggled nervously. Mallinson ignored Murdo. He was still unsure how to make best use of the young man's peculiar blend of political nous and disruptive energy, which had been evident in tutorials as well as on sessions such as these. He set about dividing the group into pairs, so that inexperienced canvassers were put out with older hands, and the disparate band made their way into the estate.

Donovan Doggett, known throughout the Penhale estate as Donkey, was eating his pasty at the red formica table in his kitchen, dropping odd morsels in the way of Spikey, his Staffordshire bull terrier, when the Labour party campaign machine reached his front door. The Doggett household was a happier place these days, since Isaac Doggett's release from prison a few months previously, and the consequent departure of his drug-dealing older son for the badlands of Bristol. Father and first-born had effectively passed one another in opposite directions, for Isaac was a largely reformed character, having begun studying for an OU degree in criminology while in prison. His return had happily coincided with, and indeed encouraged, Donkey's decision try a different approach to school, and to life in general. Neither Doggett was entirely secure in his new direction, but for the moment the two kept one another more or less upright in the manner of two heavy slabs of granite propped together at an angle, while Mrs Doggett, who did her best, looked on anxiously in anticipation of collapse.

The confident rapping of the Doggett letter box interrupted a rather one-sided discussion of the concept of personal responsibility, and set up a growling from Spikey.

"See to the dog," said Isaac, and hoisted his broad bulk from the table. He was not a tall man – Donkey got his height from his mother - but he was powerfully built. He took his pasty with him - still in the paper bag in which it had been purchased - and lumbered along the short hallway to the front door. Donkey hung onto Spikey's collar, but moved to the doorway to listen. In Jason's time a knock at the door might have meant the police, or one of a range of unsavoury characters connected with the drugs trade, and these had provided a degree of excitement and a sense of importance to the younger and impressionable Doggett sibling.

Isaac opened the door, and Donkey heard an unfamiliar accent utter a greeting.

"Mornin'! Ma name's Murdo and this is Stacey and wur callin' on behalf of the local Labour party here in Penzance and Newlyn. Just interested to know if there's any local issues that yer particularly concerned with at the moment?"

"Local issues? Well, let me see," responded Isaac. "These verges haven't been cut yet." He gestured across the road to where the grass was beginning to take on its springtime shagginess.

"Aye, we're hearing that from a lot of folk," said Murdo, making a note on his clipboard. "We're goin' to try to get something done about the bus service too. It's completely ridiculous that there's only two buses a day to the hospital."

"And how are you going to achieve these improvements, out of interest?" asked Isaac.

"Well this is the thing," said Murdo, to whom such conversations were meat and drink. "I don't know if you're aware but there's a council by-election coming up in a few weeks. We're encouraging folk to vote for the Labour candidate. As I'm sure you're aware, Labour looks after the interests of the working man – and those who would work if they had the chance."

During this conversation Donkey had joined his father in the hall, having shut Spikey with his mother in the kitchen. He regarded with interest the red-headed young man on the doorstep. Isaac Doggett, who was a talker by inclination, and who had a renewed interest in what might loosely be called sociology, was beginning to warm up.

"The working man? Do you know much about the working man? Does your leader, Comrade Corbyn, know much about the working man, how the working man thinks, and what the working man wants?"

Murdo was unabashed, but knew that lengthy doorstep discussions are the enemy of effective data-gathering. If Isaac was hoping for a protracted political argument, he would be disappointed.

"Ah reckon ah do know something about these things. Ah'm from a working-class family myself. But ah won't take up any more of your time right now. Can ah just ask how you usually vote?"

"You can ask," said Isaac. "But I won't be telling you. My vote is between me and the ballot box."

"That's no problem sir – Ah quite understand. It's been good speaking to you. Thanks for yer time. And I'll see if I can get something done about the verges." And he turned on his heel and walked down the path with his companion to where Mallinson stood with his clipboard, waiting to record the limited information that had been gleaned.

Isaac turned to his son as he closed the door.

"Jeremy Corbyn never did a proper day's work in his life."

Chapter Ten

"The L-word had not been mentioned"

On Saturday afternoon Dave played golf as planned. He was not, he insisted to Kate, a serious golfer, and cheerfully acknowledged that it was a fundamentally silly game played all too often by fundamentally silly people, but insisted that it was good fun if approached in the right spirit. Kate had once walked round with him during what he had insisted was a friendly round, and had been sufficiently unimpressed by the plethora of illogical rituals and etiquette to decide that she agreed with the first part of Dave's assessment, and was prepared to leave him to his hobby until he grew out of the second part. He only played every second or third weekend, and on these occasions she was happy to take advantage of the space it gave her to catch up with friends or pursue solitary walks along the coastal path.

Today however, once Dave had set off for his round, she drove back into Newlyn, ostensibly to visit the bank and pick up some shopping. It took her only half an hour an hour to complete these tasks, and she found herself with plenty of time before Dave was expected back from his golf. She sat now in the art gallery coffee shop, a flattened piece of paper on the table in front of her. It was the details for the Net Loft.

Kate was aware that there was an element of withholding information about the way she was going about this process, but reasoned that it was in the long term interests of the relationship that they made the right choice, or choices, for each of them. She would of course, let Dave know if she found anything that seriously appealed to her. She knew she had given the impression that she accepted that the sharing option was the one currently being explored. Well, in fairness, she did. Her mind, she told herself, remained open. Thus her conscience, if not entirely squared, was more or less appeased for the time being.

The truth was that if you left Dave out of the picture, the Net Loft appeared on paper to achieve the apparently unachievable by ticking many of the boxes that the Engine House so admirably filled. It was roughly the same size as her current apartment. It was quaint. It had a waterfront location, albeit the harbour rather than the clifftop, but that might have its advantages. It was close to shops and other facilities, and it even had its own parking space. She was bound to admit that had the Net Loft been available when she had originally been looking for accommodation the previous September, she would have seen it as ideal.

It was approximately five hundred yards from where she was sitting.

She pursed her lips. Picking up details to see what was available was one thing. Going to look round without at least informing Dave was another. But she wouldn't be looking round, at least not properly. She had never really explored the harbour area of Newlyn, which is large, and very much a working fishing port, and was important to the livelihoods of a number of her students. She was in town with time to spare. A stroll round in the general direction could surely do no harm.

She rose, settled her bill, and left the coffee shop.

Edward generally enjoyed his weekly sessions at the Roskear foodbank, but today his mind had not been on the business in hand. He had made some uncharacteristic errors, forgetting to ask for vouchers, and even dropping a carton of eggs. Now, with twenty minutes until it was due to close, things were quietening down, and the process of rationalising and storing the remaining stock had begun. It had been a busy shift, as it always was on a Saturday afternoon, there being no service on a Sunday. Edward's unease had not gone unnoticed by Moira, who was the duty manager, and she approached him now as he set about stacking the few chairs that they always put out for the convenience of customers.

"You all right Edward? You've looked a bit out of sorts today."

"Yes, I'm fine thanks – I just…didn't get much sleep last night I'm afraid."

"We'll be OK here for the last bit if you want to call it a day. The heavy lifting's all more or less done."

Edward stacked the last of the chairs and straightened.

"Well – actually I might take you up on that. If you're sure."

"No, absolutely. You head off."

"Thanks Moira. I'll see you next week."

He collected his coat and slipped out without saying goodbye to the other team members. It was only a ten-minute walk back to the Count House, but instead of turning right he crossed the road to Tyack's Hotel. It was after five and he felt in need of a beer.

The bar was busy. Roskear Town had been playing at home and the first of the rugby fans were already halfway through their opening pints. Edward considered giving up on his plan, but having settled upon the idea of a drink he couldn't quite bring himself to abandon it. In one sense the bustle and noise of the bar quite suited his need for reflection, providing a degree of anonymity and white noise against which he could mull over the events of the previous twenty-four hours. He queued for his beer, exchanging a few pleasantries with the barman, whom he knew, then found a hidden corner where he was unlikely to be disturbed. He took a draught of his pint and attempted to order his thoughts.

On alighting from the bus with Anna the previous evening, Edward had no fixed idea as to what was going to happen, nor even what he wanted to happen. As they walked the few minutes to the Parminters' house he felt himself to be floating on a gentle current of possibility that might lead to nothing more than a cup of cocoa and more time in the warmth of Anna's company. Alternatively it might lead to something considerably more significant, even life-altering. It was decades since he had been to bed with a woman. He vaguely presumed that Anna knew of his sexuality, although it had never been discussed. Perhaps that was why she felt it was safe to ask him back. He wondered if the electrical charge that he felt so clearly when they conversed over coffee after the service in St Jude's was capable, after all these years, of translation into something more tangible. None of these things seemed greatly to matter. He was, probably, a little drunk from his share of the bottle of Pinotage.

Anna's house was a substantial detached 1930's villa at the smarter end of town, set some distance back from the road, behind a wide lawn. Edward had been there once or twice for Liberal party socials, and it seemed odd now to be walking together up the drive in the dark and silence. Once they were in the hall Anna turned on some lights and took his coat, and he stood, waiting for an indication of where she wanted the next part of the scene to play out. She led the way into the large comfortable lounge and asked him if he would like a drink. He asked for a whisky and sat on the sumptuous sofa, where Anna joined him once she had fixed the drinks. She too was drinking whisky - a single malt that she poured into broad crystal tumblers.

"Thank you," she said. "I just couldn't quite face coming back here alone. I thought you might not mind."

"I don't mind," he said. And quite suddenly, he desired her. He said nothing, but their eyes met, and he knew that he wanted to make love to this woman as much as he had wanted anything these last few years of dreary, scholarly bachelorhood. And he knew in that moment that he could, that it would be all right. He had no moral scruples about the situation. He didn't doubt her story about Julian's infidelity and the request for a divorce. In any case he regarded women, married or not, as free agents. For his own part he owed allegiance to nobody.

He put his hand on her thigh, and then they kissed, still holding their drinks at first. A moment later those were put to one side. Anna said, "Not here," and led him up the thickly carpeted stair to what he knew would be a spare bedroom.

The next morning they ate breakfast together, and Anna was quiet, though not unaffectionate. There was no sign of post-alcoholic remorse, nor of an epiphany of new-sprung romance. Although up to now passivity had been his instinct,

Edward felt some need to establish how things stood between them.

"Anna..." he began.

"I know what you're going to say," she said. "You want to know what it means."

"Well…it doesn't have to mean anything," he said, "but it's possibly helpful for each of us to know what the other thinks it *might* mean."

"Would you mind awfully if we left that question for a while?" said Anna. "It was a good and a kind and a loving thing, but it wasn't something I had planned."

"Nor me," said Edward, perhaps a little quickly.

"Of course. I think I might need a bit of time to…I don't know. Process it, or something."

Edward acknowledged the reasonableness of this.

"Julian gets back on Monday. We'll need to talk about what happens next for us. I will call you, I promise, though it may not be for a week or two."

"All right," said Edward. Fifteen minutes later he was standing at the bus stop once more, wondering if the world had changed.

He had heard nothing from Anna since then, which didn't surprise him. She would have plenty to deal with in the light of Julian's imminent return. What sort of woman had the fool decided to leave her for? He thought he could guess, but he preferred not to deal in stereotypes. Certainly nobody with half of Anna's grace, or her quiet intelligence.

And what would Anna be feeling just now? He was aware that he might merely have served as some kind of therapy for her – a need for her to feel she was still attractive, or simply a need to be held by someone, or to even up the scales, though he thought she was above that consideration. Probably the least likely role he was playing was that of Long-term Future Partner, or The Man She had Always Loved. The L-word had not been mentioned by either of them.

Edward was not a man who loved easily or with abandon. He was suspicious of the claims made for the idea. There were men and woman to whom he felt a chemical attraction, something part-physical, part aesthetic and part intellectual, but he had never in his decades of adulthood felt a deep devotion to a member of either sex. During his naval career homosexual activity had been a court-martial offence, and he had learned both caution and restraint, a course made easier by the mounting losses of the AIDS pandemic, included one or two of his old Cambridge set. Habitually he avoided commitment and bold declaration. He wasn't sure he knew what love was.

He drained his pint and considered having a second. It was nearly six o'clock, and he wasn't especially anxious to encounter Murdo in his present frame of mind. He could always eat at Tyacks, though the bar was almost full now, and the noise level was becoming intrusive. Besides, two evenings in a row of eating and drinking out represented to his mind a kind of excess. He picked up his coat and made his way through the drinkers towards the door.

His mind felt clearer by the time he had walked through the town and out the long road to the Count House. The sky above him was clear too, a few stars beginning to show. In a week the clocks would go forward and the evenings would lighten. What would the spring and summer bring?

It took him a moment or two to realise what he was hearing as he approached his front gate. He stood, and listened for a moment. Yes, there it was, unmistakeably, the sound of an accordion. It was playing something different this time, not the lilting tune he had heard from his window, but something faster and more driven, and underneath it a drum beat, like bongos played rapidly and a little inexpertly. And all this was coming from inside, not outside, the house.

He strode up the path and opened the front door. The music was louder now, coming from the kitchen, whose door was slightly ajar, spilling light into the otherwise dark hall with the frenzied playing. There was a rich and unfamiliar aroma of cooking too. With a strange mixture of excitement and foreboding Edward crossed the hall and pushed open the kitchen door to find Murdo and the blonde French girl partnered in a frantic, whirling, musical duet, she standing by the washing machine, the accordion across her chest, her small blonde head lifted and her eyes closed in a kind of ecstasy. Murdo was sitting on the work surface, battering away at a small pair of bongo drums gripped between his thighs. A bottle of cheap wine, almost empty, was on the table. If they were aware of Edward's arrival, they ignored him, continuing to play frantically until the tune finished with a long open chord on the accordion and a flamboyant tattoo from Murdo. On completion of this finale, Edward's lodger jumped down from the work surface, holding his arms wide in what might have been a greeting, a gesture of love, or an acknowledgement of an appreciative audience, while the girl gave a deep bow, her eyes, as far as Edward could see, still closed.

There was nothing he could reasonably do but applaud.

Chapter Eleven

"It's not about us"

It was the Monday morning staff meeting at St Petroc's. Eighty or ninety teachers were crammed into the long, oak-panelled room, a relic of the grammar school days. This history also found expression in odd touches such as a rarely examined leather-bound set of the Encyclopaedia Britannica (c 1972) on a bookshelf, and series of faded, framed pictures of various masters' cricket elevens. It was many years now since anybody on the staff had had time for cricket, and the rather dated team photographs were in any case eclipsed by a large, and to most minds vulgar, embossed logo of the Marcato Trust, which had appeared unannounced over the course of one Easter break.

Early arrivals – those who had been free the previous lesson, or whose classrooms were close at hand - had already secured themselves a coffee and an armchair, a combination which made the entire exercise perfectly bearable, as one could more or less switch off, or think about one's next lesson, and even, if one was situated in one of the far corners, engage in a *sotto voce* commentary on proceedings. Latecomers on the other hand stood shoulder-to-shoulder around the perimeter, denied the pleasure of either comfort or caffeine, since the Head had made it clear that he objected to people "clanking around in the kitchen area" during this key moment in the school week. If the meeting finished in good time, latecomers might manage

78

a few sips of dangerously hot coffee before the unforgiving bell summoned them to their next lesson. Younger members of staff who had enjoyed a weekend of carousing had occasionally been known to spoon raw coffee down their throats in desperation. Had the Head been aware of the effect his policy of caffeine denial was having on the wellbeing of his staff, not to mention their performance in the classroom, he would almost certainly have found another solution to the kitchen-clanking problem.

At this point in the meeting, the atmosphere in the staffroom was muted, as the Head was detailing the arrangements for Vincent Narabo's funeral. As a governor of the school, Narabo was accorded a degree of formal respect, although few staff had met him. Even fewer knew or cared much about his political activities, their interest in politics being largely confined to despair at the ill-informed meddling of successive Secretaries of State for Education.

Dave Singleman was something of an exception in this regard. His recent promotion to the position of Head of Year Nine, combined with his desire to impress Kate, had led him to take a greater interest in the goings-on at the upper end of the school's management structure. In addition he ran the St Petroc's debating programme, and as such took an interest in politics both local and national. He was one of the few in the room who was already aware that Narabo had been the councillor for the ward in which the school was located, and that the unfortunate man's death would therefore trigger a by-election. He could see possibilities.

The Head sat down and Anton Killick took to the floor to summarise his statistical analysis of the Year 11 mock results. This was of interest to nobody beyond the Year 11 pastoral team, because nobody cared a great deal about anybody's performance outside of their own teaching group, and on that they were already well-informed. For his part Dave was intrinsically prejudiced against anything Killick had to say, and so he let his thoughts wander to Kate, who was one of the fortunate arm-chair occupants at the other end of the room. He was irritated to see that she was watching Killick with what was either studied attention, or a good impression of it, and with Kate, by and large, what you saw was what was there.

There was nothing surprising in her attentive demeanour. Kate had always taken things like the staff briefing seriously, and had even volunteered to join one of Killick's steering groups in her first term at St Petroc's. She saw nothing wrong, she said, with using data to drive school improvement. She was only three years younger than Dave, but somehow the different life-decades they currently occupied – he now in his thirties, she still in her twenties - seemed symbolic of intrinsic differences between them, not all of them age-related. The attention she was now paying to Killick's statistical mumbo-jumbo irritated him the more because he and Kate had argued the previous day.

Predictably enough the disagreement had arisen around their accommodation plans, and it was this very predictability, and his own failure to avoid the conflict, that Dave was really cross about. He *knew* that this was difficult territory, that he had to proceed with great patience and be prepared for a long campaign if they were to end up living together in the autumn. Any attempt on his part to force the issue would only drive a wedge between them and make the outcome he desired even less likely. Yet he had managed little more than a week before his patience had proved unequal to Kate's scepticism.

They had visited two more properties on the Sunday, one in an outlying village, (which she declared too isolated, although it was no more so than the Engine House), and one an apartment in a modern block of flats in Penzance (too modern, as it turned out, for Kate's taste.) The foreplay to the argument had begun in the form of an uncomfortable and uncharacteristic silence on the way home in the MG, and, it had reached its unsatisfactory consummation on the gravelled parking area of the Engine House.

"Can I speak frankly?" he had begun, as he turned off the engine.

"Of course," Kate said, a little too brightly. She knew what was coming.

"This feels like uphill work. I mean, it feels like you've already made up your mind and we're just going through this fatuous exercise of looking at properties to tick a box, or something."

"That's not very fair."

"It's true though, isn't it?"

"I don't think so, no. Look, I haven't made any secret of the fact that my instinct would be to find some nice place of my own. Now if that could be near you, that would be ideal. I am doing this" – here she held up the sheaf of details – "because it's what you want, and if we find somewhere that really felt big enough to cohabit in without treading on each other's toes, then I am genuinely open minded and will consider it. But if such a property exists, we certainly haven't found it yet. I mean can you really, seriously, see us squeezing comfortably into any of the places we've seen so far?"

"If we shared a bedroom, then yes."

"I really don't think that would work."

"It seems to work fine at the moment."

"That's because all I do in your bedroom is sleep and make love. And that's only at weekends. I'm not complaining by the way," she added, in an attempt to lighten the mood, but there was already an edge to their voices, which were rising a little in pitch. She continued,

"I mean they're not big, are they, these ones we've looked at? I'm not a great one for pots and potions but I do need some kind of dressing table, and somewhere to hang my decent clothes. Think what it's going to be like, both of us trying to get out to school in the morning."

"You could use the second bedroom as a…boudoir, or whatever you call it in Yorkshire."

"Then I'm effectively sleeping in your territory, night in, night out."

"My *territory*? That's a bit tribal isn't it?"

"Well that's how I feel. Look I said right at the beginning – I need my own space. It's just the way I am. Put it down to me being an only child or something. Maybe I've just never learned to share."

"That sounds ominous."

"Dave please don't try to make this about us. It's not about us."

"Of course it's bloody well about us. What else is it about? It's about whether you see me as a long-term partner, or a pleasant temporary distraction."

There had followed a pause, into which he began an apology.

"Sorry. That was unfair."

Still she was silent.

"Kate?"

"I'm sorry, Dave – that's a bit much." She opened the door of the MG, and began to get out. "I'm going to get my own supper. I'll call you later."

She hadn't slammed the door. If she had it might well have fallen off, and their relationship really would have been in trouble. But she had walked to her flat without looking back, and Dave was left sitting miserably behind the wheel of his car, wondering where exactly it had all gone wrong, and how, if at all, it could be put right.

True to her word, Kate had rung him that evening. He could hear her voice in the flat below, a fraction of a second before the digital echo in his ear. The call had been conciliatory in tone, without recriminations. They agreed it was a difficult situation, and that it mustn't be allowed to spoil all the good things that had happened between them. They had settled on a position that would allow them to go into the week in a state of relative harmony. That position was to talk no more of property until they got back from the trip to France they had planned for the first week of the Easter break. It didn't feel to Dave as if any aspect of the actual problem had been addressed.

And now Kate was gazing in rapt attention at Anton Killick, who Dave knew well had tried his luck with her the previous term.

Up on the middle school playground, Edward Tremenhere was taking a passive approach to his breaktime duty. He had been locking his classroom since the incident with the whiteboard the previous week, although this was something the staff at St Petroc's liked to say you didn't need to do. Nothing more had been heard from Toby Trott or his mother. He chose a position that allowed himself a plausible vantage point, and to reinforce the impression of an alert and dutiful schoolteacher he was staring into the middle distance. His mind, however, was occupied with the events of the weekend.

The French girl was called Sophie, and she was working for the summer in one of the large hotels in St Ives. She introduced herself in the good but accented English he had heard in the post office. Edward responded to her greeting in his own fluent French, at which she made no comment, although Murdo accused him later of showing off. Murdo's own grasp of the language apparently extended no further than a few remembered phrases from lower school, and Edward found this unusual display of ignorance in his lodger oddly touching.

All this had been established within a few moments of the ending of the duet that greeted him on his return from the pub. Almost immediately the sense of mystery that had accompanied his apprehension of the girl and her music resolved itself into the mundane and hardly startling fact that Murdo had brought an attractive young woman back to the Count House with him on a Saturday night. Edward made the required mental adjustments quickly.

"Sophie's cooking, by the way," said Murdo. "Yer very welcome to join us."

"Ees just a boeuf Bourguignon," said Sophie, rather charmingly. "There is plenty for three."

Edward had no particular supper plans of his own, and the cooking smells from the pot on the hob were enticing. He accepted the invitation, and opened another bottle of wine, this one a little more sophisticated than the plonk the pair had been drinking.

Over supper, which was delicious, and feeling that he had established himself as a relaxed and accommodating host, Edward ventured to fill in some of the remaining gaps in the story. How had Sophie and Murdo met?

"I saw heem at the hotel one night, at a folk evening," said Sophie, her facility with English apparently unaffected by the wine she had drunk. "He was with some of his Labour party friends. I recognised the badges. I am socialist, you see, and in France we hear a great deal about Jeremy Corbyn, and I am curious to find out more."

"But the funny thing is," said Murdo, "Ah nivver saw her. Which is, you know, no like me."

"I was behind the bar," said Sophie. "I don't think you ever came to the bar."

"That's always possible," said Murdo, who never seemed to have any spare money.

"So how did you track him down?" asked Edward.

"I was not trying to track him down," said Sophie. "But one day I was in Roskear and I saw him again, his appearance is – I'm not sure how you would say it in English – *mémorable*. So I followed him home. Like a puppee."

"And then you serenaded him," said Edward, mildly piqued that in the end it was indeed Murdo, and not himself, that had been the subject of the early morning music. "You play very sweetly."

"Thank you!" said Sophie with a beaming smile. "Yes I am sorry it was so early in the morning but I start work at ten and then I am working all day, and I had to catch the bus back to St Ives. I thought it would be nice for him to wake up to."

After supper Edward made his excuses and retired to the front room to read. At ten o'clock Sophie's head appeared round the door.

"Good night Edward, Thank you for having me."

He resisted the urge to get up. "You're most welcome. And I should thank you for the delicious supper. Did you learn much about comrade Corbyn."

"I learned that Murdo thinks he is a very fine man."

She looked around the room as she said this, her eyes taking in details of décor and furnishings.

"Well that's a start. Drop by another time and I'll give you my opinion."

"I think perhaps you are not socialist?"

"Not really, no. Liberal."

"Ah. You have, what is the expression… a bleeding heart? A bleeding heart makes not the revolution. *Au revoir.*"

"*A la prochaine.*"

And with that she was gone, along with Murdo, who was heard to return a few minutes later, presumably having seen her onto the bus. Edward found himself comforted that Murdo had not persuaded Sophie to join him in the basement for the night, though he was not sure why he should care. He didn't see his lodger again that evening, but when he ventured into the kitchen he found to his surprise that the dishes were all done, and the surfaces wiped.

Chapter Twelve

"St Petroc's Stripped for Action"

At lunchtime on Monday Kate had a pastoral interview with Donovan Doggett, who in addition to being a member of her English group was in her form. These sessions had been initiated the previous term, when Donkey had been considered vulnerable as a result of his father's absence and the malign influence of his older brother. Although the boy's enthusiasm for the voluntary tutorials had been initially lacking, Kate had patiently persisted with them, and in the end they had played their part in Donkey's rehabilitation.

With his father now home and Jason Doggett departed, Donkey's position seemed more secure, but Kate knew that he would need continued support if he was to stay on the straight and narrow. He sat opposite her now, slouched a little on the plastic chair, dark hair unkempt and blazer sleeves a couple of inches too short for his bony wrists. It was a caricature of the ill-at-ease adolescent, reinforced by the broad vowels of his casual vernacular. Only his startling blue eyes, clear and unblinking, spoke of some promise.

"So," said Kate briskly. "How are things at home?"

"All right s'pose."

"Is your Dad settling in? Any luck with a job?"

"He's doing a bit of labouring here and there," said Donkey, "But nuffin' regular. Says he's getting a bit old for runnin' up and down scaffolding."

"Is he keeping up with his studying?"

"Not that I can see. It's almost like his motivation's gone, now he's outside. He says he needs to be earning money, not have his nose in a book."

"Well. That's understandable. And Jason?"

"We don't hear much. He's stopped messaging me is one good thing."

Kate waited. She sensed there was more to come.

"Thing is," Donkey shifted in his seat. "He sends home money. Cash, like."

"Ah."

"The old man won't touch it. He says it's tainted. He dunno what to do with it, though. Sometimes he talks about handing it in to the police, or giving it to the dog rescue people. But he never does. So it just sits in an old biscuit tin on the shelf in the kitchen. Five hundred quid now, just sitting there, in this Scottie dog biscuit tin."

"That must be a bit of a temptation."

"I won't crack if he don't. And me Mum won't touch it. It's odd though, when, like, there isn't a lot of spare dosh around. And it's like Jase is somehow still there, taunting us."

"Perhaps that's what he intended."

"Mebbe. Mum says it shows he still cares, but I don't think she really believes it. Miss, do you know anything about this election?"

"What election?" Kate was used by now to the way Donkey's mind jumped around, and guessed he felt that enough had been said on the subject of his home life.

"Apparently some geezer's died, so there's gonna be an election to the council, to like, fill the vacancy. Someone knocked our door about it at the weekend."

"Oh. That'll be Mr Narabo. He was a school governor, but I think he was a councillor too. So it will be what's called a by-election."

"Will there be, like speeches, and debates and things?"

The highwater mark of Donkey's rehabilitation had been his participation, with Kate's encouragement, in an inter-schools debating competition the previous term.

"I suppose there might be. They sometimes have things called hustings, where all the candidates get together in front of an audience and say what they'll do if they get elected. And

86

there'll be a campaign of some sort I imagine. I don't know what it's like down here, but in Yorkshire, where I come from, these local elections can be quite lively."

"That'd be cool. Can people of, like, my age get involved?"

"I don't see why not. You need to decide which party you support."

"Like, a political party? I ain't got a clue, Miss. My dad says they're all as bad as each other."

"Well look – maybe we'll do some work on it in English. It must be quite local to us if they're knocking on your door. Anyway – time's running away with us. Well done for checking in."

"Merit?"

"Consider it done. And another one for raising such an interesting topic."

"Cheers Miss."

It never ceased to surprise Kate what value was placed on the largely theoretical currency of merits, particularly by those who had few to their credit.

There was little or no communication between Kate and Dave in the course of that day, which was unusual. While they did their best not to be too "coupley" at work, their classrooms were a few feet from one another, and there was plenty of opportunity for non-verbal communication. Sometimes, if he was bored, Dave would text her during a lesson with soppy messages or outrageous suggestions for book-cupboard assignations. Kate frowned on these electronic *billets-doux* as unprofessional, and never responded, but she also rather enjoyed them. She was very aware that the weekend had ended on a difficult note, and their drive in that morning had been quieter than usual. The idea of a unit of work around the by-election might offer a route back to harmony, or at least a distraction from the difficulties of their accommodation, so she brought it up it in the car on the way home. They were in the Fiat, and she was driving.

"So, this Vincent Narabo guy – he was a councillor, right? Is that a big deal down here?"

"Yeah, he was a Cornwall Councillor. There are a hundred or so of them altogether. In theory they make a lot of important decisions, although in Narabo's case that was generally limited to where he was going to eat lunch."

"I was just wondering – is it worth trying to do a unit of work around the by-election – you know, persuasive language, public speaking, even a look at local government? They're always looking for stuff to put in the citizenship curriculum." She chose not to mention Donovan Doggett at this point, aware that Dave had little time for the lad. She didn't wish to jeopardise her scheme before it had got off the ground.

"Well it's funny you should say that," said Dave, brightening a little. "I was wondering something similar. I was thinking we could run a mock election. You know, get the kids to research political parties, and stand as candidates."

"Well there would be room for both, I guess," said Kate. "Is the election likely to be something the kids would be aware of?"

"It'll get some coverage in the local press," said Dave. "Narabo was something of a colourful character, and the opposition against him was evenly split last time, so it might be a bit of a bunfight. There's an issue brewing around the Minor Injuries Unit too, so that should arouse some interest."

"Maybe it's something we could work on together," said Kate. "I could look at some stuff for the curricular side, and you could run the mock election."

"Sure," said Dave. "That might be fun."

She took her eyes off the road long enough to smile at him, and he smiled back.

Dave and Kate might have had less enthusiasm for their embryonic project had they been aware of a meeting taking place at that moment back at St Petroc's. Anton Killick was in the Head's office, and the two men were seated in low, comfortable chairs in the bay window, triangulated around Anton's MacBook, which was open on the coffee table in front of them. The Deputy Head was animated, leaning forward to manipulate the mousepad, his voice rising slightly as he underscored the key points of his pitch.

He was too animated to register that the Head was in fact mildly irked. Anton was the only member of his staff at any level who seemed incapable of discussing a subject without using a PowerPoint presentation, and this always necessitated the Head coming out from behind his large mahogany desk. This made him uneasy. He preferred to deal with petitioners of any sort, whether staff, parents or pupils, with the avuncular yet authoritative air of a provincial bank manager. For this to work, he needed that flat acreage of polished wood as a barrier, a symbol of the unspoken difference in status between himself and his interlocutor. Out on the open ground represented by the bay window and the easy chairs he felt exposed and vulnerable, the more so because he himself had never mastered the use of PowerPoint. He was due to retire in two years, and reasoned that until then he could get away, as he had done up to now, with the discreet support of Rona d'Allesandro. His PA cheerfully and efficiently transformed his sheets of scribbled A4 into the required format, and if necessary would change the slides at the appropriate time in response to a nod or a headmasterly wave of the hand.

Anton tapped the mouse pad a final time, and the screen returned once more to the title slide

St Petroc's
Stripped for Action

Both men sat back in their seats, the Head in relief, and Anton with the expression of suppressed triumph that his face habitually wore when he felt his case was unanswerable.

"Well I don't know," said the Head. "I mean I fully support the sentiment, and I admire the level of detail with which you've addressed the problem, but I worry sometimes that we ask a lot of young people these days as things stand, and this just seems to be piling on more pressure."

Anton considered speaking, but decided that what the Head had said was so self-evidently weak and foolish that he would allow the man time to recognise it himself. The Head, however, had further objections.

"And the title. You know what young people are like, Anton. If they can lampoon something, they will."

"It's a working title," said Anton, a little impatiently. "It can be changed. But the concept – you will agree I'm sure that the concept is strong, and appealing, too, particularly to boys. If we can just instil this sense that for those six weeks prior to the exams the whole focus of the school shifts, albeit temporarily, I think I can guarantee that our value-added will show the kind of up-tick that the Inspectors are looking for."

The school was anticipating an inspection in the summer term.

"But there will be important extra-curricular events that are already calendared – sports fixtures, plays – doesn't the junior play take place around then?"

"Sports fixtures can stay," said Anton. "They don't impinge on the interior life of the school. I acknowledged that in slide 5. The Junior play could be pushed back until after the exams. I don't mind them learning their lines quietly before then." He anticipated that Raphael d'Allesandro, who was known for his short temper, would not be an enthusiast for his proposal, and he might need to make some concessions. He continued.

"What about the wall display idea?"

"Well it will be a lot of extra work for staff," said the Head, aware that he was sounding a little as if he was reluctant to ask anybody to do anything that they didn't wish to.

"But think of the impact on the students! That sense of purpose. A moment of high seriousness in the school year. They've had pictures and poems to "enrich" them all year, if that is indeed the effect of such things. They can have them again, as soon as the exams are over. But for this six week period, everything comes down, except revision aids. It will be very powerful."

The Head felt the need to show some enthusiasm.

"I like the battle metaphor, Anton, I do. And the link with our namesake is a clever touch."

A chance discovery that there had been a frigate, a bit-player at the battle of Trafalgar, with the name of St Petroc, had sparked the idea for "Stripped for Action", and remained probably its strongest selling point.

"But I'm not going to say yay or nay now," said the Head, decisively. "I'll give it some thought and we'll discuss it next week. Now, while you are here, what sort of progress are we making with the appraisal steering group?"

It was after six o'clock by the time Anton was back in his office. The meeting had gone no better than expected, and not for the first time he questioned whether his move down to the southwest had been a wise one. It had been a significant step up in terms of salary and responsibility, but it had taken him away from the large martial arts clubs and the circles of influence in the capital. His interview with the ramshackle board of St Petroc's governors (The Chair was, of all things, a lobster fisherman), had almost persuaded him that he should turn the job down, but at the same time it had been evident that this was a school where there was a job of work to be done.

There was also the fact that prior to his interview he had received a summons to the Bristol offices of Marcato. In a spacious glass-walled room on the seventeenth floor of John Newton Tower, the former car dealer who ran the group had intimated that Anton's talent, not to mention the excellent work he had done at his London school, had been noted. It had been clearly implied that should he make a success of his time at St Petroc's, a few years at this far-flung outpost of the Marcato empire might be seen as a stepping-stone to much greater things.

Anton often wondered if the former car dealer had ever crossed the Tamar.

Chapter Thirteen

"Can we meet again, please?"

It was now just two weeks until the Easter holidays, well past the mid-point of the school year. The weather was mixed, but the sunny days had real warmth in them, and the spring flowers were beginning to appear in the hedgerows. Normally by this stage teaching hearts would lighten a little, but Edward found his spirits low, and his energy unaccountably lacking. Teaching day succeeded to teaching day without particular incident or upset (there had been no recurrence of the graffiti on his whiteboard) but he found no joy in them, and he wondered once again if he could really carry on like this for another five years. There seemed little point if he didn't need the money, and while he had always taken a quiet pride in being a good teacher, he was realistic enough to acknowledge that his students might benefit from a younger, fresher face in front of them.

What would he do if he did retire at the end of the year? Aye – there was the rub, as Hamlet might have said, had he been permitted to reach his own pensionable age. In theory Edward could fill his time by taking a closer interest in the management of the various Tremenhere properties and business concerns, but it would be a dull existence. The by-election interested him, but it could hardly be relied upon to propel him into an exciting new future in politics.

The arrival on the scene of Sophie, however, had brought to mind another possibility. Might he not return to France? It had provided a refuge for him once, when his first spell at St Petroc's had come to an unexpected end. On that occasion a respect for the ascetic life, and a recognition that particular aspects of his character might benefit from some examination, had led him to join a lay community attached to a monastery in the Dordogne. He had only remained with the brotherhood a short while, finding his character to be less interesting and, indeed, less tractable to instruction than he had hoped, and failing entirely to find God. He had drifted on down to the south, spending a few months assisting with various harvests before obtaining more settled employment in a tourist hotel. In the end he had stayed in France for three years, and had returned, he felt, a gentler and a wiser man. There was no reason why he could not now find some rural Provencal property in need of renovation, and eke out his pension by giving English lessons or doing some basic translation work.

Even as he toyed with this possible version of his third age, Edward knew that it carried with it the risk that he might end up desperately lonely. Loneliness was a condition that in recent years he had successfully kept at bay through the careful maintenance of friendships with colleagues and occasional political activity. It was another reason that he chose to let out the basement flat. He knew that if he bolted for France such sustaining strategies could not be built up overnight, and might elude him altogether. It was a line of thought that led him back inevitably to Anna Parminter.

Their night of passion (if that was indeed the right word: comfort was perhaps a better description) had largely eclipsed the issue that had led to the thing in the first place, namely whether or not he might stand for the Liberals at the by-election. Of the necessary preliminaries to that step he had heard nothing, and from Anna he had received only a brief text, assuring him she had not forgotten him, and making reference to a "difficult session with Julian." She had signed off with a kiss, but she might well have done that anyway. There were times when he yearned to hear from her with an intensity that surprised him; and other times when he felt he had got away with a rather lovely moment of intimacy with a friend, while escaping the multitude of questions and responsibilities that might be raised by an affair.

Most often, he wanted simply to hear the sound of her voice.

Edward was an infrequent user of email, and often told people, particularly at school, that he had no email address. This was not quite true - he did have an account, which he cleared of spam once a week, asking himself on these occasions why he bothered with it at all. Only when he was expecting a communication of importance would he check it daily. This was one of those times, and one evening, several days after receiving Anna's text, he found a message from her, nestling among the pleas for urgent financial assistance and the erectile dysfunction promotions, like a pearl in the roadside dust.

Dear Edward,

I'm so sorry not to have been properly in touch sooner than this. I'm afraid it's been pretty hellish at this end, and I wanted to have my head reasonably level before I contacted you again. There's so much that I want to say to you, but when I try to put it down in words, it either sounds cold, or cliched, and all the things I want to express come out as stilted versions of themselves.

Can we meet again, please? Not at my house this time I think, nor perhaps anywhere very local. The Tregarvon should be pretty quiet mid-week. Would you meet me there for dinner on Tuesday evening, at 8? My treat.

Anna.

Ps info about selection on its way. All this stuff is playing havoc with my political duties.

Edward re-read this short message several times, trying to judge what lay behind it. So the things she wanted to say came out as cold, stilted or clichéd. That didn't sound especially promising. On the other hand she had picked a hotel for the rendezvous, rather than just a restaurant. Could anything be read into that? No kiss at the end, but he rather approved of that. Anna was not a schoolgirl. He allowed a brief moment of burning hatred for the boorish Julian to flare and die before he typed his reply:

Tuesday is fine – I look forward to seeing you then.
E.

He hesitated before sending, then added "Very much." as a separate sentence. It was no less than the truth, and while he was instinctively wary of sentiment he felt there was room for a little raising of the stakes in that department. There was no harm in letting her know how he felt, and if what she intended to say was that she wanted matters to end at this point, all was in any case lost.

The promised email about selection arrangements for the by-election arrived the following day. He thought he detected Anna's precise lawyerly style in the prose, which gave him a moment of pleasure, although it was, so far as he could tell, the same letter that would be received by everyone with an interest in the selection. It advised him to complete and return the attached application form, and to await the call to attend an approval panel. This, he knew, was designed to ascertain that he was "sound", and unlikely to disgrace the party through ineptitude or illiberal behaviour.

He filled the form out, but he did not send it. It was straightforward enough, apart from one box that read "Are there any matters from your recent or past history that might lead to embarrassment for the party should they arise during the election campaign?" Ought he to make some reference to the events of twenty years ago? Sometimes it seemed to him that the whole of west Cornwall knew of them in any case. And surely anybody raising the matter now would simply be accused of cheap point-scoring. He decided that he would run it past Anna if the opportunity arose.

No more was seen or heard of Sophie during the week following their first meeting. Murdo, too, was rather elusive, and Edward wondered if there was more to the friendship than a shared political interest. The apparently reasonable explanation for the early morning serenades (which he rather missed) did not diminish his curiosity about the girl, and he looked for an opportunity to enquire of Murdo what more he might have learned.

The two residents of the Count House had been engaged in a sporadic series of chess matches since Murdo let slip, early in his tenancy of the basement flat, that he had been a Glasgow Schools champion. This was an uncharacteristic boast –

Murdo tended only to brag about areas where he was weak, and was generally modest about his genuine achievements. But he had noticed the carved soapstone chess set that sat on the coffee table in the front room of the Count House.

"Is that jist an ornament, or are ye any good?" he had asked.

Edward said cautiously that he had played a little and would happily give Murdo a game if he wished. In fact he had been a Cambridge chess Blue, and didn't particularly enjoy playing against weak opposition. But it seemed at the time a relatively comfortable way to get to know his new tenant, whom he had already found could be spiky and contrary in conversation. He had not anticipated much of a battle, but there had been a point in that first match when Murdo captured a rook out of nowhere, and Edward was forced to sit up and pay closer attention. Since then it was clear that Murdo harboured an intense desire to beat him. This was yet to happen, but Edward was often required to bring the experience and guile of decades to bear on the more unpredictable and occasionally brilliant tactical flourishes of the younger man. He knew that one day Murdo would prevail, and wondered if it would in some obscure way alter the dynamic between them.

When he finally caught up with Murdo one evening, he asked him innocently if he had the courage to face another match, knowing full well that the boy would find it virtually impossible to duck the challenge. It was obvious that Murdo might have preferred to keep his distance a little longer, but he took the bait, and feeling only a little guilty, Edward fetched a couple of bottles of beer from the fridge. At this Murdo raised an eyebrow – their games were not always accompanied by alcohol.

As was their custom, they said little through the opening moves. It was, however, a favourite trick of Murdo's , once the battle lines were drawn and a greater measure of concentration was required, to ask casually provocative questions when it was Edward's turn to play. On this occasion Edward felt no scruple at employing the same tactic, and having moved his bishop into a position where it threatened both Murdo's queen and his knight, he asked how things were going with Sophie.

"Goin'?" asked Murdo, adroitly blocking Edward's gambit. "What d you mean?"

"Well – I rather had the impression you were interested in her." Edward sat back, deciding that the contest on the board could wait while he pressed home this other line of attack.

"Dunno where you got that idea from," said Murdo. "You heard the lassie – she saw me across a crowded room and she followed me home. What can ah say? It happens."

"She is quite attractive though. You said so yourself."

"Aye well, softly-softly."

"And her political education?"

"Oh that? Well. She says she's going tae come along to the local branch meetings, but there's not a lot ah can teach her about socialism. She's quite hard-line, actually. And jokin' apart, ah was very impressed with yer French patter."

"I lived over there for a bit," said Edward. He found he was rather enjoying Murdo's slight unease, but permitted the temporary change of subject. "You must have studied French at school?"

"Ah was timetabled tae study it, but ah didnae always make the lessons."

"I see. So you buy this story about her wanting to find out more about Monsieur Corbyn?"

"Ah've no reason tae doubt it. Why, what do you think she's after?"

"Well I did think she might be after you, but unless you're being uncharacteristically coy, that's not the case. I still think it's all a bit odd."

"Well she's going tae come along to the selection meeting in Penzance. But ah'm no promising tae file a report. Now it's your move."

Edward returned his attention to the board to find that while he had been threatening his lodger's queen, Murdo had been doing something a little unusual with his King's bishop. He forced himself to concentrate. It seemed that was all he was going to learn of Sophie for the time being.

In the restaurant of the Porthmeor Beach hotel, above St Ives, the subject of their conversation was at that moment in the middle of her shift. Sophie was popular with customers, particularly the middle-aged men, who complimented her on her English and tipped her generously while their wives smiled tolerantly, or pursed their lips and busied themselves with their handbags. Occasionally she had to be firm with late solo diners, and the restaurant manager sometimes hung around at the end of the evening to offer her unnecessary instruction in silver-service or etiquette, but there was no unpleasantness. The other waiting staff, most of whom were young, were friendly enough, and had invited her to join them once or twice for drinks. Sophie had gone along out of politeness, but their talk was loud and dull, and she did little to encourage their friendship.

She had been in Cornwall for three weeks, and was quietly pleased with the progress she had made.

Chapter Fourteen

"A kiss by way of compensation"

Aside from his interest in Sophie, Murdo's principle concern at this time was the impending by-election. Idle in many areas of his life, he was capable of focus and energetic application when his interest was aroused, and following the canvassing session on the Penhale estate he had resolved to follow up on one or two of the concerns raised by residents. Now he was on his mobile in a quiet corner of the university campus, tapping his foot anxiously. He had been on hold for ten minutes and he was shortly due at a lecture. Finally, somebody picked up, and the strains of Local Hero came to an abrupt and welcome halt.

"Public Open Space, how can I help you?"

"Good Afternoon," said Murdo, in a carefully moderated version of his usual accent. "Murdo McAndrew here, community activist for the Penhale estate in Newlyn. I wonder if you can tell me when you're expecting to cut the verges down our way."

"One minute please."

There was silence for a moment, then the voice came back on the line.

"The team should get round to you in about three weeks."

"Any chance you could speed that up?"

"Well …it's difficult. As you can appreciate the grass tends to grow everywhere at the same time."

Murdo, who never liked being patronised, resisted the temptation to make a retort, and tried instead a more subtle approach.

"I just think, with Councillor Narabo's funeral imminent, it seems disrespectful to allow one of the main population centres in his ward to get in such a state. Could you perhaps bump it up the queue?"

"It's not that simple. We tend to start at Truro and work outwards, and if we start messing around with the schedules at this stage…"

"Well could you perhaps pay a contractor just to give them a quick going over? I mean presumably at this time of year there must be money left in a budget somewhere."

"Well…I dunno…"

"I think Councillor Narabo's many friends on the estate, not to mention his family, would appreciate that gesture."

"Are you calling on behalf of Councillor Narabo's family?"

Murdo made a rapid calculation, and opted for honesty.

"Not directly. But I'm confident that Mrs Narabo in particular would welcome anything you can do."

"Well I can't promise anything, but I'll talk to my upline."

"That's fantastic. Thanks very much."

"What did you say your name was?"

But Murdo had cut the call and was hurrying off to his lecture.

The clerk in the Public Open Spaces department did speak to his upline, whose grandmother happened to live on the Penhale estate, and who thought the request reasonable enough. He also knew where some money might be found. The outcome of this to-ing and fro-ing was that a short-term contract was duly placed with Pascoe Groundworks of Eglos to bring the verges up to scratch ASAP.

The Penhale estate contract was welcome news to Viv Pascoe at a time when another job that had provided a steady income through the winter was winding up. The fact that he would be going in and out to the area of St Petroc's on a daily basis offered an additional benefit. Viv had noticed that his son seemed a bit down in the dumps of late, and also that Issy was rarely mentioned these days. Rather hesitantly he raised the possibility of giving Sammy a lift over the coming week, and was gratified to find that his son seemed keen on the idea.

"I'll need to be in at 8.30, though," said Sammy.

"How's that Sam? I thought your bus didn't come to the road-end till around then."

"Yeah but if the bus is late, everyone's late, and it's nobody's fault. If it's just me that's late it looks bad."

"Fair enough," said Viv. "It'll be good for me to have a schedule to stick to. Reckon you can get us both out the door by 8.15, Maisie?"

"I can give you regular time checks, if that's any good," said Maisie.

"Well we can give it a go," said Viv. "Might be quite a laugh, eh Sam? We'll need to get some music sorted out."

"Please not Alison Krauss," said Sammy.

The truth was that Sammy's journeys in and out to school with Issy were not what they had once been. They still sat together, but the conversation was more effortful, and the occasional silences, which had been fine in the old days, now seemed tense rather than companionable. In the two or three weeks that had passed since their break-up, the news had rippled through the year group; the sympathy of some, and the quiet pleasure of others who had been envious of their state, subsided, and the conversation moved on. Sammy still felt slightly adrift, and found himself obsessed with concerns that Issy might start going out with somebody else. Travelling to and from school with his father felt not only like an escape, but in an obscure way that he was reluctant to acknowledge to himself, like some kind of retaliation. He even considered not mentioning the change to Issy, just letting her find that he wasn't at the bus stop one morning. Then he felt ashamed of his small-mindedness, and texted her the Sunday before the arrangement was due to begin.

Won't be on the bus for a bit – going in and out with the old man

He added a kiss by way of compensation for what still felt like a minor betrayal of friendship.

It was a whole hour before Issy's response came through. Then she texted.

Cool! See u at school X

That struck Sammy as a bit rich, as seeing Issy at school was now confined to their English lessons. A bit casual, too.

She could have asked how long the arrangement was expected to last, or if everything was OK.

He told himself he was making the right move.

For her part, Issy took Sammy's message at face value, and was not overly concerned by it. The ending of their relationship had been for all the genuine reasons she had done her best to explain to him. It never occurred to her that other boys in the year might be looking to occupy the place at her side that the break-up had left vacant. But of course, other boys were. As Year 9 wound its course towards the summer term, and the students grew older, more and more fourteenth birthday parties were held, some at the homes of notably liberal parents. Most of the more mature boys had regarded Issy as too bookish to be worth pursuing, but now she had shown that she could be tempted out, as it were, and by so unlikely a specimen as Sammy Pascoe, two or three of the taller, more sporty lads were assessing their chances.

One of these was Donovan Doggett.

Donkey had moved, in the course of the school year, from being perfectly comfortable in his role as hardman and lout-in-chief of the junior school, to wanting something more. He was even beginning to wonder if he should drop his nickname, in which he had formerly taken such pride. His success in the debating competition had kicked it all off, and he was beginning to discover that he quite liked English. He wouldn't go so far as to say he was good at it, but he took an interest in it, and Miss kept telling him he was making good points when he saw things in the class reader that others in the bottom set either couldn't see or couldn't be bothered to articulate.

The release of his father from prison was another factor that motivated him. He was proud of Isaac, both of his recent progress with the Open University, and still a little, secretly, of his past career as a housebreaker, which Donkey reasoned required a degree of skill and daring. He knew instinctively that his father, despite showing early promise as a boxer, was not a violent man, and he told himself that the houses he had burgled almost certainly belonged to people who had too much money anyway. He knew his father was pleased with the good report he had received at the end of the previous term, and he wanted - wanted very much - to continue pleasing him.

He also wanted a girlfriend, which he saw as a mark of maturity. He had messed around a bit at the end of Year 8 with Lily Tregunna, but then she had suddenly gone very womanly and started hanging out with older boys. And Lily lacked the class of somebody like Issy Brunel. Despite the crude tone of his interrogation of Sammy in the immediate aftermath of the break up, Donkey's fascination with Isadora Brunel was not primarily sexual. He wanted extraneous aspects of Issy – her loose-limbed grace and her intellectual prowess, her parents' Range Rover and their foreign holidays – as much as he wanted the girl herself. At night as he lay sleepless in his narrow bed, he sustained himself with fantasies of being her consort in a variety of imperfectly imagined exotic locations: on ski slopes; in expensive restaurants; on yachts. The utter and self-evident unattainability of these dreams were a torture to him, and he spoke of them to nobody.

Donkey was not the only one enduring the exquisite pangs of courtly love. Murdo's blasé parrying of Edward's questions over the chess board had masked – not all that effectively– a developing fascination for the French girl. Despite not being particularly tall (he and Sophie were more or less of a height) Murdo had never found it difficult to attract the opposite sex. His corkscrew copper hair and pale blue eyes were unusual, but in their odd way appealing, and his body was lean and hard. His quick wit was provocative but seldom cruel, and he could charm when it suited him to do so.

What puzzled him slightly about Sophie was that she made a show of being attracted to him – she claimed for example to love his accent, and liked him to deconstruct obscure Glaswegian expressions for her. She asked him earnest questions about the Labour party, and whether it could ever recover from the follies of New Labour and the disastrous adventure in Iraq. Through all this encouraging attention however she remained oddly elusive. During those few times they had spent alone, she had almost immediately taken her accordion from its bag and strapped it across her chest, picking at some tune or other with her slender fingers while Murdo tried to open up more promisingly flirtatious lines of discussion. He could see that she was using the squeezebox as a physical and psychological barrier, and he had the distinct impression that at some level he was being toyed with. It was an unfamiliar and unsettling experience.

There were other areas in which Murdo's life was not running entirely smoothly. Not all of his lecturers on the politics course appreciated his radical and idiosyncratic take on political doctrine, nor his fondness for flowery rhetoric and obscure reference. His tutor, Mallinson, was a notable sceptic. Murdo had early on put himself forward for a place on the local party executive, and word had reached him that Mallinson had spoken against him. At any rate his bid had been unsuccessful, and he had to be satisfied with running the student Labour group, and turning up regularly for canvassing and leafleting duties as little more than a foot soldier.

On Friday evening of that week, Anton Killick sat in the crowded waiting room of Kernow Veterinary, a small shoebox secured with an elastic band on his knees. He was practising a Korean breathing routine that normally eased him into a semi-meditative state even in busy, confined spaces such as this one, but still an uncharacteristic anxiety tugged at his consciousness. Around him a variety of other household pets, mostly canine and feline, sat in cages or under chairs by their owners, and whimpered and snuffled, while a cheerful veterinary nurse in a green dress came and went. Odd scraps of conversation generated and died. Anton sighed and abandoned his attempts at meditation. He looked down at the brown shoebox. He resisted the temptation to lift the lid and peer in, but he raised it to his face and placed his ear against one of the air holes punched in the side. Inside he could hear the faintest scratching. The door to the surgery opened, and another veterinary nurse came out peering doubtfully at a piece of paper.

"Um…Leon Trotsky?"

"Over here," said Anton, and rose to his feet.

Later that evening, in the silence and simplicity of the white cube that was his living room, Anton sat crossed legged on the floor in his loose black trousers and white tee-shirt. Despite the news from the vet, his head was now clear and he knew exactly what had to be done. The veterinary had, of course, offered to give Leon Trotsky an injection there and then, and would no doubt have tossed the small white furry corpse into an incinerator with scant ceremony, but Anton would have none of it, and had eased the rodent back into its box with great gentleness, explaining that he wanted to be able to say goodbye properly. The vet, who was not a sentimental man himself, nonetheless understood the attachment of owners to their pets, and had matched Anton's demeanour with his own, saying that there would in the circumstances be no charge.

Anton rose and crossed to the sideboard, where a white napkin had been freshly ironed and laid out as if for a sacrament. He lifted the box from the table and gently removed the elastic band that secured the lid. Leon Trotsky was barely stirring but opened one pink eye at the change in the light. With the greatest of care Anton eased the tiny white rodent from the straw and laid it gently on its side on the napkin, before returning the box to its place.

He stood with his legs apart, his hands together as if in prayer. Then he lowered both hands to his side and breathed slowly and deeply three times, before raising his eyes heavenward and uttering a short sentence in Korean. He was utterly calm. He knew where his responsibility lay. Unlike that of the revolutionary for whom he was named, Leon Trotsky's death would be bloodless and dignified.

Chapter Fifteen

"Did I tell you I'm in love with you, Miss Porteous?"

Dave and Kate stuck to their agreement to shelve all discussion of house-hunting until Easter, and concentrated instead on the new scheme of the mock election and associated classroom activities, which Dave was keen to present to the Head before school broke up. They were caught up with the excitement of the project to such an extent that Kate agreed to relax her normal mid-week embargo, and cooked supper for them one evening so that they could discuss the matter more fully.

"So," said Dave, pushing his plate to one side and topping up his glass of wine, "I reckon we need about three weeks to do this properly."

"When's the actual by-election? Presumably we want to run the polling days in tandem if we can."

"Yeah that's a point. I'll see if the Council website has anything to say." He took out his phone while Kate cleared the plates and put the kettle on. It was not normally her style to wait upon Dave, but she was enjoying his enthusiasm for this project.

"So…according to this…it's on Thursday 6th May. When do we get back from Easter?"

"First Tuesday after the Easter weekend."

"Right. So that's just over three weeks before polling day. We need to get clearance from the Head ASAP and be ready to hit the ground running as soon as we get back."

Kate returned from the small kitchen area with two mugs of coffee and a plate of chocolate brownies.

"I guess you'll want to brief the staff, too."

"Ideally, yes."

"Which year groups were you thinking of?"

"It needs to be a whole-school thing. It's too good an opportunity."

"It's going to be quite close to the exams. There's a bit of a gap till the GCSEs, but the Year nine tests are mid-May."

"I definitely want Year 9 involved, given that I'll be looking after them next year. And it would build on the debating work we did last term. But the upper school are the ones who'll benefit most. They're the ones who are closest to voting."

"I'll check the dates."

Dave took a bite of brownie.

"Mmm. These are good. We should do this more often."

Kate returned with her spiral-bound planner.

"Right. Let's see. Year Nine tests are week beginning Monday 17th May. A week and a bit after the by-election."

"Well that's all right," said Dave. "Don't you think?"

"I expect Frances will be fine with it but I'm not so sure about Anton."

"No, obviously Anton will do his nut. But d'you know what? I don't care. I reckon this is unstoppable, if we pitch it right. I mean it's inspection gold-dust, isn't it?"

"I suppose it is. We need to make sure there's lots of video evidence."

"We'll film all the hustings. And can you imagine how good it's going to look: queues of model citizens in their St Petroc's blazers lining up to vote in the assembly hall. The governors will love it."

"It's not going to seem a bit disrespectful, is it, so soon after Vincent Narabo's funeral?"

"I don't think so. It's all in the framing. We can pitch it as a fitting memorial to his contribution to the school."

"Did he make much of a contribution to the school?"

"Not that I'm aware of. But we'll pretend he did and that will make it even harder for Anton to stop it."

Dave took another drink of his wine. He was growing animated.

"We need to work out how we're going to do this. Do you feel up to taking notes?"

"Because I'm a woman?"

Dave looked momentarily deflated.

"No, of course not! Because… because…I've had two glasses of wine and am very excited about this and my hand might shake."

"Well I tell you what. You do the dishes, and I'll take some notes, and that way you won't feel so complicit in the patriarchy."

"It's a deal," said Dave, and got up from the table. He almost danced his way to the kitchen, and en route he leaned over and kissed Kate on the neck. "Did I tell you I'm in love with you, Ms Porteous?"

"I think you may have mentioned it."

They stayed up late making notes, until they had a detailed scheme for how the mock election would work. And then, partly because it had been fun, and partly because it was raining, but mostly because Dave said some very nice things and looked at her earnestly with his soft, long-lashed brown eyes, Kate hadn't the heart to kick him upstairs to his own flat when they finally called time. So they fell into bed in Kate's tiny bedroom and didn't get all that much sleep. Then it was all very disorganised in the morning, and Kate was a bit short and sent Dave up to shower in his own flat, the rain by that time having gone off. *This*, she reasoned as she hunted around for her school stuff, which would normally all have been packed the night before, was exactly why the current arrangement worked so well, by which she meant not only the adjacent but separate apartments, but also the ban on mid-week co-habitation. *This* was what worried her about a future spent under the same roof seven days a week.

Dave secured an interview with the Head that Friday, and pitched his proposal. He knew enough not to draw the man out from behind his desk, and felt no need to bring a laptop with him, relying instead on his own enthusiasm and a natural ability to express a strong case clearly. He focused on the widely acknowledged weakness of their existing Citizenship curriculum. He talked about how unique an opportunity this was – a by-election in the very ward in which the school was situated. He went into detail on Kate's ideas for classroom activities – analysis of the literature produced by the candidates; speaking and listening activities built around the hustings; even the mathematics of election results – percentages, vote share and so forth. He acknowledged that the exams were not all that far away, particularly for his own year group, but made a compelling case for this invaluable element of curricular leavening in advance of the hard academic slog that was to come. Finally, and this was his trump card, he invited the Head to consider how well the project would go down with the Ofsted inspectors when they descended on St Petroc's in the summer term.

The Head listened carefully, his arms resting upon the polished expanse of the desk-top, his fingers together at the tips in a steeple shape – this was his preferred posture for hearing enthusiastic plans proposed by junior colleagues. He was not oblivious to the contrast with Anton's clinical and digitally enhanced presentation of the previous week, nor with the fundamental clash of ideas that the two proposals embodied. But he liked Dave, and he liked what he had to say.

"Anyway," said Dave, "That's my proposal. If we're going to do it, I'll need to get some initial information out to staff and students before the holidays. What do you think?"

The Head smiled.

"I think it sounds wonderful. A lot of work for you, of course, but I can entirely see the benefit to the school. I'd like to run it past SMT, however, before I give it the unconditional green light. Make an appointment with Rona to see me towards the end of the week, and I'll let you know what we've decided."

Dave stood up, trying not to show his slight disappointment that the scheme hadn't been given the go-ahead there and then. The SMT were an unpredictable lot, and the strongest voice by far was Anton Killick's. This was far from a done deal.

"Thank, you," he said, "I'll do that."

The Senior Management Team met the following Tuesday, the last full week of term. Anton was up first with his "St

109

Petroc's Stripped for Action" presentation. He had found some additional images illustrating the manner in which a ship of the line was prepared for battle – decks cleared of all but cannon, the Captain's quarters converted into a primitive emergency room, and so forth. This was received politely, but without any huge degree of enthusiasm. Even his colleagues in senior management found Anton's zeal for academic excellence a little overpowering at times.

"So, I understand the principle," said Emily Flowerdew, who was the school's pastoral lead. "And it's a great tag line. However we do need to ensure we don't throw the baby out with the bathwater here. At the end of the day, this is a set of exams, not a battle for the soul of the free world. We don't want casualties."

Anton smiled tightly. "Don't take it too literally, Emily. It's designed to appeal to our under-achieving boys."

"Yes, I get that. And it may well succeed. I think the idea is good. It's a question of how rigorously we apply it. Are you suggesting we literally stop all non-academic activities of any sort from…well, when, exactly? Middle of May?"

"Oh it needs to be earlier than that," said Anton. "It's the lead up to the exams that's crucial. Once the students are engaged in them they take them seriously. But by that time it's too late. If we leave "Stripped for Action" until the actual exams are upon us it will have virtually no effect, and it won't be worth doing. But if we introduce it from the time we come back after Easter, then it's going to be really powerful. We catch the students when they've had a break, and they're in the right place to think in terms of a fresh start. They come back to corridors whose walls carry nothing but revision prompts. Form time is spent in silent study. Lunchtime clubs are suspended. Trips postponed until after half term."

"So…six weeks," said Anderson, the Director of Digital Strategy. "That's quite a chunk of the school year."

"Probably five, realistically," said Anton. "And once the Year Nine tests are over, the lower school can relax a bit. But you must see it's a change of attitude in the build-up that's really going to make the difference."

At this point the Head intervened.

"I must say I like this idea of Anton's," he said. "It shows imagination, and it's radical. And we are all aware that the exam results, while respectable, are not all that they could be. I would like to give "Stripped for Action" a try, at least in some form."

Emily Flowerdew had been about to speak, but something in the Head's tone made her pause. She had worked with him longer than anyone, and trusted his instincts.

"The question is when we instigate it, and to what extent."

"It really isn't worth doing this half-heartedly," said Anton. The Head ignored this.

"Before we settle on those details, there's something else we need to consider. One might say that exciting projects are like buses – none come along for ages and then – well, a second interesting proposal was put to me last week."

Had Dave been present, he would have been impressed with the accuracy and fairness with which the Head presented his scheme to his senior management team. No detail was omitted. They listened in silence, though Anton was shaking his head.

"This is madness," he said when the Head had finished. "This is everything that "Stripped for Action" is trying to get away from. I'm completely opposed."

"I think it sounds rather good," said Emily. "Something different that could tick a lot of the boxes we missed last time round."

"It's not the ideal time of year, though," said Anderson. "A couple of months later, maybe…"

"Well, we can't always choose when these things happen," said the Head. "And actually, Anton, I don't think it is incompatible with your own excellent scheme. I understand the by-election itself is on the 6th May. That gives you three weeks before the bulk of the GCSEs start. I think we can run the mock election on our return from holiday, then strip for action, as it were, the Monday after polling day. Surely that would work?"

Anton had gone visibly pale. "That would mean only one week of serious focus before the Year Nine tests," he said in a low voice. "It's not enough. They'll all be high from this election nonsense – we'll never get them back on task."

"They're only Year Nines," said Emily. "The rest of the world has abandoned SATs, remember. They were never thought to achieve very much."

Anton flashed her a dangerous glance. "Our year Nine tests are a central plank of our academic improvement strategy. They provide us with valuable data that enable us to track student progress and intervene accordingly. I'm surprised I need to remind you of that."

"Colleagues, please," said the Head in a placatory tone. "I think we'll call a halt to the discussion at this point – I have a sense of where we all stand. I can tell you I am minded to proceed with both projects, one after the other; I think we can enter wholeheartedly into both, and if we do I think both have the potential to bring great benefit. We might have to think a little more about when each begins and ends, but I will do that in conversation with the sponsors of each."

"Who is pushing the mock election, as a matter of interest?" asked Anderson. "Sounds like a lot of work for somebody."

The Head hesitated for only a moment.

"It was David Singleman's idea. It's a natural fit with the work he's been doing with debating."

"Mr Singleman," said Anton, expressively. "Am I the only one who thinks it odd that the incoming head of Year Nine would want to distract his charges with a lot of speechifying and posturing a week before their exams?"

"Anton," said the Head.

"I'm sorry, I'm going to have to go," said Anton, "But I should say I don't feel much enthusiasm for pressing ahead with Stripped for Action if it's going to play second fiddle to Mr Singleman's vanity project."

And with that he snapped shut his laptop, and rose from his chair. Nobody met his eye as he left the room.

Chapter Sixteen

"I'm not rigidly heterosexual"

The Tregarvon Hotel was a dozen miles from Roskear, one of the more expensive establishments on that stretch of the north coast. In a week or so it would be busy with Easter visitors, but that midweek evening it was quiet. The restaurant overlooked the bay, and Anna had booked a table by the window. She had the best of the view, across the wide stretch of Carbis Bay to where the lights of St Ives twinkled to life as dusk fell. Edward, when he chose to take his eyes off Anna, looked out onto the broad, empty Atlantic gloaming, relieved only by the occasional slow lights of a ship a few miles offshore. None of the other diners was within earshot.

They might have been taken for a well-to-do couple from the Home Counties on an early Easter getaway; Edward in chinos and a reasonably expensive checked shirt while Anna was wearing a pair of pale blue jeans that might have come from Top Shop, and a black polo neck that most definitely hadn't. Although nothing had been said in advance of the rendezvous, it had been established early on that each had taken a room, ostensibly to avoid relying on a taxi and the need to recover vehicles the following day. Drinks in the bar beforehand had been reasonably relaxed, but there was a sense too that there was business to be discussed.

It was now nine o'clock, and their desserts had arrived. The early conversation had not flagged (they had drunk most of a decent bottle of red between them) but had artfully skirted round the issues that they had supposedly met to discuss, focussing instead on Edward's anecdotes of life at St Petroc's. Anna had brought him up to date on the state of play with Julian, who had moved into a flat in Truro and was encouraging her to start divorce proceedings as soon as possible.

"More wine?" asked Edward, holding the bottle up to the light to inspect the quantity remaining.

Anna put her hand over her glass. "Not for me. Thank you. There are things we need to talk about, although to be honest, I've rather enjoyed not talking about them."

"Oh. That sounds ominous," said Edward, pouring the remains of the wine into his own glass.

"Well, I just mean...it's big stuff, some of it. Look, let's deal with the political bits first, then we can talk about the other."

"About us, you mean."

Anna met his eyes and nodded. "Yes. About us." She was being, he thought, rather lawyerly, difficult to read. He attended to the remains of his crème brûlée.

"All right then, said Edward. "Politics."

"Are you still interested in being the candidate?"

"Yes, very much. I've read up on the ward, and the recent electoral results. I'm keen to get cracking."

"Well the good news is that nobody else has come forward, so it looks as if it won't be a contested selection. I've put the word around that you're interested, and the general response has been favourable. So we just need to set up an approval panel. Once that's done, the exec will appoint you as soon as the deadline for expressions of interest has passed."

"Remind me when that is."

"Close of play Monday. So you'll be able to get on with campaigning in the holidays. You didn't have anything else planned, did you?"

"I had thought I might nip over to Brittany, but nothing's been booked."

"That's good, because time is short. The election is on 6th May. Could you attend an approval panel this Friday?"

"I think I'm free. But if I'm the only candidate, can't the executive just rubber stamp me?"

"Goodness me, no. Everything has to be done by the book."

114

"I trust they'll be gentle with me."

"It's all routine stuff. Presumably there are no skeletons in your closet?"

"Only the rather old and tired one that's been rattling around in public for so long that it's almost respectable." He said this lightly.

Anna looked at him sidelong. "Really?"

"Surely you've heard of my being bundled off to France in semi-disgrace. I thought everybody knew."

"I'm afraid I haven't. But do tell. I'm agog."

Edward hesitated. If Anna knew nothing about the events of twenty years ago, then what he was about to tell her had some bearing on their own relationship. She picked up on his reluctance.

"Or, I mean, if you'd rather save it for the approval panel…"

"No. I wanted to run it past you anyway for…all sorts of reasons."

She waited. He pushed his plate away, and straightened a crooked piece of cutlery.

"So, I'm not sure whether you're aware, or guessed, but I'm not rigidly heterosexual." The form of words seemed to invent itself for the occasion. He made himself look up at Anna, and she met his gaze candidly enough.

"Oh. OK. Well, I hadn't guessed, as it happened. You did quite a good impression of being rigidly heterosexual the other weekend."

Edward smiled at the poor joke.

"Is that it? Because, you know, we are the Liberal party. We quite like that sort of thing."

"Well, there's a bit more. A bit before the millennium, so we're talking over twenty years ago, when I was a relatively young Head of Department, I got involved…well, not exactly involved…let's just say there was some preliminary flirting…with a younger colleague. A male colleague. You have to remember the general atmosphere around homosexuality in schools wasn't quite as liberal then as it is now."

"Of course. Section 28 was still on the statute books."

"Quite. And while everyone could see it was on the way out, there was still this whiff of scandal attached to any hint of gay behaviour in staffrooms."

"And you said this was a member of staff?"

"Yes – admittedly a newly qualified one. Anyway, he was giving off pretty clear signals, or so I thought, and I responded. A student must have seen something and suddenly there were rumours flying around. The Head – the same one who's there now, as it happens - was newly appointed at the time, and didn't really know what to do. He called us both in, individually. I don't think I've ever seen a man look quite so uncomfortable.

"Anyway, the other guy must have panicked because he effectively reported me for inappropriate conduct, as if he were utterly affronted by the whole business. Then a governor with particularly narrow views got hold of it and wouldn't let it go. It got into the papers and attracted a bit of adverse publicity. It was suggested I should take a term's leave of absence, with the understanding that my job would be held open for me. I'm afraid I rather took the huff. I went to France and didn't come back for three years."

"And this other colleague. Presumably he was gay? I mean you hadn't completely misread the situation?"

"Oh, he was queer as a nine-bob note. He runs a gay nightclub in Torquay now. It only took him a year to decide teaching wasn't for him. He tried to contact me about five years ago, but I'm afraid I ignored it."

"I don't blame you. And…" Here Anna hesitated. "Since then?"

He was aware that her question might be an attempt to probe beyond the political. It seemed to Edward that they should keep the topics as separate as possible.

"Well…no scandals, if that's what you mean. And today the atmosphere is very different. I suspect most people would regard it as a lot of fuss about nothing. But folk have long memories. The party might be fine with it – I mean I should hope they would be. But it's not out the question the opposition might try to make something of it discreetly, on the doorstep."

"Well," said Anna. "Thank you for being so honest. I can't see it affecting the outcome of the approval."

"No. Well that's good"

"Look, do you want to order coffee? I'm just going to nip to the loo."

"Of course. I might have a brandy."

"Make it two."

Anna pushed back her chair. He tried to read her body language as she discarded her napkin and bent to pick up her bag. Was she buying herself time to think? Probably. He had always assumed that she knew, as he assumed that everybody knew, from the staff to the students to the traffic wardens on Trelowarren Street and the waiter who was tripping across now in response to his raised hand.

He ordered the brandies and turned his face to the darkness outside. If he listened carefully he could hear the sea on the rocks, beating its slow, timeless, broken rhythm. He had a sudden urge to be out on the black water in a wooden boat, or even just on the rocks with the sea breaking around him, harsh and unrelenting, but entirely non-judgmental. He was heartily sick of judgment, and he feared that with Anna's return, there was more to be borne.

And then she was back, slipping elegantly into her seat.

"Coffee and brandy on the way," he said, by way of resuming the dialogue.

"Good." She smiled. "It's been a lovely meal."

He nodded graciously, as if he were in some way responsible.

The waiter was crossing towards them, and they waited until he had retreated, having placed the drinks, a little ceremoniously, on the table. Edward spoke first.

"Look, I realise that whatever you were going to say about how things stand between us might be affected by what I've just told you. You might need time to reflect. You might not fancy a relationship with a bisexual man. I understand that. I should say that I genuinely thought you either knew or guessed."

"How would I have guessed? You're not exactly camp."

"I suppose not. Well. I don't really know what to say. Perhaps you didn't fancy a relationship with me anyway. Perhaps what happened the other weekend was just a one off…an act of friendship…" He realised he was talking a little too quickly.

"Edward, if you give me a chance I'll tell you what I feel."

He smiled ruefully.

"Yes, of course. I would welcome that."

Anna took a sip of her brandy.

"It's been, as you can imagine, a difficult couple of weeks for me. I haven't really had much headspace for thinking about us. Which is not to say that I didn't think what happened was important. It was. And I was aware that we needed to connect and clarify what the implications were." Here she hesitated, and he had to resist the temptation to interrupt.

"I've felt for a long time that there might be something more than friendship between us. But of course acting on that was out of the question, while my marriage to Julian was intact. Or at least while I assumed it to be. Then I found out what I now know about Julian's behaviour, which, it turns out, had been going on in one form or another for years. I'm sure you can imagine what it feels like to make that kind of discovery. It un-moors you. Completely and very rapidly. All the norms, and the assumptions, that have governed your behaviour up to that point suddenly cry out to be re-examined. But once one gets one's bearings again, one's instinct – or this is what I found – is that you want to hang on to those norms. You don't want this…betrayal…to make you into a different person. That would just feel like another kind of theft."

Edward nodded.

"Of course at the same time there are all sorts of other instincts at work. The need to feel you're not alone, that you have allies. The need to feel that there are bits of your life that are not hopelessly compromised, solid ground where you are capable of acting independently, of making choices for which you will bear responsibility. Am I making any kind of sense?"

"Perfect sense."

"The evening I spent with you – in all its aspects, felt to me like one of those pieces of solid ground. Something I chose to do independently of the situation, not because of it, and certainly not by way of any sort of revenge against Julian. And in case I didn't say so at the time, it was very lovely, and felt very right."

"But it was a one-off."

"I don't know. Not necessarily. Look, I'm forty-seven years old. I'm professionally successful, my kids are more or less independent. I'm the injured party, and knowing what I now know I have no interest in reconciliation, which in any case isn't on the table. If I choose to enter into another relationship of any sort - long term or one-night stand – that's up to me. I have that choice, and holding onto it – the choice, I mean - seems important to me. I guess what I'm saying is that it's going to be a few more weeks, or months, before I know whether or not I'm up for exploring what kind of future we might have. That's assuming you would want that kind of future. I'm very aware we haven't discussed that."

He waited. She made a gesture as if to indicate that that was all she had to say. He cleared his throat.

"Look…that all makes sense. I completely acknowledge how hellish your position is. I just…it would help me to know a couple of things."

"Go ahead."

"Let's suppose that for the next few months we continue as friends – at arm's length, as it were. I think that's what you're saying you would like."

Anna nodded.

"You're not ruling out that the relationship could be more than that in the future?"

"I'm not ruling it out."

"And…I'm sorry, but I've got to ask this. What I told you this evening…has that made any difference?"

"I don't think so, no."

"You don't think so."

"There's just...God this sounds terrible coming from the Chair of the local Liberals…I think I need to ask…if you've been in a relationship with a man recently?"

"I was seeing someone in London for a bit five years ago. There's been nobody since then."

"I see." She nodded. "OK…"

He added gently, "I think what you might also want to know, is that being gay, or in my case bisexual, doesn't make you more or less promiscuous than anyone else. Just as for any other human being, remaining faithful in a committed relationship is a matter of personal integrity, not sexual orientation."

"Yes. Yes of course. I see that. And I'm sorry you felt you needed to say it."

He smiled. "It needs to be said more often. Look - we've rather pushed the boat out tonight. Shall we split the bill?"

"Oh…I think I said it was my treat…"

Edward reached his hand across the table and put it over Anna's.

"I would rather we split it."

Chapter Seventeen

"The joke that must never be made"

Dave and Kate were working hard to be tender and considerate towards each other after their argument. They both knew that there was a fragility to their reconciliation, like a limb that has been reset after a bad break, and it seemed safest not to put too much weight on it, but to throw their energies into the mock election project. Dave planned to put the main points of the project in an email which would be sent to all staff and students before they broke up, so that would-be candidates could make their plans over the holiday. He just needed the green light from the Head.

Kate was enjoying putting together a scheme of work for use in English lessons, with suggestions for cross-curricular elements that might be used in other subjects. The more she thought about it, the more opportunities she discovered. The history department could look at the development of the modern franchise, particularly Votes for Women. Art and IT could design posters and fliers, using as a model the real literature of the candidates as it landed on local doormats in the course of the campaign. Geographers could look at the key aspects of the ward in which the actual by-election was taking place, mapping its boundaries and plotting its centres of population and employment. With exams and tests in the offing no department could be forced to pursue these options, but equally, none would be able to complain of being left without opportunities.

One day in the middle of the week Dave found himself standing behind Anton Killick in the lunch queue, a proximity between colleagues that conventionally required at the very least an acknowledgement, if not an exchange of pleasantries. Whatever animus he might be harbouring within, Anton liked to maintain the appearance of courtesy, and Dave steeled himself for some gritted-teeth politeness. He was a little shocked when Killick kept his back to his junior colleague for the entirety of their painfully slow progress from cutlery tray to custard urn, during which the Deputy kept up a stream of solicitous enquiry as to the general health of the counter staff, their children, their elderly parents and their pets. Knowing nothing at that point of Anton's thwarted plans for "St Petroc's Stripped for Action", Dave wondered what recent offence he had done to the Deputy-Head.

He was enlightened by Anderson, the Director of Digital Strategy, when he dropped into the IT suite to discuss how the school's website might be utilised in the students' campaigns.

"Ruffling a few feathers, this election project of yours," said Anderson.

"Really?" said Dave. "Everyone I've spoken to has been very positive. I mean I accept that some of the exam groups will have to keep their involvement to their own time, but that's fine. Individual teachers are completely free to set their own priorities."

"Does the phrase "St Petroc's Stripped for Action" mean anything to you?"

Dave shrugged. "Naturism as a Wednesday afternoon activity?"

"That," said Anderson, "is the joke that must never be made."

"Well go on then. Fill me in."

"It's Anton's new project. He wants the school to come back from Easter to a bare-bones, exam-focused curriculum, in and out of lessons. Wall-displays to convey nothing but dates and formulae. Form periods to be silent revision. Like a

Man O'War preparing for battle, you see. I think it's rather clever."

"Yeah I get the reference. Sounds horrific. It's not as if the kids don't get that the exams are looming. If anything they could do with a distraction."

"Well you'll be pleased to know that the Head seems to agree with you. He's told Anton he can do it, but not until the middle of May."

"So I get a clear run for the mock election?"

"Apparently so. But Anton is not a happy bunny. If I were you I would watch your back."

Dave left the IT department with mixed feelings. Normally he would have been only too happy to play the role of the thorn in the Deputy Head's side. And he had foreseen that Anton would be no fan of the mock election. But Anton was responsible for all curricular and extra-curricular matters, and the Head prioritising Dave's project over his own would undoubtedly be a provocation. He did not doubt that Killick would find some way, however petty, to make things difficult. He had not yet had the Head's response to his draft email, and he began to feel anxious. Despite Anderson's assessment, and the enthusiasm the Head had shown when Dave had originally pitched the project, there were no guarantees.

On Thursday there was a note in his pigeon-hole from Rona d'Allesandro, asking him to drop by the Head's office after school.

"He'll just be a couple of minutes," she said, when Dave arrived at four o'clock. "He's got Anton in with him just now."

"Okeydoke," said Dave, and took a seat in one of the easy chairs in the foyer.

It was quarter of an hour before the door opened and Anton emerged. He didn't look at Dave, but compressed his lips in a kind of grimace as he passed him on his way down the corridor in the direction of his own office.

Anton was followed a few seconds later by the Head, who looked, Dave thought, slightly ruffled. He began to feel uneasy.

"I'll just be two minutes," said the Head, and disappeared into his personal toilet.

The Head's personal toilet, or the Throne of Grace as it was sometimes known, was something of a standing joke amongst the staff. The door was marked only with a brass sign that read "Private", and Rona d'Allesandro assured him that nobody, parent, guest or governor, was ever offered the courtesy of its facilities, being instead directed to the staff toilets along the corridor. The Throne of Grace was kept locked at night, and the cleaner responsible for the admin block, presumably by way of a joke, claimed to be sworn to secrecy as to its appointments and decor.

When the Head emerged he seemed more composed.

"David, come in, come in," he said, taking his accustomed place behind the broad expanse of his desk, and indicating to Dave the chair on the other side. Dave sat down, noting that the Head appeared reluctant to meet his eye, instead picking up what was presumably a printout of his draft email and flicking through it. Dave could see that some sections had been highlighted.

"Now, your scheme, your *admirable* scheme for the mock election. All very exciting, and very worthwhile. I must congratulate you on the level of detail..."

"The curricular stuff is all down to Kate really," said Dave. "It's very much a joint effort."

"Ah yes, indeed. Well, please do pass on my congratulations to Miss Porteous. In fact I will drop her a note. So many opportunities here. And I do thoroughly approve of cross-curricular work – we don't do nearly enough of it..."

"I believe the inspectors like it too," ventured Dave. There was clearly a point of some sort to which all these pleasantries were leading.

"Well, of course, and particularly in the lower school. Perhaps at this time of year they would be expecting the focus for senior students to be more on the exams."

Dave felt a weight settle in his stomach. He had a momentary flashback to Anton's grim expression, followed almost immediately by a premonition of what the Head was about to say. He cleared his throat.

"The election will be over by the sixth of May. Surely…"

"A little too close, perhaps to the first of the GCSE's," said the Head. "In the eyes of some, at least. Parents, you know."

"And Anton."

"Well, he is the Director of Studies. It's his job to bang the drum for exams and so forth. The thing is, yours is not the only exciting project in the offing. Anton himself has devised a scheme – rather a clever scheme in my view, to sharpen up everybody's focus in the run-up to the GCSEs. He's calling it…"

"St Petroc's Stripped for Action," said Dave flatly.

"Indeed so. The idea is, you see, that like a ship of the line in Nelson's navy…"

"Yes…I've heard the pitch. The students are to be fed an extra ration of rum and given a tarry rag to bite on when we amputate their limbs.

"Now David. You know I dislike cynicism."

"So when exactly do we roll back the wardroom carpet and scrub down the table?"

"Well this is the point. Anton was keen to start it all as soon as we get back from Easter. Fresh start and all that. But I have insisted – largely to accommodate your own excellent scheme – that we don't "strip for action" as it were, until after the election. And I have to say that by doing that I have made my Senior Deputy more than a little unhappy."

Dave tried not to look pleased at this.

"So the mock election can go ahead?"

"It can go ahead, but only for junior students."

"But…the seniors are the ones who need to be aware of this stuff. They're the ones who will be voting in a few years' time. They're the ones – some of them anyway – who will actually have some understanding of the issues under debate. The juniors will just see it all as a bit of fun."

"Oh, I think you're underestimating, if I may say so, the effectiveness of your project. And Miss Porteous's, of course. You will be planting a seed. And your excellent Year 9 debaters – young Doggett, for example."

"I think that might be a flash in the pan…"

"I'm not so sure."

"I…I really don't know if I can bring myself to do all this if it's just going to be for the benefit of Year 9." Even as he said it Dave knew that these were not the words the Head would expect to hear from his latest appointment to the pastoral team.

"Do you know, that's almost exactly the response I got from Anton when I told him Stripped for Action couldn't start until the election was over?"

125

This went home. Dave had no wish to be placed in the same category as the Deputy Head.

"Think about it, David. Running the mock election is a big project. It's the first time you've done it – there are bound to be hiccups. This is the Year Group you'll be taking through in September – it's a terrific opportunity to build relationships. And at the end of the day we are talking about May – the very month the certificate exams begin. I'm proposing a compromise."

Dave stuck out his lower lip. Then he looked up and met the Head's gaze, now steady upon him.

"All right," he said. "Junior students only. But in all other respects we run it as I'm proposing?"

"Absolutely," said the Head. "You will have my full support."

"I think the Head's been quite clever," said Kate, as they drove home that evening.

"Really?"

"Well think about it. Anton's his second in command. It's quite a big thing to clip his wings in response to your initiative."

"Our initiative."

"Our initiative. Stripped for Action is a strong idea, particularly given the link with that ship. And he's right about the size of the mock election project – it would be a huge thing if you – we - were trying to do it at such short notice for the whole school. This way we can really make sure we get it right, and tailor it for your year group. I can't imagine the Year Sevens and Eights will be that interested, but our debaters will be dead keen to get involved. They'll have real ownership."

"Well you may have a point. I don't agree about Stripped for Action though. Don't you think exams generate enough stress?"

"I'm not sure this will increase the stress – just kind of clear the decks and give the kids room to work."

"Did you really just use a naval metaphor? Was that deliberate?"

"Oh dear. I don't think it was. There must be plenty more though."

"Perhaps you could save them until after 6th May. I have a feeling we'll be drowning in naval metaphors once we strip for action."

"Aye-aye Cap'n."

"I'll turn a blind eye to that one."

Kate snorted with laughter. They rounded the bend above Wheal Prosper, and the sun broke through the clouds. Perhaps because they were exhausted by the tensions of the last few weeks, the prospect of an endless contest to find ridiculous naval metaphors was deeply appealing, and they were both laughing uncontrollably as they pulled up next to the Engine House. It was almost the end of term.

Chapter Eighteen

"It was only an orange cream"

As the mock election was now to be restricted to Year 9, Dave was given a slot at the final year group assembly of the term in order to pitch the project. Once he had adjusted to the disappointment of not involving the older year groups, and got over his resentment at Killick pulling rank on him, he began to see the advantages of focusing on this group of students. He knew them well, having been a form tutor for the previous three years, and they were the students that he would have charge of in September, when he took on his new role as Head of Year.

He stood now in the wings as they filed into the theatre with their tutors, more or less in silence, under the watchful eye of Sheila Abbot, who was retiring in the summer. Once they were settled, Sheila spoke.

"Well, Year Nine. Here we are at the end of another term. With one or two exceptions which we won't dwell upon, it has been, I think, a good one and I would like to congratulate you on your generally high standard of dress and behaviour around the school. You are shaping up to be a really pleasant bunch of young people."

There was a pause, and Dave thought he detected a catch in Sheila's voice. She had been a Year Head for twenty-five years, and was widely respected for her fair, no-nonsense approach. She was retiring early to look after her dying husband. This couldn't be an easy time for her.

"Next term as you know, you will be sitting some important tests which will give us very useful information about how well you have been learning – and indeed how well we have been teaching you – in your academic subjects. However that is not the only significant event that lies in store, and to tell you a bit more about what we have planned, I will hand over to Mr Singleman."

Dave glanced up to the lighting box at the back of the theatre, where Sammy Pascoe was primed to cue the music. There was a second or two of dead air, then the tortured four-tone riff of Glen Buxton's lead guitar tore through the theatre at high volume. A few vaguely recognised it. Most looked bemused, and there was some eye-rolling from the sophisticates, but also a general sense of sitting up and paying attention because it seemed something interesting might be about to be said.

"I'm your top prime cut of meat, I'm your choice
I wanna be ELECTED!
I'm your Yankee-doodle dandy in a gold Rolls Royce
I wanna be ELECTED!"

Dave walked to the centre of the stage and Sammy faded out the music. He paused.

"A sweet to the first person who can tell me the name of the artist."

"Alice Cooper!" called a long-haired skinny boy three rows back whose dad played in a metal band. Dave tossed him a Quality Street from a box that that had been lurking in his desk drawer since Christmas.

"And another one to the first person why can tell me why I'm playing it."

A hand went up near the back. Dave peered into the gloom and detected the lanky form of Donovan Doggett. He would let that one pass, as it would doubtless be a smart-arse comment of some sort. He waited, but no other hands went up.

"Sir!" called Donkey from the back.

"Go on then," said Dave with more enthusiasm than he felt.

"There's a local council by-election happening because that dude croaked."

There was laughter, a smattering of ironic applause that died away as Dave stared at him, balefully.

After a few seconds Donkey added,

"Sorry sir, I mean, passed away."

"Thank you. A pity you had to spoil a good answer with inappropriate language."

The theatre settled into respectful silence once more. Out of the corner of his eye he could see Kate with her head in her hands.

"There is indeed to be a Cornwall Council by-election in the immediate area of the school, with voting on the 6th May. This means that over the next few weeks, most of you will be receiving literature through your door from the candidates, setting out why you, or rather your parents, should elect them to this important job of representing you. Now all this is interesting for its own sake, and the Head has agreed that we will track the progress of this election as it happens." He paused.

"More importantly, we're going to run our own election here in the school. And, because of the GCSEs and A levels, which are not far away, this is the only year group that will be given this privilege." Dave was aware that he was now presenting as a selling point what up to now he had considered a disaster, but that was fine. In this game, you had to adapt to survive. He continued.

"You will all have the opportunity to stand as a candidate, either for one of the mainstream political parties which you will see represented in the actual election, or as an independent, with your own manifesto telling the voters what you will do if elected." There was a buzz of interest at this, and Dave allowed it to run its course before proceeding. "There will be speeches and question and answer sessions, which are given a special name…anybody?

Issy Brunel's hand went up.

"Issy?"

"Is it…hustings?"

"Correct." He threw her a Quality Street.

"All this will take place in the three weeks after you get back from Easter, with the final ballot on the 6th May, the same day as the actual vote. There will be an email to all students giving more details, and explaining what you need to do if you wish to stand as a candidate. To avoid the whole thing getting out of control, we will be looking for no more than one candidate from each of the main parties, plus up to four independents, so there will need to be some preliminary vetting of manifestos. Every prospective candidate will need to be sponsored by a member of staff."

In the wings Sheila Abbot was pointing at her watch.

"Now I think we're running out of time, so very quickly, are there any questions?"

Issy's hand went up again, and he nodded in her direction.

"Who will the electorate be?"

"Good question Issy. All students in Years Seven to Nine, provided they've registered to vote in advance. Yes Toby?"

"Can you be, like, the Monster Raving Loony Party?"

General laughter. Dave had already considered this and decided there should be room for a bit of eccentricity.

"In theory, yes. But remember there are going to be no more than four independent candidates, so we'll be picking the ones who we think will run the best campaigns."

He was about to hand back to Sheila when he saw Donkey's hand up again.

"Yes Donovan."

"Sir I'm sorry about my inappropriate language, Could I have a sweet for my correct answer?"

Dave hesitated. He did in fact have one more Quality Street in his pocket. The presentation had gone well. And it was only an orange cream. He caught Kate's eye. She nodded.

"As it's nearly the holidays," said Dave. "But I'm not throwing it to the back row. You can come and get it after assembly."

Dave stood in the foyer as the students streamed past him, listening for evidence of enthusiasm for his project. There wasn't a great deal, but a small knot of the more bookish students, plus one or two eccentrics, hung around with questions. One of these was Donkey, waiting a little detached from the group, no doubt determined to get his chocolate. Once the enquirers had dispersed, Dave rummaged in his pocket.

"So, out of curiosity, how come you were the one who knew the answer?"

"I'm interested in politics, Sir. In fact, the mock election was pretty much my idea."

"Was it indeed."

"Yeah, I mentioned it to Ms Porteous in one of our meetings."

He recalled Kate saying that it was something a student said that had sparked the idea. She hadn't said it was Donkey. Dave decided to be gracious.

"Well," he said, "I'm very glad you did. Are you going to stand?"

"Might do. Not sure what as, though."

"Well have a think about it over Easter. Now you'd better get a wriggle on. The bell's gone."

Sammy's week of commuting with his father in the pickup was almost at an end. It was only a fifteen-minute journey, and they chatted cheerily enough. Viv was careful to make sure his son was dropped off in good time within walking distance of the school gate (he humoured without comment Sammy's request that he not be dropped at the gate itself, although that would have been just as simple). They talked music, as they always had, though the balance was shifting so that it was now Sammy who was introducing his Dad to artists he had never heard of, rather than the other way round. Viv pretended more enthusiasm for this musical education than he felt. It was conducted via the not very good speaker on Sammy's not very expensive phone, the Nissan not being blessed with Bluetooth, and between the noise of the dodgy exhaust and the unfamiliar slang and beats of the music, he was never entirely won over to the merits of Stormzy and Lethal Bizzle. You couldn't, in Viv's opinion, beat a good-looking southern woman with a sweet voice and a slide guitar.

In spite of Issy's outwardly relaxed response to Sammy's temporary absence from the school bus, she did start to miss him round about the Wednesday. This was the day she had a slightly odd encounter with Donkey at breaktime. They had never had much to do with one another, being at opposite ends of the spectrum of academic ambition. Each had traditionally regarded the other as a slightly alien species with whom an encounter of any sort was unlikely to end productively. However during the inter-schools debating competition the previous term, Donkey had demonstrated a more vulnerable side, and a keen-ness to succeed that had quite impressed Issy, and since then they had acknowledged one another more or less amicably around the school.

She had passed him at lunchtime on her way to netball practice. He was on his own at a corner of the PE block, leaning against the wall with his hands in the pockets of his slightly-too-short trousers. and he nodded in response to her cheerful "Hey Donkey." She walked on, but he called after her.

"Issy! Wait a bit."

She turned and looked back. Donkey detached himself from the wall, and took a few steps towards her.

"I was just wondering…"

"Uh-huh?"

Issy continued to look at him, her expression open, friendly. The distant sounds of kids playing football floated over from the playing fields. A member of the PE staff had come out of the building and was getting something from the boot of their car.

"Could you…maybe call me Donovan?"

"Donovan? You mean…not Donkey?"

"Thassit. It's kind of…I dunno. Not the image I want to project. Or some crap like that."

Issy looked at him with interest. This was new. Donovan Doggett *was* Donkey. He had been Donkey since Year 3, when he had been given the part in the school nativity play. Possibly he was destined always to be Donkey. As if reading her thoughts, the boy looked away, and Issy had a momentary epiphany as to what it might feel like to carry through life the burden of such an unpromising nickname.

"Sure," she said. "Donovan it is. I gotta dash. See you."

Sammy was back on the bus for the final few days of term, and he and Issy sat together as usual. Things were still awkward between them. It seemed that the only shared territory they possessed was their recent breakup, which was obviously off-limits, and their lessons with Singleman. They had been working hard in English to finish off the term's written work, so there wasn't much to talk about there either.

133

The news of the mock election provided welcome new material.

"You gonna stand?" asked Sammy.

"Definitely," said Issy. "It'll be really cool if there's hustings and so on. What about you?"

"I guess I might. Not sure what as though."

"I was thinking," said Issy. "If you decide not to stand, and obviously if you want to then you should, but if you decide not to, you could be my campaign manager."

"Right," said Sammy. He was not sure whether he was encouraged at the overture or irritated at its presumption. "Or if I stand you could be my campaign manager."

"Well…it's just you said you weren't sure," said Issy. "I didn't mean to…"

"No, okay," said Sammy irritably. "Anyway, what would you stand as?"

"Probably Conservative," said Issy. "That's how my parents vote. And I kind of agree with a lot of their policies."

"Really?" said Sammy, without making too much effort to hide his distaste. "I've never asked my parents how they vote, but I'm pretty sure it's not Conservative."

This was the first proper conversation they had had in about ten days, and it wasn't going well.

"I mean it's not the popular choice," said Issy, apparently deaf to the flatness in Sammy's voice. "Among people our age, at least. But that's maybe a good reason to go for it."

"Right. Well…I don't think I could be your campaign manager if you're going to stand as a Tory."

"OK," said Issy. "Well… see you on the stump."

The bus was pulling into the layby at Eglos, and Sammy was damned if he was going to ask what, or where, the stump was.

Chapter Nineteen

"Metaphorical fire in her belly"

Murdo sat on the train to Penzance in cheerful mood. Partly this was due to the prospect of a few hours in Sophie's company, but he was also buoyed up by an encounter that had taken place at the weekend.

On Saturday morning he had paid another visit to the Penhale estate, where he was greeted by the pleasing scent of freshly cut grass. He knocked once more on the door of the Doggett residence, which was opened by a lanky tow-headed youth an inch or two taller than Murdo.

"Mornin'!" said Murdo amicably. "Are either of yer parents in?"

"They're both out," said Donkey. Who wants to know?"

"My name's Murdo, from the local Labour party? I think we might have met before. Ah called round a couple of weeks back and spoke to your Dad. About the by-election?"

"Oh yeah," said Donkey, with interest. "I'm thinking of standing."

Murdo looked at him quizzically. "D'ye mind me asking how old you are?"

"Fourteen," said Donkey. "I don't mean the proper by-election. I mean the school one."

"Oh yer havin' a school one? That's grand. Are ye, like, standing for any particular party?"

"I dunno, maybe just the Donkey party." As soon as Donkey said this he regretted it.

"Whit, like…animal rights?"

"No. That was just a joke. It's – it used to be my nickname. My real name's Donovan."

"Right. So… you're Donovan Doggett."

Donkey scowled. "How do you know my surname?"

"Yer parents are on the electoral register. Well…" Murdo checked his phone. "Yer Mum is. Does yer dad no vote?"

"My old man's been away," said Donkey, still scowling.

"OK," said Murdo, unsure what he had done to offend. "The last time I called, yer Dad said he wanted the verges done on the estate. Well…" He gestured to the newly mown grass across the road. "Ah made a few calls and ah jist wanted to make sure he wis happy with the result."

"All right."

"And with the other thing…the school election. If I can give you any help with yer campaign, jist give me a call. Ah got into politics when ah wis your age, so ah'd like tae encourage you."

"All right. I might do that."

Donkey took out his phone and the two exchanged numbers.

"The Labour party, you said."

"That's it. Party of working men and women. Now don't forget to tell yer dad that I called. And tell him there's still time to get on the electoral register. I'd be happy to give him a hand with that. Nice to meet you, Donovan."

Since then the boy had texted Murdo, expressing an interest in finding out more. He had sent a holding reply – he would need to think of the best way to move that forward. It would be good to find out about this school election, too. Perhaps he could offer to go in and speak to the kids.

He put down his phone as the train from Roskear pulled into St Erth, where it met the branch line from St Ives, and peered out of the window. The platform was on a slight curve, and he thought he could see Sophie sitting nonchalantly with her legs stretched out in front of her, her accordion in its bag on the bench beside her. She looked as if she were waiting to meet the train, rather than board it, and Murdo with an effort returned to scanning his phone, in order not to appear keener on the rendezvous than she was. Presumably, having made the effort to be there on time, she would get on the train, and presumably she would come and find him. Or perhaps she wouldn't. He was finding Sophie frustratingly difficult to predict.

The train sat for a minute or two, then a whistle blew, the engine note picked up, and it began to move. He glanced up as they passed the bench where Sophie had been sitting, and was relieved to see that she was no longer there. He decided that looking out of the window would serve as well as studying his phone, and remained in that attitude until the connecting door hissed open and Sophie came into the carriage. She placed her backpack on the table and slid easily into the seat opposite him.

"*Salut*, Glasgow." She offered her cheek and they exchanged the traditional double kiss across the familiar barrier of the accordion, about which Murdo was beginning to feel distinctly ambivalent.

"Saloo Grenwee." It had become their standard greeting. Sophie came from a village with a complicated name, so Murdo had settled on addressing her by his best approximation of the french word for frog. This she seemed to find endearing.

"So, tonight we select the Labour candidate, yes?"

"Aye, well, you'll no get a vote, as yer no a member. But you can listen to the speeches."

"I have a little surprise for you." She fished in her pocket and drew out a small plastic card bearing the imprint of a stylised red rose and the narrow, bearded face of Jeremy Corbyn.

"Ye've joined? Nice one!"

"So now we both have a vote."

"Do you know anything about the candidates? I mean, I can give you ma views if you like."

"I have been online. Mallinson, he is your lecturer, yes? He is not I think, socialist. *Pas vraiment*. But the other one has the Momentum...what is the word?"

"The endorsement."

"Yes, the Momentum endorsement. But she is not so local. I think that is not such a good thing."

"Aye but Mallinson's a…" for a moment Murdo struggled to articulate what precisely were Mallinson's shortcomings.

"You don't like him?"

"Well I don't like his politics. And Ah'm not that keen on him on a personal level either. Ah find him arrogant – he'll think he's got this sewn up. Momentum aren't sae strong down here, so their endorsement doesn't carry so much weight. Might depend how many students turn up."

"And the other candidate? The Momentum one?"

"Ah don't know all that much about her tae be honest. Single Mum, been a union official. She's working class and she's got fire in her belly, and that's good enough for me. She'll shake the place up, which is what it needs."

"What is belly?"

"Like, yer stomach. It's a metaphor."

Sophie looked at him a little coldly. "I did not imagine it was literal."

"Naw. Sorry."

There was a silence between them for a while. The train was two miles out of Penzance, at the point in the journey when the ground to the left falls away and St Michael's Mount, lit on this occasion by the evening sunshine, seems to rise as if by magic out of the sea.

Murdo gestured towards it, anxious to restore harmony.

"Pretty smart, eh?"

Sophie was unimpressed. "It is not as big as Mont St Michel."

Murdo rolled his eyes, and Sophie grinned unexpectedly.

"OK, yes, it is pretty smart."

When she smiled like that it made him dizzy. The train was slowing, and Sophie rose and picked up the accordion, Murdo gestured towards it.

"Can ye play The Internationale then?"

"Of course. I am socialist, remember."

There were about a hundred people packed into the hall, from students to grizzled veterans. One or two small children sat on parents' knees or charged up and down the aisles. Following the hustings speeches and the questions, the vote had been taken by secret ballot, and tea was now being served while the papers were counted in an adjacent room.

Murdo thought he knew, from the general composition of the members who were there, what the outcome was likely to be. A number of students, none of whom were over-fond of Mallinson or his politics, had turned up, but it was unlikely to be enough to swing the outcome. The single mother with metaphorical fire in her belly had spoken with great passion – possibly a little too much passion - about the need to pursue a radical socialist agenda. Mallinson, on the other hand had been urbane and understated, but had demonstrated a strong knowledge of the ward and its issues. Murdo reckoned that at least half the hall would have known him personally for a number of years. He didn't hold out much hope.

The buzz of conversation abruptly subsided as the returning officer once more mounted the steps of the small platform at the front of the hall, followed by the two candidates. Mallinson's face was hard to read, but the woman from Momentum looked, Murdo thought, less pleased than she would have done had she won.

"Right ladies and gentlemen, thank you for your patience. We have a result, which has been accepted by the losing candidate, and I can tell you that the outcome of this selection is that the Labour Party candidate in the forthcoming Penhale and Eglos by-election will be Trevor Mallinson."

The candidates shook hands to a smattering of applause and one or two boos from the students.

"I'd like to thank both candidates for the spirit in which this hustings was conducted, and I'm sure as a constituency party you will all be getting behind Trevor to work for a Labour victory in this election. There will be a press photograph shortly so please stay behind for that – it's always good to have a crowd."

"Let's go," said Murdo. "Ah'm no interested in being in the picture. We've got time for a drink before the train."

"But I haven't played the Internationale," said Sophie. It was hard to tell whether she was serious or not.

"I don't think anybody will be singing the Internationale tonight," said Murdo gloomily. "We've just selected a fuckin' Blairite."

They slipped out the back of the hall in company with some of the other students and disaffected Corbynites who couldn't quite bring themselves to hold up placards and smile for the photograph. They were at the tail of a general drift towards a popular pub, and Murdo was aware that one perfectly proper outcome would be to join the group and introduce Sophie to his friends from the politics course. He was in the process of working out a way to avoid this when she said quietly,

"You know I don't really feel very sociable tonight. Can we just go somewhere quiet for a glass of wine?"

"Aye nae bother," said Murdo, unable to believe his luck. "We just hang a right here…"

They ducked into a narrow alley that brought them out on to a long hill leading down to the harbour. Ten minutes later they were sitting side by side in the corner seat of the Clipper, Murdo with his cider and Sophie with a glass of red wine. He had asked the Landlord quietly if he had something a bit up market, had baulked at the price tag, but had paid up, judging that it might be worth it in the long run.

"So," said Sophie, "Tell me about Edward."

"Edward? What dye mean? He's jist my landlord."

"I find him interesting. There is about him a sadness I think, in his eyes. Does he have family?"

"I dunno. Not of his own, I don't think. We mostly just argue about politics. And keeping the place tidy." Murdo was quite suddenly aware at how incurious he had been about his landlord.

"He likes you, I think. He is tolerant of you."

"Aye well…there might be a reason for that."

Sophie raised her eyebrows.

"I think mebbe he's gay."

"Really?"

"Ah'm no sure. I mean, he's no, like, rampantly queer."

"But you think he is attracted to you?"

"Ah couldnae say for definite. He's never come on tae me or anything."

Sophie took a sip of her wine, and then, as if to take the focus off Edward, said,

"So you are not gay?"

Murdo looked taken aback.

"Me? Naw. Ah mean ah've got no problem with it, but personally ah'm heterosexual. Jist, ye know, tae clarify matters."

Sophie looked at him sidelong, and he wondered if he had gone too far.

"Whit about you?"

"You mean my sexuality?"

"Aye, that."

"I am lesbian. Just to clarify matters"

"Seriously?"

"Yes, why not?"

"Naw, ah mean, fair enough. How's your wine by the way?"

Sophie wrinkled her nose.

"I've had worse."

"Right," said Murdo. "That's good."

They spoke little on the short journey back from Penzance, and Murdo walked home from Roskear station feeling mildly depressed and in a state of some confusion. The clocks would go forward at the weekend, and new, spring-like scents emanated from the dark shrubbery in the gardens along the road to the Count House. Change was in the air. Walking up the path he could see Edward reading in the front room, and he paused briefly at the door and studied his landlord before letting himself in quietly. He felt as if he was seeing him for the first time. It would have been easy – and perfectly normal - to simply slip down to his basement flat, but some impulse – curiosity perhaps, even a kind of guilt - made him stick his head round the door. Edward was propped against a large cushion, his reading glasses on his nose and his long legs stretched out along the length of the settee, apparently unaware of Murdo's presence in the doorway.

"That's me back."

Edward looked up from his book.

"Was democracy served?"

"Well. In the short run, mebbe."

"Did Sophie show up?"

"Aye. She came along. With her bliddy squeeze box. Anyway. I'm a bit knackered. I'll see you tomorrow."

"No doubt."

Down in the basement Murdo sat on his bed in thought for some minutes. There was new information to be absorbed and fresh perspectives to explore. Sophie; Mallinson; the by-election campaign; the substance of all these things had been subtly altered as if by a change in the lighting, and decisions as to how he moved forward in respect of each would be required. Hanging over everything was the approaching Easter break, and the question of whether or not to return to his troubled family in Glasgow. Suddenly he felt exhausted. He pulled off his clothing and climbed into bed.

Chapter Twenty

"Should she just abandon caution?"

Term ended on a Wednesday, and the final half week, despite the looming exams, was not taken particularly seriously by either teachers or students. The more diligent members of staff respected Anton Killick's embargo on the showing of DVDs and the playing of games until the final day, but most paid only lip-service. The trick was maintaining just the right balance of good humour and light-touch control that would ensure the final few days were relaxing and reasonably merry, without descending into the kind of chaos that would lead to a major disciplinary incident. By and large, this had been achieved. Now the final bell of the final day had rung, and the students of St Petroc's were streaming out of the school gates into the sunshine, joy and promise of a Cornish spring. Edward watched them go from the window of his classroom, and reflected on the events of the week that had passed since his rendezvous with Anna.

After the meal they had lingered at the table just long enough to finish their brandies, but the conversation had not flowed as lightly as it had earlier in the evening, and they departed for their separate rooms with a brief, rather formal embrace a little after ten o clock. They made no arrangement to meet for breakfast, and having settled his bill the night before, Edward rose at six to drive the short distance back to the Count House for a shower and some clean clothes before walking in to catch the early train to school.

It was a glorious morning, the sea beyond the harbour flat and blue and boundless. Although the meal with Anna had not ended quite as he had hoped, and he had slept poorly, he felt to his surprise a certain lightness, as if he were stepping unencumbered into the final week of term. A coffee and a pastry in Costa by way of breakfast had added to his vagabond mood. He had been disappointed in Anna's response to his honesty, and therefore a little disappointed in Anna, and by extension the local party. He did not at that point greatly care whether he was approved, selected, or ultimately elected. These seemed suddenly all to be things that people did to you. At the end of the day, he could if he wished put two fingers up to all of them.

There had been, after a day or two of silence, a brief exchange of texts, initiated by Anna. She thanked him for being understanding, and apologised if some of her questions had been clumsy. She promised to be in touch soon. His response had been gracious but cool. The details of the approval panel meeting had been confirmed more formally via email, and that was the next time he saw her.

The offices of the Roskear Liberal Democrats occupied the floor above a shopfront on Trelowarren Street, as they had done for decades. In fact the entire building, which was owned by a local sympathiser, was let out on favourable terms to the party, so the shop window contained posters and literature, faded and a little out of date, and there were a desk and chairs arranged as a kind of reception area, suggestive of civic formality and earnestness. These were generally unoccupied. At election time, Edward knew, it was a different matter. Volunteers old and young would spring from the woodwork, and the place would buzz for weeks with frantic activity: the duplicator running day and night; tables of volunteers stuffing envelopes as the folding machine clattered manically in the background. He wondered what level of support he could expect for the by-election.

The approval panel itself had gone smoothly enough. As the rules required it was chaired by a councillor from outside the constituency who Edward knew slightly and who greeted him warmly, thanking him for his attendance and assuring him that this was likely to be no more than a formality. The other panel members were a smart, efficient looking woman in her thirties and a student of some description, neither of whom he knew. Anna was acting as clerk and host.

Edward's insouciant mood had stayed with him. He had given some thought as to what he should put in the box that asked about incidents from his past that might embarrass the party. In the end he had simply written: "Minor scandal twenty years ago as discussed fully with the local party chair. No illegality involved." The ball, he felt, was in the panel's court.

The interview had cycled through predictable questions around his political record, his interests in local government, and his campaigning experience. He was asked if there were any party policies he fundamentally disagreed with. He replied that he thought they were a bit soft on independent schools. As to his priorities were he to be elected, those would also be educational, and securing the future of the local Minor Injuries Unit. Things seemed to be winding up when the Chairman cleared his throat and said,

"Now as to the matter of the minor scandal you have referred to, Anna has briefed me fully, and I in turn have relayed the salient facts to the panel, and we are all in agreement that your unfortunate experience should be no barrier to you getting elected, and is certainly no barrier to your approval."

Edward inclined his head in acknowledgement.

He knew Anna was trying to catch his eye from her seat at the side of the broad table, but he continued to look at the Chairman, who rose and shook his hand. Anna had shown him out of the office. Even without the slight coolness between them, any kind of intimacy in that context would have been inappropriate, and they had merely wished one another good night.

He had heard nothing from her since. On the Sunday evening he had received an email from the Chair of the panel, confirming that he had been approved as a Liberal Democrat candidate for local council and parish elections at all levels, and was free to apply for selection for any seat in the County. Now it was simply a case of waiting for the Executive Committee to confirm that he had been duly selected to represent them in the by-election.

He checked his phone again, but there was nothing. Outside, the playground was almost empty. He rose and set about tidying his classroom.

At the Engine House that evening, Dave and Kate were each putting the finishing touches to their packing for their holiday in France. They were catching the early ferry from Plymouth, and had to leave Wheal Prosper at five the next morning. There had been considerable debate as to which car they should take, Kate favouring the greater reliability and carrying capacity of the Fiat, while acknowledging that the MG would be the more romantic choice.

In the end she had given way, ostensibly for the pleasure of open-top driving on continental roads, but largely because she knew that taking the MG to France was a long-time ambition of Dave's. They were now drastically restricted in the amount of luggage they could cram in. Dave had a small rack that clipped to the lid of the boot, and that would take the camping gear, allowing them one bag each in the boot, and two small day-sacs, one of which would be lodged behind Kate's seat, and one at her feet.

She looked critically at the bulging grip on her bed. The weather was forecast to be mixed – plenty of sunshine, but also periodic thundery showers, and this complicated matters. Her small rucsac was also full, and beside them on the bed was her hair-drier, for which she had yet to find a place. She contemplated her options. She could just leave it behind, obviously. They were camping after all, but somehow this made the inclusion of the odd luxury item all the more appealing. She could ask Dave if he had room in either of his bags, but this she found herself reluctant to do. She decided to wait until they had loaded the car, which they planned to do after supper, and see if there was a corner of the boot where it would fit. She didn't particularly want it in the footwell – getting out of the MG in a dignified manner was enough of a challenge without the added complication of a hair-drier flex wrapped round her ankles.

A ping from her phone announced the arrival of a message from the upstairs flat.

All done up here. Supper ready in half an hour.

She texted back.

146

Cool. Up in a bit. X

Time for a last bit of tidying. After supper they would load the car, then she would lock up her flat and they would sleep at Dave's. It was exciting, the thought of going away together. Apart from a three-day visit to her parents in Yorkshire over Christmas they hadn't been away anywhere since the relationship started. In fact, she had never gone off somewhere with a bloke, in a sports car, with a tent. There was something appealingly old-school about it; something fugitive.

As she tidied the flat, she was hit once more by a wave of sadness that she would soon – perhaps in a matter of weeks - have to leave it. She sat down on the threadbare sofa. What would her life there have been like if Dave were not around? If, as she had initially imagined when she took it on, the upstairs was simply let to holiday makers, or if somebody lived there with whom she was only on nodding terms, would she feel the same now that she had to leave? Almost certainly not. The location was dramatic, of course, but the accommodation itself was basic. Initially she had been quite profoundly struck by the mining heritage still evident in odd holes and grooves in the metre-thick granite blocks that formed the walls. But inevitably that novelty faded, and it became simply her home, her refuge from the teaching life that was so intense, and at times exhausting.

She realised that it was Dave, as much as anything, that gave the place its significance. The awkwardness that had marked their first meeting (she had, on her first weekend in residence, accidentally locked him in the outhouse) had slowly given way to neighbourliness, and then to something more. She recalled the time he had come down to her flat one damp evening to beg a lift, the fine rain leaving droplets on his long lashes; their first kiss across a surf-board as they floated in the sea's autumn warmth. So many misunderstandings and false starts had to be negotiated before that memorable bonfire night, the brownie burning in the oven as they struggled out of their jeans, here, on this very sofa.

The details for the Net Loft lay under a pile of magazines on the coffee table. She extracted it and considered it thoughtfully. She had wandered round to look at it the day she had found herself alone in Newlyn, but had learned little more from the road than could be seen from the printed details. The

147

roof terrace was at the back of the flat, and not visible from the front. She had tried to work out when exactly it might get the sun. The smell of fish from the harbour was noticeable, but that might just have been the wind direction. Or it might be the reason nobody had snapped it up.

Was she getting it all wrong, this house-hunting? Should she just abandon caution and throw in her lot with Dave one hundred percent? He was a good man, she knew that. And he loved her. And the sex was great. A property rented together was hardly a future set in concrete. She glanced again at the description, and it seemed suddenly like just another lifeless piece of paper destined for the recycling. Kate was not one for rapid U-turns or dramatic bridge-burning, and she resolved that she would sit with these feelings for the next few days and see whether they evaporated or solidified in the course of their holiday.

Her phone pinged again.

Serving up!

She texted back.

On my way, lovely man x

It was dark and chilly when they set off the next morning, but the sky was clear, a few late stars still hanging in the west. The roof was up, and Kate was already strapped into the passenger seat, wedged in with a blanket and the rucsac at her feet, waiting for Dave to finish locking up the upstairs flat. In the end the hairdryer had been left behind. She heard his steps on the wooden staircase, the crunch of his feet on the gravel. He opened the driver's door and paused before getting in.

"All set?"

"Yup…ah no dammit! I think I might have left the light on in my bedroom." She began to unstrap herself.

"I'll check," said Dave. "You stay there."

"Make sure the iron's unplugged while you're there!"

He let himself in to her flat with his key. The iron wasn't even out. Perhaps that had been a joke. The bedroom light was off too, the bed neatly made. He was walking back across the living room to the front door when he noticed a set of property details on the coffee table – not a house or flat that he recognised. He hesitated. They needed to get off, and anyway it was Kate's business, but…he looked again at the picture. The Net Loft. He didn't remember that being mentioned. He left it where it lay, locked the flat and climbed into the MG next to Kate.

"Right," he said as he gunned the engine. "Next stop Plymouth."

It was April Fool's day.

Chapter Twenty-one

"D'ye want another tea cake?"

For those whose day began at a more civilised hour, the first morning of the holiday dawned bright and clear. It was almost a week now since the approval meeting, and Edward was still waiting for confirmation from the executive committee that he was the official candidate. Without this he could not order leaflets or begin canvassing. Nor had he heard anything from Anna, though that was perhaps unsurprising given his coolness towards her on the night of the approval. Her children would be arriving back from University and they would be dealing with the break-up of the family.

Although his participation in the by-election was still not confirmed, his enthusiasm for standing had been growing steadily, and he had already begun some tentative planning. He had bought a large-scale map of the area from WH Smiths, and this was pinned to a sheet of chipboard and propped up at the back of the desk in his study. The boundaries of the council ward were marked out in pink highlighter, with the major settlements bordered in blue. There were five of these – the Penhale estate and the adjacent private housing around St Petroc's, which accounted for perhaps half of the voters, and four reasonably large villages, the nearest only three miles distant, spread out across the area between Roskear and the school. The rest of the voters lived in scattered hamlets and on farms, and would be difficult to reach.

Edward's study was the smallest of the four bedrooms on the first floor of the Count House, and was made even more compact by the bookshelves that lined three of the walls. On top of these shelves were ranged a large number of postcards depicting writers both classical and modern; favoured works of art; and places that held some significance for him. He sat now at his desk, oblivious to the familiar décor that surrounded him, and considered once more the figures from the last election. Three years ago Vincent Narabo had won the seat comfortably enough, with five hundred and fifty-seven votes. The Lib Dems were a couple of hundred behind that, only thirty or so ahead of Labour, who in turn had narrowly edged out an Independent candidate whose name Edward didn't recognise, and Mebyon Kernow, the self-styled Party for Cornwall. The Greens brought up the rear with 87 votes. Overall turnout was forty-four percent, about average for that type of election. Narabo had been elected on only twenty-nine percent of the vote. He was lucky the opposition had been split.

Edward had mentioned nothing of his plans to Murdo. In part this was because there would almost certainly be a derisory reaction of some sort that he would need to be in the right mood to deal with, and in part because at the moment Murdo was quite happy to chatter away about Labour's plans and there seemed no reason to cut off this flow of useful intelligence. It was not particularly good news that the party had selected what seemed like a fairly moderate and sensible candidate in Trevor Mallinson. A vocal left-winger would have been far preferable from Edward's point of view.

He would need to build a campaign team – it was not clear yet what level of support he could expect from the local party, whose average age was somewhere around that of Edward's own. This was not necessarily a problem if the weather were fine – many of the party's more senior members were doughty campaigners with decades of experience who liked nothing more than to lace up their brogues and pick up a bundle of leaflets from the Roskear offices. Edward was aware that there was probably useful voting data held on a computer system somewhere in the local party HQ – he was hazy as to how these things worked, but intended to ask Anna when they were in communication once more. There might be a Lib Dem group at the university who would be willing to get involved.

He wondered if he might recruit – or even pay – some of his own students. He had read Dave Singleman's email about the planned mock election. Surely there were opportunities there? The school would need to be even-handed, but many of the parents must live within the constituency, and the fact that a member of staff was standing might well be of some interest. Edward made a mental note to get hold of his colleague and have a chat. The competitive spirit that had been an important element in his prowess at sport and at the chess board began to kick in. He could win this thing. He could damn well win it. And if he did, he would hand in his notice.

In the meantime there were plenty of Easter jobs to be done in the garden, and also on the boat, which was currently on the hard standing in a boatyard near Falmouth and had barely been touched all winter. He had booked the relaunch for mid-May, and if he didn't want to miss his slot, he had better get started with rubbing down the hull. Had the local party confirmed his selection, *Tiddy Oggie* might never have made it into the water, but as they had yet to do so, Edward reasoned that he might as well do what he could while he could. He closed his laptop and shut the study door behind him.

He dug out his boat maintenance clothes – a grubby pair of khaki shorts and a jumper with holes in the sleeves, and rooted around in the garage for the bits and pieces he would need to begin cleaning off the hull. Perhaps Raphael, who crewed for him regularly, would be free to give him a hand.

The holidays had begun for Murdo too. He was still in bed, but awake, when Edward's car left the drive of the Count House. He lay for a while watching a shaft of sunlight advance across the moth-eaten carpet of his room, and thought about the days ahead. He was expected for lunch at Auntie Rona's, which was a mixed blessing. He liked his aunt, and although she gave him a hard time over what she saw as his shortcomings, he knew that she liked him too. The problem was Uncle Raph. Auntie Rona was family. She was still close to his mother, understood her problems, and how difficult life had been for him growing up. At the same time he suspected that her move down south was an attempt to distance herself from that, to embrace a life that was at once simpler and more sophisticated. Raphael d'Allesandro, with his southern English upbringing and his Italian heritage – a heritage more recent than the streak of it that lay three generations back in his own family, had been regarded as a bit of a catch when Rona first brought him home to meet the more respectable bits of the McAndrew clan. There hadn't been all that many repeat visits, and he was pretty sure it was Uncle Raph who had put his foot down about Murdo staying with them in the cottage. He was never overtly unfriendly to his nephew, but the two tended to circle one another warily on the rare occasions they found themselves in the same room.

The d'Allesandros lived in a pretty stone cottage in Gurrian, one of the larger villages that were, as yet unbeknownst to Murdo, circled in blue on the map in Edward's study. He usually took the bus but had decided to cycle the six or seven miles, given the freshness of the morning. There were some substantial hills to overcome, and Murdo's bike, which he had picked up second-hand shortly after his arrival, was not in great shape. Nonetheless, he was in optimistic mood. He would push it up the hills if he had to. He was lightly loaded, carrying no backpack and wearing no helmet.

It took him only ten minutes to get clear of Roskear and out into the countryside. The first couple of miles were mostly flat, and he cycled along through fields that were still damp from overnight rain. He had picked out a route in advance and he had his phone to fall back on if he got lost. New flowers were out in the hedgerows now, small and startling in their beauty and brightness. They were flowers he had never seen in Scotland, and once or twice he stopped and surprised himself by taking a picture. He would never admit it, but he thought Cornwall was pretty fine. It didn't have the grandeur of the mountains he had climbed as a kid, but the coastline was impressive. The people seemed generally friendly, and more than once he was told by locals that he was all right, because he was a Celt. He quite liked that.

He reached the first long climb, and after two or three minutes of slow and tedious progress that gave rise to some unsettling creaking and clanking from his bike, he got off and pushed. If anything his progress was quicker that way. Another ten minutes brought him to the top of the rise and he turned and looked back at Roskear, spread out three or four miles behind him, its few prominent civic buildings catching the sun. What surprised him was the sea. Despite being only a few miles away it could never be seen from the town itself, but it now lay vast and open from shore to horizon. Between his vantage point and the town stretched a green and purple and brown carpet of heather and bracken, with occasional vivid splashes of early gorse.

He took some more pictures, and sent them to Sophie.

Magic Day! What u up 2?

He waited a few minutes to see if she would message back, but there was no reply. He knew she would be working, and that she didn't have a day off for at least another week. The holidaymakers were pouring into Cornwall now, and Sophie was taking on extra shifts, saving up money for her college course the following September. She said she was going to study law at the Sorbonne. Perhaps she was. To Murdo, Sophie was still such an exotic creature that he was prepared to suspend all disbelief as to her origins, essence or intentions. Even before her assertion that she was a lesbian, he had understood instinctively that any serious campaign of seduction would have little chance of success. The whole Sapphic thing at least offered him a convenient ladder to climb down and away from the notion of romantic pursuit without having to admit that she was simply out of his class.

He checked Google maps and satisfied himself that he was on track and on time, remounted his rickety machine and set off once more.

At Auntie Rona's they sat over the remains of a mince pie, the kind his mother had made when she was still fully functioning. It had been served the way he liked it, with mashed potatoes, gravy and a sensible number of peas, and it went down a treat. Uncle Raph had apparently got the call to help Edward sort out his boat.

"That wiz great Auntie Rona."

"Aye well you look as if you could do with a decent meal. Are you not eating properly?"

"Ah'm eatin' fine. We take turns at the cooking. Edward's a bit fond of his green veg, but apart from that it's all good."

"And how are you and Edward getting on?"

"We get on fine. Ah don't agree with his politics, but that's no' a major problem."

"Well I'm glad to hear it. You're well set up there Murdo. Edward's a very nice man and you don't want to be upsetting him. And the rent he's charging is very reasonable."

"I don't think I am upsetting him. We jist, ye know, have a bit of banter now and again."

There was a pause while Rona cleared the plates. Murdo wondered if he should mention at that point that he hadn't actually paid Edward his rent for April. In fact, he'd only just paid for March.

"Any news from Glasgow?" he asked instead to Rona's back.

"Your Mum's doin' all right. Getting by."

"Ah'm wondering if ah should go up?"

"She'd appreciate it."

"Ah jist… ye know. Ah can't stand being in the house with that bell-end."

"Don't call him that please."

"Ah bet he calls me a lot worse."

"No doubt he does, but that doesn't mean you go down to his level. You can do some drying if you like."

He picked up a dish towel. "When they go low, we go high. D'ye know who said that?"

"Who said that?"

"Michelle Obama."

"Ah like Michelle Obama. Ah'm reading her autobiography."

"It's good tae see you takin' an interest in politics Auntie Rona. Ah'll need tae lend you *The Ragged Trousered Philanthropists.*"

The dishes dried, he sat down at the table while Rona put the kettle on.

"There's no pudding I'm afraid. Just a Tunnock's Tea cake if you'd like one."

"That'd be grand." He waited until she joined him at the table. "Thing is Auntie Rona, talking about philanthropists…"

"Oh here we go!"

155

"If ah'm going to go up tae Glasgow, ah'm going tae need the train fare."

"And how much is that?"

"Hundred and fifty with the railcard."

"Jeepers, Murdo!"

"That's what it costs. That's what privatisation does."

"Aye no doubt. But at least the trains are clean."

"Can ye do it? Ah'm really sorry tae ask. Ah mean, ah don't really want tae go, tae be honest."

"Ah know that. It's just… we're supposed to be going on holiday next week, and Ah've just bought loads of stuff for that. Ah'll maybe need to talk to Raphael…"

"Naw leave it," said Murdo. "We canny involve Raph. Ah know what he thinks of the Glasgow family."

"Can ye blame him?" Rona's tone hardened a little.

"Naw, ah don't. And' ah'm sorry. Ah didn't mean it tae sound ungracious. Ah jist…well taking money from family is one thing. Ah don't want Raph subsidising me. It's jist a bit of a shitty situation."

"Aye, it is. D'ye want another tea cake?"

Chapter Twenty-two

"Satellite aerials and colour-matched mopeds"

Those who take their exercise over fields and hills, or in their gardens, rightly rejoice at the arrival of spring in all its floral and avian glory. For those who mess around in boats, however, humble as those boats might be, there are peculiar pleasures of which walkers and gardeners know nothing. These reside in the smell of anti-fouling and varnish, in the perfection of a freshly painted waterline and the delight occasioned by some small functional artefact of brass or stainless steel, purchased from the chandlery to solve whatever technical problem bedevilled last season's sailing.

Edward's boat was not a grand one. It was a Cornish Shrimper, one of thousands built in the County to a pleasing and distinctive traditional design, and easily spotted on moorings and under sail on the waters known as Carrick Roads, the huge natural harbour guarded by the twin castles of Pendennis and St Mawes. A Shrimper is only nineteen feet long excluding its handsome wooden bowsprit, and has a low cabin housing two bunks and a very basic galley – nothing more than a single burner stove on gimbals and a pump-action sink. Toilet arrangements are via the time-honoured system of "bucket and chuck it". Shrimpers are most easily identifiable to land-lubbers by the single porthole set a third of the way along the hull, and to sailors by their gaff rig and pleasing, compact lines, and a certain robust cheerfulness to their manner of sailing.

Tiddy Oggie was still some way from displaying any of these features to admiring observers, being currently balanced, as she had been all winter, upon eight pine stocks and a pair of railway sleepers in a tucked away corner of Tallack's yard at the top of the Penryn river. On either side of her hull Edward and Raphael were scrubbing away at her anti-fouling with squares of green scotch-brite, conducting a conversation as best they could given the substantial bulk of the boat between them. An old transistor radio on the deck was spilling Radio 3 onto the morning air, and this mingled with the birdsong, as the smell of nautical unguents from neighbouring vessels in their various states of readiness blended with the scent of the Monterey pines that surrounded the boatyard. It often occurred to Edward that if heaven were anything like this, it would indeed be something to look forward to.

They had been talking generally about school matters, which might seem odd given that the term was behind them and the morning so perfect. In fact few teachers are able to simply close their classroom doors at the end of a term and forget about that part of their life until the holiday is over. There is for many a necessary stage of decompression, both physical and psychological, and Raphael and Edward knew one another well enough to manage their discourse in such a way that it was therapeutic rather than tiresome. This involved each allowing the other space in which to conduct a monologue of matters that had to be spoken out in order to let the holiday oxygen in, while at the same time supplying undemanding utterances at appropriate intervals to maintain the illusion of conversation.

"Anyway," said Raphael, who had been burbling on for some time about his plans for the junior play, "That's roughly what we're aiming for, assuming Anton's scheme to re-enact the battle of Trafalgar doesn't get in the way." Although there had been no formal announcements, rumours of "St Petroc's Stripped for Action" had begun to leak out just before the end of term.

"I think it's a good choice," said Edward. "There's not that much Shakespeare that juniors can handle in its entirety, but

A Midsummer Night's Dream is ideal." He straightened. "Shall we break for lunch?"

"Just finishing this last bit," said Raphael. "Is Betty open for business?"

"Should be. You stick the kettle on when you're done. I'll wander up and get the bacon rolls."

Betty Tallack did a good trade at the start and end of the season selling bacon rolls and pasties from a battered van near the entrance to the yard. Edward wandered down between the ranks of boats, in which one or two gaps had already appeared from owners sufficiently determined and well organised to squeeze every day of sailing they could from the coming season. Tallack's yard catered for the small to medium budget enthusiast, and the boats that occupied it tended to be modestly sized, or longer-term projects in poor repair unlikely ever to make the short journey to the slipway. Ray Tallack had once told him that it was not unusual when owners died, and he set about the necessary arrangements for disposal of their craft and the settling of bills, to find that a family had known nothing of their loved one's secret hobby. It sometimes felt, he said, as if he was breaking the news that there had been a mistress.

Edward returned with the bacon rolls and handed them up to Raphael, who was seated in the Shrimper's generous cockpit. The kettle began its cheerful whistle as Edward hauled himself up the ladder to join him. Soon they were both chewing reflectively on their lunch, their mugs of tea on the cockpit seats beside them.

"The joy of being on holiday," said Raphael.

"You know," said Edward, "I'm thinking I might knock teaching on the head before too long."

"I wouldn't blame you," said Raphael. "I would if I could afford to."

"I just worry slightly that I might...you know, get bored."

"You need a project. There's a few around here that could do with a fresh injection of energy. And a few grand spending."

"I think one boat is probably enough. But as it happens I do have a project in mind. I'm thinking about getting more involved in politics."

"Really?" Raphael raised a dark eyebrow, and Edward noticed as he often did, what an extraordinarily beautiful face his friend had. "For the Liberals?"

"I think so, yes. I've got some contacts still in the local party and…well they're looking for a candidate for this council by-election. You know – the ward that Vincent Narabo held."

"That's exciting. Does Dave know?"

"Well it's not been confirmed yet, so I haven't mentioned it to anyone."

"I expect he'd be keen to involve you in his mock election. I mean…if you have the time."

"I'm sure I could make time to talk to the candidates, if that would help. But I'll need to put together a bit of a team. To deliver leaflets and so forth."

"Of course."

There was a pause, then Raphael continued,

"I mean I'd love to help, Edward, and all power to your elbow and all that, but we're off to Italy in a couple of days and then I'll be up to my eyes in the play."

"No of course – I wasn't really meaning…"

"Rona might be happy to lend a hand though. She's quite keen on the Lib Dems."

"Do you think? I mean even if she was just willing to deliver a few leaflets round the village…"

"I'll mention it to her if you like."

"Well…better not say anything too definite just yet. Until the selection's confirmed."

As Edward and Raphael chatted over their bacon rolls, The majestic white bulk of the *Pont Aven*, flagship of the Brittany Ferries cross-channel fleet, continued its stately progress towards Roscoff, a creamy vee of foam trailing behind it across the dark blue water of the Channel. There was now a little more than an hour left of the passage, and Kate and Dave were queueing for their lunch at the counter of one of the large bright cafeterias. They paid in euros, and carried their trays across the wide lounge to where they had set up camp in forward facing seats near to the observation deck. It had been a smooth crossing, and after nearly five hours on board Kate was accustomed to the gentle roll of the deck beneath them. She barely noticed the compensatory adjustments she was required to make as she walked, adjustments that would have to be unlearned again once they reached dry land.

She thought that Dave had seemed a little tense, but she put that down to concern at the logistical operation of getting the MG onto the ferry and leaving it on the packed car deck for the duration of the voyage. In the event boarding had gone smoothly enough, although the tiny blue sports car had been dwarfed by the motor-homes and caravans that surrounded it. Kate felt a quiet pride that they were doing the crossing in their own way, and just at that moment she wouldn't have swapped the MG for any of the vast, gleaming pantechnicons with their satellite aerials and colour-matched mopeds.

They had transferred everything they would need for the voyage into one of the back packs, then Dave checked the luggage and the roof fixings for a final time and they picked their way between the vehicles towards the stairs that led to the passenger decks.

"It'll be fine," said Kate. "They lock the car deck, don't they?"

"Not much worth stealing anyway," said Dave, a little gloomily, Kate thought.

"I don't know about you, but I'm gagging for a *pain au chocolate* and some decent coffee."

"You're still in Plymouth, remember."

"I'm on a French ship. The coffee's bound to be good."

And it was. There was something distinctly…French about it, or so it seemed. They had their breakfast while the ferry finished loading then they stood up on the observation deck and watched as, with a single shouted command that would have been incomprehensible in any language, ropes and cables snaked back down onto the quay, and the gap between the huge vessel and the jetty opened a hairsbreadth, then widened, and widened still further as the *Pont Aven* eased away from her berth and began her careful passage out towards the open sea. They stayed on deck and watched the land slip away astern until it was just a green smear on the horizon. Then, feeling the cold, they had returned to the lounge, where Dave slept for much of the trip.

Now it was the French coast that was rising in the distance before them.

Edward and Raphael did another hour's work after lunch, by which time Tiddy Oggie's hull was free of weed and barnacles and ready for anti-fouling. They agreed that they had done enough for one day, and Edward dropped Raphael back at the cottage in Gurrian.

"Thanks Raph, that's really moved things forward," he said as his friend got out the car.

"No problem. Sorry I won't be around to help you get the anti-fouling on."

"I can do that easily enough. Love to Rona. Enjoy Italy!"

"I'm sure we will. And I'll mention the campaigning thing. On the understanding it's not yet confirmed."

"Lovely job. Take care now."

Raphael closed the car door and Edward pulled away. He felt light of heart. The boat was a step nearer to launching, and he had recruited a potential supporter for his by-election campaign.

A mile or two down the road he slowed for a cyclist who was weaving a careless course along the lane in front of him. As he drew nearer he recognised Murdo's distinctive auburn curls. He tooted his horn as he passed, and raised a hand in cheerful salute. No doubt the boy had been visiting his Aunt. He wondered whether he should have a discreet word with her about the rent. He wasn't over-concerned. He was aware that his resources were vastly greater than his tenant's, and provided the principle of regular payment was more or less adhered to he was prepared to be flexible.

Back at the Count House he garaged the car, leaving the tools and boat gear in the boot. Now that the hull had been cleaned off he would press on with the anti-fouling. The fair weather was set to continue the following day, though it was forecast to be unsettled later in the week.

He washed his hands at the kitchen sink and contemplated a shower. Perhaps he would check his emails first. Nothing had come through by text during the day, but it was probable that the formal confirmation of the selection would be sent via email from the local party. He turned on the laptop in his study, casting a critical eye over his campaign map as he waited for it to boot up. He wondered if it would be too much to ask Rona to deliver the whole of Gurrian...

There was an email from the local party in his inbox. He clicked it open.

Dear Edward,

I am sorry to have to tell you there has been a change of plan with the selection for the Penhale and Eglos council by-election.

We are under pressure from HQ not to stand a candidate, essentially to make way for the Green party, who say that they in turn will step aside for us at the next General Election. As you will be aware we only lost the Westminster seat by a couple of thousand votes last time, and getting the Greens onside will be a considerable help. For this reason, and with some reluctance, the Local Party executive has agreed to comply with HQ's request.

I am sorry because I know that you were looking forward to campaigning, and you would have made an excellent councillor. The fact that you are now approved means that you are of course eligible to apply for selection as a Liberal Democrat in any other Cornwall Council election or by-election in the next four years.

Yours sincerely
Anna Parminter
Chair
Roskear Liberal Democrats.

Chapter Twenty-three

"Pas beaucoup de choix"

It had not been Dave's intention, when they set off to catch the ferry, to sulk. Still less had he wanted to provoke any kind of showdown. As he locked up Kate's flat and joined her in the MG he did not consider that the piece of paper he had seen on her coffee table held any real significance. He had registered it, but had been prepared to tuck it away as something to be considered, or perhaps raised with Kate, at some later date, but certainly not at the start of their holiday. He had been looking forward to this moment – two of his great pleasures, driving the MG and camping in France, were now to be sanctified by the presence of his beloved Kate. His cup was, at least in theory, running over.

So he had smiled, and kissed her briefly before he started the engine, and uttered that upbeat holiday-coach-driver declaration of their destination, but somehow conversation had not caught hold, and they had driven in silence along the dark empty roads to where the dual carriageway began. Then Kate had nodded off somewhere around Bodmin, and Dave found his mind going back to the Net Loft.

It might mean nothing, or it might mean everything. It might mean that she was going to cut and run. Of course he himself had glanced from time to time at property on his own account, but that was quite different. He had never followed anything up, and instead had focused his efforts on finding something that they might rent together. He no longer had confidence that Kate had done the same. For all he knew she might even now be planning a move.

He had grown gloomy as the morning brightened, and by the time they were approaching the Tamar bridge he felt distinctly resentful. How could he enjoy this holiday with the knowledge that Kate had a secret escape plan in her back pocket. The Net Loft. Even the name! You didn't get much more holiday-home chic than that. No doubt there would be wooden sailing boats in the windows and dolphin mobiles dangling from the lights.

He considered raising the matter there and then to get it out of the way, but that was so out of key with how he had envisaged the start to the holiday that he couldn't bring himself to do it. He loved ferries, and packing and early starts, and he had been looking forward to this for weeks. So he hid his bad mood behind a show of concentration on the logistics of tickets and boarding, then, once they had settled in, he declared that he needed to catch up on rest. While he could certainly have done with some sleep, he never really dropped off, instead turning over in his mind the possible significance of his discovery. The crossing, which should have been a delight given the conditions, was in consequence a misery to him, and he knew his disgruntlement was not going unnoticed.

For her part Kate was not over-concerned about Dave's ill-humour. It was he, after all, who had done most of the planning, and she had learned that with any such project he had an endearing need to nail down every detail and variable to minimise the possibility of mishap. She, in contrast, had had relatively little to do other than sit back and be driven, and this left her free to enjoy the pleasure of the trip in a way that perhaps Dave wasn't. So she had left him to his dozing and had gone up on deck, finding a sunny but sheltered spot to read and enjoy the novelty of being out of sight of land, and the tang of salt on the air.

Once they were off the ferry she made herself useful as a navigator. They had a brief debate as to whether or not to use the continental road atlas that Dave had insisted on bringing, and Kate had been a little surprised when Dave readily gave in and agreed that she could read the directions from her smartphone instead. The roof was down now, and they drew the odd interested glance from motorists as they drove through small clean towns and villages on their way to the campsite. She knew that Dave had to concentrate on driving on the right-hand side of the road, so she kept her conversation functional, contenting herself with soaking up the sun and that delicious sense of being in another country, with unfamiliar architecture and mysterious signage.

It was almost five by the time they found the campsite, where there were more transactions to negotiate, this time in French. (They had both studied the language at A-level, and had agreed that where possible they would try to speak it rather than revert to communicating in English.) They were shown to their pitch, which was sheltered and secluded, and had set about putting up the tent and sorting out the basic kitchen equipment that they had brought with them. This all went relatively smoothly. They had walked hand in hand into town, and chatted about what they might do the next day, but Dave's mood was still muted, and Kate's conviction grew that something was amiss.

Now they were seated at a cheerful little bistro on the main square called *La Bonne Etoile*. Dusk was falling, and the coloured lights strung between the poles of the awning made a cheerful picture. A fountain played softly in the centre of the square, and other drinkers and diners came and went in that peculiarly effortless and natural French manner. Kate had had a generous bowlful of *moules marinière*, and a little more than her customary half-glass of red wine. She decided enough was enough.

"So, come on, then Singleman," she said when they had finished their main courses. "We're here, the car's behaved brilliantly, the campsite looks great and you've just wrapped yourself round a decent plateful of *steak-frites* and half a bottle of red. What have you got to be miserable about?"

Dave looked as if he might be about to protest, but then he slumped a little in his seat.

"I'm sorry…I just…Look I wasn't going to say anything, but maybe it's best to get this out in the open. When I went back into your flat this morning – God, was it only this morning? - I couldn't help noticing – I mean it was sitting out on the table, it just caught my eye – a set of details for an apartment in Newlyn. Not one that we'd discussed, as far as I remember."

There was a silence, then,

"Ah. That would be the Net Loft," said Kate.

"I wasn't snooping," said Dave. "I didn't read it or anything, but it looked as if it might be…well, a bit small for two. It's just thrown me a bit."

Kate sighed. "You weren't really meant to see that."

Dave recognised this as an attempt, probably sub-conscious, to divert blame, but now that he had started he didn't intend to be deflected. They were going to have to have this conversation at some point.

"I just need to know, are you about to bale?"

"Oh Dave! No of course I'm not about to bale. I picked up those details a fortnight ago, and I haven't even been to see the place. I imagine it's gone by now anyway. I found it under a pile of magazines when I was tidying up last night. I nearly put it in the recycling there and then."

"You didn't, though."

"No." She hesitated. "I thought I would leave it until after the holiday."

"It's just…it makes me feel – again – that you're not really serious about us finding somewhere to rent together."

They both knew that this was steering the conversation back into dangerous territory.

"I am serious about it, probably more than ever actually. But I need to have a plan B. It doesn't seem unreasonable to lean against the odd door now and again."

They were quiet for a moment or two. A waiter came over and cleared their table. Dave poured himself some more wine. Kate was still nursing her glass.

"OK. Well I feel happier knowing you haven't actually been…looking around. You haven't, have you? Been looking at other flats? I'd rather know."

"No, I haven't. I thought that wouldn't be in the spirit of things."

"Because I'm just wondering if maybe we do need to think about flipping this whole thing on its back. Maybe we need to spend a few weeks looking at living separately."

"But that's the very thing you don't want."

Dave looked at her over the candle that still burned in its glass dish between them.

"What I want is for us to have a long-term future. Instinctively it's felt like that means keeping you as close to me as I can. But I know that's not good. Maybe what you need is some space to work out if you want the same thing."

"Gosh. Right. That's upping the ante a bit."

"I don't mean it like that."

"You see the odd thing is – and partly it was seeing those details again last night that's made me think this – I was kind of coming round to the view that maybe I needed to be a bit more adventurous in my own approach."

"How do you mean?"

"I mean just move in with you. At 14 Penmere Terrace, or some other version of it. The total floorspace isn't going to be that different from what we have now – it'll be a case of how we manage it."

Dave looked genuinely perplexed.

"So…let me get this straight, 'cos it's been a long day and I'm feeling a bit spacey…if I understand it correctly we're now in a place where I'm prepared to see you move into an apartment of your own – a Net Loft or whatever – and you're prepared to move into a two-up, two down in Newlyn with me."

"Yes. I think that's about the sum of it. And I don't know about you, but I think what that says about us and our future is probably quite positive."

"Wow." Dave looked baffled for a moment, then he looked at her earnestly. "But how are we going to decide which option to go for?"

"*Ça, je ne sais pas,*" said Kate. "But I'm damned if I'm going to worry about that while I'm in France. Is there any of that wine left?"

Dave topped up her glass, then looked at her and grinned.

"*Je t'aime vraiment.*" Then, mischievously, "*Voulez-vous couchez avec moi ce soir?*"

"*Pas beaucoup de choix,*" murmured Kate and moved the candle to one side so that she could lean across and kiss him.

The waiter, who had been approaching with the dessert menu, noted with approval the moment of intimacy between the young English couple, and with commendable professional delicacy busied himself with some minor adjustments to the awning.

Back in Cornwall, Murdo and Edward were also seated across a table – this one being the kitchen table in the Count House where there were no waiters, discreet or otherwise, in attendance.

Edward had been upset by the email from the local party – not just because he had been getting fired up at the thought of campaigning, but also because he thought the strategy politically misguided. Such informal arrangements as the one with the Greens were not unheard of, but they seldom yielded real benefits, and were something of a hostage to fortune. He had read and re-read the email, but there seemed little room for misunderstanding, and little hope of a reversal of the decision. He had sat for a while in his study and wondered what to do next. He was irritated too, by the fact that the email came under Anna's signature, still without any hint of warmth or recognition of what had passed between them. He had texted her to ask if they could meet to discuss the situation, but as yet there had been no response.

He had made himself a cup of tea and taken it into the conservatory. He tried to read the paper but found himself unable to concentrate. Then Murdo had arrived, hot and sweaty from his cycling, and had disappeared to the basement for a shower. Edward called after him not to hang around, as he wanted a shower himself, but Murdo either didn't hear him, or ignored him, and Edward, now feeling distinctly grubby after his day's work on the boat, had to wait an hour for the hot water to replenish itself.

Both Edward and Murdo would have been happier to have had the house to themselves for the evening, but it appeared that neither had any intention of going out. There had been some oblique conversational to-and-fro around the matter of supper, and in what might have been a moment of generosity, or possibly just a moment of weariness, Edward offered to order a takeaway for them both. It was an offer that Murdo was never going to turn down. Now the remains of the food, and the plastic and foil containers it had arrived in, covered much of the table. They were on their third bottle of beer and the conversation had slid, as it always tended to, in the direction of politics, and specifically the matter of the by-election. Edward had sat down quietly determined to reveal nothing of his own situation, but that now seemed a long time ago. It was Murdo who first offered a more personal perspective on the coming contest.

"Tae be honest wi' you Edward, ah'm not sure ah can support Mallinson. The man's no a socialist, that's for sure."

"I don't imagine many of the candidates will be."

"Probably not. Personally, though, ah mean, on a personal level, he's a bit of a shit. Jist, ye know, between you and me."

"Is he?"

"Oh aye. Ah mean...take the ither day. Ah had tae get an essay back, yeah? Ah mean, ah'd had the mark, which was pretty crap, but ah had tae go over it wae him..."

And thus began a tale that took them into the fourth beer.

Chapter Twenty-four

"Who told you about the family tradition?"

Mallinson had awarded Murdo a beta minus, far and away the poorest mark he had so far received. Murdo had booked an appointment to discuss the work on the last Friday of term, but when he turned up at the scheduled time, Mallinson was not in his office, and his door was locked. (Murdo instinctively, and without any real justification, tried the handle when there was no answer to his knock.) He had arrived in combative mood – he took his academic work seriously and had been pleased with this particular piece when he handed it in – and Mallinson's absence was a further irritation. He checked the time on his phone. He definitely hadn't arrived late. He decided he would give it ten minutes max.

There were some moulded plastic seats in the corridor and he sat on one of these for a short time, scrolling through his phone. Then he read the notices and studied the political cartoons on the walls adjacent to Mallinson's office, trying to judge the level of wit they demonstrated, and to ascertain clues as to the man's own politics. A number of the lecturers liked to parade their radicalism, some claiming to be Marxists, but Mallinson was not one of these. His style was dry, restrained and objective, as if he were above the grubby business of party politics. You would never have guessed that the man was a Labour Party candidate.

Ten minutes passed with no sign of his tutor, but still Murdo found himself reluctant to leave. He knew that if he didn't see Mallinson that afternoon, he wouldn't get his work back until after the holiday. Besides, he was in the mood for an argument. He waited another five minutes. At quarter past he muttered an obscenity to himself and set off back along the corridor.

At the top of the stairs he bumped, almost literally, into his tutor. The two stood facing one another, Murdo having a slight height advantage only by virtue of Mallinson being on the second top step. The lecturer looked taken aback, and Murdo didn't feel there was anything he could say that wasn't stating the obvious. He stepped to one side, maintaining eye contact, waiting for the man to apologise, and indicate how he wanted to proceed.

Mallinson simply walked past him, saying as he did so,

"Ah yes, your essay. I'm afraid I was held up at a meeting. I have half an hour now, if you're still free?" Throughout this he continued walking along the corridor until he reached his door, while Murdo remained at the top of the stair. He unlocked his office, then looked back at Murdo and said,

"Mmm?" raising an eyebrow as he did so.

A number of retorts came to Murdo's mind, but instead he said,

"Aye that's fine. Let's do it now."

He walked back along the corridor and joined Mallinson in his office. The lecturer cleared a pile of papers off the one spare seat and signalled to Murdo to sit down, while he took off his jacket and settled himself at his desk. He held out his hand for the essay. Murdo, resigned now to a difficult and almost certainly unsatisfactory tutorial, handed it over. Mallinson flicked through it and read again the comments at the bottom.

"Yes, well I should probably say that there's a lot of quite reasonable stuff in here. I wouldn't want you to be too discouraged about the mark. That basically reflects the fact that you haven't answered the question that was asked."

"Ah thought the premise was flawed. Ah made sure ah explained why."

172

"We don't set trick questions to first year students."

"Ah didn't regard it as a trick question."

"A foolish one, then?"

"Well – misguided. It suggests the 2014 referendum was a setback for the Nationalists. Ah doan' think it wuz. Anybody who wuz in Scotland the day after knew that all it had done was fire up nationalist passion."

"You were there, presumably?"

"Aye."

"But you were, what twelve, thirteen years old?"

"Ah was fourteen actually. And ah played a full part in the campaign."

Murdo's enthusiasm for the Yes campaign had been one of the reasons he was seldom in his French lessons. Those leaflets weren't going to deliver themselves.

"Were you an SNP member then?"

"Naw – ah wuz just a Nationalist, by instinct. Still am. Ah joined the Labour party when Jeremy became leader."

Mallinson nodded but said nothing. Then he said,

"Look – let me speak frankly. You've got a lot of enthusiasm, and a lot of campaigning experience for someone of your age. You've picked up a bit of political theory along the way, not all of it sound, in my view, but at the end of the day you're a Year One Politics student and a newcomer in the constituency. My advice is to rein it all in a bit. There are folk here you can learn from, and they'll enjoy teaching you, on or off the campus."

He handed back the essay. His tone was not unkind, but Murdo knew when he was being patronised.

"That's it then?"

"There's not a lot more to say. If you read the comments you'll see there are plenty of positives. But if you don't answer the question…" He raised his hands in an elaborate shrug.

"OK, thanks very much," said Murdo, "Ah think ah get the picture."

He had left Mallinson's office quietly furious.

"So ye see," continued Murdo, when he had related this to Edward, "Ah'm not really interested in working to get Trevor Mallinson elected."

Edward nodded. "Well…that's interesting." Then he said,

"I've had a bit of a setback myself in that regard."

"Oh uh-huh," said Murdo, going to the fridge.

"The thing is…I was actually thinking of standing myself. For the Lib Dems. In fact I was given to understand it was pretty much a done deal that I'd be the candidate. But now there's a hitch."

Murdo opened two more beers and put one in front of Edward. To Edward's surprise, his announcement was met with more interest than derision.

"Ye were hoping tae follow in the family tradition."

"In a way. Who told you about the family tradition?"

Murdo waved a hand.

"Ah take an interest in these things."

"I see. Well anyway, it seems it's no longer happening. There's going to be some kind of arrangement with the Greens."

"Wi' the *Greens?*" Murdo was incredulous. "Wass the point of that?"

"Some sort of quid pro quo at the next Westminster election, apparently"

"Yeah, like that'll ever work," said Murdo. "So, lemme get this straight. No Lib Dem candidate in this by-election."

"Apparently not. But you didn't hear that from me."

"Mum's the word. So where d'ye reckon those Lib Dem votes are goin' tae go?"

"Anywhere and everywhere, I should think. Some will go to the Greens, but not that many."

"What about Labour?"

"I doubt it. There's not a lot of love lost between the parties locally. The Lib Dem voters might just stay at home."

Murdo took a chug of his beer, then looked evenly at Edward.

"Well we wouldnae want that. Very bad for democracy. What if there was a good independent standing? Someone with a bit of profile?"

"They might do well. Independent candidates do get elected down here."

"Are ye no tempted?"

"Me?" Edward looked taken aback. "Goodness. I don't think so."

"Why not? You've got the name-recognition."

174

"Yes, but – I'd have no support. And it would be a bit disloyal to the local party."

"Ah don't know about that. The local party might be quite pleased. They'd be keeping their side of the bargain with the Greens, but the members would still have a candidate to vote for. Ah wid say that from the Liberal perspective it would be a good outcome."

Evidently the socialist in Murdo had for the time being given way to the political strategist. With something of an effort Edward brought his mind to bear on this new line of thinking.

"Yes but they couldn't campaign for me. I mean that would defeat the whole point of the thing."

"They couldn't campaign *openly* for you, no. But there's ways and means of getting the word around."

Edward got up and began to clear away the dishes, as much as anything to give himself some space to think. He knew that he was slightly drunk, but he was also a little excited by Murdo's suggestion.

"I'm not sure I would want to," he said. "And to be honest, I've never been much of a campaigner, at least not on my own behalf."

"Aye, you would need a campaign manager."

"Well exactly. Where am I going to find one of those?"

He began running water into the sink.

"Well as it happens ah might know somebody," said Murdo. "But he'd want to be paid. Have you got any decent whisky in the house?"

Across west Cornwall very few of the St Petroc's staff, students or families were concerning themselves with the more obscure workings of the forthcoming by-election. A number of the luckier ones were embarking upon or contemplating their own imminent holidays.

Anton Killick was lying in a state of near-meditation on the thin single mattress in his bedroom. He was due to drive to London the following day for a Taekwondo training week run by a visiting Korean fifth-dan. Normally this would be something to look forward to – not perhaps with excitement, for that was not the spirit in which these things were conducted, but at least with a kind of calm inner joy. Calm inner joy, however, was proving elusive. In part this was due to a lingering fury that Singleman's mock-election nonsense was to be allowed to upstage Anton's own plans, but another source of unease was Josef Stalin, his remaining white rat, who Anton sensed was suffering from loneliness and possibly even depression since the demise of his companion. A replacement would have to be found, and he had not yet had time to locate one. Then there was the matter of the journey up to London, and the business of persuading the hotel that there wasn't a problem having a rat, albeit a white one in a cage, on the premises. If they did object (he had learned from experience there was no point in enquiring in advance), then Josef Stalin would need to be billeted in his car, which would be parked out at Putney, and Anton would need to make daily trips to replenish food and water. There was nobody locally whom he would trust with his rats.

Raphael and Rona d'Allesandro had gone to bed in a state of mild disharmony following Rona's tentative broaching of Murdo's need for funds. Neither of them had a great deal of spare cash, Rona having maxed out her credit card on clothes for the trip to Italy. Raphael's family were effortlessly stylish, and while she shared their dark Italian looks she knew that her workaday wardrobe didn't quite come up to scratch. The trip itself would not be hugely expensive as there were no accommodation costs to meet, but they were taking Raphael's new Alfa Romeo, which had been purchased a few months previously and had accounted for most of his savings. There had also been presents to buy. The relative investment made in maintaining links with their respective families was one of the few points of dissent in the d'Allesandros' otherwise contented fourteen-year marriage.

The Brunels were also bound for Italy, for a chalet in the Alps that they took each Easter for some late season skiing. They would be leaving the following morning, driving no further than Bristol in the family Range Rover, and flying out from there. There was no disharmony of any sort in evidence as they settled for the night – there seldom was. A combination of wealth, health and a kind of fundamental decency, allied with a willingness to work hard towards clear and broadly worthy goals, seemed to render the Brunels immune to the slings and arrows that assailed other families. Issy knew that

176

this was at least in part an illusion – that no family is completely proof to disaster– and she understood that the hand she had been dealt in life's card game was a particularly strong one. As yet, however, she saw no reason to question her family's values or their approach to the world around them, and her anticipation of the trip was unclouded by middle-class guilt.

No holidays were planned or anticipated in either the Doggett or the Pascoe households.

Sammy was looking forward to the break from school, but knew he would be bored before very long. There were a couple of tech sessions planned for the school play in the final week, and Mr d'Allesandro had hinted he might want him to stage-manage the show, which would be the biggest responsibility Sammy had so far been given in that regard. He also needed to work out how he would approach the mock election. Without clearly articulating the thought, a determination was growing in him that whatever the outcome, his goal was to beat Issy, or Issy-the-Tory, as he was beginning to think of her. He might persuade his dad to take a couple of days off for some fishing, and pick his brains about politics. Viv Pascoe wasn't a great one for parading his knowledge, but it was sometimes surprising what he knew. His Mum, too might have something to say. He wondered how her work on the parish council fitted in with what happened at County Hall.

The Doggetts were running out of both money and ideas. As Edward and Murdo's discussions moved to the single malt stage of proceedings, Isaac was sitting at the formica table in their kitchen on the Penhale estate with a red biscuit tin in the shape of a Scottie dog in front of him. His wife and son were in bed. He stared at the unopened tin for some time, then eased off the lid with two powerful thumbs and emptied out the contents, a mixture of ten and twenty-pound notes. He counted them, as he did each night, then he put them back in the tin and replaced the lid. With a heavy sigh he put the tin back on the shelf above the cooker and lumbered off to bed.

It was still, just, April Fool's day.

Chapter Twenty-five

"The empty bottle of Laphroaig"

For Sophie, the Easter holiday simply meant more work. The hotel was full, and her hours had been increased, which she was pleased about, although it limited the scope of her investigative activities. She was happy that sufficient progress had been made on that front, however, and that her friendship with Murdo and the access it gave her to the Count House were well established. She could afford to concentrate for a while on saving money for the coming autumn while she worked out what her next move should be. The wages at the hotel were not particularly generous, but they were supplemented by her share of the tips, and by occasional busking sessions down by the harbour. Her accommodation, basic as it was, was free.

She often thought of Murdo as she went about her duties. He was useful to her, but there was also something very appealing about him – something more than his accent, which was *vraiment adorable*. He was alive and vibrant in a way that she found attractive, and she approved of his politics. He would need to be kept at arm's length, of course - their conversation in the pub on the night of the selection had gone some way to achieving that - but she was anxious not to lose his friendship. So she replied warmly to the messages and pictures that he sent her, and even agreed to meet him in St Ives on her one day off, just for the afternoon. At some stage she would need to engineer another visit to the Count House, but when she suggested they might explore Roskear on her day off Murdo had been notably unenthusiastic. There was, he said, nothing to explore. On the other hand he had never seen St Ives, and he wanted to visit the art gallery, "tae see what all the fuss is about." So they had settled for that.

By now Sophie more or less knew her way around the baffling labyrinth of lanes and alleys that lay behind the harbour, and she had swum in the still chilly turquoise waters that surrounded the town, itself little more than an island. She had read something of its significance as an artists' colony before her arrival, but had not yet visited any of the more famous galleries, all of which cost money. When she had an hour to spare she enjoyed poking around the tiny studios and shops, and once she had taken the bus out to the wild, empty country to the west, where ancient walled fields led down to the very edges of the cliffs, and the sea stretched wide and blue to the horizon. The other holiday staff had now settled into their own social groupings and seemed happy enough to leave her to her own devices.

It was dry and sunny the day Murdo came to visit, though a brisk breeze blew in from the sea. Sophie was surprised to find how much she was looking forward to his company. She had arranged to meet him at the tiny railway station that clung to the side of the cliff half-way down the hill from her hotel. There was one long thin platform and a single track, along which a two-carriage train bustled toy-like back and forth once an hour to meet the main line at St Erth. Perhaps because she was on her own territory, Sophie had for once left her accordion in her room at the hotel, and she lounged now on one of the benches and watched as the train approached and the crowds on the platform arranged themselves for boarding, or to greet the new arrivals. Murdo was one of the first to disembark, and she raised a hand in greeting.

"Hiya Glasgow!"

"Awright *Grenwee*, ya wee french brammer."

"Brammer? I do not know that word."

"Aye ye'll no find it in a dictionary, but trust me – it's complimentary."

179

They walked together back along the platform, past the hanging baskets and troughs of early spring flowers to the ramp that led up to the main road.

"So what's the programme? I'm gaggin' for a coffee by the way."

"Yes, I thought coffee first, maybe down by the harbour? Then the Tate? Although it is quite expensive…"

"Aye well that, for once, is not a problem. In fact, if you'll let me, I'd like tae treat you."

"But Glasgow you are *toujours à court d'argent*! I hope you have not robbed a bank!"

"I have not robbed a bank, no. It jist so happens I have come intae a bit of cash. I'll tell you all about it over coffee."

Back at Tallack's yard, the source of Murdo's improved fortunes was addressing himself to the matter of *Tiddy Oggie*'s waterline. This required extensive quantities of masking tape to protect the areas of hull immediately above and below. Edward stepped back from the Shrimper's starboard side and eyed the preparation work critically. Mistakes made now would be with him for the season.

He made a tiny and probably unnecessary adjustment to the section of tape just aft of the porthole, then shook the can of paint vigorously for half a minute before levering the lid off with a screwdriver. There was time to get the starboard side done before lunch. Carefully he dipped a clean brush half an inch or so into the thick creamy paint and began the steady, soothing process of applying it to the four-inch band that marked the point at which the hull sat on the water.

It was now several days since he had made what he was beginning to think of as his Faustian pact with Murdo. Possibly the single malt was to blame. They had finished half a bottle of Laphroaig between them, and by the time the midnight hour struck they had agreed terms. Edward would stand as an independent candidate, and Murdo would act as his campaign manager and election agent for the sum of £125 per week for the four weeks up to election day. This would represent ten hours work each week, to include team-building, literature design, filing of nomination papers and other legal necessities, and preparation of the expenses return. Murdo would assist with delivery and canvassing where time permitted, but the idea was that most of this would be carried out by the team, which he would train if required.

At first Edward had laughed at the sum proposed. But as Murdo pointed out, successful election campaigns generally did cost money, and the outlay would be easily recouped in Edward's first month's allowance as a councillor were he to be elected. Besides, he had argued, his pale blue eyes peculiarly intense over the rim of his whisky glass, for twelve-fifty an hour Edward was securing the services of an experienced and skilled campaigner, who could produce the necessary artwork and look after both the leafleting and the social media aspects without which, he assured Edward, no campaign in such a rural ward could possibly succeed.

Such was Murdo's confidence in the value of his services, and his powers of persuasion, that he had even managed to attach certain conditions to the deal. One was that payment would be partly by way of a rental holiday. That way no money would actually change hands, although a declaration in kind would need to be made on the expenses return. Another, rather to Edward's surprise, had concerned the content of the campaign.

"Ye'll appreciate," said Murdo, "that I'm potentially tarnishing ma political reputation here. I could get thrown outa Momentum for this."

Edward murmured that that might not be such a bad thing, but Murdo ignored him.

"More to the point, ah'm not putting my best efforts into electing some wishy-washy bleeding heart who's gonnay sit on his arse up at County Hall n' do fuck all fer his constituents. Yer going tae need to satisfy me that yer going tae work for local people. Folk like them on the Penhale estate. And that means fighting the hospital closure's got to be front and centre of yer campaign."

"Well I've got no problem with that."

"Good. Where do you stand on giving the real living wage tae all council employees?"

Here Edward was also on secure ground.

"Definitely. I'm fairly sure that's Lib Dem policy anyway."

"Aye you might be right there. Free parking for NHS staff?"

"You mean they have to pay?"

"God almighty, did they really approve you? Of course they have tae pay."

"That's outrageous!"

"Yeah, well, welcome to the real world. Well, if that's the basis of the campaign, I'm happy to put my name tae it."

And with that Murdo had extended a pale freckled hand, and Edward, with only the most momentary hesitation, had shaken it.

The next morning he had awoken late with a hangover and a sense that he had committed to undertake some dreadful felony. Hopefully Murdo would feel the same. It seemed extraordinary that after months of sparring over their political differences, his tenant was now prepared to work with him on an election campaign in which an official Labour party candidate would be standing. But as Edward stood under the shower the logic that lay behind the agreement drifted back to him like fragments of a dream, and the force of the arguments reasserted themselves.

He dressed and checked his phone. There was a text from Anna.

Hi. Sorry to be so slow to get back. And very sorry about the selection. Free for a coffee this morning if you're around. Anna x

Edward grimaced. He didn't owe Anna anything, he knew that. But in an ideal world he would have liked to have run this new scheme past her. Might she be shocked, angry even? He tried to remember why Murdo had thought this was a good outcome for the local party.

He texted back a proposal that they meet in an hour at a garden centre a little out of town that had a half-decent coffee shop. Then he dressed and went downstairs. The hall was quiet and there was no sign of his campaign manager. The kitchen wasn't in too bad a state, and he spent a few minutes tidying up the remains, looking a little wistfully at the empty bottle of Laphroaig before placing it carefully in the recycling along with the eight beer bottles. He wasn't quite ready for breakfast, his stomach still a little queasy from the previous night's excess.

He wrote a brief note to Murdo saying that he was out for the morning, and that given the level of alcohol consumed he would be willing to release him from his obligations if he felt any regret about them. Even as he wrote this he felt it was transparently a plea for Murdo to extend him the same latitude, and he felt a little ashamed at his own timidity. Sod it! Nothing ventured, nothing gained. He would see what Anna had to say, and take it from there.

Anna was remarkably sanguine.

"Well I wondered if you might do that," she said, when they had ordered their coffees, plus a pastry to settle Edward's stomach. "You're perfectly within your rights."

"So I won't be thrown out of the party?"

"You would be if there was a Liberal candidate standing, but as there isn't, nobody can complain."

"What about the Greens? Somebody's bound to clock that I'm a Lib Dem."

"Well they might, but so long as we can put our hand on our heart and say we haven't encouraged you…"

"Which you haven't…"

"Which we clearly haven't. And it's perfectly plausible that you would stand in a fit of pique at not being selected."

"I don't think that's quite what I'm doing."

"Of course not," she said with a straight face. "You realise we won't be able to give you any practical help with the campaign."

"Well as it happens that may not be necessary. I have engaged the services of a campaign manager."

Anna raised an eyebrow.

"Not one of ours I hope? That might cause problems."

"Very much not one of ours. My lodger, in fact."

"I didn't know you had a lodger."

"I keep quiet about him. He's from Glasgow."

"I see." Anna sounded as if she wasn't quite sure what she saw.

"Nothing like that," said Edward. "He's pretty, but he's far too young for me."

This last part was mischievous, but Anna looked a little taken aback and Edward wondered again if she was quite as liberal as she made out. He began to feel independence suited him. Perhaps he would leave the party altogether.

"Well in that case, I wish you luck with your campaign," said Anna briskly. "I'm afraid as Chair I'll need to be seen out and about supporting the Green candidate, but don't be surprised if word gets round the membership that there is a friend of the party in the race too. You'd be surprised how much people complain if they don't have a Liberal candidate to vote for."

And with that they had parted, still without anything having been said about how matters stood between them on a personal level. Edward returned to the Count House to find Murdo sitting in the kitchen looking blearily at his note. He looked much as Edward had felt two hours previously.

"I just thought," said Edward, "That it might be fair to offer you an exit if, you know, cold light of day and all that…"

"Aye that's very good of you," said Murdo. "But ah'm still up for it if you are."

Edward finished his painting, and cleaned off the brush, wiping his hands with white spirit. The smell of frying bacon was drifting down on the breeze from Betty's hut. Tomorrow would mark the first day of his campaign.

Chapter Twenty-six

"I'm afraid we always vote Conservative"

For Team Tremenhere, the rest of the holiday was spent getting the by-election campaign off the ground. Edward tidied his study, locking away his personal correspondence, and designated it the campaign HQ, diffidently offering his highlighted map to Murdo. His campaign manager eyed it professionally and declared it a useful starting point, then briskly reeled off a list of urgent preliminary tasks. The first of these was to take photographs of Edward at various prominent and recognisable spots across the council ward.

"I don't have a digital camera," said Edward apologetically.

"I think you'll find there's one on yer phone."

"Well yes, I think I knew that, now that you mention it," said Edward. But will it be good enough quality?"

"Oh fur God's sake," said Murdo. "It's probably best if you leave the technical stuff to me."

They spent a pleasant morning driving round the larger settlements, Edward posing sternly and benignly by turns in front of Post Offices, parish churches and village signposts. One or two local residents recognised him, which brought an approving grunt from Murdo. In Gurrian the Vicar came out of the church as Edward pointed accusingly at a large pothole for the benefit of the camera.

"Well Edward Tremenhere, how the devil are you?" boomed the Vicar, who was a low church liberal of the old school, and a former Roskear second row. "What brings you to Gurrian?"

Edward found himself mildly discomfited.

"Hello Jonathan. Very nice to see you. I'm just…passing through, really. Ah…this is Murdo McAndrew, my lodger."

"Very pleased to meet you Murdo," said the Vicar.

"Very pleased to meet you too father," said Murdo, who was not entirely up to speed on the different denominations south of the border. "Actually, Edward here is being a wee bit coy. He's standing for the by-election and we're just out taking some pictures for the campaign literature."

"Are you by Jove?" said the Vicar. "Excellent stuff! For the Liberals, I hope?"

"Well it would be," said Edward. "But they're not putting anybody up this time round, so I'm standing as an independent. But – you know – my values haven't changed. Still very much a Liberal at heart."

"A left-leaning Liberal," said Murdo without looking up from his phone.

"Quite," said Edward, shifting a little uncomfortably where he stood.

"Well that's a poor show from the party," said the Vicar. "But if there's no Liberal on the ticket you'll get my vote. Now I must dash, I'm afraid. I'm on my rounds."

"Kin ah just ask one quick question father?" said Murdo. "What would you say was the issue that most concerns folk in the village at this present time?"

"Speeding!" called the Vicar over his shoulder as he set off along the pavement towards the Post Office, "We need the limit bringing down to twenty."

"Awesome," said Murdo, and gave the Vicar's broad departing back the thumbs up.

"You need to be a bit less shy about yer candidacy," he said critically to Edward as he punched at the keyboard of his phone.

"Yes, I know. Sorry. Where to now?"

"Village boundary. We need tae find a thirty mile an hour sign for you to point at."

"Stern face again? " said Edward.

"Yer a fast learner."

Murdo spent the next two days producing customised leaflets for delivery in the various villages. These all carried the same photograph of Edward looking dignified and serious, along with a biography that majored on his local roots and his family's history of civic engagement. Each leaflet carried another photograph with the local landmark and some reference to whatever they had managed to glean about issues particular to that area. They agreed that they would start with the Gurrian leaflets on the basis of the intelligence they had obtained regarding speeding problems, and leave the printing of the others until they had a clearer picture of local concerns.

"Though broadly speaking," said Murdo, "Yer on fairly safe territory with pot-holes and dog shit."

They had a disagreement over whether to mention Edward's work at the local food bank.

"It feels like blowing my own trumpet," said Edward.

"This is politics," snapped Murdo. "You accentuate the positive and you hope tae God nobody finds out about the negatives. We don't need to make a big deal of it, but it's got tae be in there."

Reluctantly, Edward agreed, though he vetoed Murdo's suggestion of a picture of him distributing tins of beans.

"Aye okay, mebbe that would be goin' a bit far," conceded Murdo. "But ye gotta realise, This isn't the 1950's. Folk don't want tae elect some kind of gentleman-amateur. They want someone who's goin' tae roll up there sleeves and get stuck in."

"No, absolutely, I see that," said Edward. "That's what I intend to do."

To gather more reliable intelligence in the remaining villages Murdo designed what he called a "knock and drop" leaflet. These were run off on Edward's printer in black and white, and took the form of a survey that would be handed to residents and collected an hour later.

"Ideally," said Murdo, "We need a freepost address for the folk who aren't in. Your local party has probably got one."

"Yes but we can't use it," said Edward. "I promised Anna we would keep clear water between ourselves and the Lib Dems."

"Who's Anna?"

"The local party chair. And a friend."

"Well they don't need to look at them," said Murdo. "Or we could agree that we'll share the data with them after the election."

But here again Edward put his foot down.

"I'll pay for one if necessary," he said. "But I need to keep the local party out of this."

They were in his study, Edward standing and Murdo seated at the desk with his laptop open in front of him. This was becoming a familiar scenario, and Edward was beginning to feel a little as if he were being cuckooed out of his own nest. Murdo tapped rapidly at the keyboard.

"Two hundred and thirty quid for the licence," he said. "But it lasts a year."

"I can't afford that," said Edward. We'll just have to do without."

Murdo scratched his chin. "OK what we'll do is put a copy of the survey on the website."

"Do we have a website?"

"Nearly. It'll be up and running by tomorrow."

"Right," said Edward. "That's impressive."

"When you hire McAndrew Political, you get your money's worth," said Murdo and returned to his screen. "I could do wi' a brew by the way."

Edward obediently set off for the kitchen.

They agreed to deliver the knock and drop survey in Eglos the following day, and Edward was mildly surprised when Sophie turned up on the doorstep fifteen minutes before they were due to leave.

"*Bonjour Monsieur le Candidat. Ca va?*"

"*Ca va bien merci, et vous?*"

"*Oui ça va,*" said Sophie.

"I'm afraid we're just going out," said Edward.

"That's whit she's here for," called Murdo from the kitchen. "Grenwee is giving up her day off to help us with the knock and drops."

188

Sophie smiled winningly. "I am inspired by your bold decision to tackle poverty and injustice by standing for election," she said. "I wish to join your great movement."

"Well, I'm not sure it's a movement just yet," said Edward. "More of a vague stirring."

"Even Macron had to start somewhere," said Sophie.

"Capitalist in sheep's clothing," said Murdo disparagingly.

"I agree," said Sophie. "We copy only his strategy, not his politics."

The "we" was not lost on Edward. The sense that he was not entirely in control of this process was beginning to build. At the same time there was no question that Murdo appeared to know what he was doing. And team-building was part of his remit. At least, he mused as they drove over the hill to Eglos, any mis-steps would bring embarrassment only upon himself, and not upon Anna and the local party.

There were two hundred and twenty-four houses in Eglos. Once Edward had parked, Murdo produced his laptop and showed them an arial photograph screen-shotted from Google maps.

"Sophie and me will take this end, and you work north from the community shop," said Murdo. "That way you get the posh houses. On no account spend more than two minutes on any one doorstep. Long conversations do not win votes."

"I do know one or two people in Eglos," said Edward. "it would be a bit rude not to stop and chat."

"OK three minutes if it's somebody you know. But no more. You've got about eighty houses to cover and we don't want to be here all day. There's an over-run clause on my contract, don't forget."

Edward assumed this was a joke.

"Oh, and if they're not in, make sure the leaflet goes right the way through the letter box. But listen out for dogs."

"This isn't the first time I've done this, you know," said Edward petulantly as they got out the car and set off on their respective routes.

Although it was true that he had campaigned for others on many occasions, this was the first time Edward had knocked on doors on his own account. It felt different, not having the identity of the party to lend credibility to what seemed like the presumption of walking up someone's path and rapping on their door on a fine spring morning. He rehearsed a little speech in his head. "Good Morning!" This would perhaps need to be brighter than his usual rather grave baritone, but not overly cheerful. This was not after all, California. "Good Morning." (Look them in the eye, perhaps smile a little.) A pause. "My name is Edward Tremenhere." Or perhaps just "I'm Edward Tremenhere." Or should he go for the slightly more formal "May I introduce myself?" At any rate, it was important not to rush the name. That was, after all, what the voters needed to remember on polling day. So perhaps put the slight pause after his name, rather than before. But then what? "I'm standing as an independent candidate in the forthcoming by-election." That was reasonable enough. "And I wondered if you would be willing to complete this short survey…"

Edward had been walking the length of the village, while experimenting with these variations, with the intention of working his way back into the centre to meet Murdo and Sophie. Now he was almost in the countryside, standing outside the gate of a dignified looking stone villa set fifty or so metres back from the road. It was a mild, windless morning, the dew still damp on the neatly cut lawns, and the smell of the surrounding pines hung in the air like a mist. It looked, he thought, like a reasonably civilised place to begin his engagement with the electorate. He checked that his clothing was in order, then opened the gate and walked purposefully up the path, the bundle of survey leaflets in his hand.

A doorbell drilled rather louder than he would have liked, and a minute passed when he could hear nothing but birdsong. He was about to fold up his leaflet for posting when the door opened and he found himself looking down on a petite woman in her eighties. He took a step back to reduce the sense of disparity in their heights.

"Good Morning," he said. "I'm sorry to disturb you. My name is Edward Tremenhere and I'm standing in the forthcoming council by-election as an independent candidate. I wondered if…"

"You'll need to speak up," said the woman rather sharply. "Which party are you standing for?"

"I'm standing as an independent," said Edward.

"Oh, one of those," said the woman. "I'm afraid we always vote Conservative."

"Ah," said Edward, not quite ready to give up yet. "Well perhaps this time you will consider breaking that habit."

"I shouldn't think so," said the woman. "Is that one of your leaflets?"

"It's a survey," said Edward, handing it to the woman. "It only takes a minute to complete. We just want to know what issues people might be dissatisfied with in Eglos."

The woman handed it back. "Oh, I shan't bother with that. I don't find there's much to complain about myself. Shame about old Narabo, though he was a bit of a rogue. I hope the Conservatives put up somebody better this time."

Mindful of Murdo's warning about wasting time, Edward decided to cut his losses, and wished the woman good day. As he was walking down the path she called after him.

"What did you say your name was, young man?"

"Tremenhere. Edward Tremenhere."

"Well, good luck with the campaign."

The rest of Edward's round proceeded without incident. Most people were out, but every four or five doors there would be a householder who seemed willing to take a survey and agreed to put it back through the letterbox for collection within the hour. At one property a fierce pug attached itself to his trouser leg and had to be forcibly removed by its apologetic owner. Nobody was openly hostile, and one or two said they would consider voting for him. He made a mental note of those addresses to add to his database of supporters.

At the community shop Murdo and Sophie were waiting for him. The plan was to go for a coffee in Newlyn and then return to collect the surveys.

"All right?" enquired Murdo. "Anythin' to report?"

"All good," said Edward. "What have you got there?"

Sophie had a sheaf of coloured paper under her arm.

"Sophie's been pickin' up some litter," said Murdo as they walked back to the car. "Settin' a good example."

"May I see?" said Edward, although he had a good idea what the "litter" might be.

"Probably best if you don't," said Murdo, but Sophie had already handed him one of the pieces of paper. It was a flier for the Conservative candidate, an earnest-looking, clean-cut young man in a shirt and tie.

"And how did you come across these?"

"They were just…hanging out of the letter boxes," said Sophie. "It looked most untidy."

"Which is why you should always push your leaflets right the way through," said Murdo. "I expect better of the Tories, to be honest."

They were at the car.

"Just get in," said Edward. "We'll talk about this over coffee."

Chapter Twenty-seven

"Tiny red points of warmth in the distance"

Sun-tanned and happy, Dave and Kate returned from their week in France on the late afternoon ferry from Roscoff. The weather had been mixed, with one or two dramatic thunderstorms, but the last two days had been fine, and their mood was buoyant as they leaned together over the rail to watch the pretty little Breton town disappear astern. Having on that first evening pushed to one side the matter of their future accommodation, they had fallen into a state of glorious absorption with each other such as only a holiday will permit, and the voyage back to Plymouth was merely a further opportunity for proximity, gentleness, and affection. In contrast to the trip out, they were seldom apart, and their activities were now synchronised. They listened to the same music through shared ear-buds; when one read, both read, sometimes from the same book; and when one slept, both slept, curled up together like teenage lovers.

Somewhere past the Channel's midpoint, evening drifted in from the southwest on a high skein of pink cirrus cloud, and it was dark by the time they reached Plymouth. The night was by now clear and cold, and the blackness that lay beyond the harsh artificial lights of the terminal seemed somehow hostile as the little MG drove down the ramp and took its place in the queue for customs. They had visited a hypermarket just outside Roscoff, and every last nook and cranny now held a bottle of wine. Although there was in theory no limit on how much could be brought into the country, Dave felt the familiar sense of relief when their passports were returned to them and they were waved on their way.

Kate had still not driven the MG, but she felt that her relationship to the car had changed in the course of the trip. Undeniably, it had a character of its own, expressed in the throaty bubble of its exhaust and in certain intermittent quirks of its ignition system. It also leaked, as she discovered during one of the heavier downpours, but that had been remedied by a strategically positioned beach towel and had seemed not to matter. Otherwise, the ancient sports car had behaved impeccably, and had been the stimulus to a number of conversations with locals. At one small café in a remote village, they were given free coffees at the insistence of the elderly proprietor, who remembered with a tear in his eye *une tres jolie anglaise* who had given him a lift in such a car when he was hitch-hiking through Kent in nineteen seventy-two.

Now, as they climbed out of Plymouth to join the main road, Kate fancied she sensed a certain weariness in the steady beat of the engine – not anything to cause alarm, but perhaps just a point being made that this had been quite a trip, what with the distance covered, the unfamiliar road signs and the foreign petrol. She gave the dashboard a reassuring pat.

"I can't believe it," she said.

"What's that?"

"I'm anthropomorphising your car."

Dave grinned at her under the flashing orange bars of the sodium lights.

"It's easily done. I regularly talk to her. Presumably you talk to yours?"

"I try not to. Mine just does what's expected of it. I think it's generally less reliable cars that get spoken to. No offence intended, of course."

But the MG's engine at that point, as if offence had indeed been taken, missed a beat, then picked up again. Dave grimaced, and Kate felt guilty.

The car ran smoothly enough for the next forty minutes or so, but just after they joined the A30 the engine note once

194

more dipped, then did the same thing a few seconds later. Kate wanted to say something, but knew that whatever she said would almost certainly be inappropriate. She glanced at Dave, who was staring grimly ahead through the windscreen. The engine gave a cough, then another, then the power dropped dramatically. Dave slowed to a crawl, and pulled onto the grass verge just as the engine cut out altogether.

"I think that may have been my fault," said Kate.

"More likely to be the carb," said Dave briskly. "There's a couple of things I can try."

He pulled the bonnet catch and got out of the car. Kate felt the waft of chill night air and was happy enough to stay put. It had been 24 degrees when they left Roscoff, and neither of them were dressed for the cold. Through the window she could see stars, but otherwise it was black apart from the occasional sweep of passing headlights. She looked at her watch. It was nearly 11.30.

For ten minutes or so Dave tinkered under the bonnet, returning once to the car for an oily rag and once to try the engine again, without success. It was now distinctly chilly, and Kate shivered when he opened the door once more.

"Looks like we're going to have to ring the AA. Here's my card – you give them a call while I dig out the warning triangle. We're not very well parked here."

Kate did as he asked, and by the time Dave returned to the car she had established that the AA would be with them in an hour.

"Bloody Hell," said Dave. "What are they doing?"

"Not to worry," she said brightly. "We're nearly home. At least it didn't happen in Brittany."

Anton Killick was also on his way back to Cornwall, having completed his martial arts boot camp in London. He had been driving for more than five hours without a break when he began the descent from Bodmin Moor. Anton had an instinctive dislike for motorway service stations, and he regarded driving long distances as a form of discipline. He was physically tired from his week's training, but he felt mentally alert, even highly tuned. Secured by the seat belt on the passenger seat of his white BMW, Josef Stalin was curled up in his box, fast asleep.

The training camp had been just the tonic Anton needed. Long sessions in the dojo had been followed in the evening by lectures on philosophy and the principles of mastery. The System, as it was known to its western adherents, drew heavily on elements of Taekwondo, but it also incorporated the teachings of a fifteenth century Korean who was not entirely part of the mainstream. Certain principles of wellbeing developed by a Californian businessman of opaque pedigree gave the System its contemporary focus. It was the all-encompassing philosophy that gripped Anton, and which few other martial artists seemed to understand or feel drawn to.

One aspect of the teaching that had particularly challenged him had been a Korean concept that had no direct equivalent in English, but that seemed to encompass notions of both love and service. This was not in any sense a sentimental love, but a strong, uncompromising love, one that would not always be perceived as love by the recipient, although it would have their best interests at heart. Love of any sort was not something that Anton felt entirely at ease with, and like so much of the System's teaching, it was all a bit of a paradox.

He was in the process of contemplating how this principle might be applied to his professional life when the BMW's powerful headlights picked out the red warning triangle by the grass verge a quarter of a mile ahead. A hundred yards beyond that he could make out the dark shadow of a small car, its near-side wheels up on the grass verge. He put on his hazard lights and braked smoothly to bring the BMW up fifty yards or so behind the MG, whose shape was camouflaged to a degree by the luggage rack on the boot. Why, wondered Anton, did people insist on hanging on to these ugly, unreliable little throwbacks? He seemed to recall that the slacker Singleman drove something similar.

Inside the MG's cramped cockpit, morale had been dropping with the temperature. It was now almost midnight, and an update from the AA had put their arrival time back another half an hour. Conversation had dried up, and Kate had been on the point of slipping into a cold and uncomfortable doze when the cabin was lit by the white light of Anton's powerful headlights.

"I hope it's not the police," said Dave, who had a sneaking suspicion that the tread on his front near-side tyre was not all that it might be. But the figure he could see approaching in his wing mirror was capless, and unadorned by the paraphernalia of modern policing. He wound down the window.

"I was just wondering if you needed any help," said a familiar voice. Then, less courteously, "Oh. It's you."

"Anton!" said Dave flatly. "What are the flaming chances?"

"Anton?" said Kate, peering across Dave to get a glimpse of their ministering angel. "Where on earth did you spring from?"

"I hope I'm not interrupting anything," said Anton.

"Far too chilly for that," said Dave, with hollow humour. "No, we were just taking a brief comfort break."

"I see. Very thoughtful of you to put out a warning triangle."

Dave said nothing, and for a moment Anton considered returning to the warmth of his car. Then he remembered that loving service might not always be appreciated by the recipient.

"Look I presume you've broken down. I've no doubt you would rather your good Samaritan arrived in some other form, but here I am, so if there's anything I can do to help…"

"Thanks Anton," said Dave. "I appreciate the offer, but the AA will be along in a minute."

"Well, thirty minutes," said Kate. "And then we don't know if they'll be able to fix it."

"They'll be able to fix it," said Dave. "That's the thing about MGs. They're always fixable."

"I suppose there have to be some advantages," said Anton.

Dave ignored this. Then Anton said,

"Well is there any need for you both to wait? You can't be very comfortable. I'm on my way back to Newlyn now and I'd be very happy to run Kate home."

I bet you would, thought Dave, but he said nothing.

"That's really kind, Anton," said Kate.

Oh yes. Extremely thoughtful, thought Dave. He waited for Kate to graciously decline. Surely she would graciously decline. Surely she wouldn't…

"What do you think Dave?" said Kate. "I don't want to abandon you…"

"It's entirely up to you," he said, stiffly. "I suppose there's not much point in you freezing here for another hour."

"Well it is a bit chilly…but no, look, I'll just stay here. Thanks all the same, Anton. You get on home."

Killick inclined his head.

"Very well. I hope you don't have too long to wait. Good night."

"Good night Anton!" said Kate. "And thanks again for stopping!"

Dave grunted, and Anton returned to his car. A moment later the white BMW accelerated smoothly past them. In silence they watched its tail-lights shrink to tiny red points of warmth in the distance.

"You could have gone, you know," said Dave, after a bit.

"I don't think that would have been the right call," said Kate. "Maybe we could get the sleeping bags out of the boot?"

Once again the midnight hour found only one person awake in the Doggett household, but this time it was Donovan who couldn't sleep. Like his father, he was mesmerised by the Scottie dog biscuit tin on the shelf above the cooker and its steadily increasing store of used notes. He knew that Isaac counted it regularly; knew too that money was short in the household. His mother often ate little at mealtimes, and they had stopped having those Tesco chocolate puddings that he liked so much.

Half-way through the holidays, Donkey was bored. His mates on the estate spent their time at the skate-park down on the promenade , and in the amusement arcades when it was wet. Donkey had no money for the slot machines, and his skateboard needed a new set of front wheels. A couple of days ago he had texted the Scottish guy again in the hope that they might meet up and talk politics. He had received a prompt but apologetic reply. Murdo was apparently stacked up with things to do, but promised he would get back to him when he could.

If only the old man could get some work. They didn't need that much to get by on – even a few extra quid a week would surely make all the difference. A new set of wheels was only a tenner off eBay. The tin was full of tenners. He promised himself he would pay it back. He lifted down the Scottie dog tin and placed it on the table in front of him.

Where Isaac had simply levered off the lid with his powerful thumbs, Donkey held the tin to his body and pulled up with his fingernails, releasing the pressure at the crucial moment so that the lid wouldn't fly off and wake the household as it hit the kitchen floor. It was a practised technique, but even as the lid came away to the pressure of his fingers, something he suspected but had not dared to acknowledge when he lifted the tin off the shelf became unanswerably clear.

The red Scottie dog biscuit tin was empty.

Chapter Twenty-eight

"Where's the money?"

At the first staff meeting of the summer term, Dave Singleman found himself in the unfamiliar position of being front and centre, facing the massed ranks of his colleagues with their coffee cups and their open planners, their facial expressions ranging from polite interest to blank boredom. One or two were glancing surreptitiously at their phones – a liberty that he should have excused on the basis that he had done it many times himself, but which he found, now that he had something important to communicate, to be surprisingly off-putting.

The Head had, without warning, offered him the floor to officially launch the mock election. Taken by surprise Dave wisely decided not to oversell the project, but to underline a couple of pieces of essential information that had been in the original email. That communication, having been sent before the two-week Easter break, would have been long forgotten by most colleagues.

"I think I'd just like to say at this stage that I hope to announce the list of candidates at the end of the week. Then there will be some hustings sessions and some manifesto material appearing on the network. Each candidate needs to be sponsored by a staff member just to keep them honest, as it were, so I'll be looking for support in that role from colleagues who either have a degree of political interest of whatever shade, or who perhaps are form tutors to the candidates.

"As you know we've decided in view of the forthcoming exams to restrict the exercise to years seven to nine, so those year groups will form our electorate. One very important point is that all students have to register to vote in advance – more details on that will follow, but form tutors will have a key role in reinforcing the message. Kate has put together a really great pack of resources for use in lessons to support the cross-curricular element of the project, and we hope very much that lots of you will get involved that way. Polling day is 6th May, same as the actual by-election. Thanks very much in advance for your support."

Dave returned to his usual place by the kitchen. It was hard to gauge how it had gone down, but he thought he might have detected a frisson of approval.

"Thank you, David," said the Head. "This is a really worthwhile project, and I think the fact that it runs in parallel with the actual council by-election in the school's area makes it too good an opportunity to miss. I look forward very much to seeing who our candidates are. Now just a word about summer uniform…"

Kate flashed Dave a smile of encouragement. The deadline for nominations was close of play on Thursday, but they had found only two forms in Dave's pigeonhole on their arrival at school that morning – one from Issy Brunel, who was sponsored by Kate and who, to Dave's mild disgust, wanted to stand as a Conservative, and one from Sammy Pascoe, who said he wanted to stand as a Lib Dem, and who had added a note enquiring if Mr Singleman would be willing to sponsor him. Dave had hoped for more.

Up on the middle school playground, Edward was seated on his usual duty bench, enjoying the novelty of having his coffee in the sunshine. He had already done a circuit of the main teaching block, and had turfed one or two covens of Goths out into the fresh air. Now he was reflecting on the progress his own campaign had made over the holiday.

They had managed to leaflet all of the outlying villages – Rona d'Allesandro having very decently agreed to deliver the whole of Gurrian. His nomination papers had gone in, and he had been pleasantly surprised at how easy it had been to gather the signatures. On these initial indications it seemed likely that a substantial part of the Liberal vote would indeed come his way. Now that Murdo had the bit between his teeth, it was hard to see how he could have done this without his campaign manager. He wondered if even the local party machine would have been quite so focused and efficient. Murdo also seemed pleased with what had been achieved so far, but said that until they saw who was on the ballot it was difficult to determine precisely what the next stage of the strategy should be. Nominations closed in a few days, and then Edward would know who exactly he was up against.

He became aware of a small group of Year Sevens gathering shyly around him like Victorian factory workers who cannot agree who should approach the owner for a pay rise.

"Good morning," he said. "Is this a delegation?"

"Don't know what one of those is," said a boy from his own form. It was the one who had chatted to him at the station the day of the whiteboard incident.

"A delegation is a group of people sent to represent a point of view or to make a request," said Edward.

"Well we kind of are that," said the boy. "We was wondering if you would do that coin trick for us again?"

"Ah" said Edward. "I remember you asked me that a few weeks ago. Do you have a coin that you're prepared to lose?"

The gaggle turned in on itself briefly, then one of them stepped forward and handed him a ten pence piece.

"There you go, Sir."

Edward checked his watch.

"All right," he said, "Just time before the bell. Watch carefully."

He held the coin between thumb and forefinger, then passed his other hand in front of it, and held out his hands palms upward. The ten pence piece had vanished. He smiled at them, then before they could question him further, he reached out to the ringleader and seemed to produce the coin once more from behind his ear. The group wowed and applauded.

"That's awesome sir!"

"Do it again!"

"Can you show us how you do it?"

"A magician never reveals his methods," said Edward, as the bell went. His spirits were high as he rose to return his coffee cup to the staffroom. If his campaign continued to go well, that was as nothing compared to the vanishing trick he intended to perform at the end of the school year.

More candidate forms came in at lunchtime, most, to Dave's irritation, lacking the necessary sponsorship details. It was clear he would need to get everybody together and possibly extend his deadline. If he insisted on sticking to the letter of his own law, then Issy Brunel – brackets Conservative - would win by virtue of being the only candidate who had completed the paperwork correctly. While it could be argued that that was a useful life lesson for the others to learn, Dave was not prepared to see his grand scheme fail on such a technicality.

At the end of school he and Kate considered what had come in so far. There were candidates for the three main parties, in the shape of Sammy, Issy and Hardeep Singh, whose father had been a Labour councillor in London before they moved down west. Connor Pendarves wanted to stand for the Greens, and Toby Trott had aspirations to campaign as an independent for the right not to wear school uniform, and to have ice cream every day for pudding.

"Well, it's a start," said Kate, "What do you reckon to Toby Trott?"

"Much as it pains me to let him anywhere near it," said Dave, "I had hoped to have at least one independent standing. And he has, to his credit, got a sponsoring member of staff." This was Sheila Abbot, the retiring Head of Year, who no doubt wanted to encourage one of her habitual ne'er-do-wells to participate in such a worthwhile exercise.

"Are you going to sponsor Sammy?"

"I think I need to stay above it all. I'll ask Mark Armitage. He's a bit Lib Demmy. And Robbo said he'd look after anyone who wanted to stand for Labour. So we just need to find a tree-hugger for Connor."

"I've got a good idea who the vegetarians are," said Kate. That's as good a place to start as any."

It was apparent that Murdo needed as much time as possible to apply himself to the strategic thinking and background work demanded by the campaign, and in consequence he had been released from all Count House catering duties. As Edward still had school during the day, and a substantial marking load to deal with, he had reluctantly given up on maintaining his usual high standards of home cooking, falling back instead upon ready meals and occasional takeaways. If Murdo noticed the change in diet he raised no objection. Evening meals tended to morph into informal campaign meetings, and they sat now with the remains of their fish and chips in front of them.

"What's the plan for the Penhale estate?" said Edward. "I know it's not my most fertile territory, but presumably we need to pick up some votes there if we're going to beat Mallinson."

"Well it's definitely got to be leafleted," said Murdo. "But I'm not sure that door-knocking there's goin' to be very good use of your time. Your votes are probably goin' tae lie in the villages."

"How many houses on Penhale?"

"About 800. Might be worth just paying somebody."

"How much?"

"Ah'll make some enquiries. Could be a couple of hundred quid. Trouble is, ye nivver know if they've really been delivered. Plus they'll be wrapped up wi' pizza leaflets and all kinds of other crap. It's not ideal."

"I don't suppose you and Sophie…"

"Sophie's working pretty much full time these days. As am I, in case ye hadn't noticed."

"I had, I had. In fact I was going to say – you mustn't let your college work suffer on account of this campaign."

"Lectures have pretty much finished now."

"Revision then. I'll feel very bad if you get me elected but fail your first year as a consequence."

"There's nae exams at the end of the first year. Now let's get back to the campaign. There's been a bit of comeback frae Labour on a tweet you put out last week."

"A tweet? What tweet? I'm not on Twitter!"

"Aye well actually ye are, or at least the campaign is. It seems referring to Mallinson as a blow-in has ruffled a few feathers…"

"So where's the money?" said Donkey, belligerently.

"Now then, Donny," said Isaac. "Just mind your tone."

Donkey took a breath. They were seated across the red formica table. It was the evening after he had discovered that the tin was empty, and he had waited to see if there would be chocolate puddings for supper. None had appeared. As a poor substitute a packet of digestive biscuits from B and M was open on the table between them. Mrs Doggett was at the sink.

"Thing is," said Isaac, "I was finding it a bit of a temptation."

"Tell me about it," said Donkey bitterly.

"Well, we all were," said Isaac. "Your mother too, bless her. So I decided to give it away."

"You gave it away? You gave away more than five hundred twatting quid? Who's the lucky guy?"

"I gave it to the Seaman's Mission."

There was silence while this sank in. Donkey's head went down onto his arms on the table. Mrs Doggett stopped washing the dishes and turned to face her two menfolk.

"Well I'm proud of you Isaac Doggett. I think you did the right thing."

"Thank you, Mother. Donny?"

Donkey said something indistinct into the table.

"What was that son?"

He looked up.

"I said right on."

His father nodded approvingly.

"It wouldn't have been right to spend it. We all know where it came from. There's folk whose lives are being made a misery because of that money. Besides, I got some work in prospect."

"What kind of work?" said Mrs Doggett sharply.

"Plastering." said Isaac, lightly. "All legit, like. Well, I mean, it's cash in hand, but that's all right."

"Where?" said Donkey.

"Up Exeter way."

Donkey looked appalled, and when he spoke his voice was shaking.

"Dad please don't go to Exeter. I want you to stay here. I'm going to be in this mock election, and I want you to be here so I can tell you about it when…when I come back from school."

"You never mentioned that, son."

"Well I haven't put my forms in yet. I was going to…I wanted to talk to you about what party I should stand for, and that."

"What party would you like to stand for?"

"Well Murdo says I should stand as a socialist."

"Who's Murdo?" asked Isaac suspiciously.

"He's the Scottish guy that came to the door that time. The one that sorted out the verges. He says he'll help me with my campaign." He had heard back from Murdo that afternoon, and been pleased when the older boy suggested that they meet in town after school later in the week.

"Well I don't have much truck with socialism. Folk have got to make their own way in the world."

"I'd like to maybe start my own party."

"You need to think of some kind of cause you could stand for," said Mrs Doggett, in a rare intervention in the family discourse. She was pleased that the conversation had moved away from the matter of the money. "Something that you feel strongly about."

"What I feel strongly about," said Donkey, "Is that folk should be allowed a second chance."

Chapter Twenty-nine

"It's still not a crime in Yorkshire"

On Wednesday afternoon Donkey met Murdo by the skateboard park. The two walked for a bit, then leaned on the rail and looked out over the grey water. The rain was holding off, but a stiff breeze was raising white crests like sharp little teeth across the bay.

"So lemme get this straight," said Murdo. You're fourteen years old, you've kind of developed an interest in politics, but you're not sure what party to support."

"Pretty much," said Donkey.

"So what's sparked this interest?"

Donkey dug around among the mish-mash of factors that had brought him to this point to find the ones he felt comfortable sharing.

"Well, I've always just kind of messed around at school, and never thought I was any good at anything, like, academic. Then this new teacher – Miss Porteous – encouraged us to get involved in debating, even though we were in the bottom set, and I won a prize in this competition. I mean I know I'm not really good, not like Issy…"

"Who's Issy?"

"Just a girl in my class." Issy was one of the factors he hadn't intended to mention. "And my Dad…was away for a while, but now he's come back, and he's kind of changed a bit…"

"In a good way?" asked Murdo gently.

"Right, in a good way. But my brother's a bad lot, and I just don't want to end up going the way he's gone. I suppose I've just always thought I hadn't much choice, really, in how I was and that, but now I think I do." He paused. "I don't know if it's got anything to do with politics at all, really."

"Ah tell you what son," said Murdo. "If ah've learned anything in the past five years, it's that politics has to do with pretty well everything. What you learn at school, how much you get paid, whether you can get a house to live in or a bed in your local hospital. You might not realise it, and most folk don't, but all these things get decided, one way or another, by the people you vote for. And the tragedy is, lots of folk just don't vote."

"See that's the thing," said Donkey. "Six months ago that would have meant nothing to me. And now, just hearing you say it is kind of...I dunno, exciting, and scary at the same time."

"How long have you lived on that estate?"

"Penhale? I've never lived anywhere else."

"And if you don't mind me asking, is yer dad in work just now?"

"Nothing steady," admitted Donkey.

"OK," said Murdo. "That's interesting. D'ye fancy an ice cream?"

"So... I think I might have solved the Penhale problem," said Murdo after supper that evening. "D'ye know a kid called Donovan Doggett?"

"Everyone knows Donkey," said Edward, setting down two mugs of coffee on the table. "But he's not generally regarded as the solution to anything."

"Well you might need tae be a wee bit open minded here. And by the way he doesn't want to be called Donkey any more. He thinks it sends out the wrong message."

"Fair enough," said Edward. "I don't actually dislike the boy, but he has generally been a bit of nuisance."

"You should have seen me when I was fourteen," said Murdo.

"And look at you now."

208

"Right, well, banter aside, young Doggett is developing an interest in politics. Apparently there's some kind of mock election going on at the school?"

"There is. A colleague of mine is organising it."

"Well he needs a teacher tae sponsor him. And possibly because of his past behaviour, they're not actually queuing up for the privilege."

"No. That doesn't surprise me."

"Well I said you would do it."

Edward looked as if he might be about to object, but then he said.

"All right. No reason why not."

"In return, he'll do some delivering on the Penhale estate for us. I mean I didn't make it an explicit quid pro quo, but that's the understanding."

"Well – that's good. But it's a big estate, and Donkey …Donovan… is not, on past performance, entirely reliable."

"Aye but there's more. His old man is out of work."

"And out of prison."

Murdo took a sip of his coffee.

"Just what sort of Liberal are you?"

Edward looked stung. "I'm just contributing to the sum of information we hold on the situation. Actually I taught Isaac Doggett, back in the early days. He's wasn't such a bad lad."

"Yeah, ah met him on the doorstep when ah was canvassing for Mallinson, and he seemed pretty straight to me. Anyway, here's the deal. You sponsor the boy – he delivers for us. Slip Isaac a hundred quid, and he'll make sure the whole estate gets done."

"More money!"

"I think ye can probably afford it. Yer still well within yer expenses limit."

"What makes you think the father will want to get involved?"

"Well he needs the money for one thing. Reading between the lines the family's struggling to put food on the table. But also….and it gets a bit subtle here so ye'll need tae pay attention…Ah reckon both the boy and his dad will be grateful to you, for different reasons. They'll be keen to help. Isaac'll need a clear brief, but I reckon he's smart enough to know which shell-like ears on the Penhale estate are worth having a word in. He could pull us in twenty or thirty votes that wouldn't otherwise come our way."

"There's a lot of ifs and buts in there. Some families on the Penhale estate won't be over-fond of the Doggetts."

"It's only a hundred quid Edward. Even if we got no benefit from the arrangement, it would make a big difference to them."

"Fine," said Edward wearily.

"Whaddiz that mean?"

"It means you're right. It's a good thing to do. Make it so."

On Thursday evening in Kate's flat on the ground floor of the Engine House, Dave set up a spreadsheet with the final roster of candidates for the mock election. It read as follows:

Isadora Brunel	Conservative
Donovan Doggett	Second Chances
Sammy Pascoe	Liberal Democrat
Connor Pendarves	Green Party
Hardeep Singh	Labour
Lily Tregunna	Mebyon Kernow
Toby Trott	Own Clothes/Ice-cream

Kate leaned over his shoulder. "Looks pretty good," she said. "Nice blend of sensible kids and…not quite so sensible ones."

"I dunno," said Dave. I suppose it's not all that different from what I was expecting. It's just…seeing it written down – I mean it could go either way, couldn't it? I'd be happier if Donkey and Toby Trott weren't involved."

"It's Donovan, actually," said Kate. "He wants to be known as Donovan. And remember, you didn't want him involved in the debating."

Dave grunted. "Yeah well, I'm still not convinced he's changed his spots. Good of Edward to sponsor him though. Did you know he's running for the council?"

"Yes I heard," said Kate. "I guess he'll have to leave, or go part-time if he wins."

"I doubt he'll win," said Dave. "If the Lib Dems don't stand it will be between Labour and the Tories."

"Rona says her nephew is running his campaign. Apparently he's very politically aware."

Dave closed his laptop. "Ah yes, the infamous Murdo. Interesting. By the way it's also good of you to sponsor Issy the Tory. I can think of a few colleagues who wouldn't have touched that one."

"I was glad to," said Kate. "I voted Tory at the last election."

Dave chuckled. Kate's occasional dry sense of humour was one of the things he loved about her. Then a ghastly thought struck him.

"That's a joke, right?"

"Nope," said Kate. "It's still not a crime in Yorkshire."

She moved away from him and sat on the arm of the settee. Dave swivelled round and looked at her sidelong.

"OK. Wow. I'll need to digest that."

"Don't you vote Tory then?" asked Kate innocently. She didn't imagine for a minute that he did, but keeping this discussion in the realm of banter seemed the safest course.

"Um, no, I never have, actually. I mean people do down here, obviously. God knows why because the Tories do nothing for Cornwall. But, I mean…can I ask why? Why you voted Conservative?"

Kate shrugged. "Well my parents always used to, and as you know they're quite churchy, and believe in family values, and all that stuff. The local MP always seemed quite a decent bloke. Labour are pretty militant up in Yorkshire, and…well I dunno, I just carried on I suppose. I did vote Lib Dem once, if that helps."

"Right," said Dave. "That would have been in your dangerously radical student years."

"How do you vote then," asked Kate, to forestall what might have been a slightly frosty silence.

"Mostly Labour or Green," said Dave. "I did actually vote Lib Dem once too now you mention it."

"There you are," said Kate cheerfully. "Common ground! Do you want another cup of coffee?"

It was a Thursday night, and the assumption had been that Dave would stay over. When they had watched the ten o'clock news – which seemed to be more full than usual of political stories, which they digested in silence – Kate said,

211

"Presumably you're all right sleeping with a Tory?"

Dave laughed, a little hollowly, she thought.

"Provided we declare the bedroom a politics-free zone."

"It always has been up to now."

"I know," said Dave, "I know. I'm only joking. And I'm sorry. It's stupid. It doesn't matter what your politics are. You're still Kate and I still love you."

"Glad to hear it," said Kate.

But in bed that night they lay side by side, neither admitting to the other that they were awake, each wondering what this new unexpected difference that they had discovered meant for their relationship. Each silently added it to the small pile of differences they already knew about, and over which they occasionally stumbled – their different attitudes to education; their contrasting family backgrounds; the housing issue which was still not properly resolved.

Dave's tally of mismatches included what he considered to be Kate's over-friendly attitude to Anton Killick, for whom she not infrequently expressed a degree of sympathy, and of whose appraisal working party she was an enthusiastic member. It wouldn't have taken much encouragement from him, he reflected gloomily, for Kate to hop into Anton's white BMW on the night of the breakdown and zip off back to the Engine House in warmth and comfort, listening to God knows what dismal choice of music on the Blaupunkt sound system; her jeans no doubt slipping a little on the red leather upholstery. As it was, Dave and Kate had got back just before 3 am, and that, now that he thought about it, hadn't been a particularly passionate night either.

For Kate there were other issues, ones about which she considered herself to have been pretty tolerant. There was Dave's liking for an occasional spliff. He claimed these days that he only indulged this taste when he was out of the country, but Kate wasn't entirely sure she believed that line. Then there was his past relationships, notably the untied loose-end represented by Candice the ex-pole dancer with whom he had clearly had some kind of liaison in the not too distant past. Candice had once turned up at the Engine House, where she treated Dave with a provocative familiarity that wasn't entirely excused by her being at least a decade and a half older than him. These things, it seemed to Kate, were at least as

212

significant to the long-term viability of a relationship as where you put your cross in the privacy of the polling booth.

Thus they lay for some hours as the moon rose silently behind the Engine House, until the settling chill of the early dawn drew them together once more.

In the Doggett household on the Penhale estate by contrast, all three members of the family slept soundly. At a meeting earlier that evening, Murdo had explained his proposition to an initially sceptical Isaac, who had wanted to be sure that none of the literature he would be distributing would be promoting Jeremy Corbyn. Murdo assured him that it wouldn't, that Edward was standing independently of any political party, and that furthermore Isaac should only enter into doorstep discussion with neighbours who he felt would be sympathetic to his recommendation. In return (he didn't actually use that phrase), Mr Tremenhere would sponsor Donovan in the St Petroc's mock election and he, Murdo, would personally supply the boy with advice on how to run a successful campaign. Fifty pounds in notes changed hands there and then, with another fifty promised once Isaac confirmed that the leaflets had been delivered. The leaflets themselves would be dropped off by Edward at the weekend. Murdo had shaken hands with them both and left in time to catch the late train back to Roskear.

"Edward Tremenhere," mused Isaac after Murdo had left. "Who'd have thought I'd be handing out leaflets for Edward Tremenhere. He's got a dodgy past you know."

"So've we all" said Donkey. "Second chances, remember?"

Chapter Thirty

"I'd like to book a viewing, please"

On Friday the student candidates were given their first public outing at the Year Nine assembly. They were allowed a minute each to introduce themselves and, if they wished, make a short speech to kick-start the campaign, a process that would be repeated with the other two junior year groups. The results were revealing, and not in every case what Dave had expected.

Issy Brunel – Conservative Party
"I stand here as the candidate of compassionate conservatism. (An audible snort from Dave in the wings.) I believe that it is important to balance the public finances and not just continually borrow to support public spending. I believe that hard work and self-reliance should be rewarded, but I accept that not everybody is born with the same advantages. For this reason there should be a safety net for those who can't help themselves. Not everyone is aware that higher taxes do not necessarily produce more income, because wealth creators can be dis-incentivised. I believe that the United Kingdom is stronger together but I am not opposed to a Cornish Assembly. Vote Brunel Conservative on May 6th."

Polite, slightly baffled, applause.

Donovan Doggett – Second Chances Party

"My name's Donovan Doggett" (satirical cries of Don-key from the back of the theatre). "Yeah you can call me Donkey – but actually me name's Donovan. I'm standing for the Second Chances party 'cos I think everyone in life deserves a second chance and probably a third and a fourth if it comes to that. Some of you know me Dad's been in the nick, but he's out now and trying to make something of his life and I'm standing in honour of him and everyone like him who got off on the wrong foot as you might say. So

> Vote for me on the sixth of May,
> You might need a second chance one day."

Riotous applause, at which Donkey blushed as he left the stage. Still some cries of Don-key!

Sammy Pascoe – Liberal Democrat Party

"Right you all know who I am, but you probably don't know what the Liberal Democrats stand for. To be honest I didn't either till I started looking into it, but basically we're a kind of middle ground between the two main parties. We're more caring and compassionate than the privileged folk in the Tory party, who don't know what it is to struggle (here he cast a glance at Issy, to whom he hadn't spoken all holiday) – and Labour, who just think the answer is to chuck money at everything. We believe in strong local government, which is why I'm really proud of my mum who's a parish councillor. And we believe in proportional representation, which is I admit is a bit complicated but I hope to put something about it on my website. So vote for the sensible middle way – Vote Pascoe Liberal Democrat on May 6th."

Sustained, though not riotous, applause.

Connor Pendarves – Green Party.

"Our planet is dying." Pause for effect. One or two groans, but not many "The icecaps are melting and our oceans are full of plastic. The rainforest is being ripped out for profit. Everybody says they want to do something about global warming but nobody actually wants to change their lifestyle. We're all too fond of cheap flights and big cars. A vote for me

215

on May 6th will send a message that our generation won't put up with it any longer. I'm standing for a clear plan by the school to reduce its emissions and increase its recycling. I also want to see better plant-based options in the canteen. I'm building a team to fight this campaign so if any of you want to get on board you can leave your details on my website, doubleyoudoubleyoudoubleyoudotConnorforagreenerStPetr ocsdotcom. Together we can make a difference. Thank you.

Applause, and considerable cheering, particularly from the girls.

Hardeep Singh – Labour Party.

"Yeah right hello. My name's Hardeep but you all probably know that. I'm standing for Labour because it's the only party that believes in fixing what's wrong with society which is that too much of the wealth is in the hands of too few people. Now the Tories would have you believe that those with a lot of money have earned it through hard work but that's not necessarily the case. Half the time it's because they inherited it, or they've had advantages like going to a private school, or sometimes they've been really ruthless in business and screwed over their workers. And sorry Sammy but you basically can't trust the Lib Dems 'cos they just got into bed with the Tories during the coalition and that's why we got austerity. (Sammy's face remained impassive at this but he made a mental note to ask Mr Armitage what the hell Hardeep was going on about). So if you want real change there's only one choice and that's Hardeep Singh for Labour. Thank you."

Applause, but a distinct sense that the audience were experiencing manifesto fatigue.

Lily Tregunna – Mebyon Kernow.

"Right me 'ansomes. I'm standing in this election for Mebyon Kernow. Now if you don't know what that is, then shame on you, cos what it is, is the party for Cornwall. Tell you the truth I didn't know about it either until somebody told me and when I looked into it, it really opened my eyes. Turns out Cornwall isn't really a County like folk try to make out, but actually an ancient nation, same as Wales basically, with its own language which you do know about 'cos it's on the road signs. Anyway what we need is a Cornish Assembly same as

216

the Scottish and Welsh assemblies so that decisions about Cornwall are made by the people in Cornwall. That and less second homes. That's all I can tell you at the minute, but I'm looking into it more and I'll put some stuff on the website. So vote for Tregunna, which is a proud Cornish name, and for Mebyon Kernow. *Onen hag oll!*

Pockets of cheering and stamping, and quite a lot of mildly baffled applause. The flag-bearer for Cornish nationalism walked proudly off the stage still chewing gum, as she had been throughout the speech.

Toby Trott – Own Clothes and Ice-cream Party.

"Brothers and sisters the time has come to wake from your slumbers. (Despite falling out with his teacher, Toby had been enjoying his study of Animal Farm). For too long we have been oppressed by our cruel overlords and denied basic human dignity. I am talking, brothers and sisters, about the right to wear our own clothes to school, instead of the dull, grey, scratchy uniform that we are forced to put on each day. Are we conscripts in an army? Are we inmates of a penal institution? No, brothers and sisters, we are people in our own right and we are entitled to the dignity of expressing ourselves through what we wear. And ice-cream too. Not to wear, obviously, cos that would be silly. But why can't we have it as a choice in the canteen? It's not that expensive and it would make every day feel like a celebration and we would all work much harder in afternoon school. So vote for me and reclaim your rights. Own clothes! Ice cream! Toby Trott! Yay!"

Wild cheering, which encouraged Toby to bow several times before leaving the stage.

Dave allowed this to subside before stepping forward from the wings.

"Well. What a great start to our mock election campaign! I'd like to thank all our candidates for standing, and congratulate them on a fine set of opening speeches. Provided you register – and you'll be hearing more about how you go about this – you'll get one vote on May 6th. It's what we call a simple "First past the post" election – the person who gets the most votes wins. So think carefully about whose ideas you want to support. You'll be hearing lots more from the candidates over the next couple of weeks. Now before I hand back to Mrs Abbot, let's give all the candidates a big round of applause!"

Dave was genuinely surprised by the enthusiasm of the candidates and the quality of their speeches, and the buzz that was created by the assembly. Nothing quite like it had been seen before, and while not all the candidates were serious ones, and some clearly were not yet on top of their parties' manifestos, there was a sense that something quite significant was happening. Form tutors murmured approving comments as they left the assembly, and the students who had spoken were shiny with pride. He wondered, who, at the end of the day, would capture the imagination of voters, and whether novelty would win out over serious politics. He looked around for Kate, but couldn't see her.

It was breaktime when he finally caught up with her in her classroom.

"How did it go?" she asked brightly.

"Were you not there?"

"No, I'm really sorry I had a meeting. Last minute. I'd been through Issy's speech with her though. Was it all right?"

"Yes very slick," said Dave. "As you would expect. They were all really good actually. I'm a bit sad that you missed it. Nothing too serious, I hope." His tone was friendly enough, but Kate could tell he wasn't happy.

"Oh…no. It was just…an appraisal working party thing. Anton wanted us to meet, briefly, supposedly, to arrange a time for the next meeting, then Emily wanted to speak to me about a pastoral matter, and… by the time I got away there was only about a minute left."

"Right." Not so much friendliness there.

"Dave, I'm really sorry. If I could have been there I would. You know that."

"Good old Anton. He would have done that deliberately you know."

"I really don't think so…"

"No. Because you don't think he's got a malicious bone in his magnificently toned body."

"I beg your pardon?"

"Nothing. I'm sorry. It's just we've been working so hard on this and…oh never mind. It went well, and that's what matters, I suppose. Look I've got to stay on after school and
218

make sure all the manifestos are on the website. Is it okay if we go home about six?"

"Yes, of course. I'll go in and do some shopping." Then "Sorry, I've got some prep to do for my next lesson."

Quietly furious, Kate turned and cleaned her whiteboard. When she turned round again Dave had gone.

Edward was perhaps the only member of the school community for whom "the election" meant something else altogether. That afternoon the candidates for the Cornwall Council contest were also to be announced, posted on the Council website, and after his last lesson of the day, when he had tidied his classroom, he logged on. The Council site was a large and complex one, and it took him a minute to find the correct page, but eventually, there they were: his opponents.

Esme Aitchieson	Green Party
Tristan Gilmore-Forbes	Conservative
Ivan Gummow	Independent
Trevor Mallinson	Labour
Anthony Penberthy	Mebyon Kernow
Edward Tremenhere	Independent

Despite the fact that he had been campaigning for a fortnight, it came as a mild shock to see his name on the ballot, and the sight of the others, none of whom he knew, raised in him an unexpected surge of mild hatred. It seemed wrong that all these people should be setting themselves up in competition, and that he should know nothing about them. He was about to google them when his phone buzzed in his pocket. It was a text from Anna.

Great to see your name on the ballot, even if it doesn't have Lib Dem after it. Very Best of luck x.

He texted back.

Thanks!

Then, after a moment's hesitation,

Would it compromise your position to meet up for a drink? I've given my Campaign Manager the evening off.

The reply was immediate.

That sounds good. 8 at the Tregarvon?

Kate wandered into town, thoroughly miserable and still angry. After an unsociable night they had both made a bit of an effort, over breakfast and on the journey into school, to be cheerful. She had of course had every intention of being at the assembly, as she normally would be as a form tutor. The sequence of events that derailed this was exactly as she had described it, and as innocent too, though it was becoming clear that Dave's residual jealousy of Anton was going to be difficult to shift.

She knew that Dave himself, if challenged, would acknowledge that this jealousy was ridiculous. It was founded on the flimsy basis that Anton had once, before Kate and Dave had started going out, asked her to meet him for a drink, supposedly to discuss school business, and she had accepted. The occasion had been excruciatingly awkward, with Anton clearly at a loss to know how to shift out of his formal school manner, and when he had asked her out a second time she had made very clear that she wasn't interested. Since then he had made no further overtures. As to his body – well, she had a swimmer's respect for a toned physique, and Anton's was evident even when he wore a suit. It had of course been even more evident when their visits to the fitness suite coincided, as they once had. Dispensing with those gym visits was another compromise that had been made to keep Dave happy.

In the supermarket in town she had no enthusiasm for buying the kind of ingredients that might have gone into a reconciliation supper, and instead she pulled a quiche and some garlic bread off the shelves. A packet of mixed salad, and some dressing, if they could find the makings between them, would jolly well have to do. Really she wished she were just eating by herself that evening. She wasn't in the mood for small talk.

She paid for her purchases, and left the store. It was still only five-fifteen. She could get on with some marking while she waited for Dave to finish whatever he was doing. She was about to set off back up to the school when a thought occurred, and she spun on her heel and walked instead in the direction of the harbour. She had a sudden curiosity to see the Net Loft, perhaps even catch a glimpse of its new occupant at a window. Would it be someone of her own age? Or some balding middle-aged, divorced man, contemplating his own lonely supper of quiche and salad.

A few minutes' walk took her to the harbour. There was no sign of life at the Net Loft. What there was, however, was an agent's board, a different one this time, advertising that the property was available to let.

Kate stood for a while in thought, then glanced at her watch. It was twenty-five past five, and the letting agent was at the other end of town. She took out her phone and dialled the number on the board. For a while there was no response, and she feared they had turned the phones off for the day. She was about to kill the call when,

"Good afternoon, Kernow Lettings. Steph speaking. How may I help you?"

"Good afternoon. I'd like to book a viewing please."

Chapter Thirty-one

"Finish your quiche before you start to patronise me"

Edward made sure that he arrived early at the Tregarvon, and settled himself with a pint in a corner seat with a view of the door. He felt ambivalent about the meeting. At the time, it had seemed like a good idea, but now that he was in that moment of anticipating Anna's imminent arrival, it seemed to him that something had fundamentally changed. To put it crudely, he could take her or leave her. It was a month since they had spent the night together at her house, and nothing remotely akin to that surprising moment of intimacy had since passed between them. Anna might be a useful political ally, but even acknowledging that fact was to diminish any other aspect of their friendship.

He watched her come into the bar, and look around to find him. He raised a hand in greeting, and stood up as she crossed the room to where he was sitting. They kissed rather formally.

"What would you like? I'm on the ale I'm afraid."

"A glass of red, thank you," said Anna, taking off her jacket and shaking out her hair.

Edward went to the bar and returned a minute or two later with Anna's wine.

"So," said Anna, meeting his gaze directly. "How's the campaign going?"

"Well I think we're doing all right," said Edward. "We've leafleted the villages and I've done a bit of door-knocking. We haven't touched the Penhale estate yet, but that's in hand. There's a hustings next week that I could do with picking your brains about. And you might be able to fill me in a bit on the other candidates."

"You're probably further ahead than most of them," said Anna. "What's the response been to the lack of a Lib Dem candidate?"

"General disapproval, I would say. The ones who admit to usually supporting us seem quite happy to lend their vote to me. Or so they say. I'm not sure the Greens are going to get much out of it."

"I think you might be right there. I have dropped into casual conversation with one or two members the fact that you're standing, and I wouldn't be surprised if you get some offers of help."

"Anyone I should contact?"

"I'm afraid I can't go that far," said Anna. "I have to be whiter than white in this."

"Fair enough. Any intel on the other candidates? We know about Mallinson."

"The Tory's a bit of a surprise – some bright young thing who runs a tech start-up in Newlyn. Only recently moved down here."

"Bit of a change from Narabo, then."

"Yes. I think they felt their image could do with burnishing. The MK candidate's been a councillor before a little further up the county – lost his seat at the last election. Esme is perfectly decent and sensible and might pick up a hundred votes or so for the Greens. Ivan Gummow's the chair of planning on Eglos Parish Council, and has stood a couple of times before without success, so he's beginning to look a bit shop-soiled. I'd say it's wide open. Four hundred votes could win it – less if it's a wet day."

Four hundred votes. It sounded a lot when every vote meant someone turning out in what might be unpleasant weather, and making their way to a polling station just to put a cross next to his name. He noticed that Anna had barely touched her wine. His own pint was half-drunk.

"Well that's useful, thanks." He was about to move on to the question of the hustings when Anna spoke again.

"Edward, do you mind if we leave politics for a bit? I don't want to be too late, and there's something else I want to talk about."

"Of course." He waited.

"I owe you an apology."

"I'm sure you don't…"

"Well, I feel I do. I've left you dangling a bit, and I'm sorry. Partly I've been busy sorting out the domestic stuff, instructing lawyers and so forth, and partly the ongoing possibility of you being the candidate, then the negotiations with the Greens, has made it more convenient to keep you at arm's length, as it were. But that's a bit of an excuse. And also, I'm sorry if I came across as a bit startled when you explained about…your orientation."

"Being bi."

"Yes. I have no issues with it, whether we're in a relationship or whether we aren't. As you so succinctly expressed it the last time we were here, it's a matter of fidelity; integrity if you like - nothing more. And I have a high view of your integrity."

"OK. Thank you." He smiled at her. "Barely necessary apology accepted."

"Thanks. Anyway, my situation's settling down a bit. The divorce looks as if it will be straightforward. Julian appears quite happy to be sued for adultery. He assures me I'll get a generous settlement."

"How did the kids take it?"

"A bit taken aback at first. They're angry with Julian, which I'm trying to discourage. They'll be here for another fortnight and hopefully by the time they go back to university it will all be a bit more settled."

"And what about you? Are you dealing with it all right?"

"Yes, I think so. I've got some supportive friends. And I know my way around family law, so that bit should be straightforward. And now that it's happened, I'm glad that it happened when it did, when I've still got some choices to make."

Edward nodded, wondering if he was one of those choices.

"As far as we're concerned, I'm open minded, genuinely. I'm not going to rush into another serious relationship, and I don't really want to bring anybody back to the house while the kids are there. That feels premature. But I do…well, I like you very much. I like your company, and I value your friendship. I'd like to spend more time with you, doing this sort of thing, but realistically I think anything more serious is probably best parked till…I don't know, the summer maybe? Does that sound unreasonable?"

"No not at all," said Edward. His tone was light, but he was aware that they were discussing this as they might if they were considering the building of a small extension, or the purchase of a puppy. "In a way I won't know for sure what my own plans are until I know whether or not I'm on the council. And in terms of us, I feel much the same way you do. I think I'd feel happier though if I knew when we were going to see each other next, if you see what I mean. So that neither of us is left dangling, to borrow your phrase."

Anna took a mouthful of wine, and nodded. She looked relieved. Edward found that he felt relieved too. And with the relief he felt warm towards her again.

"The hustings is next Friday. Why don't you come back to the Count House afterwards. There'll probably some other members of the team there, but they're all quite good fun." He paused, then added,

"Please? It would be nice just to have you in the house. It won't be anything fancy. You don't have to stay over but there's plenty of room if you want to."

Anna smiled.

"All right. Thank you. Something to look forward to."

They walked together to the car park, where they hugged a little longer than friends would, and she kissed him briefly on the lips before breaking off and getting into her car.

"Call me midweek," he said, and she nodded before winding up the window, and turning the key in the ignition. He stood and watched as she drove out of the car park, and remained standing for some time after the sound of her engine had died away.

On Kate's return to the school to collect Dave, he had immediately apologised for his behaviour, an apology that she

225

had not very graciously accepted. The journey home was largely silent.

"I can eat at my flat tonight if you like," said Dave, in a contrite tone as they got out of the car.

"No it's fine, I've got some food in. Just…just give me an hour, will you? I need to straighten my head out."

He had readily agreed, and knocked at her door just before seven thirty. It was the first time he had done that for a while, and she noticed that he had showered and changed his shirt.

"Hi, come in," she said, and forced a smile. "Quiche is just about ready, I should think."

"Great! And I smell garlic bread…"

The table was set. There was a bowl of salad in the middle, where there was sometimes a candle. There was no candle tonight. There was no music playing either. The flat had something of the air of a stage set awaiting its actors. Dave sat down and poured himself a glass of wine from the half-drunk bottle. It looked like there was business to be discussed.

Kate brought the quiche and the garlic bread to the table.

"Help yourself." She sat down and began piling salad onto her plate.

"So…" said Dave. "I get the distinct impression I'm still in the doghouse."

"I don't really believe in doghouses," said Kate. "They're something of a misogynistic trope. But if you mean am I am still quite pissed off, then the answer's yes."

"I'm not sure what else I can say," said Dave. "I've admitted I was out of order. It's just – this mock election is quite a big thing for me, and I've really enjoyed working with you on it. I guess I was disappointed – maybe more than I should have been - that you weren't there to see it get off the ground."

"Only it wasn't just that, was it," said Kate. "It was the fact that I was at a meeting with Anton."

"Yeah, OK, that didn't help. And what I said was stupid. But cut me some slack here. I admit I get a bit jealous of Anton's interest in you, and I should be above all that because I know there's nothing to be jealous of, but can't you see it as a positive thing? An indication of how much you mean to me?"

"I think jealousy has more to do with insecurity than love."

226

God, thought Dave, this is uphill work. Kate continued.

"OK, let's talk about Anton. He can be a bit of an idiot, we all know that. And he's socially awkward. And he doesn't like you, largely because you make no secret of the fact that you're opposed to virtually everything he's trying to do at the school. But none of that makes him a bad person. And I'm on this working party, which I quite enjoy, and which is good for my career, and from time to time I will have meetings with him. You've got to get in a place where that's acceptable to you."

"It is acceptable, of course it is. This was just an unfortunate combination of events. But let me ask you something. How close were you to accepting his offer of a lift that night we broke down? Honestly?"

"I don't know," said Kate. "I did consider it. It was freezing cold and I was tired. I didn't accept mostly because I knew it would have upset you. Not that that would have been justified."

"Hmmph!" said Dave.

"I have absolutely no interest in Anton. If you can't accept that, we're in trouble."

"Really?"

"Yes. Really."

"Wow."

"And while you're at it, you also need to accept that not everybody who votes Conservative is a self-serving moron."

"I do accept that. Some of them just don't think hard enough about the consequences of their choices."

"Right. That would be me, then?"

"You tell me. You admitted yourself that the reasons you vote Tory have a lot to do with your upbringing. Well that's fair enough. But most of us are able to burst that particular bubble when we go to University. I mean tell, me, honestly, which policies of this current Government you support, and why."

"Look, I don't have your interest in politics. Frankly most people don't. I'm sympathetic to the broad principles ; law and order; family; hard work; sensible management of the economy. I just don't trust Labour on those things. Well, not all of them."

"Oh for God's sake," said Dave. "Where do I begin?"

"If I were you," said Kate quietly, "I'd finish your quiche before you start to patronise me. Because you'll be out that door before you can say Jeremy Corbyn."

Dave was about to retort, then he met her eye and thought the better of it. There was a moment or two of silence, then the chink of cutlery as they addressed himself once more to eating.

"OK," he said, "We've done Anton, and we've done politics. Anything else you want to talk about? Because I'm thinking I'll get an early night tonight."

Kate took a breath.

"Well actually, there is something else," she said. "The Net Loft has come back on the market. I've booked a viewing tomorrow morning."

"Uh-huh," said Dave. "Well perhaps that's not such a bad idea."

Kate began to clear the plates. She had expected more of a reaction to that one.

"Do you want a coffee?"

"No, I'm fine, thanks. Can I help with the dishes?"

"There's not many to do."

"Right. Well, look, thanks for the supper. It was probably good to…get some of that stuff out in the open…"

"Yes."

"I just can't help wondering…"

"What?"

"What happened to France? All that fun, and love and freedom."

He was half-way to the door. She put down the dishes she was carrying and crossed to him.

"France will always be there, Dave. We need to make sure we're still in a position to enjoy it together."

"Yes, That's the thing."

She was prepared to embrace him, but he turned and went out the door. It felt like a slap to the face. She listened as she always did to his steps on the outside stair, then his key in his own door, then the vaguer creaking as he moved around the upstairs flat.

Chapter Thirty-two

"A triad of leaping dolphins"

"It's a beautiful day," said Sue Brunel. "Anyone fancy a trip to the beach?"

The family was at breakfast, an unhurried meal of stewed fruit, granola and yoghurt, with pastries and black coffee, that they took together at weekends in their large, comfortable kitchen. Today the bi-fold doors that led out to the veranda were open. Both the girls were wearing shorts, and the mild spring air stirred around their ankles.

"Yesss!" said Phoebe, her younger daughter. "Can Maddie come?"

"If her parents will let her. What about you, Isadora?"

"Not sure," said Issy. "I need to work on my campaign."

"How did that speech go?" asked her father, helping himself to more coffee from the machine on the breakfast bar. A compact, purposeful looking gadget of polished steel and glass, it had cost around the same as Viv Pascoe had paid for his Nissan pick-up, and functioned considerably more reliably.

"OK, I think," said Issy. "I'm not sure how many votes I'll get, though. It turns out being a Tory isn't very trendy."

"Perhaps it's a bit of an uphill battle with kids of your age group," said her father. "But it seems generally popular in the country at large."

"Have you and Mum always voted Conservative?"

"If I remember correctly we both voted Labour in '97," said her mother. "That was my first election."

"Was that Tony Blair?"

"Yes – his first term. The Tories were looking a bit old and tired. Blair seemed like the guy with all the fresh ideas."

"He wasn't exactly radical though, was he," said Issy, a bit disappointed that her parents hadn't, in their early twenties, been a bit more daring in their political philosophy. But then she, at fourteen, wasn't exactly rocking the boat either.

"Can I ring Maddie now," said Phoebe.

"The countries that have tried extreme left-wing polices," said her father, "generally end up living under some kind of dictatorship. Socialism begins with high ideals, but it ends up with people eating their pets."

"Daddy! Don't be horrible. Don't worry Dougal, we would never eat you!"

The family Labradoodle remained panting by Phoebe's chair, unperturbed by his master's grisly pronouncement.

"That's a good line," said Issy. "I might use that."

On the Penhale estate, Murdo was sitting once more at the Doggett's kitchen table. He felt oddly comfortable there, and was glad he had abandoned his plans to go home to Glasgow for the holiday. Isaac Doggett, once he had got his head round the boy's broad accent and his un-nerving self-confidence, was beginning to see him as a good thing. Edward had dropped Murdo off with the leaflets at nine o'clock, and after a few polite words with the family had gone off on his own to do some door-knocking at the private housing on the other side of the school. It had been agreed that while Edward would be fine on his own among the genteel granite villas, it would be better use of Murdo's time to oversee the first Penhale delivery session. After they had done that he would spend an hour with Donkey going through his campaign plan for the mock election. Murdo hoped that the morning might cement the working relationship in manner that would benefit them all.

"Let's have a look at this leaflet, then," said Isaac. "I want to know what I'm sticking through folks' doors. I've got a reputation to maintain."

Murdo passed him one of the fliers, and Isaac studied it with a furrowed brow.

"Could I get something like this for my campaign?" said Donkey.

"Unfortunately printing costs money," said Murdo. "Specially if it's in colour. But there's no reason why you canny produce something yourself. Edward might be able to get it copied for you."

"We done something like this in IT," said Donkey. "Leaflets, I mean. I got a B for mine."

"Did," said Isaac, without looking up. "We did something in IT." Then, seeing the boy's expression,

"B's good though son."

"Aw right dad."

"I tell you what," said Murdo. "You put together something on Publisher, or whatever you use, then email it to me, and I'll add in a few fancy bits. Stuff other folk won't think of doing."

"Awesome!" said Donkey.

"Well that looks all right," said Isaac, handing back Edward's leaflet. "I didn't know about the minor injuries unit. We don't want to lose that. We been there with you a few times, eh Donny."

"Once or twice."

"I mean if we'd had to take you up to Truro that time you fell out the window, you might have bled to death."

"Yeah, thanks dad."

"Anyway," said Murdo, "Shall we make a start?"

At the cottage in Eglos, Sammy Pascoe was wrestling with the finer details of his own campaign. As usual on a Saturday the family were all in the tiny front room, the fire still in, sustained as it was by the apparently limitless supply of wood to which Viv had mysterious access. Maisie was sewing in her chair by the fire, while Viv tinkered with the pickup of his guitar. The Kernow Dixies had a gig that night and he needed to sort a minor interference problem. The table was shared with Sammy, who was busy at the family laptop.

"So, Mum. The coalition. What's that?"

"A bloody disaster, that's what," said Viv without looking up.

"Well it depends on your point of view," said Maisie. "A coalition is when two parties agree to work together, usually

231

because neither has enough MPs to form a government. In 2010 the Lib Dems agreed to form a government with the Conservatives. That way between them they had enough MPs to win the votes in the House of Commons."

"Hardeep says it's a reason not to vote Lib Dem."

"Yes, Labour are rather fond of saying that. That's because the coalition government brought in really big cuts in public spending, so a lot of people at the bottom of the heap had it very tough."

"To be fair that does sound pretty bad. What am I supposed to say if he keeps bringing it up?"

"Just hit him with Iraq," said Viv. "They don't like being reminded of that."

Sammy sighed. "OK so what happened in Iraq?"

"Tony Blair took us into a dodgy war that caused the death of a hell of a lot of people, a war which – incidentally – the Liberal Democrats opposed very vocally."

"How do you guys remember all this?"

"We lived through it, Son. It was a big deal at the time."

Sophie had excused herself from the day's canvassing on work grounds, but in fact her shift didn't begin until the late afternoon, and mid-morning found her on the bus to Roskear. She did not alight in the centre, however, but stayed on the bus until it had growled its way through town and emerged onto the road on which the Count House was situated. Here she got off.

She walked past the house initially, glancing up the drive at the side as she did so, noting the absence of Edward's car. She knew that both Edward and Murdo had planned to be out campaigning that morning, but she wanted to be sure the house was empty. She walked as far as the next corner and turned, then when she reached the Count House once more she opened the gate, closed it again behind her, and walked purposefully up the path.

She rang the bell and listened carefully. Silence. She turned and looked casually back towards the road. She was screened by the rhododendrons from anyone not standing directly at the gate. There was traffic passing on the main road, but otherwise she could hear nothing. She stepped into the porch and tried the door carefully, but it was locked. She looked round for places that might hide a key. There was a mat, but nothing beneath it. A large plant pot on the doorstep containing three sickly geraniums looked more promising, but when she lifted that it revealed only a small community of worms and woodlice, and she dropped it back with a grimace.

Undeterred, she walked quietly round to the back of the house, where a large rear garden was surrounded by the same high shrubbery. It could have been quite lovely with a bit of attention, but it waited in vain for its first trimming and pruning of the spring. Sophie ran her fingers over the fragile papery globes of the dead hydrangea blooms, and turned her attention to the back of the house.

The shabby, iron-framed conservatory ran the length of the rear-facing wall, and she walked cautiously towards this. She could see that inside the door to the kitchen was ajar. The door that gave access to the garden however was firmly closed. Cautiously, Sophie placed her hand on the handle and turned, then applied gentle inward pressure. The door stuck at the bottom but clearly wasn't locked. Gently she nudged the bottom of the door with her foot, and it sprang open. Quiet as a cat she stepped through the doorway and padded across the slate flags of the conservatory floor towards the kitchen.

Edward reached the end of a slightly run-down Georgian Terrace and wondered whether he had done enough to justify stopping for a coffee. He had completed two or three canvassing sessions now, and his spiel was becoming quite polished. He had met with no real hostility, certainly less than he was used to getting when he had canvassed for the Lib Dems in the past. It appeared that independents offended nobody, which was not necessarily a good sign. Lots of people expressed admiration for what he was doing, and wished him luck, though not all of these, he knew, would vote for him. Although by no means universal, by far the most common response was a polite "I'm afraid we usually vote Conservative." The expression itself implied a lack of consideration of the issues, or even the character of the candidate, that he found disheartening and more than a little irritating.

In any case his mind was not entirely on the task in hand. Anna had texted him early that morning, a light but warm message thanking him for the previous evening. This had initiated a running exchange to which Edward had only been able to contribute when he wasn't driving or with Murdo and the Doggetts. The texts were not exactly flirtatious but in some indefinable way they had moved beyond the business-like briskness that had characterised their recent interactions.

Edward checked his phone once more, but there was nothing new. Perhaps if he did the next block, then walked into town for a coffee, there would be a message awaiting him as a reward for his labours. He chuckled to himself as he crossed the road once more, and Puck's words from A Midsummer Night's Dream came to mind.

Lord, what fools these mortals be.

A mile across town from where Edward contemplated his happy progress towards romantic entanglement, Kate was standing in front of the Net Loft, poised to take a step in the opposite direction. She had seen nothing of Dave that morning, having left the flat at half past nine. The MG had been on the drive, but there had been no sign of life up on the veranda. He might be lazing in bed, or he might have gone for an early surf. He might have texted her, but he hadn't. Then again, she might have texted him, but she hadn't. It was the first Saturday morning in five months that they hadn't woken up in the same bed, and the thought of that made her feel slightly sick. How had it come to this? Perhaps viewing the Net Loft was a completely stupid idea. She could call the agents and make an excuse…

"Kate?"

She turned. A smartly dressed woman perhaps ten years older than her was crossing the road from the harbour car park.

"Hi! I'm Steph, from Kernow Lettings? Sorry I'm a few minutes late. Shall we go in?"

Kate nodded.

"Sure."

Steph produced a key and opened the front door.

"What you see out front is what you get – room for your recycling but not much else. So it's low maintenance."

"OK."

They were standing in what might generously have been called an L-shaped room, the main part of which was a little smaller than the downstairs area of the Engine House. This larger space constituted the sitting room, with the leg of the L, which ran towards the back, providing just enough room for a study area. The kitchen itself, which was next to this, occupied its own separate space. The sitting room was unfurnished, but the carpet was clean and an inoffensive mid-blue, and one or two details of the woodwork had been picked out in different shades of green and turquoise. It seemed light and cheerful enough. There was a wood-burning stove set into the chimney space. A triad of leaping dolphins adorning one wall was the only decoration. They didn't look quite right on their own.

"Does the wood-burner work?"

"I believe so, but I can double-check with the owners if you like. Kitchen's at the back. It's not huge."

She peered into the kitchen, which had all the basic appliances, and a reasonably up-to-date glass hob. Not a huge amount of cupboard space, but she could just nip out to the supermarket if she ran out of anything.

"Anywhere to dry laundry?"

"if I remember rightly there's a line up on the terrace."

They climbed the stairs, which were steep and narrow. The bedroom was small, having been partitioned at some stage to accommodate a shower room.

"It'll take a small double," said Steph. "And this cupboard on the landing does quite nicely as a wardrobe."

"Right," said Kate.

"And out here," said Steph, "Is the sun terrace."

A modern uPVC door gave out onto the flat roof above the kitchen, which was boundaried by a run of low wrought-iron railings. It was relatively private, although one or two of the neighbouring properties had what looked like bathroom windows overlooking it. The harbour, with the sea beyond, was visible from one corner.

"Right, thanks," said Kate. "That gives me an idea."

"It's small," acknowledged Steph, "but I think it's quite comfortable. And obviously the location is great. The previous tenant was here for about eighteen months, then moved up country. I think it worked OK for them."

"OK," said Kate. "I'll think about it." She stood uncertainly. This was it, then. This was the Net Loft.

"Are you all right?" asked Steph. "If you don't mind me saying so, you look a bit out of it."

"Yes, I'm fine. Thanks." said Kate, recovering herself. "I think I just need a coffee. And maybe a piece of cake. Are there any more viewings scheduled today or tomorrow?"

"Next one's Monday evening. We're closed Sunday, so unless someone comes in this afternoon…"

"All right," said Kate. I'll let you know later today."

Back at the Count House, Sophie had completed her investigation of the downstairs, with which she was already reasonably familiar. She had found little of interest, although she did spend some time looking at Edward's commissioning letter from the Queen. Then she climbed the broad stair and paused on the landing. Up until now she had felt no compunction about what she was doing, but somehow pursuing her investigations upstairs seemed morally dubious. She cautiously pushed open the first door she came too, which led to Edward's study.

She stood on the threshold, taking in the books, the desk with its map of the council ward, the boxes of leaflets. She spotted the rows of postcards above the bookshelves, and she considered these more closely, working her way around the room from left to right. Then she gave a small, involuntary intake of breath.

She pulled the chair across from the desk to the middle of the opposite wall and climbed on to it, holding the shelves for balance. She reached up and took down one of the postcards. She examined it briefly, then carefully adjusted the position of the neighbouring cards to fill the gap. She climbed down, replaced the chair, and looked carefully around the room to ensure it was exactly as she had found it.

Chapter Thirty-three

"Is it all going to be in Latin?"

Kate had imagined that her viewing of the Net Loft would result in immediate clarity as to what was the right thing to do – that she would either fall in love with it on the spot, or realise as quickly that she would only ever be miserable there. In fact neither was the case. When she viewed it, the property presented itself to her merely as a viable option – a perfectly workable solution to the problem she faced of being kicked out of her digs. She knew that if she had seen it back in September, when she was flat-hunting, and Dave Singleman was nothing more to her than one of several new departmental colleagues, she would almost certainly have taken it. Essentially, the choice was now a simple one. Sign up for the Net Loft, or commit to finding somewhere with Dave. Her moment of dreaminess at the conclusion of the viewing was merely the moment at which it became clear to her that this was the decision she needed to make.

She parted company with Steph outside the property and drifted round to the Art Gallery coffee shop. She ordered a flat white and an almond croissant, and found a seat. The café was crowded with assorted Saturday moochers and there was a buzz of chatter, punctuated by the squeals of toddlers and the frenetic exhalations of the coffee machines. She sat with her drink and weighed up her options, a process which required no soul-searching about her relationship with Dave.

Unlike him, she did not view it in purely binary terms. While he was liable to be plunged into despair when they disagreed, and to see any hiccup or friction as an existential threat to his vision of their shared future, Kate could see that their current difficulties were probably temporary, and could be worked around.

She saw now that the Engine House played its part in all this. From Kate's point of view it was aesthetically delightful and in practical terms ideal, whereas Dave had grown blasé about its charms as a building, and saw it more as being just one step short of what he really wanted, which was to cohabit properly with Kate. Despite what he had said in France, she knew that he saw any move into separate accommodation as a move in the wrong direction, a retreat from that ideal. Although the word *marriage* had never been mentioned, she was pretty sure that that was where Dave's inclinations lay. For herself, although marriage hovered around the periphery of her thinking as a not unpleasant or undesirable prospect, it seemed to belong to some remote future, and was not something she was inclined to examine or attempt to conjure in any great detail.

The Net Loft therefore represented a practical way forward. It solved her own accommodation problem, and it would force Dave to make a decision that served his own interests in that regard, rather than push him into some Kate-orientated compromise. At worst they would end up living a few miles apart – less if Dave were to buy somewhere in Newlyn - and they would see one another every day at work. If the relationship had a future, and she was still working on the assumption that it had, then there was no reason why such an arrangement should put it at risk. It would give them some space to get over their current differences, and if it turned out they couldn't, then it would make it easier to disengage from the relationship. Kate's pragmatic nature meant that she was able to contemplate this eventuality without the fear that she was willing it into being.

She finished her coffee and left the noise of the café to call the letting agent.

That morning Dave had listened to the receding note of the Fiat's exhaust as Kate drove in for her appointment at the

Net Loft, before emerging from his upstairs apartment to head for the golf course. The surf was good, but surfing was now an activity he associated with Kate, as did others of the beach crowd, who might enquire after her absence.

Golf, on the other hand, held some of the consolations of the man-cave.

He hung around the clubhouse drinking coffee and reading the magazines until the rush of morning games had subsided. He declined one or two offers to make up a four. When the first tee was quiet he set out for a round on his own, taking his time, sometimes playing two balls, and practising a tricky chip or a certain length of putt several times if there was nobody behind him. He found it surprisingly straightforward not to think about Kate and the possible consequences of her appointment with the letting agent. He knew that probably he was in some kind of denial, but what of that? He felt powerless to influence the course of events.

He lingered over a late sandwich lunch and a lager in the clubhouse once his round was over, but eventually there was nothing to be done but to head back to the Engine House and find out what decision had been made. On his return the yellow Fiat was back in its usual place. He considered calling in at the downstairs flat, but a kind of pride prevented him. Let Kate come to him to make her report.

He didn't have long to wait. Within five minutes, he heard her footsteps on the outside stair. He wondered if she would just walk in, but she knocked, just as he had done at her flat the previous evening. He wasn't really surprised. It was all of a piece with the script they seemed to be following.

He opened the door and gestured to her to come in, which she did. He didn't sit down, and neither did she. She stayed only long enough to tell him that she had decided after some consideration to take the Net Loft. He had merely nodded, and said "OK. Fair enough." He didn't make any move to draw her in, because he didn't feel that an evening spent in each other's company was what the situation required, or what he wanted. She asked him what he had been up to that day, and he told her. She stayed for a few further minutes of awkward conversation, then she left.

On Sunday she disappeared for the day, walking the coastal path out west. On Monday, without discussion, they took their own cars to school.

Dave now threw himself into running the mock election, arriving early at school each morning, and staying late. By this point the project was in full swing, and his breaks and lunchtimes were spent either in coaching students or supervising hustings, or in earnest conversations with Anderson, the Director of Digital Strategy, about how best the school network could be used to support the election. He was sustained by a steady stream of complimentary comments from other members of staff, particularly those who had candidates in their forms, and he responded to these in an upbeat and cheerful manner, so that friends and colleagues remained oblivious to the rift in his relationship with Kate. He took a grim pleasure from what he imagined to be Anton Killick's chagrin at how well it was all going.

And it was all going very well. The students had by now all produced manifestos, which in the case of the mainstream candidates were simplified versions of their parties' headline policies. These condensed statements of political philosophy, which were limited to one side of A4, were discussed and dissected during form periods. The independent candidates, Donovan Doggett and Toby Trott, had to fall back on their own invention, and an appeal to some practical application of their policies to the lives of the student voters.

Toby Trott found early in his campaign that there was a limit to the number of different ways you could advocate the joys of own clothes and ice-cream, and was working hard on expanding his portfolio of policy ideas. He had a small but committed campaign team of Year Nine jokers – the same crew, largely, who had participated in the legendary luggage compartment break-in on a coach-trip to London the previous term - and this gang could often be seen at breaktimes debating which policies should be added to his manifesto. The hot word among the lobby correspondents of Year Nine was that retention of mobile phones (currently banned in class) and skate-boarding as a games option were soon to be added to the policy offer.

Donkey had spent some time discussing with Murdo how the concept of "Second Chances" could be expanded into a coherent political programme. Murdo had some sympathy with the notion, having several times in his young life messed up in a variety of contexts, and having benefited from those who spoke up for him, when others believed he should be punished more severely for his transgressions. They agreed that probably the strongest approach was a highly personal one, with Donkey setting the election out as a milestone on his own path to redemption.

"The thing is," Donkey had said, a little shamefaced, "Although I've been trying really hard this term, there's quite a lot of kids who are, well… I suppose you might say… a bit wary of me."

"Oh aye. And why's that?"

"Well, because I haven't been all that nice to them in the past."

"Well this is the ideal time to convince them that yer a changed man," said Murdo. "When was the last time you 'weren't all that nice' to somebody?"

"I did threaten to punch Sammy Pascoe's head for him a few weeks back," said Donkey. "But he's standing for one of the other parties, so he's not going to vote for me anyway. And he is a bit of a twat."

"Not really the point though, is it," said Murdo. "I think you need to make a personal appeal to the electorate. A kind of *mea culpa.*"

"A *mea* what?"

"It's Latin. It basically means "My bad"."

"You mean like a kind of confession? Is it all going to be in Latin?"

"Fortunately not," said Murdo. "The first rule of political literature is that it needs to be accessible to voters of limited education."

Amid all Dave's activity and the affirmation that it generated, the conviction grew, like a dark fungus at the back of a damp cupboard, that his relationship with Kate was on the skids, and that there might well be nothing he could do about it. He knew that he should be making some kind of effort to address the problem, but it was so much easier to concentrate on something that had every prospect of being a success than on something that seemed about to fail. Of course, he knew that in terms of importance there was no comparison between the two – a successful mock election would bring him credit in the school community for a year or perhaps more, and would of course set him up well for his new position as Head of Year, but that was nothing compared to what he stood to lose if he allowed Kate to slip through his fingers. The truth was, however, that he felt she had already gone.

Kate was puzzled and a little concerned at the contrast between Dave's almost manic enthusiasm for the activities associated with the mock election, and his morose and distant manner with her. She understood that he hadn't wanted her to find somewhere on her own, but now that she had taken the decision she was so occupied with the practicalities of the actual move, which she had planned for the following weekend, and so confident that she had taken a positive step which in the long run would be better for both of them, that she found herself without the patience necessary to draw him out of what she increasingly saw as a sulk. She sat with him once or twice at lunch, where his manner was much more normal, but she put that down to the presence of others and the fact that he was surrounded by his aura of mock-election glory.

On one occasion he arrived back at the Engine House a few seconds behind her, and she waited while he got out of the MG.

"Fancy a cup of tea?" she asked cheerfully.

"Um thanks, but I've got masses to do."

"I am still your girlfriend, you know. Unless you've broken up with me and just haven't bothered to tell me."

At this he had looked pained.

"Kate, please. I know. It's just – with the election and everything – I haven't had time to get my head round your…decision."

"OK. Well that's fair enough. All the same a hug might be nice, just now and again."

"Um, yes. Of course."

He put down his brief case, and they held one another for a while on the gravelled parking area.

"That's fine, thanks," said Kate. "I'll let you go."

"Sorry," said Dave. "It'll be better when the election's over."

She wondered if he had even registered that by that time she might well have moved out.

Chapter Thirty-four

"My horse is sick"

Edward's campaign was also in full flood. Although he was back at school, it was light now until well after eight in the evening, and with Murdo's encouragement he did a couple of hours of door-knocking each night. He chose the areas where he felt personal contact was most likely to lead to voters turning out for him, and generally speaking he was encouraged by the response. He had also, as Anna predicted, been contacted by several members of the local party who declared themselves disenchanted with the decision not to stand a Liberal candidate, and who offered to help deliver leaflets. All this boosted Edward's ability to reach the electorate, and added to the growing sense that whether or not he actually won the election, he would not be disgraced by polling only a handful of votes.

The campaign activity was taking its toll on his schoolwork, and unmarked exercise books were starting to pile up. He had, however, at Dave Singleman's request, led a lunchtime session talking to the candidates about what it was like to be standing in the actual campaign, and when the Head got wind of this he asked Edward to repeat the talk in an abbreviated form at a whole school assembly. In this way he felt that his candidacy was making some contribution to school life, and giving the

Head and Frances some ammunition to use against complaints from over-vigilant parents.

In theory he was meant to be overseeing the campaign of Donovan Doggett, but as the boy seemed to be behaving more or less sensibly, and not to be engaging in any form of voter intimidation, Edward was happy to maintain a light touch. He settled on an arrangement whereby Donkey checked in with him at the beginning and end of each week to discuss any problems. In any case it was clear that the lad was in close contact with Murdo, a relationship which, as far as Edward could see, was of benefit to both of them.

The other part of that alliance was also working well, the Penhale estate having been delivered without incident. Earlier in the week he had received a call from Isaac Doggett, who was keen to tell him how much he was enjoying the delivery, and how he would be happy to do more if there was more to be done, on the same terms. He explained that he had been away for some time (Edward was perfectly aware of the nature of the absence, but didn't say so) and that it had been a nice way of getting to know some of his neighbours again. He finished by assuring Edward that he had put in a positive word for him wherever he could. Edward, who rather liked Isaac's down to earth, chapel-tinged earnestness, thanked him, and invited him along to the hustings, which was the next major event on the campaign's horizon.

The hustings was scheduled for the end of the week in Eglos Village Hall, and Edward viewed the event with some trepidation. He knew that on paper he presented as a credible candidate, but it was dawning on him that there were a number of local issues where his knowledge was likely to lag behind that of some of the other candidates. On planning, for example, while he knew the basics, Ivan Gummow would be able to run rings round him, and he needed to be better informed about the precise nature of the threat to the Minor Injuries Unit. Mallinson would no doubt be well up to speed on that. Had Edward been standing for the Liberal Democrats he would have been fully briefed by councillors who knew exactly what was going on, but as an independent he was expected to do his own research.

On Tuesday night he rang Anna. They had been in regular text contact since their last meeting, but this was the first time

245

they had spoken by phone. Her voice when she picked up was cool and measured, and he found his heart beating slightly faster.

"Hi, it's me."

"Hello." For a moment he was at a loss, then he said,

"I just thought I'd give you a call."

"Well…it's nice to hear from you."

"You sound very sexy on the phone."

"I try to sound professional."

"Well, I think perhaps that's it."

He wasn't sure if she was displeased at this line of chat.

"Is this an okay time to talk?"

"I'm just cooking supper. I've got a few minutes."

Perhaps that explained her slight reticence.

"Is everything okay with you?"

"Yes…more or less. Slightly tricky conversation with Julian about the kids. What about you?"

"I'm getting anxious about this hustings. I could do with an inside track on a couple of issues."

"Can I call you back later tonight?"

"Yes sure. About eight?"

"Ideal. Talk then."

When Anna called back later that evening she sounded notably more relaxed. He was struck again by how much he loved her voice. They spoke for over an hour about issues that were likely to come up at the hustings, and he was surprised to find that even a conversation about planning regulations could carry a faint erotic charge. Then they talked more generally about her situation, and her plans for the future, unformed though they were. She said that of course she intended to carry on practising, that she found work a welcome distraction.

"I'm sorry about my comment earlier, about you sounding sexy on the phone," said Edward. "I do see that that might have been regarded as a bit crass. I wouldn't want you to think that I don't respect your professionalism."

"Oh. That's all right. It's just – you get a bit of that from time to time as a female lawyer, and it's pretty tedious. And I was feeling a bit tired."

Edward was in his study. The door was closed. Murdo he knew was in his own quarters in the basement.

"How are you feeling now?"

"Well… I'm feeling more relaxed. I've opened a bottle of wine and I've got my feet up."

"I can hear Mozart. The third violin concerto?"

"Yes."

"And you're alone."

"Yes. All on my own. What about you?"

"Well, Murdo's here, but he's occupying himself in his dungeon. I'm feeling a bit restless."

"Ah. Restless."

"It's only nine. I could be round in fifteen minutes if you wanted some company."

"I think I'm quite happy with Mozart tonight. Thank you."

Eglos village hall was not one of those that had benefited from an exciting, lottery funded, post-millennium makeover, and thus it retained that smell of musty canvas and floor polish that characterised a building whose last significant refurbishment had been in the mid-1950s. It was, however, filling up fast, and energetic gentlemen of a certain age were wheeling out extra chairs, tubular framed models with sagging cloth seats of a colour that might once have been chocolate brown. These were, in fact, surprisingly comfortable.

Polling day was only six days away, and since the list of candidates had been published the level of interest in the campaign had increased considerably, with both local papers and even Radio Cornwall reporting upon the by-election. Edward sat now, as alphabetical order dictated he should, at the extreme right of the low platform at the far end of the hall. His fellow candidates had all turned up and were arrayed beside him for the audience's scrutiny. He wondered if the Eglos parish clerk, who was chairing the meeting, would vary the order in which they responded to the questions, which had been submitted by the audience in advance. If she didn't, then Edward would be last each time, which could be useful if the questions were particularly awkward, but might make it difficult to come up with anything original if they were straightforward.

Technical support for the evening was being provided by Pascoe and Son, and Viv had rigged a couple of spotlights from the lighting bar (a piece of equipment normally only used once a year for the village panto). These were not particularly intense, and certainly added to the atmosphere, but they did make it difficult to see much beyond the first half a dozen rows. Team Tremenhere - Murdo, Sophie and the Doggetts - had set up camp three rows back, and elsewhere he could see two or three of the local party members who had helped with delivery. Edward was surprised to find that he felt slightly nervous. He found that he was unable to look at Anna, who was in the front row.

The parish clerk took her place in the central seat and tapped the microphone. There was an immediate squeal of feedback, followed by laughter from the audience, at which the clerk looked cross. Sammy Pascoe leapt forward to make a minor adjustment to the positioning of the mic, and nodded his encouragement to the clerk to try again.

"Good evening ladies and gentlemen." No feedback this time. "Thank you all very much for coming this evening to our hustings meeting, which is, I believe, the only one being held for this by-election. We're very pleased to welcome you to Eglos Village Hall. The format of the evening is straightforward. We have had a good number of questions tabled in advance, and I will be putting each of these to all six of our candidates. If we do have any time left after that I may allow questions from the floor, but again, these should be put to all candidates, rather than targeted at anyone in particular. However, I'd like to start by giving each of our candidates one minute to introduce themselves and say a little about their background. We'll begin with Esme Aitchieson."

Edward listened with interest to the introductions from his place at the end of the row. Esme was softly spoken but articulate. The young Conservative was confident and clear. He had, he said, a Cornish aunt, and had spent many happy holidays here as a child. This, thought Edward, would be unlikely to cut much ice. Ivan Gummow, the planning man, sounded rather pompous and self-satisfied. He was of course on his home turf, and Edward wondered if the clerk would show him any favour. Mallinson had a northern accent and gave a factual and unshowy introduction. No doubt he was keeping his powder dry. The Mebyon Kernow candidate greeted everyone in Cornish. Then it was his turn.

"Good evening everybody, and to Mr Penberthy, *gorthugher da* to you too. And by the way *ow margh yw Klav*. My name is Edward Tremenhere and I'm standing as an independent, although as some of you may know, my family has been involved in Liberal politics in this part of Cornwall for something like a hundred and fifty years. I teach in St Petroc's school in this ward, and have done for two decades. I'm also a former naval officer, although that was many years ago. I'm standing because I think the Penhale and Eglos ward needs a strong independent voice, someone not tied to any of the main parties, who can be an advocate for all those who live here. I hope to convince you this evening that I can be that person."

A respectful round of clapping followed these introductions. The Mebyon Kernow candidate looked at Edward suspiciously.

"Thank you, said the clerk." And now to our first question. "How do the candidates intend to prevent the threatened closure of the Minor Injuries Unit at Penzance hospital? I think we'll start this time at the other end of the table. Edward Tremenhere".

Chapter Thirty-five

"A hat festival"

After the hustings was over the candidates shook hands, and there followed a brief period of milling around while the hall emptied. Edward thought it had gone rather well. At least there had been no obvious disasters. One or two of the audience came up to him and wished him luck, and one wild-eyed woman in rainbow harem pants and a parka asked him earnestly what he was going to do about the UFOs that she saw regularly from her bedroom window. Edward said that regrettably, keeping the skies free of alien space-ships was probably beyond what he could be expected to achieve on the Council, but that Mr Gummow, who was chair of planning for the parish, and who was standing over there with the clerk, might know more about the problem. The woman wandered off in that direction.

Anna, who had kept her distance throughout the evening, was talking to the Green candidate, and Murdo, who had been taking notes on his laptop throughout, stood off to one side with Sophie. Edward didn't think he looked particularly pleased.

"Nice one, Sir," said Donkey, ". You was very…what's the word? Articulate. Me and dad have got to catch the bus now."

"Right, Donovan. Well, thank you for coming. You too Isaac."

"I thought you did all right there," said Isaac. You was good on the hospital. One thing I'm wondering though."

"What's that?"

"What did you say to that MK bloke? He looked proper taken aback."

"Oh…that's just a bit of Cornish my grandmother taught me. It means "My horse is sick.""

"I thought it was something about a horse. Why'd'you say that?"

"It doesn't do any harm to show you know a bit of Cornish. And I was interested to see if Mr Penberthy understood it."

"And did he?"

"Actually he did. On his way out he told me to try changing its diet."

Isaac roared with laughter, and gripped Edward by the arm. "*Keslowena.*"

"*Grassow,*" said Edward, and watched father and son, the one tall and gangly, the other square and solid, leave the hall.

Sammy Pascoe had been busy de-rigging the sound system, but once the Doggetts had left, he too came over.

"Nice work, Sir."

"Thank you Sammy. And thank you for your excellent work on the sound. How's your own campaign going?"

"All right, I think. Mr Armitage is helping me. We've got our hustings on Tuesday."

"Yes of course, Well, good luck with that."

"Cheers, Sir."

Murdo sidled across.

"If you've finished with talking to yer adoring public, can we get a shift on?" he said. "Me and Sophie's starving."

So far, Murdo had passed no comment upon the proceedings. Once they were out of the car park and driving back to the Count House. Edward said,

"So, how did I do?"

"I thought you were very good," said Sophie. "You explained your wishy-washy liberal ideas very clearly." Wishy-washy was a new expression she had learned from Murdo.

"Thank you Sophie. I'll take that as a compliment. What about you, Chief Campaign Strategist?"

"You did all right," said Murdo. "It wasn't a disaster. That's the main thing."

"That's hardly a ringing endorsement."

"Well…I dunno. It's just – I mean it's one thing running a campaign, which ah'm happy to do, and ah'm getting paid an' that, but hearing you on a platform next to the Green woman, and even Mallinson, you did come across a bit like Centrist Dad, if you know what I mean. And you were mebbe just a bit pleased with yourself. All this Lloyd-George-knew-my-father crap."

"Right." said Edward. "Now I'm feeling a bit deflated."

"Murdo, I think you are being unkind," said Sophie. "Surely the point is that Edward knew what he was talking about, and he came across as somebody competent who would work hard for the electorate."

"Aye, fair enough," said Murdo. "Ah'm just used to a bit more passion from ma political icons."

"I never promised you passion, Murdo," said Edward, as they pulled into the drive at the Count House. "Competence and integrity are my selling points. And for what it's worth, I was reasonably pleased. My main goal was not to get caught out, and I don't think I was. Anyway. Let's get the supper on and open a bottle of wine. I see you've brought your accordion, Sophie."

Sophie had indeed brought her accordion, and while Edward set about fixing supper, she played softly and, it seemed to Edward, a little pensively, standing to one side of the kitchen. Edward had decided that as Anna was coming round, pizza would not do, and he had made a stew the night before, which was soon in the oven, with potatoes boiling on the hob. Murdo sat at the table with his laptop, glancing up wistfully from time to time at Sophie.

The doorbell rang.

"You expecting somebody?" said Murdo. "I thought we were gonnay have a strategy meetin'."

"The strategy meeting is hereby cancelled," said Edward. "Tonight we dine with the Chair of the local Liberal Democrats, who is a particular friend of mine." He turned down the heat on the potatoes and went to answer the door.

"Ah canny believe this," said Murdo flatly. "May Day, when the workers of the world unite, and I'm eating posh food in a big house with a bunch of liberals."

Edward led Anna into the kitchen.

"Anna, I'd like to introduce two of my campaign team. This is Sophie, who comes over occasionally from St Ives to help us, and Murdo, who is the brains behind the campaign, and lives in the basement. Murdo, Sophie, this is Anna, a long-standing friend and a fellow Liberal."

"Hello both," said Anna. "Please don't stop playing Sophie. I could hear the music from the porch – it sounded really lovely. Where shall I put this?" She was carrying a large glass bowl containing a rather fine trifle.

"Thank you," said Sophie, and she scrutinised Anna coolly for a moment. She took a sip of wine then began a new tune. Edward took the dessert bowl from Anna and found a space for it in the fridge.

"Awright," said Murdo, and looked up briefly before continuing to tap at his laptop.

"Murdo and Sophie are both socialists," said Edward, "so I have to keep a close eye on them."

"Murdo and Sophie are both young," said Anna. "I was a member of the Labour party when I was their age."

"I didn't know that," said Edward, passing her a glass of wine. "What happened?"

"Tony Blair won the leadership after John Smith's death. I didn't much care for him. I gave up politics for a while, then I got involved with the Lib Dems at the time of the Iraq war. I had a lot of time for Charlie Kennedy."

Murdo stopped typing and looked up.

"Right enough, he probably was tae the left of Blair. What do you reckon to the coalition?"

Anna considered before answering.

"Well I understand why we did it – the economy was in a mess and Labour were never going to play ball with us. Also we're a party that believes in co-operative government. But I didn't support it at the time, and obviously it turned into a bit of a disaster for us."

"Not as big a disaster as it wiz fur the millions who suffered under austerity," said Murdo.

"I'm sure that's true," said Anna. "But don't forget Labour's proposed spending plans were just as tough."

Murdo made no reply to this, but he closed his laptop.

"It smells lovely," said Anna. "Is there anything I can do to help?"

"No, it's nearly ready," said Edward. "Murdo just needs to move his stuff, and then we can put out some cutlery and napkins. Oh, and we could do with glasses and a jug of water."

Sophie slipped her accordion from her shoulders and fetched the cutlery from the dresser. Murdo cleared his laptop from the table and attended to the water. Edward smiled to himself as he drained the potatoes. Anna had survived round one.

When they were all seated and the stew was served, Anna said,

"Well Edward, I thought you did pretty well tonight. And I'd like to propose a toast that I think we can all support. To beating the Tories!"

"To beating the Tories," returned the echo. Even Murdo joined in.

Edward was not a particularly adventurous cook, but he had a few signature dishes that he knew worked well, and this stew, made with beef from the organic farm at Cusgarne, was one of them. There was lots of it, and when the second bottle of wine was opened, the disparate group slowly relaxed into one another's company. Sophie, Edward thought, was in an odd mood, uncharacteristically quiet. Murdo however seemed to have decided that there was no point in niggling, and told them funny stories about his early political adventures with the Nationalists. They dissected the other candidates, and agreed that the most competent performances of the evening had probably come from Edward, Mallinson, and Esme Aitchieson. The Tory, it was decided, although clearly a Bright Young Thing, was possibly a bit too fresh-faced and lacking in local knowledge to make much of an impact. Sophie however declared him to be *assez mignon*, at which Murdo looked up sharply.

"What's assymeenyong?"

"You know, kind of cute," she replied.

"Aw right," said Murdo. "A cute little Tory."

"I'm not saying I would kiss him," said Sophie, with a straight face.

"No, well, I thought…ach never mind."

It felt, thought Edward, a bit like a family meal, with Murdo and Sophie like bickering teenage children.

By the time they had moved onto Anna's trifle it was clear that nobody was going to be driving that evening. Anna could have walked home at a stretch, and Sophie might have caught a late bus, but somehow neither of these seemed likely outcomes. After the trifle Edward made coffee, and brought out a bottle of single malt.

"Goodness," said Anna, you'll need to pour me into a taxi."

"There's beds made up here," said Edward. "Nobody has to rush off."

They moved through to the lounge, and Sophie once more picked up her accordion. Edward put a match to the small fire he had lit against the slight chill of the evening. Sophie didn't take any whisky herself, protesting that she hadn't yet acquired the taste, and instead played softly while the others enjoyed theirs. The music and the firelight made conversation unnecessary, and for a while the four of them just sat. Then Anna said,

"Do you celebrate May Day where you come from, Sophie?"

"Oh yes," said Sophie. "In my village we would get up before dawn, and go into the woods to pick *muguets* - the little white flowers, I do not know what you call them…"

"Lily of the Valley," said Edward.

"*Oui, c'est ca*. And then we give them to family and friends. It brings good luck."

"You'll see lots of Lily of the Valley at Flora Day," said Anna.

"I don't think I've ever asked you whereabouts in France you're from," said Edward.

"I think you won't have heard of it," said Sophie, looking at him with her direct gaze. "It is a little village about twenty kilometres south of Caussade."

Edward got up and poked the fire.

"I think I've been to Caussade," he said. "Isn't that where they have a hat festival?"

255

"That's right," said Sophie "Were you there for long?"

"I only went for the day. It was quite a long time ago. Shall I stick another log on this or are folk thinking about turning in?"

"I'll head for bed soon," said Anna. "But it was nice to have a fire. Firelight and whisky belong together somehow."

"Ah've never been tae France," said Murdo.

"Perhaps you will come and visit me in Paris," said Sophie, who had stopped playing, and was watching Edward as he attended to the fire. Then she said,

"Edward, where is my bedroom, please? I too am tired."

Edward showed the girls to their rooms, which were both on the same floor as his own. He was quietly encouraged that Anna had agreed to stay, and not a little hopeful that the separate rooms thing might be for appearances only. Sophie's relationship with Murdo he knew to be officially platonic, so he was unsurprised that she didn't join him in the basement. He dug out clean towels and showed them where the bathroom was, then went back downstairs to the kitchen. There was no sign of Murdo.

He turned on the radio and found some quiet classical music, then set about clearing away the dishes. He half-expected Anna to reappear and offer to lend a hand, but after some creaking and plumbing noises from upstairs, everything went quiet. Still, all might not be entirely lost on that front. His thoughts returned again to that strange sense of a family gathering, and in the mellow state induced by the music, the whisky and the lateness of the hour, he reflected that in different ways he cared a great deal for the three people who were sleeping under his roof that night.

The house was silent as he climbed the stair, and even on the landing there was no sound to be heard from either of the other occupied rooms. He used the bathroom and retired to bed, but lay a while, partly simply to enjoy the moment, but also in case Anna had been listening for him to come upstairs. He was at the point of giving up on this, and settling down to sleep, when there was a soft tap on his bedroom door.

His heart beating, he swung himself out of bed and crossed the room. Softly, in anticipation, he turned the handle.

But it was Sophie who stood, fully clothed, on the landing. He started to speak, but she raised a warning finger to her lips.

Chapter Thirty-six

"Please call me when you get this"

"Edward, I need to talk to you," she said quietly. "Can we please go downstairs?"

"Yes, of course. You go down to the lounge. I'll just get my dressing gown. Is something the matter?"

But she had already turned and was picking her way downstairs like a cat.

Edward joined her in the front room, where the embers of the fire still glowed in the grate. She had turned on one of the large table lamps and was standing by the mantelpiece. Now that the initial shock of her appearance had worn off, Edward thought she seemed agitated. He closed the door behind him and perched on the arm of the settee.

"Sophie what is all this? Are you unwell? I can fetch Anna if you like."

"No, I'm quite all right thank you, but there is something I need to say. And I also need to give you this."

For a moment Edward was reminded of the early days of the accordion music at the window, that sense of a destiny unfolding. This, then, was the moment. He waited.

Sophie handed Edward the postcard she had taken from his study. It was a picture postcard of a hat, a straw boater. There was no writing on the back. He took it from her.

"I think this is from Caussade, yes?"

"Yes, it's from Caussade. Where did you get it?"

"From your study."

"I see. And when were you in my study?"

"That is not important. Why have you kept this?"

"Look, Sophie, I'm not sure what you're getting at, but as far as I can see you've been snooping around my house, going through my personal possessions. Unless you're prepared to tell me what this is about, I'm not inclined to put up with an interrogation into the bargain."

She said nothing, but she was watching him closely. Then, "I think that you may be my father."

Edward looked taken aback.

"Your father? I don't think that's possible."

"You were in Caussade, near the village where my mother, Anne-Marie Bourdais, was living, twenty-two years ago. She had a brief affair with an Englishman called Tremenhere. It is not a common name. I am the result of that affair."

Edward paused, and considered for a moment. Then he poured himself a whisky from the bottle that was still on the table, and sat in one of the armchairs.

"OK. This is clearly not going to be a short conversation. Would you like a drink?"

Sophie shook her head.

"Then could you perhaps sit down? I'll tell you what I know, and you tell me what you know, or think you know, and perhaps we can straighten this out."

Sophie moved to the settee. She looked suddenly tired. Edward spoke.

"It is true that I was in Central France around that time. I had left the school where I was teaching following a minor scandal involving a younger male colleague. You see, I'm…not especially interested in women."

He waited, watching her face.

"I think you are quite interested in Anna."

"Anna is an old friend."

Sophie said nothing.

"I have no memory of meeting anybody named Anne-Marie. There was a Jean-Michel for a while, but I don't imagine you want to hear about him."

"What about this postcard? You wouldn't have kept it if it didn't mean something to you."

259

"As I said, I visited Caussade for the day. The hat festival was on at the time. I bought the card as a souvenir, and I rather like it. As you will know, if you've been in my study, there are rather a lot of postcards. I can assure you they are not souvenirs of my sexual conquests. If they were, there would be many fewer of them."

"The hat festival is in August. I will be twenty-one later this month."

Edward shrugged. "You must see that proves nothing."

For a moment she stared at him, and he met her gaze steadily.

"Look Sophie, if you were my daughter, I would be thrilled. I don't have any children of my own. But as I did not have sexual relations with any women during my time in France, it simply isn't possible. What else did your mother tell you? Has she any details of this supposed encounter?"

Sophie seemed to collapse a little. She said nothing, and Edward realised with a shock that she was silently weeping. He considered going to her on the settee, but cold caution restrained him. He waited for her to bring herself under control.

"My mother was killed in a car accident last year. She had always told me that my father was an Englishman, a very handsome, educated man, who seemed to her to be well bred, though she knew nothing about him. She said it had been – just the once."

"I'm very sorry to hear of your mother's death. That must have been a great shock."

"She had always told me she did not know the man's name, but when I was sorting out her affairs with the help of my aunt, I came across this piece of paper. It was in her jewellery box."

She passed Edward a scrap of paper, no bigger that the postcard. In handwritten biro it said

E V Tremenhere RN.

Edward looked at it for a moment, then handed it back.

"Sophie, this is very strange. These are my initials. But do you know what the letters after my name signify?"

She nodded. "They are an abbreviation for Royal Navy."

"They are," said Edward. "But I left the Navy several years before I went to France. And I wasn't in the habit of introducing myself to people in that manner. Your mother could have got this from any one of a number of public documents – the Navy List, The Daily Telegraph, even. Don't you see?"

The door opened, and Anna came in.

"Is everything all right?"

"I think so," said Edward. "Sophie was upset about something but I think we've sorted it out now. We're just heading back upstairs."

Sophie rose from the settee and crossed the room. She passed Anna and Edward without looking at them and they heard her climb the stair.

"What was all that about?" said Anna.

"Oh...something and nothing," said Edward. "An odd idea that Sophie had got into her head. I'll tell you about it in the morning, but right now I'm shattered."

Edward went back to bed, but he could not sleep. He was racked with confusion and guilt. The details he had given Sophie of his brief time in Caussade were true in almost every regard except for one. He had, in fact, had a sexual encounter with a woman – one of a small number of affairs that he had enjoyed with both men and women in the course of his three years in the country. It had been brief, and sweet, and quickly forgotten, for he was only passing through on his way to the south.

Even now it was hard to recall the exact circumstances. He had been with a group of other young people, some English, but there were also Americans and a couple of Scandinavians. They had all been charmed by the hat festival, and stayed on for the dancing in the evening. It had been gloriously warm. They drank and laughed. Without any real effort on his part he had found himself paired off with a girl – a few years younger than himself, and they had walked in the public park in the summer dusk. There had been a moon, and the gardens were full of courting couples. They had lain down on his jacket behind a border whose flowers spilled scent out into the evening, while the sound of the band drifted over from the town centre.

Had her name been Anne-Marie? He couldn't recall. They hadn't talked much, but presumably they had exchanged first names. In those days he would have probably introduced himself as Ed. He didn't think he would have said anything about having been in the Navy. Where would she have got details like his exact initials? And what would the chances have been of her spelling his surname correctly, unless she had seen it written down. Perhaps she had got it from a newspaper. Any local girl who had got herself knocked up after the festive dancing might have constructed such a fiction.

Twenty-two years on, he couldn't clearly picture her face. But she had been blonde, he remembered that. In his mind she was still a young woman, which made the fact of her death the more shocking.

A combination of these uncertainties, a degree of indignation at Sophie's snooping, and a certain wariness born of ancient persecution had led him instinctively to his denial. But the brutal truth was that what Sophie had alleged, while by no means certain, was perfectly possible. He drifted off to sleep a few hours before dawn, and when he awoke, it was with the conviction that he must tell Sophie what he knew. If necessary a paternity test would settle the matter. He had been speaking no less than the truth when he said he would be happy to acknowledge her as his daughter. But that would need to be established beyond doubt.

He scrabbled for his watch on the bedside table. It was a quarter to seven. He put on his dressing gown and opened the bedroom door. The landing was quiet. He crossed to Sophie's room and knocked softly. There was no response. He knocked again, louder this time, and eased open the door.

The room was unoccupied. There was no sign of Sophie or her things. The bed was made up, and on it was a sheet of A4, with his name, including his initials and the RN suffix, just as it had appeared on the scrap of paper that she had found in her mother's jewellery box.

He snatched it up and turned it over. On the other side it read:

Dear Edward

I do not know whether I have made a terrible mistake, or whether you are indeed my father, and do not wish to acknowledge me. My instinct tells me it may be the second, but whichever of these is true, I do not think I want to see you again. If I am wrong, I am truly sorry for the embarrassment I have caused, and for entering your house without permission.

Sophie Bourdais

Edward stood staring at the note for some seconds, deeply moved. He looked at his watch again. Seven o'clock. The earliest bus she could have caught passed the house at 6.00 am. If she had taken that she would be back in St Ives by now. Which hotel had she said she worked at? Murdo would presumably know, but Murdo would be deep in slumber, and Edward had never, since his tenant's arrival, ventured down into his subterranean lair.

In a state of agitation he dressed, and as he did so he realised that Murdo would almost certainly have Sophie's number on his phone. In that case, he really had no option. He took the broad wooden staircase two at a time and slowed only as he turned down into the darkness of the basement stairwell. He knocked on Murdo's door, then opened it without waiting for an answer. A little light came down from the sunken window, illuminating a scene of surprising order. The room was tidy, and reasonably clean. Murdo's clothes were folded neatly on a chair, and Murdo himself was spread naked, face down on across the bed, snoring softly. As his eyes adjusted to the light Edward made out the line of downy red hair on the boy's back.

"Murdo!" he hissed urgently. "Murdo, wake up!"

Murdo groaned and reached out for the duvet that lay crumpled at the side of the bed. With a certain ambivalence Edward saw him pull it across to cover the lower part of his body. Probably that made things easier. He crossed to the bed and shook the boy's shoulder firmly. With a start, Murdo awoke and blinked uncomprehendingly for a moment. Then,

"Edward! What the fuck…?"

"Murdo, I'm very sorry to intrude. I'll explain later. But I need Sophie's phone number. I need you to call her now."

"What…whassatime?"

"It's just gone seven. Sophie's run off. It's a long story, but she…I'm worried about her. I have some information that she needs. Look…can I just have your phone?"

Murdo sat up. "Uh…it's over there, on the charger."

Edward followed Murdo's gaze and saw the phone connected to its cable on the chest of drawers.

"Givvus it here. You need the code."

He disconnected the phone and tossed it to Murdo, who punched a few buttons and handed it back.

"It's ringing."

Edward put it to his ear, but it cut to the answerphone. He thought for a moment, then said,

"Sophie, it's Edward. I need to speak to you again. What I said to you last night wasn't the full story. Please call me when you get this. I'm on Murdo's phone just now, but I'm going to text you my number shortly."

He returned the phone to its charger.

"Not the full story?" said Murdo. "All very mysterious."

"Yes, it is a bit," said Edward. "I'm sorry, but I can't explain just now. And I'm sorry for crashing into your room. Could you send me Sophie's number? Oh and one more thing. What's the name of her hotel?"

"The Porthmeor," said Murdo, as he forwarded the contact to Edward's phone. "It's the big one just up from the station."

"Right," said Edward. "Thank you. You can go back to sleep now."

He closed Murdo's door and returned to the kitchen. He sent a brief follow-up text to Sophie so that she had his number, and began to feel calmer. He had done all he reasonably could at that hour of the morning. He would have some breakfast, then call the hotel, and if necessary he would drive over there to find her.

Chapter Thirty-seven

"Anna Parminter, of Parminter and Holroyd Solicitors"

Anna appeared downstairs a little after eight. Edward told her briefly about Sophie's story, and his own less than honest initial reaction. She made no comment, but fixed herself some cereal, which she sat munching reflectively. There was no sign of Murdo. Despite the excitement, he appeared to have taken to heart Edward's suggestion that he should go back to sleep.

At half past eight Edward rang the Porthmeor hotel, and was told that Sophie was not due to start her shift till that afternoon. He left a message that she should contact him as soon as was convenient, then he rang her again from his own phone. Once more it went straight to voicemail, and Edward's unease returned. She might simply be ignoring him because she was angry, or she might be catching up on sleep. It was all too easy, however, to imagine her pacing in a state of despair along the cliff tops.

When his call to the hotel produced no further information, Anna pushed her cereal bowl to one side.

"Sophie might well be vulnerable," she said. "I think you need to find her. At least make sure she's gone back to the hotel."

"I think so too," said Edward. "I'm going to drive over there now. Would you come with me?"

"I'm supposed to be meeting somebody for coffee at 11," said Anna. "But I can cancel that. I'd appreciate if we stopped by my house on the way so I can freshen up a bit. It'll only take me five minutes."

A quarter of an hour later they were on their way to St Ives. They took Anna's Golf on the basis that Edward could always find his way back by train or bus. Anna seemed to have little to say, and by way of making conversation, Edward said,

"Have you had much to do with paternity claims? In your professional life, I mean?"

"I've dealt with a couple. They're relatively straightforward when the child, as it were, is an adult, and where the adult doesn't have their own family. In theory, if Sophie were to prove paternity, she could make a claim against you for retrospective maintenance, but it doesn't often happen. It depends what she's looking for."

"Sophie's wishes have always seemed rather opaque to me," said Edward. "I don't think Murdo has found her easy to fathom either."

"Given the circumstances we can hardly blame her for being less than straightforward."

"No, of course," said Edward, feeling once again that he was adrift somewhere on the dark side of Anna's moral compass.

They pulled up outside the Porthmeor Hotel.

"You go in," said Anna. "I'll find somewhere to park."

Edward entered the lobby, nodding at the commissionaire's greeting. There were one or two people at reception checking out, and he stood back until the desk was free. An efficient looking woman smiled a professionally hospitable smile as he approached.

"Good morning, Sir. How can I help?"

"I need to get a message to one of your employees – a Sophie Bourdais?"

"Ah yes, French Sophie. She's on this afternoon, I think. Let me…"

"Yes, that's my understanding too," said Edward. "But I'm afraid I need to speak to her urgently. I believe she has a room in your staff quarters. I wonder if I could…or perhaps if you would…just see if she is up and about?"

The receptionist's manner became marginally more professional and marginally less hospitable.

"We prefer not to intrude on our live-in staff if we can avoid it. Don't you have a phone number for her?"

"Yes, we've tried that," said Edward, feeling his impatience rising. "The fact is I'm a little concerned about her. She spent last night at my home in Roskear…"

The woman raised a professional and now almost entirely inhospitable eyebrow.

"Look I don't mean…" said Edward in exasperation, but at that moment Anna glided in and joined them at the desk. She placed a business card on the counter.

"Anna Parminter, of Parminter and Holroyd solicitors. I'm with Mr Tremenhere. This is potentially a legal matter and we have some concerns for Sophie's safety. I wonder if you could just arrange for somebody to check her room."

The receptionist examined Anna's card, looked narrowly at Edward, then picked up a telephone.

"Barbara. Could somebody from housekeeping just check if Sophie Bourdais is up and about? She's in seventeen. Stick your head round the door, would you, if there's no reply?" Then to Anna and Edward. "Would you like to take a seat while you wait?"

They retreated obediently to a plumped-up settee set against a side wall of the reception area, and waited. After five minutes a chambermaid appeared and crossed to the reception desk, where she spoke in a low voice to the receptionist. A moment later the woman came over to them.

"Please follow me."

She led them round the corner into a side room where a conference table was set up with mints and mineral water. She closed the door behind her.

"We've checked her room. There's no sign of Sophie or her things. She appears to have…gone. Barbara asked some of the girls but nobody has seen her since yesterday morning."

Edward looked at Anna.

"The station," he said. "Let's go." As they hurried past the receptionist, he said over his shoulder,

"Thank you! We'll call you if we hear anything."

"St Ives station?" said Anna as they left the hotel. "Or would we be better going to St Erth?"

Edward stopped.

"God, I don't know. Let's think. It's what…nine forty-five. St Ives station is just down the road. I'll run down there and ask about train times and if anybody's seen her. You get the car. If that's okay?"

"Yes of course," said Anna.

Edward ran the three hundred yards down the hill to the station, where holiday-makers were spilling out of a recently arrived train. He scanned the platform, calculating desperately in his head. If she had caught the 6am bus from Roskear, she couldn't have picked up her stuff and got to the station much earlier than 7.30. She would then have to connect with the main line at St Erth. If she was going for the ferry at Plymouth she could conceivably be there by now, or else well on her way to Bristol or London.

He waited until the embarking passengers had dispersed then approached the ticket collector.

"Excuse me. What time was the first train to St Erth this morning?"

"That would be the seven forty-five. Connects with the eight ten to London."

"Were you working that early this morning?"

"Yes, I start seven on a Saturday. Don't knock off till six tonight, neither."

"Did you happen to notice a girl, about twenty, blonde, carrying luggage?"

"I did too. She were about the only one on it. Nice looking maid. Bought a ticket to Plymouth."

"OK. Thanks. And if she picked up the 8.10, what time does that get into Plymouth?"

"Well it's two hour from Penzance near enough, so knock off the ten minutes your looking at 'bout ten o'clock. I can tell you exactly if you give me a minute."

"No that's fine. That's all I need to know."

"Daughter, is she?" said the man, sympathetically. "I got two of those myself. Run you ragged they do."

"Yes. Thanks," said Edward.

He wandered disconsolately back up the ramp to where the Golf was waiting with its engine running. He got in and closed the door.

"There's no rush," he said. "She's gone to Plymouth, and she'll get the midday ferry comfortably. It looks like she's going back to France."

"Back your way a bit," said Kate, from her slightly awkward position half-way up the stair of the Net Loft. "That's it. You okay?"

"Ar I'm bloody champion," said Dave in his best Yorkshire accent from the other side of half a section of bed. Kate had once told him his best Yorkshire accent wasn't too bad at all.

"Straight on up then. We can rest it on the landing, then there's a bit of a tricky corner."

"Great, I love tricky corners."

Kate had negotiated with the Brunels to buy the furniture from the Engine House, and they had been happy enough to agree, given that they were planning a complete refurbishment. Dave's assistance with the removal, and his banter, were indicative of a certain patching up that had taken place between the two of them following Kate's announcement that she was moving out. He was still a little hurt, and aware that their relationship was less secure than it had been, but he recognised that retreating into a huff was not going to improve matters. He had made an effort to convince Kate that he was on side with her decision, and willing to embrace the new reality. Kate in turn had been grateful for this and was making her own efforts to reassure him that the relationship would proceed on all the same assumptions that had held good before.

They picked up pasties from the independent bakery along the street (a convenience that was not lost on Dave), and ate them out on the little roof terrace in the early May sunshine. The sounds of traffic and the bustle from the harbour provided a cheerful backdrop, and it felt to Kate that she had made the right decision.

"So, tonight," said Dave briskly. "Any plans?"

"I was thinking," said Kate, "that I could cook us a really nice meal at yours as a thank you. And a celebration of our eight months as…well, as neighbours."

"Won't you be a bit tired for cooking?" said Dave. "We could always get a takeaway."

269

"I was thinking of doing something simple, but a treat. Maybe get a couple of decent steaks. There's a butcher just round the corner who's supposed to be good."

"Pretty much everything's just round the corner here. I'm getting a bit jealous. Steak would be lovely, thank you. Any chance of a few *frites*? "

"Goes without saying. And a crisp green salad with a garlic dressing. Then some nice cheese."

"I might get in a bottle of something special."

"I might even drink some of it. If…if I'm staying over, that is."

"I would *really* like it if you did stay over. But, you know, we can see how it goes. No pressure."

"None felt."

They sat in the sunshine in silence for a few seconds.

"Kate," said Dave. "It's going to be all right, isn't it?"

"Yes, my lover, it's going to be fine."

In the face of Sophie's letter and her precipitate action, any doubt in Edward's mind regarding her story fell away, and he began to think of her as his daughter – his only child. The odd detail of his name on the scrap of paper, with its correct spelling and naval suffix still puzzled him, not just because he was sure Anne-Marie did not have that information at the time of their brief liaison, but because the combination of words and letters had a certain coherence in his mind, as if he too had seen them written down somewhere. Of course while he was in the Navy they would have been used all the time, usually with his rank attached. But four years after he left…perhaps she had indeed tracked him down via some public record or other.

On Saturday afternoon he did his stint at the food bank, and on Sunday he went to church, partly because he was in contemplative, even penitent, mood, and partly because he hoped Anna might be there. She was not. He sang the hymns without enthusiasm, and heard nothing of the sermon, his mind preoccupied now with Sophie. Every detail of their conversation, every line of her face and lilt of her voice that he could recall from their brief acquaintance was now precious to him. He thought too of Anne-Marie, and how he would never meet her. He wondered if her life had been hard, bringing up

270

Sophie alone, or whether she had remarried. There had been no mention of a second family. He checked his phone surreptitiously every few minutes, but there was nothing from Sophie.

On Sunday afternoon he went out door-knocking with Murdo, but neither of them was in the right frame of mind. After some deliberation he had told Murdo the truth about the previous night's revelations. The boy had been initially astonished, and then, it seemed to Edward, genuinely moved. He had hoped that Murdo might be able to supply clearer details of Sophie's history or home address, but it appeared that all they had between them was her phone number. Edward had gone back to the hotel in the afternoon to seek a forwarding address, but they were uncooperative in the absence of Anna, and he was not ready yet to explain fully the reason for Sophie's sudden departure.

It was towards the end of the weekend that the final piece of the puzzle fell into place. Edward had been ironing shirts for the week ahead, as he always did on a Sunday evening. He took them up to his room and pulled open the door of his old-fashioned mahogany wardrobe when a thought struck him. He laid the shirts on the bed, and dragged to one side the hangers that held his workaday clothes. In a corner of the wardrobe, in a pair of ancient suit covers, were his old naval uniforms, never worn since he left the service, but somehow never thrown out either. Behind these were some other clothes from that era. He pulled out a crumpled blue linen jacket. It had been expensive at the time, but had hung elegantly upon his rangy frame, and he had worn it as a summer jacket for many years. It was the jacket he had casually lain on the damp grass of the park on the night of the hat festival.

He laid it now with greater care on the bed beside the shirts, opening it out as he would have done that night before he and Anne-Marie Bourdais folded into one another's arms in the moonlight. He closed his eyes, and for a brief moment he heard the band once more, and tasted the faint bitterness of French cigarettes on her lips. He knew before he looked what was woven onto a cotton name tape and sewn onto the lining of the jacket, just below the inside breast pocket on the left-hand side.

EV Tremenhere RN

271

Chapter Thirty-eight

"I'm the most 'ansomest candidate"

It was the final week of the by-election campaign. At the school and in its immediate neighbourhood election fever was gathering pace as polling day approached. Posters from the better resourced parties began to appear in windows and on stakes in gardens. Some even found their way onto prominent lampposts and roundabouts, although this was against the rules. At Penzance station on Monday morning a student thrust into Edward's hand a flier with Mallinson's serious face on it, and the words "Save our MIU" emblazoned across the masthead. Edward could remember a time when that had been the centrepiece of his own campaign. It could have been years ago, for all the interest he now felt.

He had left earnest, urgent messages and texts for Sophie, none of which she had answered. He stopped short of addressing her as his daughter, and signed himself simply as Edward, but the temptation to go further was there. He began to feel the first stirrings of a phantom grief for Anne-Marie, although he had barely known her. If only she had imparted the crucial information to Sophie at an earlier stage, or even initiated contact with him herself. Then they might slowly have built a relationship, almost certainly nothing more than a friendship, but nonetheless something valuable and meaningful to offer Sophie, and to take with him into his retirement. Instead, he was left with this muddle.

They had done little canvassing at the weekend, although this was the most important stage of the campaign if he was serious about trying to win. Now only the evenings remained. He might have expected Murdo to carry him through with his robust brand of encouragement and cajoling, but his campaign manager also seemed to have lost enthusiasm. Through the fog of his own preoccupations, Edward recognised that this change in attitude preceded Sophie's departure, and in fact stemmed from the Friday night hustings. He sensed that for Murdo the sight of his man ranged against opponents for whose policies he had considerably more sympathy had aroused a degree of regret and even shame. And although nothing had been said, he knew that Murdo, in his own way and for his own reasons, was also worried about Sophie.

On Monday evening Edward raised the matter of the campaign. It was the first proper conversation the two had had since Edward told him the reason for Sophie's sudden departure. The boy had not appeared at mealtimes since then, and Edward was forced to descend once more to the cellarage to knock on his tenant's door. When Murdo answered his expression was not particularly welcoming.

"I think we need to have a chat," said Edward.

"Have ye heard from Sophie?"

He shook his head.

"I'm afraid not. But we need to talk about the campaign."

Murdo sighed, and followed Edward back to the kitchen. They seated themselves at opposite sides of the table.

"We seem to be losing momentum," said Edward.

"Aye well, yer mind's no exactly on the job, is it?"

"No."

"D'ye even want tae win?"

Edward said nothing.

"Ah thought not. Well, that's fine by me. Ah don't particularly want ye to win either, if ah'm honest."

"I see."

"Don't get me wrong. Ah'll fulfil the terms of my contract. By my reckoning I owe you another four hours' work. Ah can do that in one canvassing session, plus the count."

"You don't need to worry about that," said Edward. "I got my money's worth. You did a good job."

Murdo nodded in acknowledgement.

273

"There, um… isn't any danger that we will win, is there?"

Murdo shrugged. "We canny rule it out. Depends what the opposition do in the next couple of days."

"I think, from my point of view, it's probably best if we…if we just regard the hustings as the culmination of a well-fought campaign, and suspend operations, as it were."

Murdo nodded again, but said nothing.

"If you're bothered about your hours, I'll donate them to Donovan's campaign."

"Fair enough," said Murdo. "Maybe second chances is no a bad thing to be investing in right now."

Edward smiled wryly.

"I take it yer still goin' to go to the count?"

"I think I have to."

"Ah'll see you there, then."

At school Edward avoided colleagues as best he could, and responded to enquiries as to how his campaign was shaping up with vague platitudes about it being difficult to tell, and having to wait and see. It was odd, as his own enthusiasm drained away, to watch it building among the student candidates and their teams. Dave Singleman's mock election was undoubtedly a huge success, and there was evidence everywhere of the effort that the young politicians were putting into the project. Predominant among this, courtesy of Murdo's influence, was Donkey's name and face, on fliers in registers, on posters on noticeboards and sellotaped to windows. It was odd to see the boy's adolescent features, frozen in classic half-profile in what was presumably meant to be a statesman-like expression.

He had his last meeting with Donkey on Wednesday lunchtime.

"So, tell me Donovan. How do you feel the campaign has gone?"

"Well I'm pretty chuffed, Sir. Murdo's been great. We've got the best posters by miles, partly because I'm the most 'ansomest candidate, and we've fliered all the junior form rooms. I'm maybe not as good at the hustings as the likes of Issy, but I reckon I've done all right."

Edward had attended the school hustings, and had been impressed himself at Issy's mastery of policy detail. He had heard, however, that she was more or less a one-woman campaign team.

"Word did reach me that accusations of bribery had been made."

"That's just Hardeep being a twat. I mean, what am I going to bribe kids with. I ain't got nothing."

"I heard you were promising a months' free protection."

"It wuzza joke sir, honest. I look out for everybody these days."

"I'm glad to hear it. Well – keep up the good work. I'm sure you'll be rewarded on polling day."

"How's your own campaign going, Sir?"

"Well…we'll find out on Thursday. By the way, has your father had any luck finding work?"

Donkey's face clouded.

"Naw. He tried for a job at the harbour but he didn't get it."

"I might have something for him. It's nothing permanent, but it would keep him going for a bit. I'll give him a call."

"That'd be great, Sir. He's really enjoyed the campaigning."

"Good. I've appreciated his help. Now remember – keep it all legal and above board these last couple of days."

"Right on, Sir. You too."

The weather, which had been generally fine through Easter and the start of the new term, now turned unseasonably miserable as a series of Atlantic lows clawed their way up the southwest peninsula, trailing their weather fronts behind them, and drenching Cornwall with two days and nights of rain as they passed through. Edward drove to school rather than take the train and risk a soaking on his way to and from the station. He peered through the windscreen at the lashing rain with a degree of ambivalence. It was the perfect excuse, if an excuse were needed, to avoid campaigning, but it also meant that his opponents would be limited in what they could do, and that made more likely the outcome that he feared most, which was that he might actually win.

By Thursday the last of the fronts had passed through, and polling day brought blue skies once more, and the freshness of a north-westerly breeze. It was chilly for May, but the sunshine was welcome. At school Dave Singleman had decreed that the polls would open at 8.30am, and close at 5.00pm, to allow those who had after-school activities to cast a last-minute vote. He had managed to obtain an old-fashioned black metal ballot-box, and this now stood on a table in the library in stately isolation, supervised by a rota of sixth formers upon whom Dave knew he could rely. He had managed to arrange informal cover for himself so that he could be present for much of the day.

His team had been briefed that they should be rigorous in enforcing the rule that only those whose names were on the list would be allowed a vote, and voter registration had closed at 4.00pm the previous day. Inevitably there would be disappointed students, and one of the first of these was Toby Trott, who swaggered in at breaktime with his small team of supporters to cast his vote. Fortunately, Dave himself was on duty.

"Yes Toby," said Dave as the lad reached the front of the queue.

"Come to vote."

"OK. Let's just find your name… so you're in 9L… Oh dear. It appears you're not registered."

"How'dya mean?"

"You had to register in order to vote. As was explained many times."

"But I'm a candidate."

"You still need to register. I did make that clear in the briefing last term. It's how it happens in the real world."

Toby turned to his band of followers.

"Did you guys register?"

Nods and murmurs of assent all round. Toby shook his head in exasperation.

"I'm not happy about this, Sir. It's well harsh. It could cost me the election. I don't know what my Mum's going to say."

"I expect we'll find that out in due course. Now do you mind moving on? I've got a queue of good people here keen to exercise their democratic rights."

All day form groups came down at pre-arranged times to cast their votes. Dave never got bored of watching this simple and unvarying process – give name to prefect; receive ballot paper; borrow pen from friend; find surface and ponder briefly; apply cross; approach the mystical black receptacle on

276

the table, pause, and deposit ballot. This was the iconic and essential act of democracy, experienced early and, Dave hoped, in a way that would not be forgotten when these students had their first opportunity to exercise the right for real at the age of eighteen, nineteen or twenty.

Various members of staff dropped by in the course of the day to see what was happening, and at lunchtime the Head himself appeared, in company with two of the governors, who smiled and nodded their approval at Dave over the line of voters. Anderson, the Director of Digital Strategy, took some photographs for a press release that Dave had prepared.

Kate had been teaching all day, but at the end of afternoon school she appeared with two mugs of tea and a brown paper bag of chocolate doughnuts. The library was quiet.

"I'm hearing great things," she said. "How's it going?"

"Well…I'd have to say it's going pretty well," said Dave, fishing a doughnut from the bag. "Something like seventy-five percent of the students who were eligible have registered, and there's only a few of those that haven't voted."

"That's awesome."

"Have you seen much of the candidates?"

"Yeah, lots of last-minute activity. I caught Toby Trott bribing some Year 7's with Haribo. Any idea who's going to win?"

"Well we haven't done any exit polling. I have to say Donkey's run a very impressive campaign, but I'm not sure his manifesto's up to much. What about your candidate?"

"Hmm. I think Issy is beginning to think she may have backed the wrong horse. Sammy's been working quite hard though. I heard him trying to explain proportional representation to a group of kids the other day. And Hardeep's been solid too."

At that point the door opened and Sammy came in.

"Hi Sir, Miss. Just wondered how it's going?"

"We were just discussing that ourselves," said Kate. "What do you reckon?"

"I reckon Hardeep might get it. I don't think it'll go to an independent. When do you think we'll get the results?"

"Well, the polls close at five, and we'll start counting straight away," said Dave. "There are only a few hundred ballots, so it won't take that long. Should be all done by six."

"Cool. I might nip into town and grab a burger. I've really enjoyed it, by the way. The mock election. Thanks for organising it."

"You're welcome."

Sammy left, and Dave and Kate were alone again in the silence of the library. Motes of dust danced in a shaft of afternoon sunlight. Dave took the mugs back to the staffroom, and Kate took out some marking. It was now almost a week since she had moved into the Net Loft, and she was enjoying her new situation. It felt good to be closer to the heart of things, and she could walk to school when the weather was fine. She and Dave hadn't really discussed what might happen next, but she hoped that soon he would also rent, or perhaps buy, somewhere in the town. Somewhere nearby.

Dave returned just as three late voters in muddy games kit arrived to cast their votes. They were followed by a Year Seven girl with bunches and a cello almost as big as she was.

"We haven't asked anybody else this," he said, after they had deposited their voting slips, "but out of interest would you be prepared to tell us who you voted for?"

The three footballers looked at each other.

"Donkey," said one. Another nodded. "Me too."

"I voted for Sammy Pascoe," said the third.

The girl with the cello said,

"I'd rather not say."

"That'll be Issy the Tory then," said one of the boys.

"Well done you," said Kate. "Who you vote for is your affair."

"That's what my Mum says," said the girl, and walked out, wrestling briefly with her cello in the doorway.

"When's the count, Sir?" asked one of the boys.

"Five o'clock. I'm just going to set up now. Are you going to stay?"

The muddy triumvirate exchanged glances.

"Might as well."

"Excellent," said Dave. "You can give me a hand."

Chapter Thirty-nine

"The one result nobody wanted"

By half past five the library held a small crowd of students and staff. They were gathered round a bank of tables that Dave had arranged in such a way that the ballot box, and the trays into which the ballots would be sorted, were out of reach of the watchers. On the business side of this barrier sat the tellers, four Sixth formers who had volunteered their services. There was one tray for each of the candidates, labelled accordingly. The Head was there, and half a dozen other members of staff who had stayed behind to see the result. Edward Tremenhere stood at the back with the d'Allesandros.

"Thank you all very much for coming," said Dave. "And before we begin the count I'd just like to say congratulations to all our student candidates, who have conducted themselves, generally speaking, with great maturity and enthusiasm throughout the campaign. My spies tell me that bribery and intimidation, while perhaps not entirely absent, have been minimal. Whatever the result tonight, you can be proud of what you've done."

There was a murmur of agreement from the staff.

"I'd like to say thank you to the Sixth formers who have helped with polling day, and who will be assisting with the count tonight, and also to all the staff mentors, some of whom are here. I'm sure the candidates will take the opportunity to thank them personally, if they haven't done so already. In a moment I'll open the ballot box, and distribute the ballots between our four tellers. They will then sort them into the candidates' trays. Once we've done that, we'll run a quick check to ensure no ballots have been mis-allocated, then we'll begin the actual counting. We should have a result for you within thirty minutes or so. It's more or less exactly the process that you will be able to watch on a larger scale at Eglos village hall later tonight, where, of course, one of our own members of staff is on the ballot."

There was a brief switch of focus to Edward Tremenhere, who looked, Dave thought, slightly uncomfortable.

"So without further ado…"

He lifted the hasp of the ballot box and eased open the lid. He upended the box, and the ballots tumbled out onto the table, where they were divided roughly evenly between the sixth-formers, who began the process of sorting. The students craned forward eagerly, alert for early indications of who had managed to pull in the votes.

At the back, Edward's phone pinged. He detached himself from the group and retreated behind one of the rows of shelving. It might simply be from Murdo, who he would pick up from the station later that evening. Or it could be from Anna, though he had heard little from her since the weekend.

It was from Sophie.

His heart pounded as he read two brief sentences in French.

Je t'ai trouvé. Tu me trouves.

I found you. You find me.

His fingers trembled as he punched out his reply.

Je te trouverai ma fille.

I will find you my daughter.

He leaned back against the shelving, and it was perhaps fortunate that the attention of the crowd was on the steadily growing piles of ballot papers, for it would have been strange for either student or teacher to observe that "Fiction A-H" was perceptibly shaking, as if moved by some profound but invisible force.

By the time Edward had gathered himself and re-joined the throng, the sorting was complete, and it was clear where most votes had been cast. Sammy, Hardeep, Issy and Donkey had all amassed respectable piles, with the other three lagging some distance behind. Kate and Dave conducted a quick check for misplaced ballots, and this gave further opportunity for unofficial counting by the audience. It looked very much as though Issy had polled slightly fewer votes than the others of the front four. Some students muttered Donkey's name, and others Sammy's…

The counting began in earnest.

And five hours later, In Eglos Parish hall, much the same process got under way in the other election, the one that would decide who would represent Penhale and Eglos ward at County Hall. This time Edward was at the front of the crowd of candidates and supporters, not at the back, watching with a combination of fascination and dread as the ballots were unfolded and checked against the numbers originally issued. Although they were not sorted at this stage, the process was conducted with the papers face up, so that onlookers were able to make a rough estimate of how the votes had been cast. A few feet along from him, Murdo too was watching intently. Anna was some way behind him, her interest in the outcome being more academic. The clear and worrying picture emerging from the verification process was that Edward and Mallinson were the front runners, and that Edward appeared to be narrowly in the lead.

He had as yet told neither Murdo nor Anna about Sophie's message. He had passed the evening alone, first in an Indian restaurant in town, then in a pub, where he would have liked to get quietly drunk but was prevented from doing so by the necessary business of the evening ahead. He had looked at Sophie's text several times, even though he knew it by heart from first reading. His own response had produced no further communication. Over a succession of sickly soft drinks, he alternated between maudlin self-pity and wild fantasies of rescue and reconciliation.

There was a short break while another ballot box, from the last of the three polling stations, was brought in and its seal broken. Murdo caught his eye and they moved to the back of the hall.

"Ah've got you jist ahead."

"Can't we stop it?" hissed Edward. "Can't I just withdraw, or concede, or something?"

"Nope," said Murdo. "Once you're on the ballot the election has to run its course. Yer only option is to resign once the result is declared and trigger another by-election, at a cost to the council of several thousand pounds. Ah wouldn't recommend doin' that on the night."

"That's absurd," said Edward, still under his breath. "I mean, what if I had been knocked down by a bus during the campaign?"

"It happens, said Murdo. "And the same rules apply. The dead man is in effect the winner, and you call another by-election. Of course, if yer knocked down by a bus, yer spared the embarrassment of having wasted everybody's time and money, not to mention their votes."

Edward swore softly.

"Yer one hope," said Murdo, "Is that Mallinson pulls back up on this last box. It's from the Penhale polling station, so in theory it's possible."

Edward groaned. "And I paid Isaac to deliver all those leaflets."

"If I were you," said Murdo, "I'd put some thought into a gracious victory speech."

Murdo set off back towards the tables, where the verification of the Penhale ballots had begun. Then he turned back.

"Who won the school election, by the way?"

"Donovan," said Edward. "He beat Sammy Pascoe by five votes."

"Excellent," said Murdo. "Another result for McAndrew Political. Let's see if we can't do the double."

Donkey had in fact won with 67 votes. Behind Sammy's 62, Hardeep had polled 51, and Issy 47. Then, after a bit of a gap came Lily Tregunna, who despite having done little campaigning had tapped into a seam of Cornish nationalist sympathy, and narrowly beaten Connor Pendarves for the Greens. Toby Trott, to almost everybody's satisfaction, brought up the rear with seven votes, his considerable last minute investment in Haribo all in vain. All this Edward had barely registered. He had stayed just long enough congratulate Donkey, and to ask Rona D'Allessandro if she could get him in to see the Head the following day, when he intended to hand in his resignation. If he could only snatch defeat from the jaws of victory tonight, he would head for the continent as soon as he could terminate his employment at the school.

He was about to follow Murdo back to the counting tables when Anna came over.

"Hello. You seem to be doing rather well."

Edward pushed his features into what he imagined those of a candidate on the verge of a possible victory might normally resemble.

"Yes, well – they're just checking the Penhale votes now. I imagine Mallinson will pull back on those."

"Anything from Sophie?"

"Actually I have heard something…can I call you about it later? Looks like they're about to start counting."

"Of course."

Despondently Edward re-joined the throng and eased his way to the front once more. The tellers had begun casting the open ballot papers into the relevant trays like dealers in a Casino, pausing every now and again to count the votes into bundles of ten, which were then clipped together. The trays were laid out alphabetically, so that at each of the three counting stations his own and Mallinson's trays were separated only by that of Penberthy, the MK candidate. Edward looped between the tables, trying to count up the paper-clipped bundles of ten as they stacked up steadily. The arrival of the Penhale ballots had clearly made some difference - it was now impossible to discern whether he or Mallinson was going to win.

Eventually the tellers sat back in their seats, their job complete for the time being. The bundles now had yellow post-it notes on them, with figures scrawled in biro. Edward could not bring himself to attempt a tally, although various of Mallinson's team appeared to be doing just that, leaning as close to the trays as they dared, and peering with narrowed eyes. They didn't look entirely happy. The returning officer, a tall thin woman with something of the dignity of a retired magistrate, was speaking quietly to her deputy at the back. The room settled into a tense silence, then the returning officer turned back to face the hall, and cleared her throat.

"Could I have a word with the candidates, please, and their agents if they have them?" She moved to an area to one side, but still behind the tables. Edward made his way round to where she stood, followed by Mallinson and a woman who was presumably his agent. The other candidates, who could all see that tonight was not going to be their night, followed behind. Edward looked around for Murdo, but he was nowhere to be seen. The three of them stood and waited for the returning officer to speak. She had a precise, clipped manner that left little room for dissent or discussion.

"So what we have on first count is a very close result for first place between Mr Mallinson and Mr Tremenhere. We currently have Mr Tremenhere ahead by two votes. We're going to follow standard procedure at this point and do a bundle check just to make sure no ballots have been mis-allocated. If the result is still as close then either of you will be entitled to request a recount. Are you both happy with that?"

"Presumably you'll check the ballots of all candidates," said Mallinson stiffly.

"Of course," said the returning officer.

Edward nodded grimly. Unless they found two misallocated ballots in Mallinson's favour, which was unlikely in a count of this size, he was heading for County Hall.

They returned to the public side of the hall, where the returning officer re-stated her intentions to the wider throng. Then the checking of the bundles began. Murdo was once more at the front of the crowd, watching closely. For want of anything better to do Edward looked around at his fellow candidates. The young businessman, who had effectively lost the seat spectacularly for the Conservatives, was doing his best to look cheerful, but one or two of the local Tory grandees who had come along were clearly furious. The Green candidate, for whom Anna's party had stepped aside, looked to have secured about a hundred votes, an increase on their previous showing. He was pleased to note that Gummow, the independent who was on his home turf, had fared poorly. The MK candidate appeared to have done quite well…

There was an intake of breath from the front of the crowd, and an audible "Yess!" from Mallinson's agent. Edward's height allowed him to see over the shoulders of those in front of him. A rogue ballot was ceremoniously extracted from his own pile like a piece of contaminated evidence, checked by the returning officer, and transferred to Mallinson's tray. Little would the Labour agent have imagined that Edward's delight

284

was as great as her own. The two leading candidates were now tied.

The check was completed without any further irregularities coming to light. This time the returning officer addressed the hall as a whole.

"This now puts the two leading candidates in a dead heat, which is probably the one result nobody wanted, least of all me." A certain light in her eye suggested to Edward that this was in fact exactly the sort of knotty conundrum in which she specialised.

"So the next step is a recount. If the candidates remain tied, then the matter is decided by the toss of a coin."

Edward joined Murdo at the front of the table, and watched as the bundles were methodically counted once more. He found himself now in a state of Zen-like calm, and when the recount produced no change in the result, he permitted himself a small smile in Mallinson's direction. The Labour candidate's face remained expressionless.

"Right!" said the returning officer briskly. "Are you both happy that we proceed to the coin-toss without further re-counting of the ballots?"

Both men nodded.

"In that case can I suggest we move up onto the stage so that everybody can satisfy themselves that this is being fairly done. I will provide the coin, which I will give you both to inspect. I will allow the coin to fall to the floor. Are you both in agreement?"

They nodded again. Edward felt still the calm that had descended upon him during the recount. Now the matter was truly in the hands of fate, and fate was leading him to France.

The returning officer led the way to the platform. The atmosphere in the hall now changed subtly, the action taking on something of the flavour of a public entertainment. Edward was reminded briefly of a time when, as a child, he had been called onto the stage from the audience in the course of a pantomime.

"Now if you would just stand here, Mr Tremenhere," said the returning officer, positioning Edward to her left, "and you here, Mr Mallinson, just so that everyone can see what we are doing."

The returning officer now stood centre stage, facing the hall, with Edward and Mallinson on either side of her. The whole group was six feet or so back from the edge of the platform. She gave the ten pence piece to Mallinson to inspect, and he turned it over gravely, as if there was the remotest likelihood of the Queen's head appearing twice. He then passed it to Edward, who smiled and returned it to the officer without further inspection.

"Who would like to call?"

Edward gestured to his opponent. "Please, go ahead."

Mallinson shrugged.

"Heads."

The returning officer flipped the coin expertly, so that it spun in the air in the classical manner before falling with a clunk onto the wooden stage. It landed on its edge and set off on a rolling arc, coming to rest at Edward's feet.

Edward looked down. He could see that the coin showed tails, that Mallinson had lost. He bent and picked it up by its edges, doing so with exaggerated slowness so that no one might accuse him of impropriety. He straightened, and looked across at Mallinson.

"Congratulations," he said.

All eyes briefly swung to the Labour candidate's face, so that the moment of prestidigitation which followed, sleight of hand learned decades ago on a frigate in the South China sea, was all but indiscernible. When Edward extended his arm to present the coin for inspection, it was the Queen's head that faced Mallinson and the returning officer.

The returning officer looked taken aback, and for the first time in the proceedings appeared slightly at a loss.

"You should properly have left the coin on the floor for myself and Mr Mallinson to inspect as it lay," she said. "Had you won the toss, I could not have allowed the result to stand."

"But as it is," said Edward, "I lost. And I accept the result. So unless Mr Mallinson wishes to make an objection...?"

"We have no objection," called Mallinson's agent, from the floor.

The officer looked at Mallinson, who shook his head.

"None whatsoever."

Edward extended his hand to his opponent, a benign smile upon his face. Those who were there remarked afterwards at his graciousness in defeat.

Chapter Forty

"A summer motoring trip through France"

Three weeks later Edward and Anna were seated across from each other in one of the many restaurants scattered around Plymouth's Theatre Royal, three quarters of a mile from the ferry terminal. Edward was studying the bill while Anna searched for change in her handbag, and neither looked up as a smartly dressed, clean-cut man was shown to a seat at the corner table a few feet away from them.

The man had driven down from London that evening, and was stopping in Plymouth overnight before continuing his journey to the southwestern extremity of the country – certainly the most remote school that he had visited in his twenty years as an Ofsted Inspector. His usual patch was the Home Counties, but the colleague who had been originally scheduled to undertake the visit had been taken ill, and the idea of Cornwall at this time of year had a certain appeal. It was, in any case, only a preliminary visit, and these, unlike the full inspections, which were hard work, could often be both interesting and enjoyable.

The inspector of schools prided himself on being a student of his fellow humankind, and as he waited for someone to come and take his order he glanced around at the occupants of the tables in his immediate vicinity. His eyes lingered upon Edward and Anna, gauging their status and provenance. It was too early for them to be theatre-goers - those would still be enjoying the final act of the evening's performance. Holiday makers, then – they had a certain transitory look about them. There was a third seat at the table, unoccupied for the moment but with a jacket hung across its back and an empty dessert plate on the table before it. A grown up child, perhaps, or a friend dropping them at the ferry terminal. The man watched as Edward settled the bill, then he returned his gaze to his menu card, although he continued to listen as the pair resumed their conversation, and to watch them from the corner of his eye. They were speaking in a desultory way about some obscure political matter that the inspector found difficult to precisely pin down, and this intrigued him.

"I hope Mallinson does a decent job," said Edward. "He looks reasonably capable."

"I've heard he's already cut down his hours at the University, which I suppose is a good sign. With a bit of luck he'll knock some sense into the Labour group, though I'm not sure how they'll take to him."

"Yes, he's an odd fish. Apparently he's an unapologetic Blairite."

"Aren't you a bit sorry that you missed out so narrowly?"

Edward shook his head.

"No. Once the facts about Sophie became clear, there was really only one thing on my mind."

The inspector leaned a little closer. Who might Sophie be? What facts? But the conversation was moving on.

"You ran a good campaign, though."

"Yes, well that was really down to Murdo. And most of our lot seem to have turned out for me. How do the Greens feel about it all?"

"They're claiming it as a success, because their vote went up. But it hasn't really shifted the dial for them. And we'll hold their feet to the fire for their part of the bargain when it comes to the General Election."

At that moment the pair were joined at the table by the third member of the party. The inspector saw a young man of about twenty with a short, wiry frame and distinctive auburn curls. He didn't remotely resemble either of the older pair, so the precise relations between the three remained something of a puzzle. The young man's accent, too, was quite different. The inspector was reminded of a character in the radio soap opera he had listened to on his way down from London.

"How are we doin' fur time?"

Edward looked at his watch.

"Just coming on for nine. We don't have to be onboard till nine-thirty."

The overnight ferry, then. A summer motoring trip through France, no doubt, along with hundreds of others of similarly fortunate families. The inspector could see the attraction, though he favoured Bali himself.

"Better get a shift on."

There was the sound of some coins being placed on a plate, then the three rose and made their way to the door. He heard them thanking the staff as they left the restaurant.

Deprived of his diversion, the inspector looked round for the waiter.

In the very establishment that the inspector was scheduled to visit, Anton Killick sat alone in his office over his wafer-thin MacBook. It was by no means unusual for him to be still at work at nine o'clock or even later, and he had long ago come to an arrangement with the caretaking staff over the setting of the alarms. Anton's mood was buoyant. The irritation of Singleman's mock election, which at the time had been larded with ludicrous quantities of praise from students, governors and even parents, was now but a memory. St Petroc's was finally stripped for action, and as if the universe were rewarding him for the boldness of his vision, one of the summer inspection team was due to visit them the very next day.

It was the preparation for this visit that was keeping Anton late in his office. The man would only be with them for a little over half a day, but a precious forty-five minutes of that time was scheduled to be spent with the Deputy Head, discussing baseline data. Anton fully intended to make the most of this. He would dazzle the inspector with the Mother of all PowerPoints, and as the man was shown around the school he would see corridors and classroom walls that displayed an unrelenting focus on the academic curriculum. The intention was to set the stage for an improved Ofsted grade in the summer. Anton did not yet dare hope for "Outstanding" – there was much work still to do – but surely, *surely,* it was perfectly reasonable to aim for "Very Good".

There was another reason for his good humour. A chance conversation with a martial arts acquaintance had led him to a companion for the recently bereaved Josef Stalin. Anton had felt a degree of anxiety about how the newcomer would be received, and as a precaution he had continued to bring the rats in to work with him, setting the cage on the window ledge behind his desk. The early signs, however, were good, and now the tapping of Anton's fingers on the keys of his MacBook was underscored by the companionable scratching of Josef Stalin and his new cell mate Ho Chi Minh as they snuffled in their straw.

A few miles away on the Net Loft's roof terrace, Dave and Kate sat hand in hand, watching the stars come out. They were ensconced in the garden swing that Dave had bought Kate as a house-warming present, a gift that he had insisted upon putting together under her tolerant and amused gaze. The tradition of the Thursday night sleepover had been reinstated, and their future once more wore a settled aspect. Dave was rapidly being won over to their new arrangement, given the proximity that Kate's flat offered to the bars, clubs and theatres of Penzance. Several sets of property details, all for houses or flats in the immediate area, were on the striped cushion beside them.

In Eglos, Sammy Pascoe was seated at the table in the one public room of his parents' cottage, poring over a book of stagecraft. He had got over the indignity of being pushed into second place in the mock election by Donkey (of all people) and he had a new challenge to face. Mr d'Allesandro had confirmed that he wanted him to stage-manage the junior play – an ambitious production of A Midsummer Night's Dream that would involve literally hundreds of sound and lighting cues. Sammy had enjoyed his foray into politics, and was delighted to have beaten Issy the Tory, but he was looking forward to once more getting to grips with the marginally more predictable world of theatre tech.

Issy – who had never really been a Tory by any kind of settled choice – was in her own home, up in her bedroom. She had discovered in the process of defending Conservative party policy that she disagreed with rather a lot of it, and was feeling the first stirrings of a need to critically examine some of the assumptions she had, up to now, happily embraced. Like King Lear, she felt there were perhaps things of which she had taken too little care.

One of these things was Donovan Doggett. Issy was at that precise moment pondering a text message from Donkey, whom she viewed in a new and interesting light since his triumph in the mock election. The message was polite, and correctly spelled, which was unnecessary given the medium, and surprising given its source. It was the latest in a series that had passed between them since the election, all of which her correspondent had signed, rather touchingly, "*Your friend, Donovan.*" This one asked her if she would meet him for a coffee in Costa on Saturday afternoon.

She was rather minded to say yes.

On the promenade deck of the *Pont Aven*, Edward stood alone and watched the lights of Plymouth recede until they were no brighter than the stars overhead. A cold white disc of moon was rising to the east, and the clear skies carried the promise of a calm crossing. He had booked a cabin, but was in no great hurry to turn in.

The day after the election he had met with the Head in his office, the same office, give or take two or three bouts of modernisation and re-decorating, that had borne witness to his last departure from the school, twenty-two years ago. His interview then had been with the same Head, newly appointed, and although the matter had never subsequently been discussed, Edward understood it to be acknowledged that he had not been treated entirely fairly on that occasion. That had undoubtedly given him a degree of moral leverage in securing release before the end of the summer term. As Edward pointed out, his exam classes would all be on study leave, and given the highly unusual circumstances, he was in any case prepared to walk away if an amicable agreement could not be reached. In the end the two men had shaken hands and agreed that Edward could leave the school at the end of May.

And now here he was, free at last of the burden of work, his pension applied for and the Count House entrusted to the care of Isaac Doggett, who had been engaged to work at the property for two days a week over the summer months, to care for the garden and undertake a schedule of renovation to the exterior, and to generally keep an eye on the place. The instinctive liberalism that led Edward to entrust this task to a former burglar was not entirely untempered by caution, and certain items of value had been removed to the sanctuary of Anna's house for the duration.

They were now out of sight of land. The temperature was dropping, and the promenade deck was empty, but Edward lingered a little longer, and found his mind wandering to scraps of Channel-inspired poetry: Hardy's Channel Firing; Wordsworth on his way to France to meet the mother of his own illegitimate child; Mathew Arnold's Dover Beach.

Ah love! Let us be true to one another!

Edward lifted his face to the moon a final time, then turned and walked back across the deck to join his travelling companion in the lighted interior of the vessel.

The End

Thank you so much for reading *The Unbinding of Edward Tremenhere*. If you enjoyed the novel, please do leave a review on Amazon – just google the title and click on the Reviews icon. You can read the funny, heart-warming story of how Dave and Kate first got together in *Mentoring Mr Singleman*, also available from Amazon as a paperback or download.

KS.

Printed in Great Britain
by Amazon